JORDAN
WELLS

HERO

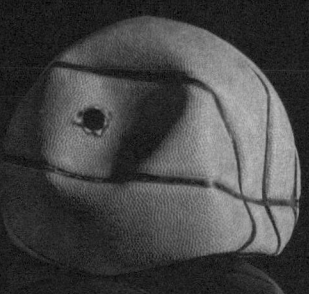

Other works by Jordan Wells

LOGGED OFF: MY JOURNEY OF ESCAPING
            THE SOCIAL MEDIA WORLD
MIRRORS AND REFLECTIONS
THE HEALING
A LONELY ROSE
THE RING PACK
THE RING PACK 2
IT'S FUN BEING A HUMAN BEING
MADAM PRESIDENT
THE SECOND SON
HE'S HERE: LET'S CHERISH HIS FIRST YEAR
SHE'S HERE: LET'S CHERISH HER FIRST YEAR
MY BABY BOY IS HERE
MY BABY GIRL IS HER
MY BABY BOY
MY BABY GIRL'S FIRST YEAR
A PRINCESS HAS COME: LET'S CHERISH HER FIRST YEAR
A PRINCE HAS COME: LET'S CHERISH HIS FIRST YEAR
A KING IS BORN
A QUEEN IS BORN

(*Stage Plays*)

HERO
THE BIRD AND THE BEE
THE WILL

Signature

HERO

A Novel

JORDAN WELLS

Scott and Scholars Press
An imprint of Scott and Scholars Press LLC

Scott and Scholars Press® is a registered trademark of
Scott and Scholars Press LLC

Publisher's Cataloging-in-Publication Data

Names: Wells, Jordan Scott, author.
Title: Hero / Jordan Wells.
Description: East Orange, NJ: Scott and Scholars Press, 2025.
Identifiers: LCCN: 2025911595 | ISBN: 978-1-955975-70-4 (hardcover) | 978-1-955975-71-1 (paperback) | 978-1-955975-72-8 (paperback) | 978-1-955975-73-5 (paperback) | 978-1-955975-74-2 (Kindle)
Subjects: LCSH Police--Fiction. | Police shootings--United States. | Law enforcement--Fiction. | Victims of violent crimes--Fiction. | Racism--Fiction. | Psychological fiction. | BISAC FICTION / General | FICTION / Mystery & Detective / Police Procedural | FICTION / Psychological | FICTION / Thrillers / Suspense | FICTION / Thrillers / Psychological
Classification: LCC PS3623 .E55 H47 2025 | DDC 813.6--dc23

First Edition 2025
Jacket design by Jordan Wells
Cover photograph by Cipariss/iStock by Getty Images/istockphoto.com
Author Photograph by Donald Bernard Jr.
Art illustration Copyright © 2025 by Jordan Wells
For special inquiries, please email us at scottandscholarspress@yahoo.com

Printed in the United States of America

10 9 8 7 6 5 4 3 2 1

I dedicate this book to the late Darren Jones.
Mr. Jones, you were my mentor, a dear friend, and a father figure.
I cherish the conversations we shared and I am forever grateful that we crossed paths in life. Thank you for all the love and support, for taking the time to read my work and give feedback, and for inspiring me to title this book, "Hero."
I thank you for that and greatly appreciate you for everything. You will truly be missed.

Author's Notes

Hello, my readers. We meet again for another story. If you have been following my work, you would see that I never run away from a challenge regarding controversial topics. In *this* story, I face one that I believe is one for the books—no pun intended—but intended at the same time.

When I wrote *Madam President*, I thought I could not go through writing another book that would be so emotionally draining. But then I wrote *The Second Son*, and after *that* story, I had to take a break from writing. *Hero* was in my mind for months and would not go away. It entered my mind when thinking of a new story to write. Usually, I sit on it when nothing comes through. But like clockwork, this idea channeled in, and I had a clear, vivid vision of this story. When I have a clear vision, I let it take over, and *that* is when the magic happens.

At first, I had no idea how I would go through with it. But after some time, I came to my senses, and a voice said, "*Get out of the way and let the story write itself.*" And that is precisely what I did. It was sometimes brutal, but I managed to get through it and delivered. But listen… I have no idea what you will get out of this story. This is a story from a different perspective. But anyway, I am not going to keep you in suspense any longer. Let's get right into it.

But before we begin, I must warn you, the reader, of this book's content and graphic nature. The content will be heartbreaking, which may hit home for many people. There is profanity (Perhaps an excessive amount of *f*-bombs in the dialogue), so please forgive me. And there are situations in this story that may cause some discomfort. But that's life—full of unsolicited discomfort. If this story is too heavy for your heart, I understand if you refrain from reading further. But I ask that you read this book to the very end. You will have a very long journey ahead of you. But it will be well worth it.

I put my heart and soul, everything I had into this story... and it drained me. It drained me because I had to embody Officer Pete Gant. I saw what he saw, I felt what he felt, and I must say, after writing this story, my views on police officers have changed forever—in a *positive* way. I truly hope you enjoy *Hero*. This may be a once-in-a-lifetime story. What I *hope* you get out of this story is some clarity. Clarity and understanding of what our law enforcement officers go through daily, and I hope you will learn to be more sympathetic and empathetic towards them. Keep this in mind; even heroes need a hero.

This story also unravels our world's hidden illnesses, exposing our society's poisonous prejudgments and leaving you with this question: "How can we change the world?"

Can we change the world? Or are we too late? I'll let you be the judge of that.

Acknowledgments

Before you read this story, I would like to take this time to acknowledge a few people.

I thank my mother and father for their love and support.

I want to thank my family and my friends for *their* support. You all know who you are.

I want to thank my teacher, mentor, father figure, and dear friend, Stephen Davis, for his contributions and for being my extra set of eyes. Thank you for everything, Steve. I love you dearly, and I am forever grateful.

I want to thank my high school teacher, Shea Richardson, for sparking my imagination and inspiring me to write poetry.

I want to thank my college English professor, Henry "Hank" Stewart, who assisted me with my writing craft.

I want to thank Ursula Liebowitz-Johnson again for helping me and our conversations about this story. As always, thank you for everything, Mrs. LJ.

I thank my college buddies, Matt and Nick, for your insight and our discussions. I also thank Detective Rick, Detective Sanders, Daniel Stover, and Pierre. I couldn't have written this book without you all. And for any law enforcement officer who ever crosses paths with this book… I understand now. This one is for you. I thank you for your service.

I also want to thank my dear friend, Mr. Howard Barshop.

Lastly, I want to thank Mr. Shawn Kirkley, one of my former students from Montclair High School, and MHS music teacher, Sammy.

And now, my readers, thank you again for your support. I leave you with this message: Let your blessings echo.

I now present to you… *Hero.*

HERO

1

DECEMBER 19th, 2025, FRIDAY EVENING:

<u>PRACTICE IS OVER</u>

The swift sound of squeaking sneakers echoed throughout the gym—beautifully decorated in triumph as championship banners hung high for the Newark Tech Terries. Basketball prodigy, eighteen-year-old Tyshawn Brendan, was on the court, hitting bucket after bucket from beyond the arc. Tyshawn counted down as he dribbled the basketball. "Three… two… one," he said, pretending he was going for the game-winning buzzer-beater. He shoots… nothing but net. He raises his hands in celebration. "Ahhh," he softly said as if the crowd was going wild. "Ladies and gentlemen, the greatest basketball player in the *world… TYSHAWN BRENDAN*!"

Tyshawn had a tall frame—six feet five inches—handsome and deeply melanated. He had finished practicing with his teammates a half hour ago. Tyshawn, however, was always the first to show up and the last to leave. Suddenly, he heard a loud voice from behind as he went for another shot.

"BRICK!"

Tyshawn turned and saw his homeboy, RaJohnn Mitchell.

"*Oh…*" Tyshawn said. "Yo Rah, what you doing here?"

"Well, *damn*, it's nice to see you, *too*, bruh," RaJohnn responded as he dapped up Tyshawn. "How you livin', superstar?"

"I'm chillin', man. Just getting some extra shots in before I dip out…. Yo, Coach Dutch know you in here?"

"Nah. I was just looking around. Looking at the trophies and shit."

"Well, you better get up outta here, Rah. If Coach Dutch sees you, you gonna have some problems."

"Man, ain't nobody worrying about no Coach Dutch. I just came to check on you. See how you doing. Heard about your commitment to Duke. Congrats, gang."

"I appreciate it," Tyshawn smiled. "Yeah, I was waiting for that one to come in."

"Shit, you're the number one prospect in the country. *Everybody* wants you."

"Nah, not everyone. I haven't heard anything from Georgetown."

"That's because they're holding a spot for *me*," RaJohnn laughed. Tyshawn scoffed, "Yeah, a'ight. Whatever you say. How bout you stand by the basket and catch the rebounds?"

"Say *what*?" RaJohnn responded with a twisted face.

"Come on, I just want to take a few more shots."

RaJohnn looked Tyshawn up and down. "I ain't your damn ballboy."

"Man, just shut up and grab the boards."

Tyshawn looked at his friend and observed his distasteful presence. RaJohnn was several months younger and a few inches shorter. He had long dreadlocks braided down to his back. Tyshawn had not seen RaJohnn since he was kicked out of school for bad behavior several months ago. Tyshawn knew of RaJohnn's temper and tried to keep his distance from his friend—only seeing him sporadically. Suddenly, Tyshawn stood at the foul line in a daze.

"Yo, you're gonna shoot or what, gang? What the fuck?" RaJohnn said.

Tyshawn shook his head and shot a free throw… swish.

"You mean like that?" Tyshawn smiled.

"Yeah, *just* like that. Cornball ass," RaJohnn chuckled. "So, tell me… is Coach Dutch still mad at me?"

"Well, you *did* quit the team, Rah."

"I ain't quit the team. He kicked me *off* the team, remember?"

"Because you weren't *eligible*, bruh. Coach had no choice. I *told* you to bring your ass to class."

"Come on, you know how it is, *gang*… you know I can't leave the block alone."

Tyshawn shook his head. "And that's always been your problem, Rah. Can't leave that bullshit *be*. You're street-struck, my boy."

"I ain't street struck, man. I just stand on business, you feel me?"

"*Anyway*," Tyshawn sighed as he took another shot. "What you doing over here on this side of town?"

"I was just in the area… to keep it a *buck*, I was over Ebony's."

"*Ebony*?" Tyshawn enthusiastically said. "Yo, you rizzed up *Ebony*?"

"*Hell yeah*," RaJohnn chuckled.

"Ain't you with Latifah?"

"Yeah but Ebony's a *baddie*, gang. I *had* to bag that."

"*Bro*… you *knew* I was on that."

"Hey… don't hate the playa… hate the *game*. You too shy for her anyway."

Tyshawn scoffed. "Yeah a'ight… but you know Latifah ain't with that cheating shit, Rah. She's crazy—for *real*, for real."

"She ain't crazy, she just be on her light-skin shit."

"*A'ight*," Tyshawn gestured. "I ain't saying nothing else. It's your funeral, bruh. But if Latifah catches you, your ass better call Po-po."

RaJohnn caught the rebound and held the ball.

"Man, don't even bring those pigs up, gang. Fuck those bitch ass cops."

Tyshawn scoffed. "See, there you go."

"Nah, fuck 'em."

"Yo, Rah—"

"Nah, and I'll tell you why. Earlier today, when I left Ebony's crib, right? I didn't even get *two blocks* from her house, and I got pulled over. Some ho ass white cop made me get out the car and shit. I had to check his bitch ass. Trying to size me up and shit with his little ass."

"Man, you better *chill* with that shit, bruh."

"Nah, yo. That cop was just being racist—just like the rest of them. See, what *happened* was he gave me a ticket saying that the tint on the windows was too dark. So, I gave it to my sister, right? Because *I* don't know what to do with that ticket shit. Then she started acting all shady—saying I can't drive her car no more. I mean, it's really not *her* car—well, like it's in her *name* and shit, but her boyfriend pays the note. And he's a truck driver, so he's not always around."

"Well, then don't drive the car."

"Nah, I *need* it. I got things to do, you know what I'm saying? I got the g-ride outside right now."

"And she doesn't know you got the car?"

"Nah. Niecy's asleep right now. She works the night shift. But she don't have to be up until ten. So, I'll just bring it back before she leaves."

"Oh, a'ight…. But for *real*, though, Rah. You gotta watch your tone and delivery out here on these streets—*especially* with these cops. They've been trigger-happy ever since that cop got killed."

"Yeah, I know. That pig probably had it coming to him anyway."

"Rah, come on, man. Don't say that. That was somebody's father."

"*Fuck* 'em. They can *all* die for all I care. Bitch ass pigs. I *stand* on *business*, you know what I'm saying?"

"Nah, you saying some real bullshit right now, Rah."

"Bro, it's *all Gucci*. I know what to do now if I get pulled over again."

"Nah, but I'm *saying,* though—"

"*Bruh-bruh*… spare me with your lectures. I ain't tryin' to hear it."

4

Tyshawn sighed. "Whatever, bro."

"You know what? Check the rock," RaJohnn said as he chest-passed the ball to Tyshawn. "We need to play a little one-on-one."

Tyshawn laughed. "Rah, try not to get your ass whipped right now."

"How about you stop talking and play ball?"

"Oh, you really *want* this ass whipping, huh?"

"Come on, Mr. Duke University. Show me what you're going to do at the collegiate level."

"Oh, you ain't saying nothing but a word."

No time was wasted as Tyshawn went into assassination mode. In less than a minute, he was up five to zero. Tyshawn looked at RaJohnn's eyes and saw how gassed he was as he could not keep up with his elite friend. Tyshawn, however, was not going to let up.

"What's wrong, Rah?" Tyshawn chuckled. "Smoked too many blunts?"

"Man, fuck you," RaJohnn responded, gasping for air. "I ain't finished."

"*Yes*... you *are* finished," a man's voice shouts.

Tyshawn turned and saw his basketball Coach, Coach Dutch, standing with his hands on his waist. Coach Dutch was a no-nonsense man—a couple of inches taller than Tyshawn, with a receding hairline and glasses. In his purple and white tracksuit, Coach Dutch walked toward them sternly as if he wanted to keep Tyshawn away from RaJohnn. Coach Dutch stood in front of Tyshawn as if he was his bodyguard, protecting him from RaJohnn.

"What up, Coach," RaJohnn said as he raised his hand for some dap.

"What you doing in my gym, boy?" Coach Dutch said with an aggressive tone.

RaJohnn lowered his untouched hand. "*Boy*? Damn, Coach, it's like *that*? Ain't you happy to see me?"

"I take *no pleasure* in wasting time with juvenile delinquents who piss off *all* their potential—*just* to gain some *bullshit* street credibility."

RaJohnn, now offended. "Coach—"

"Time and time *again* you disappointed me. No matter how many chances I gave you, you let me down—you let *everybody* down."

"Yo Coach, why you runnin' *down* on me like this?"

"Because you're *scum*, Rah... *scum*! And Tyshawn? You *know* better than to be hanging with this menace."

"Hey Coach, come on," said Tyshawn. "This is *Rah* we're talking about here."

"He's a loser, son. And we don't have time to waste on fucking losers."

"*Loser*? Yo, who the *fuck* you calling a loser?" RaJohnn said as he pushed Coach Dutch.

"Yo, Rah, chill out! *Chill out*!" Tyshawn said as he stood between them.

"Nah, *fuck* him!"

"You have five seconds to get your sorry ass up outta my gym, or I'm calling the cops on ya ass."

"I don't give a fuck! Call them bitch ass cops—"

"Four, three, two—"

"A'ight, Coach, *a'ight*!" Tyshawn said. "We're leaving."

"No, you're not going *anywhere* with this bum. You keep your ass right here. *I'm* taking you home."

"Nah, he comin' with me—*fuck* you!"

"I said, 'Get the *fuck* outta my gym, boy!'"

"A'ight, old man," RaJohnn said as he stepped back toward the door. "That's fucked up, Coach. You always told me you'd care for me—said, '*I'll always have your back, Rah*,' *no* matter what.... But now I know that was all *bullshit*—just like my sorry-ass father. But it's all good, gang. I see how it is. Yo, Ty... I'll be waiting outside."

Just as RaJohnn left the gym, Coach Dutch gave Tyshawn a piece of his mind.

"Ty," said Coach Dutch. "What the *hell* are you doing hanging around that low-life? Are you *trying* to ruin your future?"

"Oh, come on, Coach," Tyshawn sighed. "This is *Rah*. He ain't on that type of time—"

"*Bullshit.* He's *always* on that type of time, and it's going to be *prison* time for him—real soon. And *you* do *not* need to be around that type of energy. Do you hear me?"

"I *hear* you, Coach, damn. *Relax*."

"Son, listen to me… you have *such* a grand future ahead of you. All you have to do is play one year—just *one year* of college ball, and *you* are going to the mountaintop. *You* will be playing with the elite of the *elite*. The whole world will be your oyster, son. Do *not* waste your energy on *fucking losers* like that. He's no good for you. Trust me when I tell you. There's no saving that boy. I know it, and you know it… *leave* that thug *behind* you."

"He's my best friend, Coach… my brother. I can't just kick him to the curve like that."

Coach Dutch shook his head. "He's a *bum*, son. Leave the garbage on the *streets*…. I'm going to close up my office. You keep your ass right here and wait for me. *I'm* going to drive you home… do you *hear* me?"

"I *hear* you, Coach."

Coach Dutch walked across the gym and pushed open the double doors. Tyshawn stood there, feeling stuck between a rock and a hard place. Suddenly, there was a vibration coming from his gym bag. As he opened his bag, he pulled out his phone and saw a text from his mother, Jada. After he read her text, they began a brief conversation:

Mom Dukes
Hey King, I'm working overtime tonight.
I should be home at around 9ish, okay? If

you want, you can go ahead and eat
dinner without me. How was practice?

Tyshawn
Hey, okay, no problem. And practice
was a'ight. We play our first game
tomorrow. I was getting some extra shots
in before I left the gym. But I'll see you
when you get home. I love you.

Mom Dukes
I love you more, King. And I love your
dedication to your passion. But make sure you
take care of business and do your homework
when you get home. Books before baskets,
baby.

Tyshawn
You already know, Ma. I got you. See ya later.

Tyshawn then picked up his bag and headed for the door. He stopped right before the door as he saw himself in the reflection of the glass. He looked at himself, contemplating whether or not he should leave or stay. Suddenly, a voice spoke in his mind, pleading with him not to leave. Coach Dutch was nowhere in sight. Then, a sudden honk of a car horn went off, snapping Tyshawn out of his thoughts. He sighed and walked out the door. The cold wind hit his face like a stingy kiss from winter. He looked down from the top of the stairs and spotted RaJohnn waiting in the car. As Tyshawn descended the stairs, he began having second thoughts about getting in the car. He knew of his friend's troubled behavior but did not want to bail out on him.

As Tyshawn approached the car, that inner voice began to roar in his subconscious, yelling at him, saying, "Don't get in the car!" That is when Tyshawn looked up at the gym doors, hoping that Coach Dutch would walk out and rescue him from his peer-pressured instinct. "Yo?" RaJohnn said. "Get your ass in the car, bruh. It's *brick* out here." Tyshawn pinched the bridge of his nose and snapped out of the daze. As he got into the heated car, RaJohnn immediately pulled off.

"*Damn*, man," Tyshawn said. "Let a brother get his seatbelt on first."

"Yo, *fuck* Dutch," RaJohnn said. "*Fuck* him. He ain't no coach to me anymore.... Ty... he acted like I wasn't even part of the *team*, bruh. Like I wasn't a champion, too."

"Rah, you can't let that get to you, man. *I* know you helped us get through some tough games. We couldn't have won that championship without you."

RaJohnn scoffed. "Ty, you just saying that shit. You know damn well you would've won the ship even if I *wasn't* ballin'."

"Nah, for real. We were like Jordan and Pippen."

"But why *I* gotta be Pippen?"

Tyshawn laughed. "Because you weren't putting up forty points a game."

"There you go, bragging again. A'ight, I see how it is."

"I'm not braggin', bro. I'm just saying that... you mattered, man. Fuck what Coach Dutch said back there."

RaJohnn gives Tyshawn a pound. "Respect, gang... respect.... Yo, I can't believe it, man. You're going to Duke University, and then after that, the league."

"Yeah, man," Tyshawn smiled as he spun his basketball in his lap. "I'm gonna make it, Rah. I can't wait... I can't wait to be in the league with Lebron and Bronny James, Kyrie Irving, Ja Morant, Andrews, Curry, *and* SGA? I can't wait. They're going know who Tyshawn Brendan is."

"Shit, they already do. The whole knows who *you* are."

"Nah, but I'm saying like... I want to *dominate* the league. I'm not trying to be in nobody else's shadow."

"Well, you damn sure as *black* as a shadow," RaJohnn laughed.

"Man, kiss my ass," Tyshawn chuckled.

"Sike nah, though. All that you said? *Facts…* we gonna make it out the hood, bro. And live the *good* life."

Tyshawn raised his eyebrows. "*We?*"

"Hell *yeah*," RaJohnn said with an irritated tone. "What, you think you're going to leave me here in Newark to *die*? We boys, right?"

"Yeah, for *sure…* shit, we *brothers*."

"Word—like some *Kenan & Kel* shit."

Tyshawn laughed. "Yeah."

"*A'ight*," RaJohnn smiled. "That's what's up, gang. Shit, you had me scared for a minute…. Yo, let's get some food real quick from that Seven-Eleven. I'm hungry as hell."

"A'ight, bet," Tyshawn said as he continued to spin his basketball.

Tyshawn grew silent as they were on the road—looking out the frosted window at Newark's cold-blooded streets. Even though the voice in his head faded out of his mind, the weird sensation in the pit of his stomach was still there—growing. Tyshawn felt something horrible was about to happen, but he just could not put his finger on it. On the outside, he looked fearless, but on the inside… he was terrified.

2

DECEMBER 19^{th,} 2025, FRIDAY EVENING:

<u>THE NIGHT SHIFT</u>

The delightful aroma of freshly brewed pumpkin spice coffee had never smelled so good. But for Police Officer Pete Gant, he liked his coffee black: no sugar or cream. Pete had been waiting for his sausage, egg, and cheese croissant sandwich for the last five minutes at the Dunkin Donuts pickup line. As he waited, he called his wife, Claire. The phone rang but there was no answer.

Before Pete would began his shift, he would always call Claire and talk with her. He never called while on duty unless there was an emergency. At thirty-eight years old, Pete was a sixteen-year veteran on the force. Pete was attractive—piercing light blue eyes, a clean-shaven face, and the jawline of a male model. He was always clean-shaven for work. He believed that having a clean-shaven face kept his character clean. He would often sport a classic brown taper haircut. His arms had several tattoos. One tattoo, in particular, was of a cross, and right beside it was a phrase written in Edwardian script that read, "*Man of Faith.*"

Pete was a father of three. His oldest son, Michael, just

turned sixteen last week. His daughter, Elle, was a beautiful fourteen-year-old girl, and his youngest, Leo, was six. Pete named him Leo because it reminded him of the acronym "Law Enforcement Officer."

Pete had transferred from Cedar Grove to Newark three years ago. His reason was not because he hated the area. It was because he did not believe in being neighbors with a convicted pedophile. And with Pete having kids of his own, he was not taking any chances. He put in a transfer to Newark and played the waiting game. Because of his exceptional record in Cedar Grove, he was welcomed into the Newark Police Department with open arms. One would ask, "Why Newark?" His friend and fellow officer, Jesse Holm, recommended that he transfer to Newark because a position had opened, and he got in. Pete loved the idea of being stationed in Newark. It was such a big city and the home of his favorite hockey team, the New Jersey Devils. Occasionally, Pete would take the whole family to a hockey game—wearing Devils' Jerseys.

Newark was rough for Pete. That first week, he wanted to quit every day. He had never seen so much action in just seven days—so much violence. Pete's seasoned conscience had endured some traumatic events on the streets throughout his career: shootouts, murders, drug busts, and even the suicide of Bruce Martin. But no matter what, Pete never brought work home to his family… never. He kept it all bottled in. But the bottle would soon tip over the edge and shatter into a thousand pieces.

In Dunkin Donuts, Pete grabbed his sandwich and coffee and headed out the door. As he walked to his patrol SUV, Claire returned his call.

"Hi, honey," Pete said as he answered his phone. "How are you?"

"Hey, babe," Claire responded. "I'm fine—just living the LEO-wife life. I was in the basement when you called. You didn't start your shift yet, did you?"

"I *did*. But I radioed in early. I just left Dunkin to grab my coffee and sandwich."

"Oh, great. I saw on the news that the temperature will drop to twenty-one degrees around midnight. But it'll feel like *twelve*. Are you wearing your compression shirt?"

"I am. Thanks you for washing it. I appreciate it."

"You're welcome, baby."

"Did Michael finish cleaning the basement?"

"He fell asleep—*in* the basement," Claire chuckled.

"Oh, *Jesus*," Pete chuckled. "That's your son."

"Well, at least his grades are picking up. So, I can't complain too much."

"Well, yeah, that's true. I'm grateful for that."

"He did finish the garage, though."

"Oh, good. He was mad at me for telling him to clean out the basement. But he doesn't realize I'm just teaching him to be responsible."

"Indeed. But I think he's getting the gist of it."

"Yeah… and how's our princess?"

"So, Elle was *supposed* to help Michael with the basement until they played one-on-one."

"Wow. Really?"

"Yep, and whoever won had to clean the basement—alone."

"I take it she won?"

"*Oh yeah*, she kicked his butt. Maybe *that's* why he's passed out in the basement."

Pete chuckled. "She's still mad at me for missing her game, huh?"

"No. That girl loves you too much to stay mad at you."

"Yeah. I wish I could've been there to see her score her career-high thirty-five points."

"Oh, she was red hot from that three-point line. I've never seen anything like it."

Pete sighed. "Way to rub it in my face, Claire. I *wanted* to be there."

"Oh, no. I'm sorry, honey. I wasn't trying to make you feel bad."

"It's all right. I need to make some changes with my priorities again."

"Listen, Elle knows your job is very demanding of your time. She understands. And she loves you, Pete."

"Not as much as she loves her Harry Styles posters," Pete laughed as he sipped his coffee.

"Oh *please*, don't even get me *started* with that. You should see her. Every morning, before she leaves her room, she blows kisses at the posters. It's like a ritual."

"Ha… what the hell are we going to do with those kids?"

"I'll tell you what we're going to do… we will keep feeding, clothing, teaching, forgiving, and loving them for the rest of our lives."

"Exactly," Pete smiled. "Until the day we die, right?"

"Right."

"Yeah… all right, baby. I'm going to get this night started. I'll see you in the morning, okay? Love you—"

"Wait, honey?" Claire said before Pete hung up.

"Yeah?"

"Aren't you forgetting something?"

"Um… I don't *think* so. I said 'I love you.'"

"*No*, silly," Claire chuckled. "You know we pray every time before you go on duty."

"Oh," Pete responded as he forgot. "Yes, of course. How could I forget that?"

"Okay, close your eyes."

"Honey, I can't close my eyes out here."

"Okay, fine, I'll close mine…. Heavenly Father… I pray that this evening, you watch over my husband, the father of my children, my lover of a lifetime, Pete. Watch over—"

A staticky voice channels through the radio frequency—breaking the prayer.

"Oh, Claire? Honey, wait. I'm sorry, just one second…. 821 to dispatch. Can you 68?"

"821," said the dispatcher. "What's your twenty?"

"I'm at the intersection of Elizabeth Avenue and East Runyon Street."

"Please be advised that I have a possible 10-37 in the area. The vehicle is a two-door, black Kia Forte Coupe, plate number Echo-Zulu-5-2-3-Tango. The owner of the vehicle comes back as Shanice Mitchell. Vehicle taken without owner's consent."

"10-4, received. Thank you."

Pete returned to Claire. "I'm sorry, honey. We'll have to cut this short."

"Okay, no problem. You be careful out there tonight, okay?"

"Promise. I love you, Claire."

"I love you, too… *Petester*."

"Oh my *God*," Pete laughed. "Would you *please* stop calling me that?"

"Nope, sorry. You're stuck with it now."

"All right. I have to go. Good night."

"Good night," Claire said, giving smooches through the phone.

After Pete ended the call, he sat in his patrol truck for a few minutes as he devoured his sandwich and sipped on his coffee. As he observed the streets from the parking lot, he saw a silver Mercedes Benz SL 350 at the light. At that moment, Pete looked at the palm of his right hand and reminisced about Bruce Martin and that crazy Christmas morning.

Five years ago, it was Christmas morning, and Pete had an hour left to go on his night shift. As Pete was squatted on the side of the road, a Silver Mercedes Benz SL 350 went flying by—doing ninety-one on the road with a forty-five-mile speed limit. Pete immediately pursued the vehicle and attempted to make a stop. As the vehicle pulled over, Pete stepped out of his patrol unit and walked to the driver's window. Within *seconds*, the window rolled down and a cup of scorching hot coffee was aggressively tossed at Pete. With Pete's quick reflexes, he managed to block the coffee with his right hand.

Pete, along with several other patrol units, went on a chase with for fifteen minutes until the driver finally stopped. Ten minutes after that, the Mercedes Benz was surrounded in an enclosed location. It was only minutes later that Pete and the other officers heard a gunshot from inside the Mercedes Benz. As Pete and the officers approached the vehicle with their guns drawn, they noticed the windows were splattered with blood. As they opened the door, they discovered a man with a self-inflicted GSW (Gunshot wound) through his temple. The man was later identified as Bruce Martin, CEO of *Martin Enterprises Inc*. Martin went on the run as he was afraid of being a possible suspect for the murder of his estranged wife which they later investigated and concluded that he was the killer.

When Pete came home that Christmas morning, he tried to leave everything that happened right outside his front door so that he could peacefully spend Christmas with his family. But as he sat there with Claire and his kids, he could not help but envision Bruce Martin's brains—*slowly* sliding down the windows, and his bandaged hand. Pete had severe second-degree burns to the palm of his right hand. For two weeks, he could not shake hands with anyone due to the excruciating pain. As an alternative, Pete gave a salute.

For Pete, that was one for the books. And yet, he had many cop stories—very few were good, but the rest were horrific. Pete knew that his job would be perilous at times. He knew days would challenge him mentally, emotionally, physically, and even spiritually. But he also knew that he was a man of faith. He always had moral values and integrity… no matter what.

HERO

As Pete finished his coffee, he took his truck out of parked and hit the road to start his shift. Pete was a nightcrawler—an owl who loved fighting crime at night. Some nights, as he drove the Newark streets, he played the song *Freaks Come Out at Night* by Whodini to get him charged. And that was precisely what he did. As he stopped at a red light, Pete looked at his iPhone to check the time. It was 8:13 p.m.—thirteen minutes into his shift. He smiled as he looked at the picture on the lock screen—a picture of him and Claire on their wedding day. Pete loved his wedding photo. He told Claire that it reminded him daily how blessed he was to have a strong, intelligent, and beautiful wife with whom he can share his life with. Pete kissed the screen of his phone and placed it on the passenger seat. As the light turned green, he began to drive around—following up with dispatch on the suspicious vehicle. It was a smooth ride as he patrolled the streets of Newark in the dead of winter—a place of business and opportunity, but also where trouble could lurk at every corner.

3

DECEMBER 19th, 2025, FRIDAY EVENING:

HOW COULD I HAVE KNOWN?

It was quarter to nine. Pete was only forty-five minutes into his night shift. The night was smooth: no traffic stops or malicious occurrences. But as Pete hit the light, he looked to the left of a two-way road and noticed a black Kia waiting at the light—facing the opposite direction. As the light turned green, the Kia drove off. Pete had to drive a few feet before making a U-turn. As he kept a reasonable distance, he radioed in the dispatcher.

"821 to dispatch," he said. "Be advised, I have a visual of a black Kia. Plate number: Echo, Zulu, five, two, three, Tango. I'll be attempting to make a stop on that vehicle."

"10-4, received," the dispatcher responded.

"Who's the registered owner of this vehicle again?"

"The owner of the vehicle belongs to Shanice Mitchell. She called in claiming her brother, RaJohnn Mitchell, took her car without her consent."

"Ten-four. I'm stopping that vehicle now at 8:46—an unknown number of occupants. We'll be stopped on Hunterdon Street between 14th and 15th Avenue. No additional units needed at this time."

18

Red and blue lights shine bright—flashing on the back of the Kia. As the Kia came to a full stopped, Pete parked his black and white Ford Police SUV behind it. Unbeknownst to Pete, the passenger inside this black Kia was the number one basketball prospect in the nation, Tyshawn Brendan.

"*Fuck* me!" RaJohnn infuriatingly said as he looked in the rearview mirror. "These motherfucking pigs ain't got *shit* else to do."

"*Ah shit*," Tyshawn said as he looked back at the police truck with startled eyes. "Yo, Rah, I'm telling you right now, keep your head and you *better* not crash out on me."

"Yo Ty, don't be telling me what to do, bruh—"

"Nah, nah, nah, nah, nah—be *cool*. For real."

Still sitting inside his truck, Pete patted himself to ensure he had everything. As he placed his pen inside his vest compartment and opened the door, he received a call from his son, Michael. Pete has a rule never to answer his personal phone while on duty—especially while on call. He declined the call and placed his phone inside his vest uniform compartment. For a moment, he sat there, thinking about these situations—knowing that anything could go down in a split second as scenarios like this happen all too often in his line of work. Pete put on his thin blue line American flag beanie and looked at his Apple watch. It was 8:49 p.m. He then stepped out of his SUV.

Back in the Kia, there was vile commotion between RaJohnn and Tyshawn. RaJohnn had a mouth full of choice words. Tyshawn, however, was nervous, trying to neutralize his friend down.

"Bro!" Tyshawn yelled. I'm *not fucking playing* with you. *Calm the fuck down!*"

"Nah, *fuck* that!" RaJohnn shouted. "I can't *wait* til this pig pulls up to the window so I can go off on him."

"Yo Rah, I'm *dead serious*! *Keep your head*!"

Pete adjusted his vest and duty belt—leaving the lights on with the engine running—just in case the driver tried to make a fast getaway. In the years of doing stops, Pete has always made it a rule to unbuckle his holster before approaching the vehicle—just in case he had to draw his weapon. He walked toward the car—hearing rap music blasting from the inside—a rap song called *Gang Gang* by rappers Moneybagg Yo and Yo Gotti. He pulled out his flashlight—shining it on the tinted windows. Pete was calm, but even after sixteen years on patrol, startling situations like this always require serenity and precaution. Pete approached the driver's door and flashed his light on the tinted window. After giving it a few knocks, Pete stepped back and waited with a precautious demeanor.

Inside the Kia, RaJohnn did not budge. Tyshawn looked at him with a fiery face and said, "Roll the window down, man!" RaJohnn rolled the window down—barely two inches—and greeted Pete with a mischievous frown.

"*What*, yo?" RaJohnn maliciously shouted.

Pete looked down at RaJohnn. "First off, turn the music down—"

"Nah, *suck* my *dick*!" RaJohnn yelled as he rolled up the window and turned the music louder.

"You, what the *fuck* is *wrong* with you?" Tyshawn shouted, grabbing RaJohnn's arm.

"Man, *fuck* this pig ass cracker!"

As Pete stood beside the car, he rolled his eyes and sighed as he knew there would be trouble. Ten seconds went by. But it felt like an hour. The adrenaline was rising within him. Pete then stepped away from the car and radioed in the dispatcher.

"Dispatch," he said. "Another unit to my location."

"Ten-four," the dispatcher responded. "Any available unit, 821 is requesting back-up on Hunterdon Street, between 14th and 15th Avenue. Time now is 8:50 p.m."

The music was at its maximum volume in the car, and RaJohnn

had lost his cool. Tyshawn feared for his life as he had no control over his short-tempered friend.

"Are you *trying* to get us *killed*?" Tyshawn said with anger.

"That cracker cop from earlier had me on the ground, bro! I ain't *about* to let *this* motherfucker do the same to *me*. I *told* you I stand on *business*! Fuck this pig, and *fuck* Coach Dutch! Yo, I *got* something for his bitch ass."

"What you reachin' for?" A startled Tyshawn said as he looked at RaJohnn reaching into his coat pocket. "NO!"

Pete reapproached the driver's door, unaware of the threat that lied within. As the window rolled down, RaJohnn quickly extended his arm—an *instant* flash. Pete immediately stepped back, gripped, and discharged his gun.

"NOWWHAT,PIG—"

"*DROP YOUR WEAPON!*"

POP, POP, POP, POP, POP, POP!

Six... six shots—*echoing* throughout Hunterdon Street. Life or death—him or me—that was all that could fit in the milliseconds between Pete drawing his gun and opening fire. Pete rushed back to his patrol unit as he quickly discharged his magazine. His hands shook so hard that he dropped the second magazine on the ground as he tried to reload. "*Fuck!*" Pete shouted as he picked it up and reloaded. He cocked his gun as he took cover between the a-frame of his car door, expecting a shootout. "SHOTS FIRED! SHOTS FIRED!" Pete screamed in his walkie. "CODE THIRTY-THREE! I NEED EMS TO MY LOCATION *NOW*! STEP IT UP!"

Pete was in instant shock as everything happened in a matter of seconds. His heart was racing like he was running from a hungry lion—chasing after him at full speed. The adrenaline invaded his body. His freezing hands trembled as he held his gun—pointing it at the Kia. His deep breaths created heavy frost floating aimlessly in the air. It was a very eerie scene as the music echoed throughout the street, but no movement was happening in the car. Suddenly, the driver's door opened on the Kia. Pete immediately pointed his gun towards the door.

"*God… damn* it," RaJohnn shouted as he fell out the car onto the ground. "You pig mother… *fucka!*"

RaJohnn was on the ground, grunting in extreme pain. "*Show me your hands!*" Pete said as he kept his gun pointed at him—music still blasting from out of the car. It was as if a shooting took place at a nightclub. RaJohnn, now lying face down on the street, lifted his bloody hands. Pete, still shaking, approached him with caution. He stood above him as he uncocked his gun, holstered it, and pulled out his handcuffs.

"Don't move!" Pete said as he cuffed him.

"Ow, my arm!" RaJohnn screamed. "You fucking shot me, you bitch ass mother*fucka!*"

"I said, '*Don't fucking move!*'" Pete said as he patted him down. "Where's the gun? *Where's* the fucking gun?"

"There *ain't* no fucking gun, man! It was my phone, *pussy!*"

"A *Phone?* That was *stupid!* That was really *fucking stupid!*"

"Man, *fuck* you, bitch—*ow!*"

"I said, '*Don't move!*'"

After Pete detained him, he ran to the trunk of his SUV and popped it open. He unzipped his bag and pulled out scissors, gloves, and a tourniquet. After putting on his gloves, he searched for the GSW. RaJohnn, however, grew aggressively resistant.

"Get the *fuck* off me, you fucking *pig!*" RaJohnn screamed in pain.

"Stop *moving!*" Pete shouted.

Pete looked sharply for the wound. He discovered that the driver was hit *twice*: once in his left elbow and once in his hip area. Pete hurried and placed the tourniquet around his elbow.

"Ow, man!" RaJohnn screamed as he became emotional. "Help, he's going to kill me!"

"*Stop moving*! I'm trying to *help* you!" Pete said as he secured the tourniquet around his elbow. "Tourniquet applied, it's 8:51 p.m."

As per Protocol, whenever a tourniquet is applied to a GSW, the officer has to check the time it was used. He did not realize that this scene happened in precisely one minute and eighteen seconds. Suddenly, RaJohnn emotionally screamed out to his friend, who had gone silent.

"Ty," he cried. "*Ty*, talk to me!"

"Who you talking to?" Pete said, oblivious that a second occupant was in the car.

Everything happened so fast and Pete had no time to scan the vehicle. Once again, he discharged his gun from the holster, cocked it, and picked up his flashlight from the ground. As Pete flashed the light inside the car, he saw his worst nightmare. Tyshawn was crotched over in the passenger's seat like a cat on his ninth life. There was broken glass scattered over the black leather seats. The smell of gunpowder filled the heated car, and the basketball on his lap was deflated as it was struck by one of the bullets. Tyshawn was also hit—his white sweater growing red from the bleeding wound.

"*Jesus Christ*!" Pete said. "DISPATCH, I NEED A *FUCKING* AMBULANCE, NOW!"

Pete had no idea if he was still breathing or not. He uncocked his gun, holstered it, and immediately turned off the car. Now, there was silence—eerie silence. Tyshawn's seatbelt was not attached. Pete then pulled his tall body from out from the driver's side of the car.

"Stay with me, all right!" Pete screamed as he laid Tyshawn on the ground.

Another minute went by, but the ambulance was nowhere in sight. Pete immediately cut open Tyshawn's bloody sweater—right down the middle. He quickly observed and saw that Tyshawn was hit twice—both shots to the left side of his body.

"Ty! Talk to me, *please*!" RaJohnn cried.

Pete had a thousand thoughts racing through his mind. Everything happened so fast—*faster* than half a blink of an eye. It was freezing out, and he was all alone—waiting for help to arrive. "Talk to me, buddy," Pete said, kneeled beside Tyshawn. "EMS is on their way, okay? Just stay with me."

Suddenly, Tyshawn, with his bloody body trembling on the ground, looked up at Pete. He gave Pete this clear look, an emotionless look. It was a look that Pete had never seen before. A look that said, "*Why?*" Pete looked directly into his dilating brown eyes. It was as if their souls connected, and he was about to tell Pete something.

"Talk to me, buddy," Pete said.

Tyshawn inhaled a deep breath, looked Pete dead in his eyes, and with aggressive emphasis, he said…

"*FUCK* YOU!"

Blood shot out of Tyshawn's mouth like a geyser and hit Pete dead in his face—blinding him instantly.

"AHH FUCK!" Pete screamed as he stumbled back and planted himself on the ground. "I can't see! I can't see!"

Moments later, another unit pulled up. The officer got out of his patrol car and was taken aback by the scene as he saw a crying RaJohnn detained on the ground and his fellow officer screaming that he could not see. The ambulance and paramedics were heading down the street. The officer took out his flashlight and waved it down to get their attention. As they stopped, the ambulance and paramedics rushed out of their truck and took over.

As for Pete, the shooting was finally hitting him. The officer helped Pete up and took him away from the scene. The officer who came as a backup unit, Officer Daniel Siwinski—already knew Pete.

"Gant, you okay, brother?" Officer Siwinski asked as he held on to Pete.

"I—I don't know, man," Pete said with exhaustion. "I feel—I feel like I'm going to pass out."

"Woah, easy—okay, okay," Officer Siwinski said as he kept Pete from falling. "Okay, let's walk you over there... here, take a seat—right up against the fence."

"Oh, God... oh my God."

"Just *breathe*, Gant. Take deep breaths... are you hit?"

"No."

Officer Siwinski looked at Pete's face. "How'd you get blood on your face?"

"It's... it's not my blood. It's... the kid's."

"What happened here, bud?"

"I... the kid pointed something at me," Pete said as he gasped for oxygen. "It was black and... there was a flash. I... I don't know. It happened so fast—I—I can't, my mind is all over the place—"

"Okay, okay, Say no more. Just relax—right here, up against the fence."

Several more units had arrived at the crime scene. Pete was in complete disbelief. It was as if he was in a nightmare he could not wake himself from—a *nightmare* he dreaded his whole career. As he sat on the ground—leaned up against a steel fence, he saw paramedics working on Tyshawn. At that moment, Pete took a panoramic look at the crime scene. He saw shell casings—scattered on the ground. People were coming from outside the apartment complex, forming a growing crowd of onlookers. Suddenly, as Pete looked briefly at the ground next to the Kia, he noticed the deflated basketball was on the ground... covered in blood. But Pete did not think anything of it. He focused back on the paramedics as they were still working on the kid he shot.

Pete was distraught and highly fatigued—trembling with adrenaline and anxiety. Multiple patrol units and police officers had surrounded the area. The onlookers were becoming intensively vocal as they noticed two black males were on the ground shot. At that moment, Pete realized that something—that only took a split second—caused this unsolicited chaos. In less than five minutes, a crime scene was established. He sat on the ground with a stampede of thoughts rumbling in his mind. But one thought in particular stood out the most...

"Oh dear, God... what have I done?"

4

DECEMBER 19[th,] 2025, FRIDAY EVENING:

THE AFTERMATH

Minutes later, the crime scene was swarmed with police. Paramedics wasted no time as they rushed Tyshawn Brendan to University Hospital—which was two blocks away. The EMTs unit transported RaJohnn Mitchell as he was in stable condition. Pete remained silent—still sitting up against the fence—shaking as the adrenaline consumed his weary body.

Yellow caution tape was set up to block off the angry citizens as they held up their phones and recorded the crime scene. The Major crime scene unit and homicide detectives had begun their investigation, photographing the crime scene and socializing among themselves. Multiple officers approached Pete, saying, "Are you okay, brother? Are you okay?" But Pete was not okay. As he leaned up against the fence, Officer Siwinski, along with police supervisor Captain Kenneth Bernal, approached him.

"Gant, you okay?" Officer Siwinski asked.

"I—I'm okay... I think," Pete responded, still discombobulated.

"Son," said Captain Bernal. "Can you tell me what happened here tonight?"

"It was a traffic stop... no... I... it was a 10-37... and the driver was becoming hostile, and... he pulled out a black object and pointed it at me. I opened fire… I hit both of them."

"Where's your gun?"

"It's—it's in my holster."

"Give it to me… I'm going to need your body cam as well."

"Al—all right… I just need a little help getting up."

"Yes, of course. Hey, can somebody give me a hand over here?" Officer Siwinski projected.

Another officer hurried over to help Siwinski with Pete. They grabbed Pete's arms and lifted him. Pete, however, could barely stand.

"Are you okay to walk, son?" Captain Bernal asked.

"I'm a little light-headed," Pete said as his mind fogged.

"Straight to the hospital—get him *straight* to the hospital," Captain Bernal ordered. "He should've *been* at the hospital."

"Yes, sir," Officer Siwinski said.

Pete was stripped of his Axon body cam and gun and was escorted into Officer Siwinski's patrol car. As Pete walked, he looked over at the Kia and looked at the bullet holes that went through the window and the door. Pete kept replaying the moment in his head, thinking if he could have taken another approach and handled the situation differently. He also thought about his wife and kids, as well as the kid he shot. As he entered the passenger seat of Siwinski's patrol unit, Pete suddenly broke down and cried. Siwinski got in the car and noticed him sobbing with his hands covering his face. He patted and rubbed Pete's back as he said, "It's going to be all right, bud. You did what you had to do… huh? You protected yourself. There's no shame or blame in that. We're going to the hospital right now."

Pete was filled with emotion that he could no longer contain. Even though Officer Siwinski gave him words of comfort, the sense of guilt was too overpowering as he had no intention of shooting the kid. It would take less than a minute before they arrived at the hospital.

But at that very moment, all Pete wanted to do was go home to his family.

5

DECEMBER 19[th,] 2025, FRIDAY EVENING:

THE HOSPITAL

It was 9:21 p.m. Pete was alone with his thoughts, waiting in the exam room—still in full uniform. His trembling hands were unstoppable as the adrenaline had taken over. He sat silently and heard nothing but the heart monitors from the other rooms—beeping pulse after pulse. At that moment, Pete thought about the kid and hoped he was okay. He also thought about Claire. He wanted to call her and tell her about what had happened. But he knew she would already be asleep. So, instead, he called the one person he knew would be up: his father, Montgomery. Montgomery would go to his next-door neighbor's house every Friday evening and play poker. They would play for money—*big* money. Pete pulled out his phone from his vest compartment and called him. The phone rang several times before Montgomery picked up.

"He—hello?" Montgomery answered in a soft tone.

"Dad?" Pete said. "Were you sleeping?"

"Yeah. Jerry didn't feel like playing poker tonight. So, I called it quits and went to bed early. You're on your shift, right?"

"Dad… something bad happened."

"What?" Montgomery said as he sat up in his bed. "Are you all right?"

"No," Pete said as he grew emotional. "Dad... I was involved in a shooting."

"Oh my *God*, you were *shot*?" A startled Montgomery asked.

"No, no, *I* shot them. They were kids. Oh, Dad, I fucked up."

"Okay, okay, calm down... calm down. Where are you?"

"I'm in an exam room. They're going to investigate me. Dad, you gotta call Uncle Freddy."

"Right, right, okay, I'll call him."

"Call him right now."

"Yeah, I'll call him right after I get off the phone with... oh *shit*."

"What?"

"I just remembered that Freddy is away on business in L.A...*fuck*—okay, I'll just tell him it's an emergency, and he'll be here as soon as possible. But *you* don't say a *word* to *any*one. If they start asking questions, you keep your mouth *shut*—*d*o you hear me?"

"Yes, sir," Pete responded, wiping his tear-stained face.

"Okay. Are you in a hospital? Where are you?"

"Yeah, I—I'm at University Hospital in Newark."

"All right, son. I'm on my way—"

"Dad, wait... don't tell Mom anything. I don't want her to worry."

"You let me worry about your mother. Just make sure you don't talk to them. Assert your fifth amendment privilege, just as Freddy instructed. Do you understand?"

"Yes, sir."

"All right. I'm on my way, Pete... I love you."

"I love you, too, Dad."

Pete hung up his phone and looked down, tears falling. He noticed the bloodstains on the palms of his hands and uniform. His hands smelled of blood and gunpowder. Pete wanted to wash it off, but due to protocol, he had to be examined first, swabbed down, and give a blood sample for toxicological purposes.

Pete saw Officer Siwinski through the door crack as he sat on the hospital bed. Siwinski was talking to one of the doctors. They were too far away for Pete to understand what they were discussing. But after what transpired, he felt that it was nothing good. Still trembling, Pete sat there—counting the beeps coming from the monitors—trying to distract himself from the shooting. He was at seventy-nine beeps. Moments later, Siwinski began to walk towards Pete's exam room. Alongside him was the doctor he was talking to. Pete took a deep breath as Siwinski entered the room with the doctor.

"Hey, Gant," Siwinski said. "You okay?"

"I can't stop shaking," Pete responded. "But I'm okay, I guess."

"You want some water or anything?"

"No... I just want to go home... I want to go home to my family."

"We'll get you out of here as soon as we can," said the doctor. "I'm Dr. Steve Archer. I'm going to be examining you: check your vitals and everything. Are you in any physical pain?"

"No... I'm just very anxious."

"That's the adrenaline. We'll give you something for that."

"The kid," Pete softly said. "Where's the kid? How's he holding up?"

Dr. Archer gestured as he looked at Officer Siwinski—hoping he would break the news to Pete. "Do you wanna..."

Siwinski took a deep breath and sighed. "Pete... I have some bad news... we lost him."

"Wha... what?"

"He's gone... he was pronounced dead about five minutes ago. They did everything they could to save him, but it was too late. And the other kid—the driver—he's in stable condition."

Pete, now crying. "He's dead?"

"Yeah, Pete... he died."

"*No*... oh, no, no, no, no—*God*, no."

"Hey, *hey*—*look* at me. It's *not* your *fault*. Okay?"

"The kid pulled something out of the window… I—I thought he was armed. I thought he was going to shoot me."

"It's going to be fine. You did what you had to *do*."

"But the other kid… I didn't mean to shoot him. I didn't know he was in the car. Oh, *God*, what have I done?"

"Pete," Dr. Archer said. "I'm going to examine you now, okay? I'll need some swabs on your face and hands. Then, I'll need some blood samples—possibly a urine sample. I'll be right back to check your vitals."

At that moment, Pete wanted to get the rest of the process over with and head home. He had hoped the kid would pull through. But after hearing that he did not make it, Pete felt that he had blood on his hands—metaphorically and literally. Pete continued to sit there in the exam room—sobbing in the diming depths of his sorrow. Officer Siwinski placed his left hand over Pete's right shoulder and said, "Pete, look at me. This situation right here… doesn't make you a killer. That kid put your life at risk, and you had to defend yourself. Yes, it's unfortunate that the other kid was hit in the crossfire… he was just in the wrong place at the wrong time… it *happens*… it happens every day." Pete was listening to Officer Siwinski, but it was tough for him to accept it that way. A few minutes later, Dr. Archer returned to examine Pete. Standing outside of the exam room was crime scene detective Robert Winterburn.

Dr. Archer placed the arm cuff on Pete's left arm as he checked his vitals. As the cuff started to inflate, Pete sat there, still shaking, lost in his thoughts.

"Try to hold still, okay? As best as you can," Dr. Archer said.

"Sorry," Pete responded. "What does it say?"

Dr. Archer read Pete's blood pressure. "*Jesus*…. your pressure's 187 over 119."

"Is that bad?"

"You're hypertensive. We have to get that down right now."

"One-eighty-seven, huh?" Pete said as he shook his head. "My body's in tune with what I'd done... I'm a killer."

"I'm going to have one of the nurses give you some Lorazepam."

"La—what?"

"Lorazepam. It'll help with the anxiety."

Detective Robert Winterburn stepped in. "Wait, Doctor. Before you do anything else, I'll need his uniform."

Detective Winterburn had Pete undress out of his uniform and collected it for evidence. One of the nurses then proceeded to inject the IV of Lorazepam and take some blood samples from Pete. She then took swabs of the blood from his hands and face. As Pete laid in the hospital bed, Dr. Archer had returned.

"How are you feeling so far?" Dr. Archer asked.

"Better," Pete said. "I'm not shaking as much anymore."

"That's good... so—"

"When can I leave?"

"Soon... we'll keep you here for a little while to ensure you're stable enough. After that, I can discharge you. Is there anyone who can pick you up?"

"My father's on his way here."

"You've spoken with father?"

"Yes," Pete answered, now feeling sedated. "The medicine's starting to kick in. Thank you, Doctor."

"You're welcome. Just relax yourself, all right?"

"All right."

It was a surreal moment for Pete. In his sixteen years on the force, he had discharged his weapon eleven times—firing it seven. But this was the first time he shot anyone in the line of duty. Unfortunately, he hit the wrong target. The reality had now settled in. As Pete laid in the hospital bed, Robert Winterburn came forward and began to converse with him.

"How are you feeling, son?" Detective Winterburn asked as he adjusted his glasses.

"A little better," Pete responded. "Except that I'm probably going to prison for this."

"*Prison*? Oh, no, son... let me explain this to you... you're not a suspect, *nor* are you a victim. Once we investigate the shooting, the prosecutor will determine what the next step is going forward. But don't worry about that right now. Get you some rest and clear your head. We'll proceed with everything within the next twenty-four hours... okay?"

"Okay."

"And son? I must warn you... when you get home, do *not* watch the news. Do *not* turn on that television. I mean it... the media... it's the Devil we *don't* know. It's his *eye*."

"Yes, sir."

Detective Winterburn looked at Pete sincerely, his eyes piercing through the lens of his clear-framed glasses. His salt and pepper hair was combed back, sporting a thick, grayish mustache. Detective Winterburn had Pete's uniform in his possession. He explained to Pete the importance of his rights and why he should not watch the news. He told Pete that when the time comes, he wanted him to explain the shooting—how *he* remembered it, and not by watching any media coverage. As Pete laid on the hospital bed, he heard a buzzing sound from his phone. He picked it up and saw that it was a text from his father:

Dad
I'm on my way, son.
Did you need me to bring anything? Food? Water?

Pete
No. Just clothes. Please hurry. I want to get out of here.

Dad
Okay, son. I'm on my way. Did they try to question you?

Pete
Dad, just get here ASAP. Please?

Dad
Okay. I'm sorry. I'll get some clothes together, And I'll be there shortly.

Pete
Thank you.

Pete laid there in his blue hospital gown as he began to think about everything that had transpired. As a cop, Pete had been verbally attacked by the phrase "*Fuck* you" more times than he would want to remember. But this time was different. *This* time, it was a kid's final words. No matter how Pete looked at the situation, it was a tragic blur. A horrifically vivid nightmare that continued to play in his mind.

6

DECEMBER 19^{th,} 2025, FRIDAY EVENING:

A CONCERNED FATHER REUNITED WITH HIS SON

It was a quarter to eleven. Pete was still waiting in the exam room—deep in devastation as the shooting repeatedly played in his head—seeing the haunting image of the kid lying on the ground. Pete kept seeing his face and the look in his eyes. Knowing that the kid was now deceased, Pete was terrified of the possible consequences that awaited him.

Moments later, in the lobby of University Hospital, Montgomery rushed through the automatic doors with a bag of clothes. He then went to speak to the woman who sat at the desk.

"Excuse me," Montgomery anxiously spoke. "I'm looking for my son, Officer Pete Gant? He told me they brought him here."

"Pete Gant?" The woman asked.

"Yes, he's a police officer."

"Okay, let's see…."

Montgomery's patience was thin as a thread as the staff member looked up the room number. He wanted to see his son immediately.

"Look, maybe if you could just tell me what room he's in, and I'll find my way to him," he anxiously said.

The woman responded, "I'm so sorry. I'm just not getting a room number. Let me call someone and see where he is…. Pete *Gant*—correct?"

"Yes, Pete Gant."

Montgomery waited—pacing back and forth as the woman made a phone call. "Hi, Mary," said the woman. "I'm looking for Officer Pete Gant. Do you know where they have him? Just one second, sir." Montgomery looked as if he was blowing out steam.

"Ma'am, *please*," Montgomery irritatingly said.

"My *apologies*, sir… yes, Mary? Do you know where he is? Okay, C170G—C170G, sir. It's on this floor. Just go through those doors."

"Thank you," Montgomery said.

Montgomery rushed through those doors, looking at every direction, wondering where to go. He saw a doctor and said, "Doctor, I'm looking for my son. Officer Pete Gant? Where is he?" The doctor escorted Montgomery to the room where they were keeping Pete. Montgomery turned left, then right, and left again. It was like a maze of panic.

Montgomery finally made it to the exam room where Pete was in. As the door opened, Pete lifted his head and saw his father. He immediately burst into tears. "Dad," he cried.

Montgomery rushed over and hugged his son like they had not seen each other in ages. The last time Pete and Montgomery embraced each other like this was when Pete graduated from the academy. Montgomery was not much of a hugger. He would always shake Pete's hand—with a gentle tap on the shoulder. But this time, he held onto Pete for dear life.

"I got you, son," he whispered in Pete's ear. "I got you. It's going to be all right."

Pete was in bad shape, emotionally. All he could muster out through the traffic of anguish was, "I just want to go home, Dad… take me home to my family."

7

DECEMBER 20th, 2025, SATURDAY MORNING:

THE RIDE HOME

It was after midnight. The temperature was twenty-one degrees, just as Claire said it would be. Montgomery kept looking over at Pete, who was silent as a dead man's whisper. Pete stared out the passenger window, with tears in the reflection. As Montgomery drove, he began to talk with his son.

"Pete," said Montgomery. "Son, I know you don't want to talk right now. But I need to know if you're okay. You've been quiet since we left the hospital."

Pete, however, did not respond. He sat there and continued to look out the window. As Suddenly, a car quickly pulled out of a gas station and cut off Montgomery.

"Holy shit!" Montgomery shouted as he slammed his foot on the brakes and pressed his horn.

They were stunned; just before the driver in the other car pulled off, he shared some malicious choice words with Montgomery.

"Didn't you see me coming out of the gas station?" The driver yelled. "Watch where you're going, asshole!"

"*FUCK* YOU!" Montgomery aggressively responded. "*Jesus…* can you believe that son of a bitch?"

Suddenly, Pete rolled his window down as he began to hyperventilate. Montgomery looked over and saw him with his head sticking out the window.

"Hey… hey, what's wrong?" He asked.

"I think I'm having a panic attack," Pete responded as he gasped for air.

"Okay, okay, hold on. Take it easy, all right? *Breathe*."

"Pull over, Dad. Pull over now."

Montgomery pulled over by the curve. Pete quickly opened the door and vomited on the side of the road. After regurgitating, he walked over to the corner of and sat near the curve. He stared at the ground as he exhaled his frosty breath. Montgomery then got out of his car and stood beside him.

"Are you all right?" Montgomery asked.

"I'm sorry," Pete said as he wiped the vomit residue from his mouth. "I just… I felt something when you said… the f-word."

"That upset you?"

"The kid… he… never mind. Let's just go home."

"Here, let me help you up."

Montgomery took Pete's hand and helped him up from the curve. As they stood there, he looked at Pete with immense concern. Montgomery did not know why he was so triggered by him saying the f-word. But he knew not to pressure Pete by asking. Pete combed his fingers through his hair as he walked back to the passenger seat— carefully stepping over his vomit. He got in and planted his forehead in the palm of his hand.

As Montgomery got in, he looked at Pete—staring at him in silence. He did not know what to say to ease Pete's anguish. But he felt he had to say something. "Listen, son," he said. "I spoke with Freddy. He's hopping on the next available flight. Your Uncle Freddy knows the law like the back of his hand. He's cutthroat. When he gets here, he'll walk you through everything. We're going to get through this, son… together. All right?" Pete remained silent as he looked out the window. Montgomery tried to get something out of him, but no one was home. He did not know what Pete was feeling inside or what he was thinking.

"Come on, Pete… talk to me, son," Montgomery begged.

"Dad," Pete spoke. "Can I ask you a favor?"

"Yes, anything."

"Please don't treat me any different. I will go *insane* if you treat me differently. I need you to treat me as if I'm *still* the same Pete… even though I'll never be the same again."

"What do you mean, Pete—"

"Just *please*, Dad… treat me as if nothing's changed."

"Okay… I'll do my best."

"Thank you… I want to go home now to my wife and kids."

"You got it, buddy… we're almost home."

Montgomery started the car and drove off. Not another word was said between them for the rest of the drive. All Pete thought of at that moment was Claire and the children. Even though they would be asleep, Pete could not wait to get home and see them in bed— knowing they were safe from all the world's evil.

8

DECEMBER 20^{th,} 2025, SATURDAY MORNING:

A GRIEVING MOTHER

A walk down the hospital aisle had never been so painful. Tyshawn's mother, Jada Brendan, was informed of the worst news a mother could ever receive. Her one and only son was dead. Jada, however, demanded that she see her son in the hospital before they transported him anywhere. She was accompanied by her sister, Constance, and her best friend, Keshia, whom she asked to stay behind as she wanted to see Tyshawn alone. Jada was a beautifully spirited woman—long black twist braids down her back with a beauty mark on her left cheek. At thirty-seven, Jada's flawless, melanated skin made her look ten years younger. Yet her face was drained of all youthful happiness and replaced with a melancholy decal.

Jada was numb and silent. She could not believe that this was reality. She had spent the last thirty-five minutes—texting and calling—trying to contact Tyshawn's father, Morris Clark. But he was not responding. That is when Jada remembered that she did not have his new number. Jada and Morris were not together, but she had a good relationship with Morris's mother, Beatrice. She called Beatrice and told her the tragic news. Beatrice screamed through the phone as she went hysterical. All Jada asked of her was to tell Morris what happened.

Jada continued to walk down the aisle at a devasted pace, following behind the doctor, Dr. Levy. She asked the doctor if she could hold his elbow—just in case she passed out. Dr. Levy was very kind and supportive. He held Jada's hand as he led her to the operating room where Tyshawn's body was. As they were getting closer to the double doors of the operating room, Jada was beginning to breathe a little heavy. She stopped just a few feet from the doors and leaned against the wall. Dr. Levy turned to look in her eyes— seeing a distraught mother.

"Ms. Brendan," said Dr. Levy. "You don't have to do this alone."

"No… this is what I want," Jada said. "I want to be alone with my son. Can you give us some privacy, please?"

"I'll be right outside these doors, Ms. Brendan."

Jada stood there, five feet away from the double doors— standing in her mauve sweatsuit. Before she took another step, she closed her eyes, took a deep breath, and exhaled. "Lord Jesus… give me strength," she said as a tear streamed down her right cheek. Jada was about to take the most difficult steps a parent had ever taken. One step at a time as she walked toward the double doors—every inch of every step was like walking on acupuncture needles with novocaine—every step she took made her legs numb and weak. Jada placed her hands on the doors, gently pushed them open, and walked inside to witness her worst nightmare vividly.

There he was, lying on the table with a white sheet covering his body from the neck down. All Jada could do was stand there, not making a sound as her tear-stained face said it all. There was a solid ten feet between her and Tyshawn. But the distance began to decrease as she moved forward. Step by step, she walked—each step getting heavier as if she was sinking into the floor. Jada stopped as she felt she was going to collapse, only a few feet away from her son. She did not want to take another step, as another step was closer to her new reality. She then closed her eyes as tears descended. With her eyes still closed, she took the most difficult steps she ever had to take. Her body was shaking as she stood there. As she opened her eyes, she looked straight ahead. All she could hear was the sound of her breathing. Slowly, she looked down and saw her son. Tyshawn looked like he was sleeping peacefully, not a care or a bother in the world. He looked like an angel. But Jada looked like her soul had imploded in the dark, heavy depths of her pain.

Jada placed her hand on Tyshawn's right cheek. She felt coldness, stillness; she felt death... the death of her son. She kept looking at him. She then kissed him on his cold forehead and cheek. Then, she went underneath the sheet and held his hand. She *kissed* his hand—over and over again, and then his foot. But Jada wanted to see more as she lifted the sheet and discovered the gunshot wounds. She gasped as she saw the coagulated wounds. Tyshawn was hit twice: once in the rib area and the other near his left kidney.

Jada's hands were shaking as she touched around the wounds. She began to have flashbacks—thinking of the time when Tyshawn was a baby, and she would change his diapers. And now, her baby was gone. Through her tears and sniffling, Jada began to speak to her son. "*Oh, King*," she cried. "Wake up. Baby, wake up... come on. You can't leave Mommy... we just talked. Oh God... what happened, baby? How did this happen? Why did it have to be you? We were so close, King. We were so close to the promised land.... You always told me that I was the strongest woman you ever met. No matter what, you always told me that I was strong. But right now... I'm so weak.... Oh, King... why did you have to leave Mommy? *Why*? I guess God had other plans for you. I don't know what his plans are, baby. I truly don't. I just pray that I'll have the strength to carry on. Mommy's going to miss you so much. You rest now, baby... until we meet again."

Jada laid her head on Tyshawn's cold chest. The absence of his heartbeat was heartbreaking. As she cried, she thought about all her memories of the two of them together, from when he was in diapers to when he went to his junior prom. One time, back when Tyshawn was five, Jada took him to Burger King after basketball camp. She ordered him a kid's meal. He loved the chicken nuggets. As they ate, Jada took one of the Burger King crowns off the table and put it on Tyshawn's head. She had a love for crowns ever since she was introduced to Jean-Michel Basquiat's artwork.

As Jada adjusted the crown on Tyshawn's little egghead, she said this to him. "Baby… you are a *king*. Do you know what it means to be a king? It means you will grow up and do great things with your life. You will be put in a position of power, honor, and responsibility. *You* will shape this world—not just with basketball, but with knowledge. Knowledge will take you farther than basketball *ever* will. So, use this game as a tool, baby… as an instrument—a compass that will lead you to the promised land—to freedom. From here on, I'm going to call you King. Do you know what it stands for? It stands for '**K**eep **I**nspiring, **N**ever **G**ive up.' That's who you are." Sadly, Jada had to do what a black mother always feared she would *have* to do in her lifetime… to say goodbye to her fallen king.

9

DECEMBER 20th, 2025, SATURDAY MORNING:

THE COP WHO MADE IT BACK HOME

The car had just pulled up in front of Pete's house. The house was completely dark as the Gant family was asleep. The porch light was on, but that was it.

"Looks like everyone's asleep," said Montgomery.

Pete and his family reside in Glen Ridge. Michael and Elle attended Glen Ridge High School, and Leo was in first grade. The house was a three-story modern-style residence with gorgeous landscaping and a lantern on each side of the walkway; it was a beautiful house. But as exquisite as the house was, Pete grew hesitant to go inside. Montgomery sat there with him in silence as Pete had no words; neither did he. He had never seen Pete like this before. Seeing his son defeated and vulnerable, unable to do anything to help him. It hurt him as a father. Suddenly, the silence was broken by Montgomery's phone ringing. It was Pete's mother, Melissa.

"Yes, Melissa?" Montgomery said.

"Monty," Melissa responded. "Monty, oh my God. Is everything all right? Where's Pete?"

"He's right here, I have him."

"Let me speak to him, please."

Montgomery handed Pete the phone. "Your mother wants to talk with you."

Pete put the phone to his ear. "Mom?"

"Oh my God, Pete—sweetheart, are you okay? Are you hurt?"

"I'm *fine*, Mom. I'm not hurt."

"Oh, thank *God*," she cried. "Honey, I was so *worried*. What happened?"

"Mom, I really can't talk about that right now."

"Okay, well, when you can, please call me, okay? *Please*?"

"Okay, Mom, I will. I gotta go. Goodbye."

"All right. I love you."

"Love you, too," Pete said as he ended the call.

"You want me to come in?" Montgomery asked as he placed his right hand on Pete's left shoulder.

Pete shook his head. "No."

"You okay?"

Pete looks at Montgomery. "No, Dad... I'm *not* okay... *this* is not okay."

"Son, listen—"

"Dad—"

"No, no, no... just listen to me for a minute... all right? You were very fortunate tonight, son. You know that? And do you know *why*? Because *you* came home. You made it *home*, son. If they *had* shot you out there, we wouldn't be having this conversation. We wouldn't have *any* conversations... ever again. There's a cop out there who didn't make it home tonight. There are families—right now, as we speak, who got that dreadful phone call or that knock on the door. But *you*... *you* are *home*. You get to walk inside your home and be with your family."

"Yeah... yeah, I understand that, Dad. And I'm grateful. But some kid is *not* going back home... because of me."

Pete opened the car and got out.

"Pete... Pete, buddy," Montgomery said as he got out of the car and walked up to Pete. "Pete, wait!"

Pete turned around. "What, Dad?"

"Freddy wanted me to tell you that you are in good hands. He's the best, son. I know my brother, and he will *not* let you down."

"I just want to go inside now, Dad."

"Yeah... I'll call you later when he gets here."

"Okay, do that," Pete said as he walked away.

Montgomery grabbed onto Pete and hugged him. It was like they embraced for an hour. "I love you, son," he said as he kissed Pete on the side of his head. Montgomery looked at his son as he walked away silently, like a wounded soldier leaving the battlefield. "I know, son, I know... life's not fair." Montgomery returned to his car and made a U-turn. Pete turned around and saw his father drive off. Now facing the front door, he took a moment as he stood there and realized he was home. What his father just said to him was beginning to sink in. Pete thought about all the situations throughout his career when he could have been killed and not be able to stand in front of his house like he was. He closed his eyes and breathed in and out as the chilled wind began to blow, tasting the fresh air as if he were just born. Pete knew deep down how lucky he was to be home. But the shooting and death of the kid had invaded his conscience, and it was there to stay.

As Pete stepped to his front door, he put in the code to unlock it. Pete had his whole house equipped with all the modern tech appliances: cameras, locks with codes, and some extra in-house security: the family dog, Brownie. Pete was a firm believer in security. He did not take chances, especially when it came to his family. And there was a reason for that. When Claire was pregnant with Michael, Pete had a nightmare that his home was invaded when he was on duty during a night shift. Claire was being held hostage by a masked man. Pete was slowly running down the dark street, trying to get home. But by the time he reached his house, it was too late. The masked man had murdered Claire. Pete screamed when he saw Claire lying in a pool of blood as she was shot once in her forehead and twice in her womb. Pete woke up from his nightmare, screaming at the top of his lungs. He sat up in the bed, soaking wet as if he ran on a treadmill for four hours. Claire jumped out of her sleep, panicking as she did not know what was happening. Pete looked over at her and just hugged her tight. He told her about what happened in the nightmare. It was his first "night terror," as he called it. But it was far from his last.

Pete walked into the house and was greeted by Brownie. He kneeled and hugged him like a child hugging his best friend. "Hey, buddy," Pete quietly said. He looked at Brownie as he rubbed the back of his ears. Brownie has been a member of the family for the last five years—a full-grown Liver German Shepherd. Most German Shepherds have the familiar black and tan look. But Brownie had the color of a warm amber sunset. Pete's second son, Leo, was, in fact, the one who named him Brownie. When Pete came home with the puppy, Michael and Elle were so happy. Leo was eleven months old then. That same day, as Leo stood up in his playpen, he pointed at the puppy and said his first word, "Brownie." Pete and Claire thought it was too precious of memory and decided *that* was what they were going to name the puppy. Claire believed Leo's first word was *brownie* because she would feed him little pieces of her homemade brownies. Leo has been eating brownies and other snacks ever since.

Pete continued to rub the back of Brownie's ears. Brownie had a sixth sense. He knew something was wrong with Pete. Brownie would not normally expect Pete at this time of night. Pete would usually greet him at dawn and get him a treat from the kitchen. But this time, there were no treats... no smiles. As Brownie began to lick Pete's face, Pete began to talk to him. "How was your night, my friend?" Pete asked, still petting Brownie. "Good, huh? How was *mine*? The worst night of my life, buddy... worst night of my life." After Pete finished talking to Brownie, he headed for the stairs. Brownie, however, was not happy as he was still expecting his treat. His sudden whimpering made Pete go into the kitchen and fetch him one of his bacon-flavored dog treats.

As Brownie feasted like a savage, Pete headed up the stairs, glancing at the photos on the wall. There was one particular photo that Pete focused on—a family photo of them on vacation at Disney World three years ago. All five of them were wearing the Mickey Mouse ear hat. Pete remembered that day. It was a great day for him. It was the first time in a *long* time he felt free. He was able to take his mind off what happened a several days before that day when the body of fourteen-year-old Gabriella del Alto was found.

Pete remembered that morning vividly. He received a call from dispatch, reporting that someone called in, saying they found a dead person in the woods. When Pete went to check it out, he found her lifeless, naked body covered with wet leaves. A horrific stench came from the body. Medical examiners determined that her body was there for several days before anyone found her. Days after her body was found, Pete received information about her. Gabriella was a sex worker who was raped and beaten to death. At fourteen, she was already a mother of a one-year-old infant. But being that she was a minor and was not willing to cooperate with the police and tell them who impregnated her, the baby was taken from her and entered into foster care. Gabriella was all alone. No family, no friends, there was no one. To support herself, she solicited her body. Ironically, Gabriella was not raped and killed by one of her customers. She was raped by her father, who was also the *biological* father of her baby. After Pete heard about Gabriella's story, he packed his bags and took his family on an impromptu vacation to Disney World.

When it came to policing, Pete was a workaholic. He loved his job passionately and would never take a day off unless he had to. At that point in his career, he had four weeks of vacation. Pete, however, would not use them. He had seen a lot up to that point in his career but would not let it affect his work. It was as if he became desensitized to the violence. But after Gabriella's case, he realized that life was just too short not to enjoy it with his family. Also, being that Pete had a daughter, he could not imagine losing her in such a horrific way. It traumatized him deeply—to see a teenage girl lying dead in the woods after she was raped and beaten to death by her father. The experience of that incident helped Pete build a closer relationship with Elle than he did with Michael and Leo.

Some weeks after the Gabriella del Alto incident, Pete noticed something strange was happening. During that fall season, whenever he took Brownie for walks and walked past a batch of leaves on the ground, he would smell that same dreadful stench from Gabriella's body. It smelled as if her body was right there—buried in the batch of leaves. Pete did not understand why that would happen. He thought he was being paranoid. But the stench was so strong, so real. To this day, Pete has never mentioned Gabriella del Alto to his family.

At the top of the stairs, Pete took a panoramic look at the doors of each bedroom. Leo's bedroom was the closest. As Pete quietly walked in Leo's room, he saw Leo asleep with a pack of Oreo cookies on the floor. Leo was a junk food junkie. He loved anything sweet. Pete walked over and kneeled at Leo's bedside. All Pete wanted to do was hear the gentle sounds of Leo's breathing. He looked and looked at him—thinking of the reality that he would not have been able to do this had that kid pulled out a gun and taken his life. Pete gently combed his fingers through Leo's hair and kissed him on his forehead. "I love you, Leo," Pete softly said.

Pete began to reminisce about the day Leo was born. He remembered it vividly because he was on duty when Claire entered labor. Claire's due date was October the seventh, but Leo decided to show up a little early. As Claire was busy bringing an eager Leo into the world, Pete was busy dealing with a deadly car crash that killed four people—including a three-year-old boy. Claire's mother called him over ten times within five minutes. But Pete left his phone in his patrol unit. Hours later, he entered his patrol unit and saw that Claire's mother called him over twenty times.

At first, Pete grew nervous, thinking that something had gone wrong. He immediately called Claire's mother back and asked if everything was okay. She told him, "Your baby boy's here." It was bittersweet for Pete. On one hand, he was filled with immense joy, but on the other, he was devastated that he missed his son's birth. Not to mention seeing that three-year-old boy lying dead in the backseat. A day that was supposed to be so special was split with tragedy. Pete felt awful for missing Leo's birth, and every year, he tried to make it up to him and Claire.

In Leo's bedroom, Pete picked up the Oreo cookies from the floor, placed them in the packet, and took them with him. After Pete closed the door, he looked down at the cookies and ate one. His appetite, however, had vanished hours ago. And the dreadful aftertaste of his vomit was not a great combination for his tastebuds. Pete then placed the cookies on the table in the hallway and walked over to Elle's bedroom. As he opened her bedroom door, he saw her lying in bed, her dirty blonde hair wrapped in a messy bun. Pete stood in the doorway and just looked at her. He did not go in initially; he just wanted to observe his darling princess while she was dreaming. Pete could see her Harry Styles posters on the wall through the dark. It made him smile momentarily, thinking about what Claire had said earlier. Still standing there, he closed his eyes and slowly shook his head in sorrow. The crime scene kept circling through his mind faster than the bullets he shot off—instant flashes of the kid were playing in his head. At that moment, all he wanted to focus on was his family. He quietly walked over to Elle and kissed her cheek. He looked at her face. Elle was gorgeous—a beautiful spitting image of her mother. She was a daughter that any father would be proud of. Elle started varsity last year as a true freshman—point guard for the girls' Glen Ridge High School basketball team.

As Pete continued to look at her, he thought of the crime scene—thinking, what if things went left and he *was* shot and killed? He thought about all the things he would have missed out on with Elle—missing out on seeing her dressed for her junior and senior prom, missing out on walking her down the aisle of her wedding, grandchildren, everything.

As Pete stood in the doorway, he thought about when Elle was seven years old, and how he took her out trick or treating on Halloween night. Michael had caught a stomachache because of too much candy the night before. Elle was upset because she thought there would be no trick-or-treating for her. But Pete made sure that they would go. Elle was so excited, and so was Pete. He loved the idea of having a father-daughter night. Elle's favorite movie was Aladdin, so she went as Princess Jasmine. Elle went door to door, filling her plastic pumpkin bucket with candy. Pete just remembered walking down the street, holding her little hand as she looked up at him with that beautiful smile that could melt any father's heart. It was a moment of love and innocence that Pete could hold on to and cherish in his mind forever. Pete would have kept Elle as a seven-year-old girl forever if he could. But he knew that his sweet, innocent little girl would one day grow into a beautiful young woman and that innocence would be lost.

"I love you, Elle," Pete said as he kissed his fingertips and left her room. As he closed the door, he walked over to

Michael's bedroom. As Pete gently opened the door, he discovered that Michael was not there. At first, it alarmed him. He thought Michael had snuck out to a party. He was notorious for sneaking out in the middle of the night. That is when Pete remembered Michael falling asleep in the basement earlier that evening.

Pete looked straight ahead at the wall; Michael had some posters of his own. One poster was of Stevie Ray Vaughan holding his guitar, and the other was Jeff Buckley holding a vintage microphone. After Pete closed Michael's door, he went to *his* bedroom to see Claire. He opened the door to his bedroom and saw Claire lying under olive-green bedsheets. Pete made it a house rule that no one, under any circumstances, could use white bedsheets, and there was a complex reason for that.

One night, about eight years ago, Pete came home after a sixteen-hour shift. He was dog-tired—damn near delusional as he entered the house. When he walked upstairs and opened his bedroom door, he saw Claire under white bedsheets. Claire had fallen asleep on her back, and the sheets were up to her neck with her feet exposed at the bottom. It looked as if she was a corpse under a white sheet. Pete *freaked out*—instant panic attack. He called for Claire as he fell to his knees and began to hyperventilate. Claire was petrified as she was ripped from her sleep. She got out of bed and rushed over to him as she tried to figure out what was happening. Luckily enough, he did not wake up Michael or Elle. Up to that point in his career, Pete had seen dozens of corpses covered with white sheets. It was as if something traumatic had triggered a subconscious that he was not aware of, and it had caught up to him. From that moment on, Pete did not allow anyone in the family to use white bedsheets.

Pete walked over to the right side of the bed and kneeled next to Claire. Claire had the left side of her face buried in the pillow with her left arm under it. Pete gently held her left hand as he stared at her wedding ring. He kissed her hand and quietly said, "I love you,

Claire." He then kissed the side of her head and left the room, as he did not want to wake her.

After placing the cookies back in the pantry, Pete headed to the basement. The basement was made into a fun space for the kids to hang out in. There were several arcade games, a pool table, and a big flat-screen television. Pete saw Michael lying on the couch in front of the TV—holding his black Fender acoustic guitar. Pete stood there as he stared at his firstborn as he shed silent tears.

What was so crazy about that night was how fast everything happened. Pete was not even an hour into his shift before the shooting occurred. But it finally sunk in for him. He realized how lucky he was to make it home after another day as a police officer—to be at home with his family and everyone was safe. Suddenly, that feeling took a turn as he looked at the television and saw breaking news coverage.

Pete walked over to the front of the couch and grabbed the remote from the coffee table, turning the volume up a smidge. As he watched, he saw the crime scene on Hunterdon Street between 14th and 15th Avenue. Detective Robert Winterburn warned him not to watch the news or any media. Pete, however, chose not to heed his warning.

Pete watched as the video showed crime scene markers next to the shell casing and magazine that came from his gun. There were multiple people as onlookers, standing behind the yellow caution tape as they were outraged at the sight of two black teens who were shot on the ground. As the news cut to the next scene, they showed the news reporter talking to one of the residents who lived in the apartment complex where the shooting occurred. She was a middle-aged African American woman wearing a pink flamingo bathrobe and her hair in a purple bonnet.

"I was in my house," said the resident. "I heard all this loud music. When I looked out my window, I saw a bunch of sparks, and I... I ducked down because I thought the gunshots would come through *my* window."

Pete could feel his heart rate increasing. He immediately cut the television off and sat there in the dark, in silence—minus the loud fart from Michael. He looked up at the digital clock on the wall, which showed 3:29 a.m. Even though the whole family was asleep, Pete could not sleep a lick. He was restless, considering he would still be on his night shift had none of this occurred. At that moment, he decided to take Brownie for a walk.

Ten minutes later, without waking anyone up, Pete changed into warmer clothes and a heavier coat. He then grabbed the leash and took Brownie outside for a walk. The temperature was nineteen degrees. But Pete did not care. He just wanted to walk, but not alone. He walked down the sidewalk as Brownie sniffed around the gaslights. Most of the time, Pete would be armed and carry his badge if he ever had to walk Brownie in the wee hours of the night. However, his mixed martial arts background made him feel he could defend himself physically if needed.

There was a part of Pete who just wanted to keep walking without stopping, not caring where he would end up. What scared him more was that deep down, he thought he would be prosecuted, convicted, and sent to prison for the death of the kid. He still had no idea who the kid was or even his name. All he knew of him were two simple words… *"Fuck* you!"

An hour went by as Pete walked Brownie around several blocks. The shooting was all he thought about. Strangely enough, Pete did not even remember pulling the trigger. He just kept hearing the kid's voice. He felt like he was sleepwalking—having a night terror. There was a part of Pete that did not want to go back home. He wanted to stay outside and do his job—ride in his unit and patrol the streets. But deep in the back of his mind, in the depths of his fear, he felt that privilege was now destined to be doomed.

10

DECEMBER 20^{th,} 2025, SATURDAY MORNING:

<u>CLAIRE</u>

It was 6:30 in the morning—dark and cold. Claire had just turned over in her sleep—rubbing her left hand on the vacant space of the bed. Suddenly, the alarm on her iPhone went off. With her eyes closed and back turned, she reached behind and grabbed her phone. After hitting snooze, she placed the phone on the bed and stretched her body. Claire would have a Saturday schedule for herself. Every Saturday morning, she would take Brownie out for a walk as that was the only time she had to exercise and clear her head before making breakfast for the kids.

Usually, Claire would be woken up by Pete coming in from work. She would hear the Velcro from his vest ripping off, giving her immense satisfaction that her husband had made it home. But as she got up from the bed and turned around, she saw Pete sitting on the floor, looking straight ahead. As Claire observed the devastation on Pete's face, she knew this morning would be unpleasant.

"Pete?" Claire softly said.

Pete, however, remained silent. He did not even bother

removing his coat after walking Brownie. The troubled look on his face was a face she had seen many times throughout those sixteen years on the job. But *this* time, Claire saw nothing but pain in Pete's eyes. She quickly got out of bed and kneeled next to him.

"Pete?" Claire said as she held his cold hand. "Baby… what in God's name happened?"

Pete slowly turned his head and looked at Claire. "*Oh, Claire…* I really messed up this time."

"What happened, baby?"

"I shot two people… kids."

"Oh, God… but… what happened—*how*? Did they have a weapon? Were you in danger?"

"I… everything happened so fast. I don't know how to describe it."

"But what *happened*? How old were the kids?"

"I don't know. Late teens, maybe."

"Are they okay?"

"No," Pete said as he began to shed tears. "One of them is dead."

"Jesus," Claire said as she covered her mouth with her hand. "But… okay, wait a minute, when—"

"This all happened after I got off the phone with you. My father picked me up from the hospital and—"

"What? You didn't call *me*?"

"I didn't want to wake you. And I didn't want to scare you, calling late at night, thinking something bad happened to me. The last thing I want to do is cause you any panic."

"But you were supposed to call *me*. You said that if anything ever happened to you, Scotty, Martins, or Bilal would contact me or *you* would call me if you needed me. That was our agreement."

"I know, I know… I'm sorry. I just… I fucked up, Claire… I'm in a lot of trouble."

"Okay, let's just slow down with this… all right? How about we discuss this after breakfast? I think that's best."

"I can't eat right now, Claire. I just can't."

"Yes, you can. You have to eat something, honey."

"Please don't tell the kids anything, okay?"

"I won't."

"I'm serious. Don't say a word."

"I won't say anything… come on, I'll run you a warm bath, okay? Just soak in for a half hour, and then I'll get breakfast ready."

Pete sighed. "Okay."

Claire took Pete's hand and helped him up. She then went into their bathroom and ran the bath water. As she stepped back into the bedroom, she looked at Pete as he undressed. Claire stood tall at five foot seven. Her sun-kissed blonde balayage hair went down to her back. She had full lips like Angelina Jolie—a cleft chin and deep brown eyes. She had German and Italian roots in her family tree. Her father was part German, and her mother was Italian and Dutch. She loved fashion and cosmetics and was a model in her teenage years. Claire had a promising future in modeling, but what she wanted more than anything was a loving family. Her choices in men, however, were rather sour and destined for trouble. Most of the guys she dated had a reputation for being a bad boy. As a *teenager*, Claire found those types of guys attractive and addictive. But after her first boyfriend was busted for drugs, she realized that this was not the life she wanted. She wanted to be a mother and a wife. But she knew she could not have that quality of life with a hostile man. Then, one day, the *right* man came into her life.

When Claire was twenty-two, she went to a state fair with her sister, Valentina, and her niece and nephew, Jenny and Ryan. Jenny saw this giant blue stuffed unicorn as a prize for one of the state fair games. The game was to score a basket into a hoop that was twelve feet high. Claire could have been better at basketball, but Jenny *had* to have that unicorn. Claire and Valentina gave it their best, but they failed. That was until this young man came out of the restroom and saw Claire. That man was Pete. Pete stood there for a second—chuckling as he watched Claire shoot airballs. He knew she would not win a prize with shots like that and thought he could be a helping hand.

As Pete approached Claire, he said, "Excuse me? Hi. I see that you're having a little trouble… mind if I try?" Claire looked at him—an instant burst of butterflies began to flap in her stomach. She had never been more attracted to any man than to Pete. "Can you make it?" Claire asked with a smile. Pete responded, "Yeah, I can make it. No problem."

Funnily enough, it took Pete eight attempts before he finally made the shot and won the unicorn for Jenny. What Claire loved about Pete was his willingness never to give up until he succeeded. She saw that in him when he kept trying to sink the shot. They were close in age. Pete was twenty-three. He had just finished his shift working as state fair security. For the rest of the night, Claire and Pete walked and talked. They talked about everything, from their favorite bands to what they wanted in the future. Pete told her that he was signing up for the police academy. Claire thought about that. She thought about how she was always attracted to the bad boy image. But after the first seven months of dating and seeing Pete's six foot-two image in uniform, she realized that she no longer had an interest in bad boys because now… she was with a badass.

Claire, however, was young and naïve. She knew very little of what she was in for. She could not prepare herself for what was to come in a relationship with a police officer, but she did not care. Claire was deeply in love with Pete. And almost seventeen years later, their love for each other was genuine and tender. Their bond was strong, and to this day, she has been proud to be a police wife.

Back in the bathroom, Claire stayed by Pete's side and joined him in the tub. It was quiet and calm—except for the sound of water as she gently rubbed the lime-green loofah sponge over his shoulders—squeezing the suds down his back. As Claire washed his back, she began to look at his massive tattoo of angel wings with clouds in the background. Pete got this tattoo early in his career after he was involved in a shootout. As gunplay was going on, the suspect opened fire—barely missing Pete's head by a few inches. It stunned Pete at first, but what shocked him even more was when a fellow officer opened fire and hit the suspect in the face. The whole left side of the suspect's face exploded like a firecracker filled with blood. That was the first real gruesome experience Pete had as an officer. He realized that had that bullet been a few inches to the right, it could have been *his* face that exploded. Pete believed that there was an angel on his shoulders who was protecting him—which inspired him to get the angel wings tattooed on his back.

The silence lingered as Claire continued to wash Pete's back. Usually, whenever Pete had a rough shift, Claire would give him a quiet home filled with serenity. She would never ask him what happened during his shift. She preferred it that way. To Claire, ignorance was total bliss. But this time was different. This situation was something Pete could not mask. As Claire lay behind Pete in the tub, comforting him, he began to speak.

"Claire?" Pete said.

"Yes, baby?"

"Why did you marry me?"

"*What*?" Claire said, stunned by the question.

"Why did you marry me?"

"Because I *love* you, *that's* why…. I've been in love with you since the very first moment I laid my *eyes* on you. Why would you ask me that?"

"I just thought that maybe, at some point in your life, you may have some regrets being married to a cop."

Claire held Pete tight. "Babe… I have absolutely *no* regrets in marrying you. Okay? I am in this with you until the very end. I'm never going to let you go, baby. Never. Do you hear me?"

"Yes," Pete said, taking Claire's hand and kissing her wedding ring.

"We're going to get through this, okay?"

"Okay."

"Baby… you know I don't like to ask you questions about what goes on out there… but I want to know… what happened last night?"

"It… it all happened faster than the speed of light…. When I was on the phone with you, and you were praying, I got a call from dispatch about a suspicious vehicle. Not even an hour into my shift, I saw the car. I radioed it in and pulled it over. When I got to the driver's window, he was already aggressive. I didn't even get a chance to grab his license. I don't even know the kid's name. That moment is just a blur to me now. All I remember is the loud music… and a flash, and… 'Fuck you.'"

"*Fuck* you? Why would you say something like that?"

"No, no, no," Pete said as he looked at Claire. "I—I'm not saying that to you… that's what the kid said to *me*. The last thing that kid said to me was, '*Fuck* you.'"

"Wait, I'm confused—"

"There were two kids in the car. I don't know how many rounds I shot off. I just… I know that I hit both of them, and the one who didn't make it, *he* said that to me. But I didn't even know he was in the car. It happened so fast and I had no time to react any other way than I did. He extended his arm out the window so fast—I thought it was a gun. But it was a goddamn *phone*, Claire… that fucking kid."

"Jesus," Claire said. "Baby… can I ask you something else?"

"What?"

"These kids… were they black?"

Pete slowly nodded, "Yes."

Claire sighed. "I see."

"See what?"

Claire shook her head. "Nothing... I was just curious... you haven't been watching the news, have you?"

"When I came home earlier this morning, I went to the basement. I watched for about fifteen seconds and turned it off."

"Let that be the last time you watch the news, okay?"

"I know. I—I—I won't."

"Okay... I'm going to get out and get dressed. I'll make us some breakfast. You're coming down, right?"

"Yeah, you go ahead. I'll be down in a minute."

"Okay... give me a kiss," Claire said as she turned his head and kissed him multiple times. "I love you."

"I love you, too."

Claire kissed him once more and got out of the tub.

"Babe," she said as she put on her bathrobe. "I need you to promise you won't watch the news. It will only drive you crazy... promise me, okay?"

Pete looked up at Claire and responded, "I promise, I won't watch it."

Claire smiled and walked out of the bathroom, leaving Pete alone with his thoughts—dark thoughts. The shooting kept playing in his mind. Even though the bathroom was quiet, he could still hear the sounds of the gunshots: Pop! Pop! Pop! And, *Fuck* you!" That was all he heard. Pete could not erase the kid's voice. It was trapped in his subconscious. The scene was very fresh and very real. As his body soaked in the lukewarm water, his mind soaked in despair. Pete wanted out of this nightmare. But this was a nightmare he could not escape. This was a nightmare he now had to live through. A nightmare that was just beginning.

11

DECEMBER 20st, 2025, SATURDAY MORNING:

BREAKFAST WITH NO APPETITE

Pete walked down the stairs in his chocolate-colored moccasins, smelling the aroma of bacon, eggs, and pancakes. He entered the kitchen and saw Claire flipping the pancakes before the stove. She then turned around and looked at him.

"Hey, honey," Claire smiled. "Breakfast's almost ready. Take a seat."

Pete gave her half a smile—trying to show some positivity. But on the inside, he was hurting. He took a seat at the kitchen table and looked out the window. He remained silent as if he read his Miranda rights. He stared at the trees, hearing the birds chirping in chorus. Claire then came over to the table and poured black coffee into his favorite coffee mug. It was a coffee mug with a saying engraved on the side that said, "Proud to be a LEO." Pete, however, did not feel proud at all.

"Claire," he said.

"Yes, baby?"

"Can you hand me another coffee mug, please?"

"Uh… yeah."

Claire was confused as she did not understand why Pete asked for another coffee mug. But she gave him a new mug and went back to the stove. She could not take her eyes off him. She looked as he poured the coffee from one mug to another and placed the "LEO" mug in the kitchen sink. At first, Claire thought that was strange, but she did not want to cause any confrontation about it. A few moments later, their younger son, Leo, entered the kitchen.

"Daddy!" Leo said with enthusiasm, surprised to see his father in the kitchen.

"Leo... hey, buddy," Pete said as he hugged him.

Usually, Pete would spend the rest of the morning sleeping after working the night shift and would not interact with the kids until the afternoon.

"Daddy, why aren't you sleeping?" Leo asked.

"Oh... Daddy got off work a little early last night, bud. So, I'm going to have breakfast with you guys."

"Really?" Leo smiled.

"*Really*, yeah," Pete smiled back.

"*Great!*"

Leo was a very optimistic little boy. No matter what, he always found a way to enjoy the moment. Pete loved that about him. He loved Leo's positive views on life. It gave him a reason to smile. As Claire was occupied with cooking, Pete continued to chat with Leo.

"Ready for some breakfast, bud? Mommy's making some pancakes, bacon, and eggs."

"Eh," Leo shrugged. "I just want cereal."

"Oh... well, go have a seat, buddy. I'll pour you a bowl."

Leo went to sit down at the kitchen table while Pete walked over to the pantry. As he opened the pantry, he grabbed the box of Honey Nut Cheerios and began to pour them into a bowl.

"Daddy, no!" Leo said. "I *hate* Cheerios. I want Lucky Charms."

Pete looked at Leo with confusion. "Oh… I'm sorry, bud. I'll have this bowl for myself. I like Cheerios."

Pete grabbed another bowl and poured in the Lucky Charms. He then placed the two bowls on the table. Seconds later, Michael came up from the basement. "Dad," he said, surprised to see his father up. "What are you doing up so early? Pete walked over to Michael without uttering a word and hugged him. He hugged his son for what seemed like forever. Michael, however, did not understand his father's impulsive affection.

"Bad night at the office?" Michael asked.

"Oh, son… we'll talk later," Pete said as he touched Michael's shoulder. "Let's just have some breakfast. You want some cereal?" "The pancakes and eggs are ready, you guys," Claire interjected. "Michael, go upstairs and tell your sister breakfast is ready?"

"She's on her way down, Mom."

"Mommy," Leo said, chewing a mouthful.

"Leo, honey," Claire said as she poured a glass of orange juice. "What did Mommy say about you talking with your mouth full? Eat first, talk second."

"*Okay*," Leo responded, chewing like a baby calf.

As Pete, Leo, and Michael sat at the kitchen table, Elle came into the kitchen with a sad look as she scrolled her thumb up and down her phone.

"Elle?" Claire said as she placed pancakes on the plate. "Elle, what's wrong?"

Elle looked at her mother and said, "Mom… one of my teammates just texted me about a basketball player who was shot and killed last night."

"Oh my *God*, that's *terrible*," Claire responded. "Did you know her?"

"It's a guy. His name was Tyshawn Brendan. I met him once. He was the top basketball prospect in the country. He just committed to Duke."

"Wow… that is awful news, sweety. I'm sorry to hear that."

"Here's a picture of him."

Claire stood next to Elle as she held the phone, looking at the picture of Tyshawn Brendan. Pete was utterly oblivious to the fact that Elle was talking about the kid he shot. But then, as he overheard Elle, he remembered the deflated basketball with the bullet hole that he saw at the shooting. Instantly, his body began to quiver. His knees shook underneath the table as he feared that Elle was talking about the very same kid.

"Elle," Pete said. "Can—can I see what he looks like?"

As Elle walked over to the table, Pete began to breathe heavily. It was as if she walked in slow motion—holding the phone. She handed the phone to him, and he saw the photo of Tyshawn Brendan. Pete went silent again. He froze—looking at the picture of the kid he shot. He could barely keep the phone steady as his hand was shaking. He was becoming nauseous and dropped the phone on the table. Everyone looked at him with concern. Then, he quickly stood up and said, "I'm gonna to bed." Pete rushed out of the kitchen and headed up the stairs—feeling the heavy chunks regurgitate up his throat. He ran straight into his bathroom and vomited—barely making the toilet. After the nausea settled, he flushed the toilet and leaned against the brown tiled wall. Back in the kitchen, Claire talked with the kids as she made their plates. "Hey guys, your dad had a rough shift last night. I'm going to go up and check on him. But you go ahead and eat. I don't want your food to get cold."

A minute later, Claire walked into the bathroom. She saw Pete sitting there with a gruesome look of guilt. She grabbed a washcloth and ran warm water over it—twisting and squeezing until it was damp. She gave it to Pete to wipe off the puke residue from his mouth. Claire was a shrewd woman. She knew there was a connection between the picture Elle showed him and the shooting. She sat beside Pete and attempted to dialogue.

"That was the kid, wasn't it? In the picture?" Claire asked.

Pete nodded his head. "Yeah... that was him."

"*Jesus...*"

"I don't know if the other kid is all right."

"Wait—what other kid?"

"There were *two* of them in the car. I shot *both* of them."

"You shot *both* of them?"

"Yes, I told you earlier what happened."

"Yeah, but... okay, wait a minute. Tell me again what hap—"

"Claire, please... I don't want to talk about it anymore... please?"

"Okay, I'm sorry... so, what's going to happen now?"

"I have to call Dad and see when Uncle Freddy is coming. I need him to represent me as my attorney for the investigation."

"What should we tell the kids?"

"Absolutely *nothing*. I don't want the kids to be affected by this at all."

"But *you're* affected by this. And they will notice certain changes in you. I don't want to lie to our kids, Pete. This is going to get ugly. We should sit them down and tell them."

"Not right now... let's wait until I finish this investigation. All right?"

"Fine."

"Just... go on downstairs and be with the kids. I'm gonna try to get some rest."

"Baby, I really think we should tell them—"

"I *just need* some *rest*... okay? I'm going to have some very stressful days in the next few weeks. The last thing I need is for the whole family to be on edge."

Claire sighed. "All right. Do you need me to do anything?"

"Yes... yes, I do."

"What?"

"I need you to love me. I need that more than anything."

"Of *course*, honey… that's *never* going to change."

Claire leaned toward Pete and kissed him. She knew this situation would be a roller coaster of emotions for him and did not know how she would prepare for what was to come. She understood that Pete would go through his phases of distress and exposure. But the one thing she needed him to know was that she loved him. Claire loved Pete very much.

12

DECEMBER 20th·2025, SATURDAY AFTERNOON:

THE FAMILY MEETING

It was the afternoon. Pete had been in bed—tossing and turning for the last four hours—barely able to sleep. Whenever he closed his eyes, he saw Tyshawn Brendan's face spitting up blood. He laid on his back as he stared at the white tray ceiling, thinking about what the detectives would ask him during the investigation. Suddenly, his phone rang.

"Dad?" Pete answered.

"Hey, son," Montgomery said. "How are you feeling?"

"My mind's all over the place. But I'm hanging in there, I guess. I tried to get some sleep, but all I did was lie here in bed."

"Well, listen, I just picked up Freddy from the airport, and we're on our way to you. So, get yourself together, huh?"

"All right."

"And you've been staying away from the news, right?"

"Yes, Dad… I haven't been watching the news."

"Good… we're on our way, son."

As Pete hung up his phone and got out of bed, he turned on

the television, hoping that a college football game was on. But as he was changing the channels, he came across the news. At first, they were discussing the war that was still going on in Israel. They mentioned how over 1,500 people have been killed since the October 7th attacks two years ago. Pete watched all the chaos and shook his head in disgust. As he laid back down, looking at the ceiling, he thought, "What kind of a world are we living in?"

But then, the news correspondents segwayed into the shooting of RaJohnn Mitchell and Tyshawn Brendan. They showed video footage of Tyshawn Brendan's highlights and his high school accolades. Pete's heart was racing as the anxiety was coursing through his veins. "How could I fuck up so badly?" Pete said as he watched. "They'll never let me live me after this." The news showed candles and shrines of Tyshawn Brendan on Hunterdon Street. It was becoming too much for Pete. He grabbed the remote and immediately changed the channel.

The next channel he turned to was showing the classic Superman movie starring Christopher Reeves. It was Pete's favorite movie growing up. Pete had an undying love for superheroes. He loved them all: Superman, Batman, Spiderman—he idolized them. He was an avid comic book reader *and* collector. Pete loved superheroes so much that he wanted to be one.

One time, when Pete was eight years old, he went to school wearing a Superman cape that his Aunt Carla made for him for his birthday. When he walked into his classroom, all his classmates laughed at him. One of his classmates pointed and laughed, saying, "You're not Superman; you're a clown." Even Pete's teacher disapproved of him wearing the cape and told him to remove it. Pete, however, was a rebellious kid and refused to take it off. His teacher grew aggravated and sent him to the principal's office. His classmates continued to laugh and point as he walked out of the classroom. But Pete did not go to the principal's office. He went to the boys' bathroom, sat in one of the stalls, locked the door, and cried in his cape. He never felt so embarrassed and humiliated. He just stayed in that bathroom and cried. As he sat in that stall, an epiphany dawned on his mind.

At that young age, Pete realized that the world was *not* what it seemed to be: happy, loving, trustworthy, or even beautiful. Pete saw the horror of the world, but most of the ugliness came from people. He knew that heroes would not always be appreciated for their good deeds. He also knew that, in reality, wearing a cape would make all of the kids laugh at him. But Pete was determined, even at eight years old, that he would *be* a hero. At that young age, he decided that he would be a police officer—someone who could serve his community, protect the innocent, and make the world a better, more beautiful place, even if he was never appreciated for it. Pete also understood that not every hero wore a cape... some wore a badge.

Twenty-five minutes later, Pete was dressed in casual clothing as he waited for his father and Uncle Freddy. He figured they would be a while before they arrived at his house. He then made his way downstairs to the kitchen. As he walked into the kitchen, all the dishes were washed and put away, and the food was gone. But Claire was sitting with a sobbing Elle at the kitchen table.

"Elle?" Pete said with concern. "What's wrong?"

"What's wrong?" Elle cried. "What's *wrong*? Really, Dad? You know *exactly* what's wrong. It was *you—you* killed Tyshawn Brendan."

Pete looked at Claire. "You told her?"

"No... she figured it out."

"It's all over social media, Dad. I can't believe you. My own father killed one of my idols."

Elle stormed out of the kitchen and headed upstairs. Pete and Claire felt the vibration of Elle's bedroom door being slammed shut. He looked over at Claire with disappointment.

"I asked you *not* to tell her—"

"I didn't *tell* her, Pete. She connected the dots… and I couldn't just *lie* to her… and you running out of the kitchen like that?"

"So, now the kids know… *perfect*!" Pete said as he sat down.

Claire sighed. "I'm going to go check on her."

Claire left the kitchen, leaving Pete alone with his devastating thoughts. Suddenly, the doorbell rang. Pete got up and walked to the front door. Expecting just his father and Uncle Freddy, Pete was stunned at the sight of his brother, Gregory, whom they called Greg.

"What the hell is he doing here?" Pete said, not happy to see Greg.

"*Hey*…" Greg smiled. "Is that any way to treat your brother? That breaks my heart, man."

"This is not the time for your sarcastic *bullshit*, Greg. So, if that's what you're here for, don't even bother stepping a *toe* in my house."

"*Your* house," Greg scoffed. "You hear that, Dad? He thinks this is *his* house—"

"Greg… now's not the time," Montgomery spoke. "We have other important things to talk about. Can we come in, son?"

"Are you going to be respectful, Greg? Because if not, you can wait out here in the cold. Do we understand each other?"

"You got it, little bro," Greg winked. "I won't say a word."

"Wait, where's Uncle Freddy?" Pete asked as they walked in.

"He's in the car on an important phone call… how are you doing?"

"I'm all right. Dad, let me talk to you in the kitchen."

"Well *damn*, it's like *that*, bro?" Greg said, feeling left out.

"Hell yeah. It's *always* been like that."

"Hey, come on—*both* of you," Montgomery said. "Not now… all right?"

Pete walked with his father to the kitchen. "Dad, they've already started talking about the shooting on the news."

"You've been watching the news?"

"No… not necessarily. Just a few glances at it. But they're already talking about it. And the kid? Who didn't make it? His name is… was, Tyshawn Brendan. He played basketball."

"*Ah, shit…* um… oh, there's Freddy," Montgomery said as Freddy walked in.

"Pete," Freddy said as he hugged Pete. "How are you doing? You okay?"

"Freddy… I'm in a lot of trouble."

"No, no, no. We're not *thinking* like that. Okay? All I need for you to do is to relax and let me take over… did anyone ask you about the shooting last night?"

"No, not really. Dad told me not to say anything. I had a detective there at the hospital. He collected my uniform. But I didn't say anything to anyone."

"Good. That'll make my job *much* easier."

Greg came into the kitchen. "You know, I just *love* what you guys did with this… rather *pricey* house. Remind me, how much did you pay for this house?"

"You haven't even been in my house for *one goddamn minute,* and *already*, you're starting with your bullshit."

"*Your house*? Do I need to remind you who *paid* for this fucking house?"

"It wasn't *you*."

"Well, it damn sure wasn't *you, was* it? Dad, you can jump in anytime here."

"Greg," Montgomery irritatingly responded. "I'm *warning* you. Knock it off."

"What? I can't tell the truth? That *you* paid for this house with *your* hard-earned money? One-point-one million dollars *cash*?"

Freddy intervened. "Greg! Now's not the time to be *dick-*measuring with your brother."

"Oh, *come* on, Uncle Freddy. *Enough* with the delusion. You *know* the truth."

"That *my* dick is bigger?" Pete retorted.

"The *fuck* it is. You wanna put money on it?"

"Ah, *typical* phrase of a *gambling junkie*. You want to put money on *everything*—most of the time, someone *else's* money. Don't sit there and pretend like Dad never bailed *you* out. And what about Mom? Huh? How many times did she have to go into *her* savings and pay off those crooks?"

"Really? You're going to go *there*? I *paid* my debts, okay? Every last one of them. And it's really ballsy of you to bring that shit up about Mom's savings. I'm not fucking proud of that."

"Yeah, well, you shouldn't have walked into my house talking that bullshit—"

"There you go *again*! *My* house! *My* house! News flash, Pete! This wouldn't *be* your fucking house it if wasn't for *Dad's* money. You think you're fooling your neighbors walking into a house like this on a *cop's* salary? Get the fuck outta here. That's what I'm talking about, that delusion—"

"*HEY*!" Freddy shouted. "Will you cut this shit out? This has gone on long enough between you two. Greg, *we* are dealing with a crisis here? Your brother's career and life are on the line. This shooting is a serious issue."

"Serious *issue*?" Greg chuckled. "Two blacks shot in the ghetto? That shit happens every goddamn day. Uncle Freddy, you said it yourself: the driver was a *thug*—probably a bastard child with no parents... and I have to be honest, Pete, you screwed up. I made a lot of money betting on that Tyshawn Brendan kid."

Pete shook his head. "You bet on high school games? Jesus *fucking* Christ, Greg."

"Hey! Welcome to the world of elite sports, brother. That wasn't some ordinary *hoodlum* on the block you killed. That was *Tyshawn fucking Brendan*. You didn't know?"

"I *didn't know* he was in the *car*, Greg."

Suddenly, there was a knock on the door. Freddy went to open the door, revealing Pete and Greg's grandfather, Dwight Gant. But Pete and Greg always called him Poppa Dee. Poppa Dee was an septuagenarian southern man with an old-school mindset and had no filter.

"Pop?" Freddy said. "What are you doing here?"

Poppa Dee came inside with a smile on his face. "Debra dropped me off," he said. "I came to see my grandson." Poppa Dee made his way into the living room and saw Pete. "There he is," Poppa Dee smiled, extending his wrinkled hand. Pete, however, refused to shake his hand. "Pete," said Montgomery. "Shake your grandfather's hand." Pete sighed as he shook hands with his grandfather.

"*Attaboy*," said Poppa Dee. "Now, was that so difficult?"

"Yes, it was."

"Oh? It couldn't have been more difficult than pulling that trigger last night, was it?"

"Hey, Pop, come on," said Freddy. "That's uncalled for."

"Oh, *zip* it, Freddy. Pete should be *proud* he shot those animals. One less uppity bastard to worry about."

"He shot a basketball star, Poppa Dee," Greg chuckled. "Not your typical 'Boyz in the Hood,'"

"They're *all* thugs, Greg. And don't you forget that—nothing but a race of parasites."

Pete grew enraged. "You sound like a goddamn Nazi, Poppa Dee."

"*Woah*... who do you think you're talking to—"

"I'd appreciate it if you just leave my house—and take this asshole with you."

"*Oh*... Monty, you're going to let him talk to us like that?"

"Pete, come on," Montgomery pleaded.

"No, I want them out of my house."

"My house," Greg laughed. "You hear that, Poppa Dee? He thinks this is *his* domicile. You gotta love this guy."

"Yeah, I hear him," Poppa Dee grinned. "Sounds like he forgot his place. And I *told* him about that. Just like I told your father. Don't forget your place."

"Poppa Dee, *spare* me your nineteen-fifties, Jim Crow philosophy. I got enough shit on my mind to deal with."

"Son, I didn't come over here to sympathize with ya. And you're wasting your time feeling sorry about shooting those hooligans. That's what you signed up for, isn't it? To do the dirty work and wipe out those who are a menace to society?"

"*Goddamn* right, Poppa Dee," Greg added. "Prime example, I spoke with a friend of mine who lives in Chicago. He *told* me that the crime rate has gone up over the last couple of years. Just this weekend *alone*, there were *a hundred and nine* shootings in Chicago—twenty-one of them were fatal. And guess what? Not *near one* of them was done by a white man."

"And what argument are you trying to make there, Greg?" Freddy asked.

"*Exactly*, Uncle Freddy. *Exactly*. That's my whole point right there. *Who* gives a fuck, right? I know *I* don't."

"Damn straight," Poppa Dee added. "They live like animals and behave like animals—and kill each other like it's a sport. Then they wanna blame the *"White"* man and the *system* for their hypercritical *bullshit*. I wouldn't dwell on it, Pete. Like you said, you have other pressing business to worry about."

"Yeah, like how's he going to keep this house after they *fire* his ass,"
Greg laughed. "How much you wanna bet—"

Pete slams his hand on the kitchen table. "How much you wanna bet that I'll *kick* your ass right here—*right fucking now*—bet that!"

"Bring it on, motherfucker—"

"Bet that! Bet that! Bet that!"

"Oh, *fuck* you, Pete! *Fuck* you!

Montgomery immediately stood between Pete and Greg as the sibling rivalry grew hostile.

"HEY!" Montgomery shouted. "*Enough*! *Both* of you! You're *brothers*, goddamn it!"

Silence in the room. Pete, however, felt nauseous. He quickly stepped outside to his back porch to get some air. Suddenly, Claire came storming down the stairs as if she had something to get off her chest.

"There she is," Poppa Dee smiled. "How are you, beautiful?"

"Gentlemen," Claire vaguely said. "I have my children upstairs. Could you please keep your voices down in *my* house!"

"I'm sorry, Claire," said Montgomery. "We're leaving now."

"Hey, uh, Monty," said Freddy. "Give me a minute alone with Pete, huh? I want to talk to him."

"All right. Greg? Pop? Let's go. Claire, sweetheart, once again, I sincerely apologize for all the commotion."

"Claire," Freddy said as he stayed behind. "I know you're worried. But don't be. I will make sure that *nothing* happens to him. I *swear* to you that I'll take care of this."

"You better," Claire said as she headed back upstairs.

Freddy kept his distance from Pete in the backyard—observing Pete's demeanor. Freddy was a character. He was five years younger than Montgomery. His hair combed back with a white streak on the left side, which was a rare birthmark. His colleagues at his firm would often tease him, saying he was Robert Kardashian's reincarnation. They said it so much that Freddy started to believe it, which boosted his ego. As he continued to observe Pete, he began to speak with him.

"Brothers can be assholes, Pete," Freddy said. "Pay no mind to him."

"I don't know *how* the hell we're related, Freddy," Pete said. "Greg and I are cut from two different cloths."

"It's the same as your father and me. We don't always get along."

"Freddy... what am I going to do? I killed that kid."

"Okay, listen... we *can't think* like that."

"But—"

"No, no buts, son... look, before we go, I need you to have a clear head. Now, I'll be beside you to ensure you don't incriminate yourself. These interrogations can get tricky if you're not careful."

"So... what do we do?"

"Well, first of all... I need to know what happened. Tell me what happened, Pete. As much as you remember. No details left out."

Pete took a minute before describing the shooting. He hated that he had to relive everything in his mind, but he went through it and told Freddy everything he remembered about last night. Unbeknownst to Pete, Freddy had already done his homework on the incident. He watched news coverage of the shooting the entire flight back from L.A. He knew all about it up to that point. But he needed to hear it from Pete's perspective.

Freddy was very in tune with how cops were portrayed when it came to police shootings—especially when it involved a *white* police officer who shoots a black person. But in *this* case, the fact that Tyshawn Brendan was a high school basketball superstar, this case became an overnight catastrophe. Freddy knew he had to do his best and protect his nephew—just as he swore to Claire he would.

13

DECEMBER 20th, 2025, SATURDAY AFTERNOON:

THE INVESTIGATION

Pete sat quietly in the interrogation room as he waited for Freddy to return. He had everything on his mind: Claire, his kids, and everything that happened less than twenty-four hours ago. He also thought about the deflated basketball. He only glanced at it once at the scene but remembered seeing the bullet hole that went through it. What was beginning to conflict him was not knowing how many shots he fired. And even though everything happened so fast, Pete had no recollection of firing his gun. The door suddenly opened, and Freddy had returned.

"Sorry to keep you waiting," Freddy said as he closed the door. "I had to talk with the homicide detectives before we get started—so we're all on the same page."

"What are they going to ask me?"

"The usual: before and after the crime scene and possibly some general questions about yourself."

"How about the detectives? Do they seem fair?"

"Well... *one* of the detectives, we communicated well. As far as the other... I'll just say he has a big chip on his shoulder. But not to worry, nephew. Your Uncle Freddy will be right beside you for every question. And if they give us any bullshit, we're outta here."

"All right," Pete sighed. "I'm ready whenever they are."

"Okay... just hang tight. We'll get started shortly... everything's going to be just fine."

"Thanks, Freddy."

Freddy touched Pete gently on his right shoulder and stepped out of the room. Pete lifted his head and sighed deeply—closing his eyes as he relieved some stress. He kept his eyes closed as he took deep breaths. Even though the shooting scene was still fresh in his mind, he felt relieved that he would clear the air. Pete had this vision of the detectives coming in with compassion and support. But as the door opened, and he saw the two detectives' faces, that vision quickly disintegrated like a pure white dandelion getting blown away in the dark abyss.

The detective entered. "Pete Gant?"

Pete stood from his seat. "Yes, sir."

"I'm Detective Bison. This is Detective Baldwin."

Pete looked at both detectives: Bison was white, and Baldwin was black. From his observation, Pete had an inkling which one had the chip on his shoulder, and it was not Detective Bison. Baldwin had a look of disgust on his face. The fact that two black teenagers had been shot, and one of them was dead, Baldwin looked like he wanted to rip Pete's head off. However, Pete felt somewhat safe as Freddy sat beside him. Freddy looked at Pete—giving him a quick smile of comfort as he held his notepad and pen.

"Okay," Detective Bison said as he cleared his throat. "I'm just going to document the date and time of this investigation. The date is Saturday, December 20th, 2025, and the time is 2:36 p.m. Okay... and if I can get your full name for the record?"

Pete was hesitant, "Oh, *my* name?"

"Yes, sir."

"Peter Gant."

"Thank you… and if I can get your badge number and the precinct you report to?"

"Yes, my badge number is 821, and I report to Newark police 5th precinct."

"And what is the location of that precinct?"

"Uh… 480 Clinton Ave… Newark, New Jersey."

"Okay, thank you—"

"How—how long is this going to take?" Pete impulsively asked.

"It'll be a little while, Mr. Gant."

"Right. Sorry, sir."

"No, that's okay… now, Mr. Gant… walk us through what happened on the night of December 19th, 2025."

Pete looked at Freddy. Freddy gave Pete a head nod to speak.

"I received a call from dispatch."

"Around what time?"

"It was around eight. I was just starting my shift."

"And what was the call for?"

"A 10-37."

"Okay… and for the record, can you say what that is?"

"Yes, it's the code for a suspicious vehicle."

"Thank you… proceed."

"So, I told dispatch that I would be on the lookout for it. I drove around for about twenty minutes. Nothing was going on. Then, as I was at the light, I saw the car."

"Can you describe the make of the vehicle?"

"It was a black Kia Forte Coupe."

"Four doors—two?"

"Two."

"And what did you do after you got a visual on the vehicle?"

"I radioed it in—to dispatch—notified them that I found a vehicle that matched the description from earlier."

"At what time did you discover the vehicle?"

"It was… after eight."

"Well, you just said you started your shift *at* eight, right? And you drove around for about twenty minutes before you spotted the car… is that correct?"

"Yeah… something like that."

"So, can you give me a time frame of when you pulled the car over?"

"I don't know… maybe eight-thirty, possibly—no… actually, it was a quarter to nine. I remember calling dispatch and letting them know that I was attempting to make a stop on the vehicle. It was around eight—forty-five or six."

"Okay. So that's a little more than twenty minutes that you drove around…. So, you stopped the vehicle at around eight-forty-five… is that accurate?"

Pete nodded. "Yes."

"And where did you stop the vehicle?"

"I pulled the vehicle over on Hunterdon Street… between thirteen—no… fourteenth and fifteenth Avenue."

"All right," Detective Bison said as he wrote his notes. "Now… after you stopped the vehicle, walk us through what happened."

"I sat in my patrol unit to make sure I had everything I needed before stepping out. I remember my son—my *oldest* son, Michael, calling me on my personal phone. But I didn't answer it. I muted the call and put it in my vest compartment. That's when I stepped out of my patrol unit and walked to the car. I was flashing my light on the window—"

"I'm sorry; what time did your son call you?"

"I don't know the exact time off the top of my head. But it was not much after eight-forty-six."

"Okay. So, it's eight-forty-six, you're flashing your light at the vehicle… what happened next?"

"As I approached the vehicle, I knocked on the window. Maybe a few seconds later, the driver rolled the window down and said something like, 'What, man?' I remember the loud music, and I asked him to turn his car off… and that's when he said something else to me. I don't know if you want me to repeat it. It was a pretty vile."

"Yes, please, tell me exactly what was said. Leave nothing out."

"So, the driver said… 'Suck my nuts,' no, wait… that wasn't what he said… *dick*… suck my dick."

"That's what the *driver* said?"

"Yes—yes—I'm not saying that to *you*."

"Right, right, yes," Detective Bison chuckled.

Detective Baldwin, however, did not crack a smile as he sat with his arms folded, *grilling* Pete like a crocodile eyeing its prey. Detective Bison continued, reading his notes, saying, "So… you pulled the car over now. You knocked on the window, the driver rolled the window down… and after you asked him to turn the car off, he said *to you*… 'Suck my dick.' Is that accurate?"

"Yes," Pete confirmed. "Up to that point, yes."

"All right, and *then* what happened?"

Pete was now hesitant as he was getting closer to the shooting. He sighed and continued on with his story. "I stepped away from the car and radioed for backup. By the time I returned to the vehicle, the driver had rolled the window back down… oh, wait a minute… there's one part I forgot. After the driver made the 'Suck my dick' comment, he rolled the window back up, and I couldn't see him. So, after I radioed in for backup, I walked back to the window, and…."

"Mr. Gant?" Detective Bison spoke as Pete faded away in his mind. "*Mr. Gant!*"

"I—I'm sorry," Pete said, pinching the bridge of his nose as if he was getting a headache. "Can—can we just take a break, please?"

"If you need one. That's not a problem."

"And can I have a minute with my attorney, please?"

"Absolutely. We'll be outside."

Detective Bison got up and headed for the door. Detective

Baldwin, however, remained seated—still staring at Pete. "Yo, Baldwin," said Detective Bison. "Let's give them a minute." Baldwin stood up with his arms still folded and walked out of the room with a malicious frown. As the door closed, Freddy pulled his chair closer to Pete, and they conversed.

"How am I doing so far, Freddy?" Pete asked with concern.

"You're taking it well, champ. I'm proud of you," Freddy smiled.

"That Baldwin guy hasn't taken his eyes off me this whole time."

"Oh, he's just trying to intimidate you. You pay no mind to him. Just remain calm. You're doing great."

"Okay… I'm ready to get this over with. Let's bring them back in."

"All right, son."

Freddy opened the door and invited the two detectives back into the room. But *this* time, Detective Baldwin took over for Bison. It was like a drastic pendulum shift. Baldwin was more aggressive, sterner, and no bullshit. As Baldwin looked at Pete, he continued the interrogation.

"Let's go back to the 'Suck my *dick'* part," Detective Baldwin spoke. "When the driver said that, how did that make you feel?"

"Excuse me?" Pete responded as the question threw him off.

"How did it make you *feel*? Were you angry? Upset? Pissed off?"

"I wasn't *happy* with what he said… I felt that was uncalled for."

"Okay, let me rephrase the question. Did what the driver *say*— *motivate* you to shoot him?"

"No, absolutely not. That's *not* what happened."

"So, let's talk about what *did* happen—the shooting. How did the shooting transpire?"

Pete, now confused and irritated. "When I stepped to the tinted window for the—"

"Oh, so it was *tinted windows*?"

"Yes, they were tinted."

"Are you aware of the policies of tinted windows?"

"Yes, sir."

Detective Baldwin grins. "Go ahead... continue."

Pete looked over at Freddy with concern. He did not like where the investigation was leading and wanted it to end. Freddy, however, encouraged Pete to proceed as he said, "Go on, Pete." As Pete cleared his throat, he continued, saying, "After I radioed in for backup, I stepped toward the window—for a *second* time, and the driver rolled down his window, and... there was a flash... that's all I remember."

"What do you mean that's all you remember?" Detective Baldwin asked with a twisted face.

"I don't remember discharging my firearm and opening fire. That part is all a blur to me. It happened so fast."

"Can you tell me how many rounds you fired off?"

"No, I can*not*... as I said, I don't remember shooting my weapon. When I get to the shooting... my mind goes blank."

"Well... to help refresh your memory, it was six... you fired off *six* rounds. You hit the driver twice—as well as the passenger. But what you're *telling* me is that you don't remember *any* of it?"

"I'm sorry, but no... I don't."

"And you expect us to *believe* that?"

"I don't know what else to tell you. I *don't remember it.*"

"*Hmm....*" Detective Baldwin grunted as he shook his head.

"Let's shift gears here, okay? I would like to know a few things about you *specifically.*"

"Like what?"

"How long have you been stationed in Newark?"

"A little over three years now."

"And where did you transfer from?"

"Cedar Grove."

"*Cedar Grove*, huh? That's an *auspicious* environment. Nice neighborhoods, grass in the front yards. But you know, Mr. Gant? I can't help but ask *why*... why transfer from such a peaceful town like *Cedar Grove*—where hardly *any*thing ever happens, to *Brick City*?"

Looking at Detective Baldwin angrily, Pete responded, "Because I wanted to."

"*Wow....*" Detective Baldwin retorted, sensing Pete's cynical demeanor. "Because you *wanted* to... is that right?"

"Yeah, that's right."

"Or maybe it was because you wanted to hunt down unarmed, promising *black* boys and *shoot* them in cold *fucking* blood, right?"

"*HEY!*" Freddy shouted, now infuriated. "Are you *fucking* kidding me right now?"

"Woah, *woah*, take it easy, Freddy!" Detective Bison said as he stood up.

"No," Freddy responded as *he* stood and put on his jacket. "We're done here. That was *way* out of fucking line! And I will *not* have my client be treated in such an unlawful manner! How *fucking* dare you?"

"Okay, *Freddy*, there's no need to use all this foul *language*! We're just doing our jobs here."

"Yeah, well, we all have a fucking job to do, *don't* we? And *my* job is to look out for my client's best interest. That last question was a slap in the face, and I *will not* allow *my* client to be accused of racial profiling or *any* other *ridiculous* prejudgments of injustice... we're done here."

Freddy and Pete collected their belongings and left the interrogation room. Freddy was cursing like a sailor to his car—motherfucker this, motherfucker that; the detectives were a whole bunch of motherfuckers the entire ride to Montgomery's house. Pete was deeply offended by that last comment from Detective Baldwin. It was like he sparked something deep into his subconscious. He made Pete think about his decision to transfer to Newark, an area with a predominantly black population. The comment was so triggering that

Pete began to question himself, thinking, "*Am* I a racist? Do I hate black people?" Those wicked thoughts were dancing in his mind, and he had no idea of how to turn off the music.

14

DECEMBER 20^{th,} 2025, SATURDAY EVENING:

FAMILY TIME

Later that evening, Pete and Freddy settled in at Montgomery's house. The house was a Tudor mansion that Montgomery had built back in 1989. Pete had many treasures of memories in the house. One was of chopping firewood with Montgomery as a teenager. Another was when a bear was lurking in the backyard and Pete had to scare it off with banging pots.

Pete walked down the long, sophisticated hallway, looking at the expensive artwork and family photos on the wall. As he looked, he saw one of the photos of him, Montgomery, Greg, and his mother on a beautiful yacht that Montgomery purchased back when Pete was a teenager. They sailed off the Marina Rivieria Nayarit at La Cruz in Mexico. Pete had an exquisite time there. From a financial standpoint, the family lived very well. Montgomery was a successful businessman who made valuable investments with a hedge fund company in the eighties. Those investments served him well and made him millions in the process. Montgomery always believed that a man made his own luck, and that was what he tried to bestow upon

Pete and Greg. But when Pete told his father that he wanted to be a police officer, Montgomery disapproved. Pete, however, was adamant about being a cop. He felt that it was his true calling and that no amount of money would change his mind about his destiny. This decision created a falling out between them, and they did not speak for a year. But when Pete and Claire had Michael, he reached out to Montgomery, telling him he was now a grandfather. The great news melted the ice-cold ocean mass of tension between them and they have been solid ever since. As Pete entered the kitchen, his mother, Melissa, sat at the booth, enjoying a glass of white wine.

"Hi, Pete," Melissa smiled.

"Hey, Mom," Pete responded as he walked over and kissed her.

"How are you doing, honey? I really would like to know."

"I had a rough day, Mom. The investigation was a disaster. It was going okay at first, but then that other detective took the conversation in a different direction. That's when Uncle Freddy shut everything down, and we left."

"What was said?"

"I really don't want to talk about it right now, Mom."

"I understand," Melissa said as she sipped her wine. "How's Claire?"

"She's fine... under the circumstances. She's been very supportive."

"That's good. A strong man always needs a strong woman by his side. I always made that my mission—to be a strong woman."

"Mom... can I ask you something?"

"Sure, honey, how much money do you need—"

"Mom, no," Pete said as he shook his head. "What I'm about to ask you has *nothing to do* with *money*."

"Oh, I'm sorry, dear," Melissa said as she put away her checkbook. "Go ahead. I'm listening."

"What do you think about black people?"

"What do you mean, Pete?"

"I mean, just… what do you think of them?"

"Well… I have black *friends*—if *that's* what you're asking."

"No, Mom… I was just… nev—never mind."

"Is everything okay, sweetheart?"

Pete gave his mother a startled look and responded. "*No*, Mom… everything's *not* okay—okay? I shot two black kids in the middle of Newark. I'm in *deep shit*."

Melissa sat there, stunned, as Pete never used this tone of voice with her. He saw the frightened look on her face and knew that he crossed the line. "I'm sorry, Mom," he said, looking down at the marble kitchen island. "I'm just in a terrible situation here. It's not you. I'm sorry for raising my voice." Pete stepped away and walked out of the kitchen to clear his mind. Being that he came from an upper-class family living in a very sophisticated bubble of wealth and privilege, Pete knew they would not understand the social dilemma of his job.

Pete headed upstairs and went to the doorway of his old bedroom. As he turned on the light switch, he saw that it was made into a storage room—filled with boxes and papers—preventing him from having a nostalgic moment of his old room. As he walked in, he looked in one of the boxes and found something he had not seen since he was twelve years old: his old Superman cape. Pete was taken aback as his mind imploded with childhood memories. For old times' sake, he tried it on. By having it on made Pete feel like a kid again—filled with innocence and optimism. Unbeknownst to Pete, Montgomery was standing behind him.

"Gotten *taller* since then, huh?" Montgomery chuckled as the cape only reached halfway down to Pete's back.

"Dad," Pete said as he undid the cape from his neck. "I didn't know you were behind me."

"Oh… sorry… I didn't know you were having yourself a nostalgic moment."

"Yeah, well… it doesn't fit anymore. So, I guess you can just get rid of it."

"Now why would I do a ridiculous thing like that? You used to eat, play, and even *sleep* wearing that Superman cape… remember?"

"Of course, I do… I've had a lot of memories with this cape."

"I remember one time when you were about… *nine*. You and your little cousin Brittany were outside playing with the kids next door. You were wearing that cape, and they thought you were *nuts*. But then, one of the kids was choking on a piece of… *candy*, was it?"

"Yeah… yeah, it was a gumball. It got caught in her throat."

"Right, right. You told me you wrapped your arms around her and performed the Heimlich maneuver you learned in school. You said it popped right out."

"Yep… she said that I was her Superman. I was Clark Kent; she was Lois Lane… now look at me. Some hero I've turned out to be."

"Pete, son… you can't just keep putting yourself down like this. It's not healthy."

"I should just go home, Dad… and be with my family."

"All right… I'll take you home."

"No, it's late. I'll catch an Uber ride."

"Oh, don't be ridiculous. Come on, *I'll* give you a ride."

"No, Dad. Really… I'll get an Uber."

"No, wait, Gregory's still here. I'll have *him* take you home—"

"I'd rather walk backward, in the opposite direction of freeway traffic—wearing a *blindfold*—than to ride *any*where with him."

Montgomery sighed. "You know… someday, you two will need one another. Whatever beef you have with your brother needs to be fed to the pigs."

Suddenly, Pete developed a stomachache. It was as if he was triggered all over again. "I'll back right back," he said as he rushed into the bathroom and sat on the toilet. Unbeknownst to him, Pete was suffering from diarrhea. He was puzzled by what triggered him until it hit him. His father mentioned "pigs." Pete connected the dots and felt that the night of the shooting, when RaJohnn called him a pig, it created a traumatic episode that triggered him.

"Pete?" Montgomery said as he knocked on the bathroom door. "You're okay in there, son?"

"Yeah… I'm all right. It must've been something I ate."

"All right… I'll be downstairs."

"Okay. I'll be down in a minute."

Pete knew he had a long road ahead of him. But what he feared the most was that he would eventually walk this road alone. Ten minutes later, Pete was at the front door, putting on his coat. His Uber driver was two minutes away. Just before heading out, Pete had a word with his father.

"Are you sure you don't want me to drive you home? It's not a big deal."

"No, that's okay," Pete responded. "I can get home."

"All right… Freddy said he'll be in touch. Call me if you need anything, all right? *Anything*."

"I *will*, Dad… thank you."

"I love you, Pete."

"I love you, too."

Montgomery reached out, grabbed his son, and held him tight. He loved Pete with all his heart and wished he could understand what he was going through. However, Montgomery and Pete lived different lives. But regardless, Montgomery always loved his son.

"Okay, Dad… let me go," Pete said as Montgomery held on.

He kissed Pete on the side of his head and said, "You're a good man… exactly as I raised you to be… you remember that."

"My Uber's outside… I'll see you later."

Pete walked out of the house and headed to his Uber ride. Just as he was halfway down the walkthrough of the front yard, he turned around and waved goodbye to his father, and Montgomery waved back to him. As Pete approached the back seat of the silver Honda CR-V, he opened the door and saw the Uber driver's melanated face.

"Pete?" The Uber driver asked.

"Yes, you're Andre?" Pete responded.

"Yes, sir."

Pete got in the car, and Andre took off. Andre was wearing glasses and a black Kangol bucket hat. Pete noticed something a bit odd about Andre. As he looked at Andre in the rearview mirror, he saw that Andre had this sinister smirk on his face, which made Pete a little hesitant to continue the ride. But he shrugged it off as he refused to let his paranoia get the best of him. Pete always had great intuition about peoples' demeanor and would use it wisely. But he neglected his intuition. He put his guard down and trusted Andre. Something that he would later regret.

15

DECEMBER 20th, 2025, SATURDAY LATE EVENING:

<u>THEY KNOW NOW… EVERYONE KNOWS</u>

Seven minutes into the Uber ride, Pete was in the back seat, looking out the window as they drove past the naked woods. He received a text from Claire—which showed up as "*Amore Mio*," which is "My love" in Italian, being that Claire had Italian roots in her family:

Amore Mio
Hey, where are you?

Pete
I'm on my way home.
I should be there in fifteen minutes.

Amore Mio
Okay, because something came up, and we need to talk.

Pete
What happened?

Amore Mio

We'll talk when you get home.

Pete had yet to learn what Claire was talking about. But the fact that she did not want to speak about it over the phone, he knew there was a problem. One would wonder why Pete had an Uber account. Some nights, when he was off duty, Pete would go out with fellow officers at a bar called "Code 23," a code for when police arrived at a scene. Whenever he went to Code 23, he would have a few beers and socialize with his brothers and sisters, talking about life and what they go through on the streets. Pete thought having an Uber account would be necessary just because he never wanted to put himself in a DWI situation.

Usually, Pete would keep the conversation short between him and his Uber drivers. But this night, his driver, Andre, was a social butterfly... or more like a wasp.

"Ayo, Pete, how was your night, my man?" Andre asked.

"Could've been better," Pete responded. "Yours?"

"Oh, it was fine. I was gonna call it quits before you came across my radar. And then I just said, 'I'll do one more.'"

"Well... thank you, I appreciate that."

"Oh, the pleasure's all mine... *Officer Gant.*"

Pete looked at Andre with startled eyes. "How... how did you know I'm an officer?"

"Well, any cop who shoots and kills the number one basketball prospect in the *country*, it's only a matter of *time* before they put your mugshot all over the internet. So, tell me, *pig*, how many more black people have you shot?"

At that moment, Pete felt his life was in danger and that Andre would be hostile. Though he had no idea where he was, Pete wanted out of the car immediately.

"Stop the car, man," Pete demanded.

"Nah," said Andre. "How about you answer my question."

"*Stop* the *car*!"

"No, answer my *question,* pig!"

"Either you stop the car or—"

"Or—or *what*? You gonna shoot me, too, *pig*? That's what you wanna do? Shoot *another* black man—"

"Just *stop* the fucking car and let me out!"

"A'ight, I hear ya, playboy. Yeah, you know what? I'll stop the car and let you out. I don't wanna drive you *no* goddamn way. Fucking pig."

As Andre pulled over on the side of the road, Pete got out and slammed the door—now walking in the opposite direction of the car. Andre, however, was not finished with Pete. He put his car in reverse and caught up to him. "You're a *motherfucking* disgrace, you know that?" Andre shouted. Pete, however, remained silent and kept walking. Just before Andre pulled off, he said, "Don't you worry about it, pig. You're going to *get* yours one day. Karma's a *bitch*, and so is your *wife*!"

Pete stopped in his tracks and aggressively responded. "Leave my wife and my family the *fuck* out of it, okay? I got out your car. Now go on about your business."

"I hope they throw your cracker ass *under* the fucking jail. I'm *sick* of you motherfuckers killing us. Go to *fucking* hell, pig! *Fuck* you!"

Andre then drove off, leaving Pete in the chilly dust. Once again, he was triggered. Pete immediately thought of Tyshawn and started to breathe heavily. It was cold and dark, and he had no idea where he was. He then took out his phone and opened his map app. As he typed in his home address, Pete realized that he was sixteen minutes away from his house by car. But walking distance, he was an hour and twelve minutes away. "Fuck," Pete said as he looked at his phone. He could have easily called his father and told him the situation. But Pete was a stubborn man. He hated to ask for favors or have people do things for him. And he was *not* going to book another

Uber ride. That is when he decided to walk home. He set up the map to direct him back to his house and began walking.

As Pete walked, he searched on his phone to figure out what the hell Andre was talking about. Initially, he did not find anything. But then, his photo came up as he typed his name in the Google search engine. The picture was taken by the crime scene detective, Robert Winterburn, the night Pete was at the hospital. He could not believe they released his photo. But then, he went further and looked on the app X, formerly known as Twitter, and discovered something horrifying. People posted Pete's picture and called him the most atrocious words he had ever seen. He scrolled through multiple accounts and saw what they were posting about him, and nothing was pleasant:

@bulldogBrady1204
> This fucker deserves to rot in hell for killing that kid.
> Damn, these pigs.

@CameronDaGreat98
> This is the pig who shot Tyshawn Brendan. Damn. RIP King. He was on his way to being the next MJ. Police brutality is real, bro. It's hunting season on us black men.

@JacktalkinSMACK34
> This was some Illuminati shit. No cap, bro. Tyshawn Brendan was a blood sacrifice. Everybody knows that. It's definitely a conspiracy.

@SamoneTheQueen27
> OMG. I can't believe it. This is the police officer who shot those two black kings in the car. I heard one of them died, and the other is still with us. They really killing us for nothing now, and they're killing our talented young black men.

@JonesTheKingoftheCourt03

Bruh… I can't believe this. I was just talking to Ty two nights ago at the game. I was congratulating him on his Duke commit. He was legit. The truth on the court. Nobody could compete with him. And his handles? He was a magician, bruh. Damn, RIP, Ty. And fuck this pig who killed him.

@BeckyGotThemCheeks69

OMG, can we please stop with this "pig" Talk? We don't know the full story of what happened. None of you were there, okay?

@BradleyTheGamer297

Those black thugs got what they deserved. Newark is a shit show. They probably had drugs in the car and everything. I guarantee the shooting will be ruled justifiable.

@DevonMCTriggerHappy

It's cracker cops like this one I be talking bout in my raps. I be telling y'all that these fucking pigs be wildin'. Like you said, *@CameronDaGreat98,* it's hunting season on all of us. R.I.P Tyshawn Brendan.

@WillwiththeDribbleSkills946

Damn. #JUSTICEFORTYSHAWN Tyshawn was my guy. Unbelievable. I couldn't stop crying when I heard about it.
I woke up this morning and saw it on the news. Why they have to kill this king, man? He was so close to making it out the hood. They keep killing us. Why do they hate black people so much? Why? Rest in Peace, Ty. I love you, bro. I hope Heaven got a basketball team for you to shine on.

For the last thirty minutes, a devastated Pete scrolled his cold feet up the dark road while he scrolled his trembling thumb up the *glassy* road of his screen—reading hateful comments. Pete's eyes grew watery from both the cold air and his emotions. His anxiety increased as did his blood pressure. He tried to stop looking at people's comments but the temptation pulled him in at every scroll. Claire kept texting and calling, but he would not respond. He scrolled and scrolled and read. Even though everyone warned him about the media, Pete knew it would eventually trap him.

But then, Pete did something unexpected... he looked up Tyshawn Brendan's page on Instagram. Tyshawn Brendan's profile was under the name *TyDah11*—an expression of "Ta-dah." Tyshawn Brendan was considered a magician on the basketball court and intertwined his name with the phrase magicians would say to get the audience's attention as they worked their magic. The number eleven represented his jersey number.

Pete looked at Tyshawn Brendan's Instagram page and noticed that Tyshawn was a superstar with over five million followers. His page was even verified with a blue check. As he kept walking, Pete began to look at some of Tyshawn's highlight reels. Tyshawn was unbelievable. His ball handles were impregnably scary, ingenious, and not of this world. He dribbled like a spider with eight different hands. His crossovers were elusive and slippery. Defenders were terrified to guard him. His three-point jumper was unstoppable—*any*where beyond the arc, he was good for three. The crowds cheered him on like a god. And to *them*... he was a god.

As Pete continued to scroll down Tyshawn Brendan's profile, he saw pictures of Tyshawn with his family. One post was a Mother's Day tribute to his mother, Jada Brendan. It was two pictures: the first picture was of Tyshawn when he was three years old—sitting on his mother's lap. The second was a more recent photo of the two hugging each other as Tyshawn wore a Blue Devil hat and Jersey as he announced his commitment to play for Duke University.

Playing in the background of the post was a song by Tupac Shakur called *Dear Mama*. In the caption, Tyshawn wrote this short but oh-so-sweet note to his mother:

Happy Mother's Day, Mom.

You know I'm not the kind of kid who knows what to say when it comes to speaking from my heart. But for you, I'll do my best right here. Your sacrifices as a mother were beyond unbelievable. Every month, you would have just a few dollars to your name after paying all the bills. You were a single teenage mother taking care of your son. You took those last few dollars you had and made sure that I had everything I needed. Whether it was food, basketball gear, notebooks for school, or even to pay for basketball camp. You sacrificed everything for me. You were just a baby raising a baby by yourself. But somehow, you made it work. And I thank you so much for all you've done for me. You're my rock, my Queen, my everything. We've been great companions to each other for these eighteen years. You worked those miracles through all the struggles and setbacks, and I wouldn't trade any of it for the universe. The hard work has paid off, and I've made it. And don't you worry. Once I sign that NBA contract, I'll take care of you for the rest of your life. We're going to travel the world together, Mom. But just like Pac said, "There's no way I can pay you back... but the plan is to show you that I understand... you are appreciated." I love you, Mom. Happy Mother's Day.

After Pete read that caption, he dropped his phone and fell to his knees, sobbing in his hands. At that moment, he felt this dense sense of guilt aggressively coursing through his veins. He realized that his split-second decision tragically cost the life of an up-and-coming, remarkably talented young kid. And he was sincerely sorry for it.

Fifty minutes later, Pete was finally home. When he turned his key and opened the door, Claire stormed over to him and went ballistic. "*Where* have you *been*?" Claire cried. "Do you have *any idea* what I've been *going* through? I've called and texted you over thirty *fucking* times, and you don't *respond*? Don't you *ever* do that to me again!"

Pete, however, did not utter a word as he looked like he was in total despair. Claire looked at him as she saw her distraught husband desperately needing love and affection.

"Pete?" Claire softly said. "What's happened? God, you're *freezing*. Did... *Jesus*, did you *walk* home?"

"They know," Pete said as tears fell down his cold cheeks. "The world knows.... Oh, *God*, Claire... *what* have I done?"

Claire said nothing else as she held Pete's cold body—keeping him warm as he sobbed. This was a moment that she was too familiar with. There were plenty of nights when Pete came home in the wee hours of the morning, and Claire was that shoulder to cry on. Claire was a strong woman, but the shooting of Tyshawn Brendan was like no other situation she had been through with him. She knew about Pete's photo being posted on social media, as did the children. As Pete said... "They know now... everyone knows."

16

DECEMBER 21st 2025, SUNDAY MORNING:

GLOOMY SUNDAY

Another night of tossing and turning as Pete had woken up in a cold sweat. His t-shirt was damp, as was his boxer briefs. He looked over at Claire's side of the bed and noticed her absence. As he listened, he heard running water coming from the bathroom. He then got out of bed and went into his walk-in closet to change his underwear. In the closet, there was a window that displayed a beautiful view of the sunrise from his backyard. Often, Pete would look out the window to see the rising Sun. But as he looked, it was like a gloomy painting of a sky with a flock of birds flying across the billowy clouds.

As Pete walked back into the bedroom, he went over to the bed and saw something he would see whenever he woke in a cold sweat: a wet stain on the bed. Pete felt embarrassed by that. It made him feel like a little boy who still wets the bed. He quickly took off the sheets and looked for replacements. As he looked around, Pete discovered how unorganized he was when it came to where things were in the bedroom. Because of his busy and demanding schedule, Pete never took the time to figure out where Claire placed things in the house. Instead of pulling things out, he waited for Claire to finish in the shower. As Pete waited, he clicked on the television and went to the news channel.

Initially, the news was talking about the Israel-Hamas war and the rising death toll. They showed footage of bombs going off—drastically lighting up the night sky. Pete used to watch the news devotedly to keep up with what was happening worldwide. But the world became too sad for him—too evil, and he had enough to deal with on *his* soil. So, the news was nothing more but a bottomless cesspool of depression.

But as they switched stories, they showed the shooting of Tyshawn Brendan and RaJohnn Mitchell. Pete held the remote in his shaking hand. He wanted to change the channel, but strangely, he could not fix his mind to push the button. It was like one of his night terrors from the past. Pete would have a nightmare where he was chasing after a suspect, and as he drew his gun, he could not pull the trigger. That was the same feeling with the remote… he just could not push the button. Pete watched as they showed the families of Tyshawn Brendan and RaJohnn Mitchell, along with a crowd of people behind them with picket signs that said:

JUSTICE FOR TYSHAWN!
NO JUSTICE, NO PEACE!
BLACK LIVES MATTER!
WE WANT THE BODY CAM!
NOT ONE MORE!

They showed RaJohnn Mitchell, whose left arm was in a sling—sitting in a wheelchair. As news reporters held the microphones, they began interviewing RaJohnn's sister, Shanice "Neecy" Mitchell.

"I'm here with the sister of one the victims, Shanice Mitchell," said the reporter. "Ms. Mitchell, thank you for talking with us. You said off-camera that you feel somewhat responsible for all of this. Can you explain why?"

Neecy wiped the tears from her face and responded, "I made the call... I called the police because my brother had taken my car after I told him not to because he had received a ticket earlier that day. I was just frustrated because I had to leave early for work. I would've *never* thought something like this would happen. And I feel that had I never called the police... my brother and wouldn't have been shot and Tyshawn would still be alive."

The reporter continued. "And RaJohnn, you were hit twice, and your friend, Tyshawn Brendan, was *also* shot twice but didn't survive. Could you tell us, in your own words, what happened that night?"

"It all happened so fast," RaJohnn cried. "It's like... it's like we didn't even get a chance to *do* anything... he just started shooting for no reason. We weren't even doing nothing. I was just taking Ty home... and now I gotta learn how to walk all over again. He killed my best friend, man. Why he had to shoot us?"

Pete could not believe it. It was like day and night how RaJohnn switched up his behavior. Pete was enraged; he wanted to take the remote and throw it through the television. He felt that RaJohnn was lying about what happened and was playing the victim. But then, the reporter went to Tyshawn Brendan's father, Morris Clark, a handsome, bald man with a full beard. Morris had an aggressive vibe to him. As the reporter put the microphone to his face, he began his rant. "Hey, listen, man," Morris spoke. "All I'm going to say is this... we will not rest, we will not go quiet, and we *will not stop* until that cop is in handcuffs and thrown *under* the jail. That was *my son*. Newark police? We want the body cam, we want the cop who shot these two kids—*unarmed* kids at that, and we *demand* justice."

Pete sat there and watched the crowd roar in fury—chanting justice for Tyshawn Brendan. Pete could not move his legs as they went numb. Suddenly, Claire opened their bathroom door and saw Pete gazing at the television screen. She quickly approached him, grabbed the remote, and turned the television off.

"Pete," she said. "What are you *doing*? I *told* you, 'Don't watch the news.' You *promised* me that you wouldn't watch it."

Pete sat there in an eerie silence as Claire looked at him. He he was out of it; in a daze as if nobody was home.

"Pete?" Claire softly said as she touched his face. "Honey, *talk* to me... tell me what's bothering you."

"*Everything*," Pete cried. "*Everything's* bothering me. That kid lied. *He* was the one who was out of control. They're already painting me to be this crooked cop or something. But it's *lies*, it's *all lies—*"

"I *know* it's all lies, baby. That's why you shouldn't watch it—*none* of it."

"But I—"

"But *what*?"

"I can't help it. The father of Tyshawn Brendan... he said they won't rest until I'm in jail... they're going to put me in jail."

"No, no, they're *not*. Listen, what happened to that boy... that was an accident. I know you didn't intend to shoot him. But the fact remains that the driver was the aggressor, right?"

"Yes, but that's not how the media's perceiving it. It's... oh, God... do the kids know?"

Claire shook her head. "Yeah... they saw the picture of you last night. That's why I called you. I can't believe they would even release the goddamn photo of you so fast."

"They're going to throw me to the wolves, Claire—I know it."

"Don't *say* that... I don't want to hear this talk anymore. You are *not* going to leave us. Do you hear me?"

Pete sighed. "Yeah... I won't leave you... I won't."

Claire kissed him and gently pressed her thumb on his bottom lip.

"I love you… and don't you dare think you're going to leave me. Because I need you here with me. We're going to be all right. It'll just take time to heal… okay?"

"Okay… I just need a minute alone here."

"All right… I'm going to head down and make breakfast."

"That sounds good… I'll be down in a shortly."

"Don't turn the television back on… I mean it."

"All right, all right. I won't."

Claire went into the bedroom closet and put on some casual clothes. Pete swore that we would not look at the news anymore. But his wall of resistance was fragile and weak, and the media was a wrecking ball ready to demolish it. Pete was hooked, at a point of no return.

Twenty minutes later, Pete was fresh out of the shower and fully dressed in his navy blue sweatpants and thin blue line American flag t-shirt. As he went down the stairs, he headed to the front door. Every Sunday, Pete would go outside and grab the newspaper off the front lawn. As he looked around the front lawn, he saw the newspaper on the sidewalk and walked over to pick it up. As he picked up the newspaper and opened it up, he was stunned as he saw that the whole front page had Tyshawn Brendan's picture with the bold headline that read:

RISING BASKETBALL STAR FATALLY SHOT BY WHITE NEWARK COP

Even though Pete promised Claire he would not *watch* the news anymore, that did not stop him from *reading* it. As he stood barefoot in the grass, Pete read the article. Lies upon lies were written. The article began to enrage him. One paragraph said this about the shooting incident:

The two black teens were driving home after a hard practice when police officer Peter Gant suddenly pulled them over. RaJohnn Mitchell, 17, was the alleged driver of the vehicle. Mitchell said that they were approached by a racist white cop who harassed them and pulled out his gun and opened fire. "I didn't even have a chance to get my license out. He just shot us," Mitchell said. Mitchell was shot twice, as was Tyshawn Brendan, 18, who was allegedly seated in the passenger seat. Brendan was taken to University Hospital and was pronounced dead shortly after. Brendan was the country's #1 high school basketball prospect and had recently announced his commitment to Duke University.

Pete was so enraged that he could barely hold the newspaper steady. He viciously tore up the paper and threw it across the lawn. With his hands on his waist, Pete looked up at the front window and saw Leo looking right at him. Leo had never seen his father behave that way, and Pete had no other response than to look back at him. Seconds later, Leo just walked away. Pete turned around and placed his hands on his head and closed his eyes. "Goddamn it," he sighed. Pete felt that the media was planting wicked seeds in a garden: a garden *not* of beautiful flowers but of fertilized chaos and blossoming lily-white lies.

Pete went back into the house and closed the door. The house was quiet as if no one was there except for Pete. Now that the kids knew what had happened, Pete had no idea how he would confront them. As he walked into the kitchen, he looked at the whole family sitting at the table eating breakfast. Elle looked at Pete with mixed feelings. She did not know how to feel other than the devastation of her father shooting and killing one of her idols. Suddenly, Elle stood up from the table and walked past him without a word. She walked past him so fast that he could smell her flowery scent from the wind coming off her body. Pete heard Elle's heavy footsteps going up the stairs plus the slamming of her bedroom door. He then stood there: no words, no emotions. Michael glanced at him, but nothing was said. "Pete," said Claire. "Go to talk to her."

At the top of the stairs, Pete heard the soft sniffles from Elle's bedroom. He approached the door and looked through the opening. He saw Elle sobbing on her bed. He held his head down with his eyes closed as the gluttoned guilt within began to eat at him from the inside. Pete felt solely responsible for his children's pain. He then gave a gentle knock on her door.

"Elle?" Pete said. "Elle, sweetheart… is it okay if I come in?"

"If you want… it's your house, remember?" Elle said through the traffic of tears.

Pete walked in and sat next to Elle on her bed. She laid there with her back turned to him, wiping tears away with her fingertips. Pete was at a loss for words. He did not know how to communicate for her to understand the details of what happened the night of the shooting. But he knew Elle very well. He knew she would not initiate the conversation, and decided to break the ice.

"Elle, I know you're angry with me," Pete said with a look of sorrow.

"I'm not mad at you, Dad," Elle said. "I'm just upset. Why didn't you tell us?"

"I didn't want you guys to worry. It's bad enough that *I* have to deal with this incident. But I *don't* want my family to suffer."

"What happened, Dad? How did you end up shooting Tyshawn Brendan?"

"It's rather complicated to explain, sweetie."

"Dad… I've been looking on social media. People are saying terrible things about you—calling you a *racist*… are you?"

"Am I *what*?" Pete said with startled eyes.

"A *racist*?"

"Why in God's name would you ask me that?"

"Dad, I—"

"You *know* me, Elle. I'm your *father*."

"That's just it, Dad… I *don't* know you like that anymore. I mean… I *love* you, of course… but sometimes… I don't feel like we know each other anymore. And it bothers me when you work so many hours. My friends would ask me, 'What does your dad do for work?' I would just tell them that you work for the state. It's like I can't even be proud to tell my friends that my dad is... a cop."

Pete looked at Elle with guilt in his eyes. He knew she was right about the consistency of his absence at home. But what made him feel awful was that he did not know much about his daughter— besides her love for basketball and Harry Styles.

"Elle," said Pete. "Everything you just said? You're right. We *don't* know each other the way we once have. I'm sorry that our relationship has become that. Being a police officer is a very demanding job, honey. Every day, when I walk out that door, I put my life on the line with no guarantee that I'll come home. I do that to serve and protect my family and my community. But I've sacrificed years of precious time away from you guys. You kids have grown so fast... and I've missed a lot. I admit that now, and I'm so sorry. And—and if it's not too much to ask, I need the biggest favor... I need your love. Daddy's in a lot of trouble, and I don't know what's going to happen moving forward. But as long as I have you guys' love... I know I'll get through this. Okay?"

Elle turned and looked at her father, looking into his eyes like she was trying to read something in him. Pete, however, was feeling uncomfortable with the way she was looking at him.

"Why are you looking at me like that?" Pete asked.

"Like what, Dad?"

"Like... you're *judging* me."

"I just..."

"Just what, honey?"

"Nothing."

"No, please. Come on, if there's something on your mind, just communicate it with me... please."

"I just wish none of this happened... Tyshawn Brendan was a good kid, Dad. He was the best player in the country. I mean, ESPN The Magazine called him the second coming of Michael Jordan. In his Junior year alone, he averaged nearly forty points a game. Do you know how crazy that is to achieve such an accolade in high school?"

"Oh, Elle," Pete sighed. "It's very complicated."

"Yeah... you already said that... I just want to lay back down now," Elle said as she slid her legs under her lavender bedsheets.

Pete stood up from the bed and looked at her. Elle then turned her back to him. Pete, however, took no offense to it. He brushed his fingers down her hair and leaned in to kiss the back of her head. "Daddy loves you, Elle... very much," he said. Pete slowly walked backward and left Elle's room. As he walked out of the hall, he saw Claire standing there as if she was listening the whole time. In her right hand was his phone.

"What's wrong?" Pete asked.

"You got a phone call from your supervisor. They wanted to inform you that the agency has placed you on administrative leave... *without* pay."

"Without *pay*?"

"Yes... he said to call him if you have any other questions. Otherwise, they'll be in touch."

"Did you... did you listen in on our conversation?"

"I wasn't really listening. I just didn't want there to be any commotion."

"She told me that she doesn't know me. And she's right. I don't really know her either. The other morning, when I was fixing some cereal for Leo, I picked up the wrong cereal box. I thought he *loved* Honey Nut Cheerios. But his favorite cereal is Lucky Charms. I should know these things about our kids, Claire—the *little* things. And Michael? Since when did he have an interest in playing the guitar? Hell, who *bought* him that guitar?"

"*You* did. Remember? Four Christmases ago? You had to work

Christmas day, so you bought the kids something very special. You bought Elle the basketball hoop and Michael the guitar."

"Jesus," Pete said, gripping his forehead in disgust. "How could I forget that."

"Pete, listen… the kids love you. They know your schedule has been crazy since you transferred. I talked to them so that they understand."

"I just feel like I've put so much pressure on these kids… *and* you. It's like you've been a single parent for years now."

"Well… I'll take that over being a widow—*any* day of the week. Quite frankly, I didn't care if I was a single parent for the day. So long as your key hit that door at the end of the night, and I hear that Velcro rip off your chest… that's all I cared about."

"Claire," Pete said as he held Claire's shoulders. "This kid was loved by many. Tyshawn Brendan was *special*."

"It was an accident, baby… an *accident*… you didn't know he was in the car. Look… just go downstairs and have breakfast with the boys. Don't worry about Elle… I'll talk to her."

"Okay. I still haven't found my appetite just yet."

"Just try to eat, baby."

"I know, but… every time I eat something, it goes right through me like a bulle… *shit*."

"It's okay."

"You know what? I'm just going to take Brownie for a walk."

Pete headed down the stairs, grabbed Brownie's leash, and put on his coat. Claire came after him down the stairs and said, "Pete, wait… I have an idea. Being that you have been placed on administrative leave… maybe this could be the perfect time to get reacquainted with the kids. And the holidays are here. Now you can spend some quality time with us." Pete looked at Claire and gave her a quick head nod as he liked the idea. He felt that with the holidays coming up and him being placed on administrative leave, he could shorten the dysfunctional gap between them. Unfortunately, it was easier said than accomplished.

17

DECEMBER 22nd, 2025, MONDAY EARLY MORNING:

REGRETS IN THE BASEMENT

It was the wee hours of the morning and Claire was tossing and turning in her sleep. She touched Pete's bedside, expecting to feel his body's warmth. But what she felt was the damp spot of the bed. Claire sat up and began to blot her hand on the oval-shaped spot where Pete was sleeping. Pete was nowhere in sight. She thought to herself and realized that he must have had another nightmare. Whenever Pete had a nightmare, he would get out of bed and go to the backyard to get some fresh air. Sometimes, he would even meditate. But as Claire got out of bed and looked out the window, she did not see the backlight on.

At first, she thought that he went for a walk. But she saw that he left his phone on the nightstand. Pete always took his phone with him whenever he stepped out for a walk. After putting on her bathrobe, Claire quietly descended the stairs. The lights were off and everything was quiet. "Brownie?" She said. Brownie, however, was fast asleep on his dog bed in the living room. Claire had no idea where Pete could have been until she heard noises from the basement.

She opened the basement door and said, "Pete? Are you down there?" But there was no answer. Claire then grabbed one of Michael's old baseball bats and carefully stepped down the stairs. She called for Pete every step of the way, but still, no response. That is when she got to the bottom and saw Pete sitting on the couch, staring at the television.

"Pete?" Claire softly said as she dropped the bat and walked towards the sofa. "I was *calling* for you. You scared me... what are you doing down here?"

Claire sat next to Pete as he still had not uttered a word. She looked at the television screen and saw Tyshawn Brendan's highlight reel on YouTube. Since Elle was a basketball player, Claire had a reasonable knowledge of the game. She was blown away when she began to look at Tyshawn Brendan's highlights. She saw his elusive moves—moves she had never seen before on a basketball court. Tyshawn Brendan could not miss from the three-point arch. His crossovers were impeccable, and his fadeaway shot was impossible to shut down. Tyshawn Brendan had such a charismatic style of play. As Claire watched, she heard Pete's broken voice say, "He's incredible... absolutely... incredible.... I've never seen anyone like him. It's like watching God play." Claire looked at Pete as tears streamed down his blue-lit face—the reflection of the screen glared in his glassy eyes—witnessing a troubled man.

"Pete," Claire said as she paused the video. "How long have you been down here?"

"Since one," Pete sniffled. "What time is it now?"

"It's 4:15 in the morning... this is what you've been doing? Watching videos?"

"I couldn't go back to sleep... I was too scared to go back to sleep."

"Another nightmare?"

Pete nodded. "It was awful."

"What was it about?"

"*Me*.... I was running down the street, running to the crime scene. It was so foggy. I could barely see what was in front of me. As the fog cleared, I saw a bunch of officers running around and then...."

"And then what, baby?"

"I saw myself lying on the ground, all shot up... and the paramedics performing CPR on me. It was like I was a ghost—watching them work on my corpse. That's when I woke up. I wanted to wake you up and talk about it... but I just got out of bed and came down here."

"Oh, Pete," Claire said, rubbing his sweaty back. "Just... just come back to bed, honey."

Pete shook his head. "I can't, Claire... I just can't. Every time I close my eyes... I see him. I see Tyshawn Brendan—looking up at me. He's looking right at me, and it's like he's saying, 'Why? *Why* did you shoot me, Officer?'"

"Please don't do this to yourself, baby. You don't have to sit down here and watch these videos, the news, or *any* of it. We love you... it wasn't your fault that this happened."

"People keep saying I'm a racist, Claire. Post after post, they leave comments saying that I hunted those kids down and shot them just because they were black... am I?"

"*What?*"

"A racist? Did—did I shoot those kids because I'm a white guy who hates black people?"

"What are you *talking* about? Why would you suddenly think that?"

"Claire... I don't even have black friends. How the fuck did that happen?"

"We *have* black friends—our neighbors down the street are black."

"They're *Mexican*, Claire."

"Oh," Claire said, feeling shitty.

"And even if they *were* black, we don't even speak to them as much."

"Pete, listen to me. I think you're making something out of nothing.

What happened that night has nothing to do with race."

"That's not what the *media* is painting it as. Have you read some of these headlines? '*White racist cop shoots two black teenagers,*' '*Mr. Blue Devil, Shot by White Devil.*' This is so bad, Claire. Oh, God... why did I have to take that call? Why me? Why Tyshawn Brendan? *Why* did *any* of this have to happen? And why did I pull the goddamn trigger?"

Claire looked at Pete as he sobbed in his hands. This situation broke her heart as she felt useless—unable to help her despondent husband. She moved closer to him on the couch, placed her chin on his left shoulder, and held him. They sat in their dimmed-lit basement as Pete cried for the next five minutes. At that moment, Claire knew she could not handle this alone. She needed someone who understood what she was going through as a LEO wife. The only people she could talk to were the wives of other police officers with whom she had established a relationship with over the last several years.

"Baby?" Claire spoke. "Come on... let's get you upstairs."

"This kid was unbelievable, Claire," Pete cried as he looked straight ahead at the dark television screen. "He was *so good* on that court... he was great."

"Come on, baby... let's go."

As Claire and Pete made their way up the stairs, he stopped and said, "Claire... what am I going to do about Elle? I think she hates me now."

"She doesn't hate you, Pete. She's just distraught.... Listen, why don't you two do something tomorrow?"

"Like what?"

"Well... usually, right before her games, she practices her shots in the driveway."

"She has a game tomorrow?"

"Yeah... tomorrow night. Maybe the two of you can play."

"Okay... I guess I could try that."

"You should. I think that'll be good for the both of you."

"Thank you, sweetheart… that makes me feel a little better."

"We love you, honey… and we'll get through this—*together*."

"Okay… and I love you more," Pete said as he kissed Claire.

Pete felt he had something to look forward to with Elle. He knew Elle finding out about the shooting had now put a gap between them. But with Claire's advice, he felt that this could be his chance to rekindle their father-and-daughter relationship, and Pete wanted that more than anything… he needed it.

18

DECEMBER 22^{nd,} 2025, MONDAY MORNING:

WHAT'S THAT SMELL?

It was morning, a quarter to eight, to be exact. Pete had just woken up and made his way up to the kitchen. Claire was already up as she just brewed some fresh coffee. As Pete entered the kitchen, he leaned in for a kiss. But Claire rejected it as she swiveled her head and walked away from him. Pete looked at her—knowing why she gave him the cold shoulder.

After a little intimacy in the bathtub earlier that morning, Claire attempted to finish what they started in the bedroom. She kissed him all over his chest as she tried to seduce him. Pete, however, could not meet her halfway. It reached the point where he shouted at her and told her to stop. Claire became emotional and left the bedroom. Pete was very apologetic for snapping at her. He felt that it was too soon as the shooting was only three days ago. Being that Tyshawn Brendan was still fresh in his mind, Pete was in no mood for romance. Claire, however, took it personally. As she sat down, drinking coffee, Pete poured him a cup and joined her.

"Morning, sweetheart," he said as he tapped his index finger on the rim of his coffee mug. "How did you sleep?"

"Okay," Claire responded after taking a sip. "You?"

"I slept for like an hour or two.... Look... I'm sorry about what happened in the bedroom. I know you were just trying to... cheer me up. But I'm not ready for all that right now... do you understand?"

"I do... I just don't want you going down this dark rabbit hole—watching videos of this kid and the news—when you *promised* me you wouldn't."

"I know. I know I promised you, and I'll *keep* my promise."

Claire looked at Pete as she grabbed his left hand and rubbed her thumb on his wedding ring. "I'm scared, Pete... I'm scared that I'm going to lose you over this."

"Don't be afraid, honey. I'm going to be okay. I just need some time on this."

"We're *all* going to need some time."

"You're right... you're right."

Suddenly, Pete heard a basketball dribbling alongside the house as they sat there drinking coffee.

"Is that Elle?" Pete asked. "She doesn't have school today?"

Claire responded. "Yes, she has school. It's the last day, actually—before the holidays. But she doesn't have a first or second period on Mondays. So, she usually practices her shot before she goes to school."

"Oh."

"You know... this would be the perfect time for you to connect with her. Why don't you go outside and shoot around with her for a little while?"

"Yeah... yeah, maybe I should."

Pete quickly put on his hoodie and sneakers. As he walked outside, Elle turned around and saw her father. But then she turned back around and face the hoop.

"Hi, honey," Pete said.

"Hi, Dad," Elle responded as she held the ball.

"Shooting some hoops?"

120

"Yeah... just getting some practice shots in before the game tonight."

"Oh, okay. Cool... cool," Pete said with his hands in his pockets.

"Was there something you wanted?"

"No—well... yes. I just thought that maybe you'd want to play a little one-on-one? Shoot around?"

"With *you*?"

"Yeah, with me."

"Um... if you want, I guess."

"Great."

Pete stood next to the basket to grab the rebounds for Elle while she began to shoot. She took her first shot... nothing but net. "Good shot, babe," Pete said as he passed the ball to her. Elle took a few dribbles and took another shot: swish. "Excellent," Pete smiled. As Pete passed Elle the ball, she stood there in silence.

"What's the matter, Elle?" Pete asked.

"Dad... can I ask you just one question?"

"Of course."

"Why did you have to kill Tyshawn Brendan? I mean... I'm sure it was an accident. But why did *you* have to be the one?"

Pete sighed. "Elle... I know you're very angry with me. I'm angry at myself. If I could go back to that moment, I... I would've approached that situation differently. I thought the driver had a gun. I thought he was going to shoot me. I responded the only way I was trained to respond. That's our policy. To use deadly force if necessary.... There was a saying in the police academy, 'You delay, you die.' I didn't want to die that night. I didn't want that night to be my last. Do you understand? Sometimes, in my line of work... there's just not enough time to make a choice. And our actions don't always give us the results we hoped for."

"But what about Tyshawn Brendan, Dad? He didn't deserve to die."

"He *didn't*... and I *wish* he didn't. But what can I do? I *can't* bring him back."

Elle sighed. "No… you can't. Let's just forget about it, all right?"

"Elle, I'm sorry—"

"Dad, I just want to practice. I have a game tonight."

"I know. Your mother told me… you know what? I'm going to come see you play."

"You're just saying that."

"No, no. I mean it. I really want to come. And I *am*. I'll be there."

"Really?"

"*Really*. I promise."

"Dad, you know how you are with promises."

"Well, I won't break this one. I *promise* I won't."

Elle smiled. "Okay… it'll mean a lot to me for you to be there."

"I'll be in the stands cheering you on… come on… you shoot and I'll grab the… boards? That's what they're called, right?"

Elle chuckled. "Yeah, Dad… boards."

Elle continued to shoot around as Pete grabbed the rebounds. Suddenly, he began to discover an odious stench coming from the ball. As Elle took another shot, Pete grabbed it mid-air and put the ball to his nose as he sniffed it like a dog. "Dad?" Elle said as Pete continued to sniff the basketball. He could not believe what he was smelling, and it was getting stronger by the second.

"Elle," he said as he brought the ball to her face. "You smell that?"

"Smell what?" Elle said as she smelt the basketball.

"*Blood… gunpowder*. Do you smell it?"

"*Blood?* Dad, what are you talking about—"

"Smell it, Elle!"

"Dad, you're starting to scare me now. I don't smell anything—"

"It's right here—*smell* it!"

"*Stop yelling* at me!"

"Just smell the ball!"

"Mom!" Elle shouted.

Claire came running out of the house as she heard the commotion. "Hey! What's going on here?" Claire said. Elle ran into the house, leaving Pete behind as he held the ball. Claire looked at him as he had his back turned, sniffing away at the ball.

"Pete?" Claire said. "What the hell is going on?"

Pete dropped the basketball. "I smelt it."

"Smelled what? What are you talking about?"

"Elle was shooting the ball, and I smelled something coming off of it. It smelt like gunpowder and burnt pennies… it smelt like blood."

"*Blood*? But… why would you think you were smelling that—"

"No, I wasn't *thinking* it, I was *smelling* it—coming off the ball."

"But why would you smell gunpowder coming from a ball?"

"I don't know. Maybe it was… oh, *Jesus*."

"What?"

"I know where it's coming from… that night at the shooting, when I pulled Tyshawn Brendan out of the car, there was a basketball that fell out on the ground. I remember seeing it. It was deflated. I think it was hit by one of the bullets, and… I saw blood on it."

"Are you telling me Elle's basketball made you smell gunpowder and *blood*?"

"Yes… and not only that, as I held the ball, my pulse started to go fast… it was as if I was still at the scene."

Claire got closer to Pete. "Pete… Pete, look at me. Honey, I think you need to see someone."

"See who?"

"A doctor. I think you need to see a therapist. Didn't they provide you with counseling or something?"

"I don't trust those head doctors, Claire."

"But they can help you, Pete."

"Oh, yeah? And what do they know? What are those doctors going to say that I haven't heard already? 'Oh, it wasn't your fault, Pete. It *happens*—it happens every day. Black people get shot *all* the time.

Don't worry about it. Just take these pills, go to sleep, and *pretend* it didn't even happen.' I took that kid away from his family *and* his gifts. I *robbed* him of his destiny, Claire... I hurt a lot of people. The underlying truth is I don't *deserve* to be here. They're going to put me in prison for what I've done."

"*Don't say that*!" Claire cried. "You have to be *here*—with *your* family—*that's* where you belong. You have to take care of *your* family now. *We* are hurting. And I've *told* you to stop watching the news— *don't look* at any *media*. It's no good for you—for *any* of us."

"It's not that *simple*, Claire. I can't just block him out and pretend this never happened. Tyshawn Brendan wasn't some low-life criminal who had it coming. He had a future—a *life*! And I took that away from him. I took him away from the *world*... they *won't* let me walk away from that."

"What are you saying, Pete? It's like you're giving up."

"Claire—"

"Do we have to remove all the TVs from the house? If that's what it takes, then we'll do that."

"No, I just... they're going to come after me, Claire. And they won't stop until I'm behind bars or *dead*."

"*Don't say that*! It was an accident, Pete! You didn't wake up that morning and say, '*Oh*, let me shoot a black kid today.' You did what you had to do—for *your* protection. What if he *had* a gun and shot *you*? What if they knocked on the door and told me you weren't coming home? Do you know how many nights I went to bed *thinking* that? Thinking that you might not make it home? Do you have *any* idea what that's like? For *sixteen years*, I've dealt with that—*sixteen years*, I had to face that reality, and I *faced* that reality with you. *I've* shared those nightmares with you—*I've* cried with you—*I've* mourned all those fallen officers with *you*: Stanley, Brooks, McDaniel, Ferguson, and *Clayton*—your best friend—your brother... I've walked through *hell* with you, Pete. *Every day*!

124

Because I love you. And those kids love you... you were *never* alone."

Claire grew so emotional that she ran into the house and slammed the door—leaving Pete behind in the cold wind with burning thoughts. "*Shit*," he said to himself. Pete did not know what to do. He did not know whether or not he should go after Claire and apologize or reconcile with Elle. All he knew was that the solid bond of his family was beginning to break, and so was his heart.

It was a quarter to two in the afternoon. Pete had just woken up as he slept for four hours—the most sleep he has had since the shooting. As he laid in bed, he heard music coming from Michael's room. Pete got up and went to Michael's bedroom. He saw Michael lying on his bed as he played his guitar. Pete knocked on the open door to get his attention.

"Hey, son," he said.

"Hey, Dad," Michael responded, gently plucking his guitar strings.

"Out of school already?"

"Yeah. Today was a half day since tomorrow's Christmas Eve."

"Oh, right. I didn't even realize it was Christmas Eve already."

"Yeah... so, what's up?"

"You tell *me*. I'm hearing all this music... sounds good."

"Thanks," Michael grinned.

"Where's your brother?"

"In his room playing video games."

"Oh, you didn't want to play with him?"

"Dad... playing video games with a six-year-old is like going to a playground and picking on a little kid. If I beat him in a game, he'll start crying."

"Really?"

"Yes, he does it all the time. Whenever we play and he loses, he drops the controller, goes to Mom and cries about it. Then she tells me to let him win a few games, and I do. But he's gotta learn how to take a loss *sometime*."

"I guess the age gap can be a little difficult for brothers. But listen, you guys have to be close. That's important. As a *big* brother, you have to make sure you look out for him, you know?"

"I know, Dad... but don't you think that's your job?"

"What do you mean?"

"I mean, just...." Michael shrugged his shoulders.

"Say what you mean."

"I just meant like with all that's going on, maybe *you* can look out for *us*. People are talking, Dad. When Elle and I are in school, other kids give us strange looks. What are we supposed to do?"

"Just be yourselves. This has nothing to do with you and your sister. Just be yourselves, and if anyone asks you *anything*, just say that you don't know anything about the situation... all right?"

Michael sighed. "Whatever."

"Michael... let me ask you a serious question... what do you think of black people?"

"What do you mean, Dad?"

"I mean, just... what do you *think* of them? What do you think about black people when you see them?"

"Well... there's some black kids I'm cool with at school. We like the same music. They seem to like me. I never really had a problem with them."

"Do you consider them your friends? The black kids you're cool with?"

"Yeah, I guess. Maybe not the *closest* of friends. But... why are you asking me all of this?"

"I want to make sure your mother and I are raising you kids right."

"I mean... like *I've* never had a problem with black people."

"Oh. Okay, well, I just wanted to know what you thought. That's all."

"Yeah, Elle and I don't think like that. It's a different generation, you know."

"Yeah… I know."

"What about you?"

"Me?"

"Yeah… what do *you* think about black people?"

Pete looked at Michael, unsure of how to respond. "Uh… I'll be honest with you, Michael… I haven't had the best experiences with black people. As a police officer, it's been complicated to get black people to trust me. A lot of them are bitter towards cops. Some cursed me out, threw things at me, spit on me—some even shot at me. And after all that has happened… I'm sure many of them don't give a damn about me."

"No offense, Dad, but you kinda sound like *you're* playing the victim."

"I *do*, don't I? But I'm not a victim, son… I'm just in a terrible situation. And I think it's going to get ugly before it gets better. But I want to make sure that you're doing okay and that *we're* okay."

"Yeah… I'm fine."

"Good… and *we're* okay?"

Michael smiled. "We're okay, Dad."

"Okay… I love you. You know that?"

"Yeah, I know. I love you, too."

Pete rubbed his fingers through Michael's hair and kissed him on his head. After leaving Michael's bedroom, Pete went across the hall to check on Leo. Leo, however, was not in his room. Pete entered Leo's room and looked around as he discovered new things about his son. He noticed Leo's quality in art. Leo had pictures he drew hanging on his wall. One drawing in particular was of Pete in his police uniform. He drew Pete with a small body and a big head—looking like a bobblehead. Pete picked up the picture and smiled as he saw Leo's choice of colors. But what made him smile even more was the writing above Pete in the picture:

"My Dad, The Hero."

It warmed Pete's heart to know that Leo still considered him a hero. But after the shooting death of Tyshawn Brendan, Pete felt the farthest away from heroism. He took the picture to his bedroom and placed it on his nightstand. As he laid there in bed, Pete felt relieved. And even though he was under fire, he was grateful to know his kids still loved him.

19

DECEMBER 22nd, 2025, MONDAY AFTERNOON:

THE BODYCAM NEVER LIES... PEOPLE DO

Pandemonium had emerged all over the news and social media as the body cam footage was released. Pete was by himself down in the basement. He was warned not to watch the news. But the temptation had a firm grip on his conscience and drew his attention to the television screen.

The body cam footage was uploaded to every news channel on YouTube. Countless videos had been posted by content creators who shared their furious and emotional reactions. Pete clicked on one of the thumbnails of the CNN news channel. As he watched, the anchorman spoke:

Body cam footage of the shooting of Tyshawn Brendan and RaJohnn Mitchell has been released. Before we show you, we must warn you that what you're about to see is extremely graphic and may not be suitable for all viewers. Please be advised.

Pete's adrenaline raced throughout his body as he was about to relive that night. The Axon body cam had started to record from inside Pete's patrol unit. He remembered patting himself down, checking to ensure his gear was in order. He watched as he was about to leave the car, and then Michael called him. The body cam showed Pete declining Michael's call as he stepped out of the truck. You could hear the music blasting from the black Kia. Pete's knees shook uncontrollably. He folded his hands, pressing them over his mouth as he watched the body cam footage. The video showed Pete knocking on the window. Seconds later, RaJohn Mitchell rolled the window down, and that brief dialogue began:

"What yo?"
"First off, turn the music down—"
"Nah, suck my dick!"

Pete remembered vividly that intricate moment. Then, the body cam showed him turning away from the car as he radioed in for backup. Seconds later… it happened. The body cam was back on the vehicle; RaJohn Mitchell rolled the window down and extended his arm out the window with his phone. Then there was the flash, and then… the rounds went off:

POP! POP! POP! POP! POP! POP!

In fractions of a second, the driver's seat window went from a dark tint to a shattered piece of glass. Pete was in shock as he saw the bullets go through the window and the door. The body cam began to rumble out of focus as Pete returned to his patrol truck to take cover. He heard his voice as he yelled:

"SHOTS FIRED! SHOTS FIRED! CODE THIRTY-THREE! I NEED EMS TO MY LOCATION NOW! STEP IT UP!"

Tears fell from Pete's face as he did not remember the shooting. But seeing it shocked him as it happened in the blink of a second. Pete did not even realize he had fired off six rounds. Being that he spent hours upon hours in the shooting range, his exceptional accuracy created a trajectory of tragedy.

As Pete continued to watch the body cam footage, he saw RaJohn Mitchell hit the ground. Pete heard everything he said in the

130

video. It was like a horror film to him—seeing RaJohnn Mitchell's bloody hands. The body cam showed how Pete detained RaJohnn Mitchell and asked him where the gun was. As that night was still fresh in his mind, Pete began to feel nauseous and rushed to the bathroom and vomited. He stayed in the bathroom for about five minutes as the combined chunks of food and mucus kept dumping out of his mouth. Pete hated what he had done and wished he could take it back. But the thought of him being killed reminded Pete that his decision was valid.

After he rinsed his mouth with water, Pete flushed the toilet and stepped out the bathroom. By surprise, Claire was sitting down on the couch with her hand covering her mouth and tears falling down her face as she replayed the video.

"Claire?" Pete said. "Wha... what are you doing?"

Claire turned and looked at Pete but said nothing. She then got up and slowly went up the stairs. Pete did not know what was going through her mind. But the sudden slam of the basement door gave him an inkling of how she felt. As the footage continued to play, it showed the moment Tyshawn Brendan was on the ground. Pete looked with his startled eyes and saw the moment when Tyshawn Brendan looked at him and said, "*Fuck you!*" Pete immediately turned around and covered his ears as he was triggered. That was when he realized that the words "Fuck you," would forever be a trigger for him—his Achilles' heel.

A half hour had gone by. Pete was still in the basement as he repeatedly watched the body cam footage—on mute. But then, he began to read people's comments, and many were deliberately disturbing:

@ProphecytheProfit2387

Give this fucking white supremacist the electric chair. He shot these two black kids over a phone? These cops out here are

131

DEMONS! Facts!

@JaneButterflyLibra

OMG! Why would he just shoot them like that? Over a cell phone? Damn, these cops have no soul. I hope the families of Teyshawn Brendan and RayJon Mitchell gets some justice.

@KandanceWilliams93

@JaneButterflyLibra It's TYSHAWN and RAJOHNN. Get there names right, you dumb bitch!

@JaneButterflyLibra

@KandanceWilliams93 Coming from someone who doesn't know the difference between "there" and "their." LOL!

@Holygrail2004

Wow! This cop is ruthless. He didn't even bother to ask for a license or anything. He just started bustin his gun and killed homeboy. RIP Tyshawn Brendan. #BLACKLIVESMATTER

@MAGA4Life2025

I really don't know what people are seeing. I mean, are you guys blind? That bastard pointed a phone at the officer (Which could've been a gun), and there was a flash. If you know anything about policing, cops are trained to take out a suspect who becomes a threat. Obviously, that driver didn't know any better, and his ignorant actions cost him the life of his friend. But this OIS is 100% justifiable. PERIOD!

@Robin4Real45

@MAGA4Life2025 How could you possibly call this shooting justifiable? Are YOU blind? That cop literally executed them. Thank God one survived. I hope they put that cracker cop away for the rest of his life. I'm so tired of these racist ass cops killing us. When is this shit going

to end? And you call this justifiable? Go to hell, you fucking Trump supporter.

@ MAGA4Life2025

@Robin4Real45 So… my political views have nothing to do with this police shooting. Calling me a "Trump Supporter" doesn't hurt my feelings in the slightest. I'm not saying what happened to the basketball player isn't a tragedy. But the camera doesn't lie. People do. Look at the video! The driver was clearly the threat. The officer did what he was trained to do. It's that simple.

@Robin4Real45

@MAGA4Life2025 You see? This is why black people don't even bother talking with white people about anything. You just don't fucking get it. If that cop was black and they were white, we wouldn't be having this conversation, would we? They would throw him under the jail and melt the key. And that basketball player's name is Tyshawn Brendan.

@ MAGA4Life2025

@Robin4Real45 You're speaking from emotions and hypothetic narratives. I'm speaking from logic. The fact remains that the driver was in the wrong here. He reached his arm out with a phone and pointed it at the officer. What do you THINK is going to happen? That's why I said the driver didn't know any better, which cost him dearly. But hey, I'm not your enemy. I'm just stating the facts here. Take it or leave it.

@EvelynWilson1968

My heart truly aches when I see this video. My sincerest condolences to the families of these Two young men. I am a white woman who supports the Black Lives Matter movement. But I'm afraid that I have to side with the officer on this one right here. The driver reached his arm out with something in his hand (Which looked like a gun, I must say) and aimed it at the officer. You should never do that. I think this is just simply a tragic situation that cost the life of a very talented young man. Hopefully, something can change about how law enforcement officers are perceived in today's society.

@NatBlackandProudTurner

After watching this video, it's been made quite clear to me that black men in this country are nothing more but an obsessive commodity and just simply target practice. I bet you all the money in the world that this cop has not shed a tear, not ONE TEAR since he shot those kids. We are nothing more than a commodity that they can buy or sell, transfer around like product, and if we can't be sold, they'll just kill us off. We've all seen how they obsessed over Tyshawn Brendan. Measuring his body at the combine like a slave: measuring his hands, his arm length, it was sickening. And then they fed him to the wolves. Rest in peace to this young king, Tyshawn Brendan. I'm so tired of them killing us. They're not going to be satisfied until they kill us all.

@MAGA4Life2025

@NatBlackandProudTurner FYI, sir, black people have been killing each other and are STILL killing each other every single day. What are you going to do about blacks killing blacks? Because I'm sick and tired of the hypocrisy.

@NatBlackandProudTurner

@MAGA4Life2025 I'm going to block you. That's what I'm going to do.

@MAGA4Life2025

@NatBlackandProudTurner WOOOWW! What a great

scapegoat, avoiding answering such a simple question. But I'll ask it again. WHAT ARE BLACK PEOPLE GOING TO DO ABOUT BLACKS KILLING BLACKS? PLEASE, someone answer that question for me. I'll just say this since nobody else has the nerve to say it: "Black Lives WON'T matter if Black Lives pull the triggers." I'm done now.

Pete was in disbelief as he scrolled and read the comments. He read dozens of them before he shut off YouTube. The racial division had metastasized all over the internet. Pete felt responsible for such catastrophe. The body cam footage was out, and his name was known throughout the nation as the cop who shot and killed basketball phenom, Tyshawn Brendan.

20

DECEMBER 22^{nd,} 2025, MONDAY AFTERNOON:

<u>JAYMEL COOK-LYNN</u>

A video of civil rights activist Jaymel Cook-Lynn had been released on social media. Jaymel has been speaking publicly about the shooting of RaJohnn Mitchell and Tyshawn Brendan. His team had gathered the black community together on the streets of Newark as he prepared to make a speech.

Pete was in the basement as he had the video playing on the television. He made a second bedroom out of the basement and no one was allowed down there. The table was covered with empty Heineken and Hennessey bottles as his drinking became routine and addictive by the hour. As Pete looked at the television, he watched Jaymel reach the podium. Jaymel was more on the short side, but he had the presence of a giant—a larger-than-life figure with a Napoleon complex. He had a colossal following on social media and was loved by the black community. He had a melanated complexion and a full beard. As Jaymel approached the podium, he began his speech:

Brothers and sisters—kings and queens... I can't let this one go. I don't know about y'all, but I *cannot* let it go. This shooting has *crushed* me. It has been on my conscience *all night long*. Whenever I see a picture of my young brother, who is now deceased, it just makes me want to *scream*. It *angers* me because it keeps *happening* to *us*—and *only* us! We're always the people who catch a bullet from these wicked ass cops. Now, I know some kids are out here, so I'll be cool with the profanity. But brothers and sisters, *please* understand my pain… because I understand yours. I know y'all want revenge. So do I. I *know* y'all are tired of these cops taking our young kings and queens from us. So am I. That's why we're here today. We… want… *justice*.

Tyshawn Brendan was *our* king—*our* superstar. And that *cop*— I'm going to say his *real* name—Pete "The Pig" Gant. *That's* his name. Pete "The Pig" Gant took *our* superstar away from us. He shot and killed one of *our* promising kings. I'm *so sick* and *tired* of these *racist ass pigs ruining* our families. That pig probably went home that night, had dinner, played with *his* kids, and slept like a baby. Not a care in the world. That's how they do us. He probably doesn't even *think* about Tyshawn Brendan. How many more police shootings are we going to *see*? How many more: Sean Bell, Trayvon Martin, Michael Brown, Philando Castile, Breonna Taylor—Sandra Bland, Sonya Massey, Eric Garner, George Floyd— *Amadou Diallo*—remember him? Forty-one shots—shot nineteen times? The list goes *on* and *on*. How many more '*I can't breathe'* do we have to witness? *How* many more marches do we have to *march*? How many more kings and queens do *we* have to *BURY*? *How* many more? *I'm* here to say, '*NOT* ONE MORE!'

Pete watched on with a dense weight of sorrow and guilt. Hearing Jaymel call him Pete "The Pig" Gant was devastating. Not only did it diminish Pete's character… it crushed his soul. The narrative of Pete being a racist cop was like terminal cancer that could not be treated. The media had become manipulatively wicked—turning the shooting into yet another case that contributed to the agenda of police brutality. Even though the body cam footage showed RaJohnn Mitchell being a threat, the public was not convinced that it was justifiable. The footage showed the truth, but through the eyes of the black community, all they saw was a white cop shoot two black, unarmed teenagers. Pete continued to watch the television as Jaymel continued:

Brothers and sisters... Tyshawn Brendan was on his way. He was on his way to *greatness*. He was going to graduate high school early in January, as he had all his credits. He was in the top three percent of his graduating class. We didn't just have the next Michael Jordan. We had the next *Einstein*—the next George Washington Carver, a *genius beyond* his time. But does the media want to share any of that? No... they only talk about how great of a *ball* player he was. *Not* his intelligence, just what he could do on the court. They only see us as a *commodity*, brothers and sisters— something they can control—mentally, physically, *and* financially— treating us as if we are these disposable beings from whom they profit, but we *don't matter*... not to *them*. We're just thugs with ball handles and some rhymes. I guess this is just the way it is in this country. They're going to keep killing us until black excellence *ceases* to exist. But we're not checking up outta here without a fight, are we? *Nah*... we're *not* going out without a fight. *Bet* that. Pete "The Pig" Gant is still out there, *enjoying* his life, probably on vacation right now, sipping on some damn piña coladas— *happy* because he shot one of us—no, he shot *two* of us! *Killed* one. You see? These crooked ass cops don't have our *backs*. All they do is *shoot* us in the back—or the front—or wherever they have to—to make *sure we* are no longer breathing.

But let me tell you something about Pete "The Pig" Gant... he has a daughter. *Michelle* Gant. And *she* plays basketball. Word through the grapevine is she's pretty good. But she's *damn* sure no Tyshawn Brendan. I tell you this: her basketball career is over. If they *think* she'll be able to still play after her father shot the number one prospect? They got another damn thing coming. Brothers and sisters... I'm here to say, 'No more.' *Nobody* has our back. Nobody. Only *we* can hold each other down. And we *have* to. We *have* to protect our own before they kill us all. If *we* don't protect our boys and girls, these wicked pigs are going to finish us *off*. Do you *hear* me? It's time to fight *back* against police brutality, fight *back* against racism, fight *back* against those who don't give a *damn* about *any* of us, and fight *back* against this *sick, corrupt, trigger-happy,* genocidal *system* that is supposed to *protect* and *serve* the people—yet it *punishes* and *slaughters* the people—*just* because they *can* and *get* away with it—*Lord have mercy*! *Not* one more… it is time that *we* get *black justice.*

Pete grabbed the remote and turned the television off, having heard enough of Jaymel Cook-Lynn. Pete hated what this man initiated and what he said about Elle. As he looked at his phone, he began to read what the public had to say on social media—scrolling up the screen as cruel comments showed the deplorable darkness in people.

@JazmineDaAfricanQueen0331

Salute to the God, Jaymel Cook-Lynn. I just saw his speech. I'm 100% behind him. These racist cops need to be stopped and removed from the police force. I'm sick of them killing us. Pete "The Pig" Gant, just do the world a favor and kill yourself. You'll never be forgiven for your sins. You're a racist and a murderer. The world would be a better place without you. And when you kill yourself, go straight to hell.

@BrotherMilesBaker0512

I hope that Pete "The Pig" Gant offs himself. He doesn't deserve to live. He knew exactly what he was doing that night. I bet he even knew that Tyshawn Brendan was in the car. On God, it was a setup. They saw Tyshawn's greatness and they wanted to shut him down. Why? Because America loves tragedy. It loves to build black athletes and then destroy them. We're nothing more but pawns on their wicked chessboards. RIP to the young God, Tyshawn Brendan.

@MonicaJones0714

Jaymel Cook-Lynn was right on point. We need

to have some black justice. Pete "The Pig" is indeed a racist. He robbed Tyshawn Brendan of his destiny. I have no sympathy for this despicable, sorry excuse for a cop and human being. Bigotry has no place in our community. I hope they throw him behind bars and keep him in a cell for the rest of his wasted life. RIP TB.

@BlackandProud2DaBone0724

#JusticeforTyshawnBrendan, and shoutout to Jaymel, bro. He keeps it real with the black community. I love what he said about Black Justice. That's exactly what we need. Some BLACK Justice against these racist pigs. And Pete "The Pig?" You better watch your back, motherfucka. Because we're coming for you, you bastard.

The more Pete read, the more he drank. The alcohol was his way of coping with all the backlash from the media. Pete was always vital when it came to insults. He would never allow people's words to bring him down. But with the death of Tyshawn Brendan—that guilt had overpowered his true character—losing himself in the process.

21

DECEMBER 22nd, 2025, MONDAY EVENING:

THE GAME

It was close to a packed house as East Orange Campus Jaguars hosted the girls' basketball *Deck the Halls* tournament. Glen Ridge and Newark Tech were the guests who played the first game, with East Orange playing Montclair right after. Pete and Claire had just entered the gym. Michael did not feel like attending the game and decided to stay home with Leo.

Pete felt a sense of relief as he was unrecognizable, walking among the others wearing a facemask. But there was another side of him that felt shameful and mortified. There he was, a cop, hiding in plain sight—sitting beside Claire on the red bleachers.

"You okay, Pete?" Claire asked.

Pete nods and responds through the facemask, "Yeah… I'm okay."

"Well, it's good that Elle's game is up first. Once they're done, we'll get out of here."

"All right… I'm good, though… really."

"Okay," Claire smiled as she held his hand.

The players took the court as they began to warm up and shoot around. Pete tried to adapt to the environment—nodding his head to the music, even though he was not the biggest fan of hip-hop. So far, no one recognized him through the mask. He felt at ease because several other people were also wearing masks. As the buzzer went off, it was time for the game to start. The announcer then stood up from the turntable and spoke in the microphone.

"Testing, testing…. All right, good evening, ladies and gentlemen. Welcome to the *Deck the Halls* girls' basketball tournament. We have two games lined up for you this evening: first, we have the Glen Ridge Ridgers versus Newark Tech Terriers, followed up with our own East Orange Campus Jaguars versus Montclair Mounties. Before we begin, we ask that you rise and join us in a moment of silence as one of Newark Tech's own, Tyshawn Brendan, was tragically taken from us three nights ago."

Suddenly, Pete froze, and the entire gym went silent. Pete's heart raced as he looked around at the wave of melancholic faces in the crowd. And yet, no one could see his face. The moment of silence felt like forever. Pete turned to look at Claire as *she* looked how he felt. All he could do was stand there and feel the guilt cruising through his conscience like a wrathful hurricane over the ocean. "Thank you," said the announcer. "Justice for Tyshawn."

"JUSTICE FOR TYSHAWN!" The crowd said in unison.

Pete felt that he could not stay in that gym much longer. But as he looked at the court and saw Elle, he knew he could not break his promise. The announcer then asked everyone to remain standing as they played the national anthem—a pre-recording of Whitney Houston's singing the national anthem from Super Bowl XXV.

At that moment, Pete raised his diagonal hand and saluted the American flag for the duration of the song. No matter what, Pete would always salute the red, white, and blue during the national anthem. He truly believed in the American dream and protecting and serving his community. For Pete, it was a moment of honor. Even though he was in a bad situation, Pete did not forget that he was still an officer of the law who sincerely obeyed and honored his oath. But then, he received a phone call that would change that. It was a call from Captain Bernal, who was there the night of the shooting.

"I'll be right back," he said to Claire as he stepped away and answered the call. "Hello?"

"Gant," Captain Bernal responded. "I'm going to need you to come in. Director Louis would like to speak with you."

"Sir... um... can this wait?"

"I'm afraid not. Director Louis wants you in his office immediately."

"Sir, um... I promised my daughter that—"

"Gant... he's expecting you to be in his office within the next half hour... be there."

"Sir, I really can't—"

"That's an order, Gant. Don't keep him waiting."

Pete sighed. "Yes, sir."

After Pete ended the call with Captain Bernal, he called his father and told him what was happening. Montgomery suggested that Pete call Freddy to accompany him, and Pete agreed. Pete, however, was going nowhere until he watched some of the game. After he called Freddy and told him the situation, he returned to Claire. Claire was curious about who called.

"Who was that?" Claire asked.

"Huh?" Pete responded.

"Who *was* that?"

"It was the captain. I have to go meet with the Director."

"Right now?"

"No... I'm going to watch some of this game. I'm not going to break my promise to Elle."

The tip-off was underway. Elle was part of the starting five for Glen Ridge. A minute had not passed, and the opposing team delivered a foul to Elle. As Elle's teammate took the ball out, Elle was immediately fouled again. She went to the free-throw line to shoot two shots. Suddenly, the gym was roaring with an avalanche of boos. Pete looked around at the crowd, mortified at their behavior. Elle, however, made both free throws. Four minutes passed and Elle had already been fouled several times. Pete sat there, livid as he watched his daughter take a beating. He could see the redness on her arms and face. He felt that Elle was being targeted because of him.

"This is fucking ridiculous," Pete said to Claire. "They're just going to let her get fouled like that?"

"It's okay, Pete—"

"No, it's *not* okay."

"She's taken tougher fouls before. It's part of the game."

"No… this is personal."

Suddenly, as Elle obtained the ball, she went for a layup and received a gruesome, flagrant foul as two players knocked her to the ground. "Son of a *bitch*!" Pete shouted. "Jesus, call timeout, Coach!" Elle was slow to get up off the ground—banged up from the dreadful blows. Pete's anger was getting the better of him. He wanted to walk on the court and take Elle out of the game. It was then that he had an inkling that word got out of Jaymel Cook-Lynn speaking on Elle and that was why they were attacking her on the court.

"They're fouling her on purpose, Claire," Pete said. "I'm…" Pete suddenly became silent as he smelled a familiar scent. He smelled gunpowder and blood. He looked around and noticed two teenagers behind him holding basketballs. "*Shit*," he said under his breath. The smell was growing stronger as it seeped through his facemask. But then, something even more disturbing happened. During the timeout, the DJ played a familiar tune that Pete recognized instantly. It was the rap song *Gang Gang*—the same song blasting from the car the night of the shooting—making it a haunting coincidence.

Pete felt shortness of breath as the scene from that night was recreated. He stood up from the bleachers as he felt dizzy—heading down the stairs—bumping into people. "Pete!" Claire said, calling out to him. Elle just happened to turn around and spotted Pete heading to the exit. It took everything in her power not to show emotion and focus on her free throws. Claire quickly ran out of the gym—running after him. She went outside in the cold—her frosted breath was heavily visible as she called to him.

"Pete!" Claire said as she ran after him. "Pete, wait!"

"Claire, I have to go. The director's expecting me."

"Pete, wait a minute—"

"No! I'm sorry... but I can't do this right now. I have to go."

"Fine... fine, go."

"I'm sorry... can you get a ride with one of the other parents?"

"Don't worry... I'll find a way home."

"I'm sorry."

"You already said that."

Pete got into their black Jeep Liberty and started the car. Claire then joined him in the car as he waited for it to warm up.

"Claire, please—"

"No, just stop... relax yourself for a minute. What was going on in there? Why did you leave so suddenly?"

"I told you, I have to meet the director—"

"No, no, no. There was something else bothering you. I can see it in your eyes. Something triggered you in there. What was it?"

"*Everything... everything* was a trigger. The announcer, the basketballs, the rap music... it's like everything was coming back to haunt me. That song that was playing in the game was the same fucking song playing in the car that night. I thought I was going to pass out or something... I just had to get out of there, Claire."

"I see... I'm going to go back inside now."

"Are you sure you'll be able to get a ride home?"

"Yeah, Marcia's inside. She'll bring us home."

"All right… I'll see you when I get back."

"Fine."

Claire got out of the car and returned to the gym. Pete took a moment as he laid his head back on the headrest and closed his eyes. But the shooting suddenly reappeared in his mind, as did the song. The song that was playing that night was had now become a haunting tune trapped in Pete's head. It kept playing over and over. Sitting there, Pete looked at his phone and saw a text from Freddy:

Uncle Freddy
I'll meet you over there, Pete.
Be there in about 20 minutes.

Pete then went on X, a decision he would immediately regret. As he opened the X app, a skullduggery of posts about him appeared. Pete scrolled through the comments and was utterly appalled at what people were saying about him:

@JamaalJones1058

> Somebody ought to have your badge
> after shooting those black kids, you fucking pig.

@Tiffanywiththegoodafro0153

> Another racist cop shoots down black people. I hope you
> fry in hell, you son of bitch.

@PatrickDelman1369

> Shame on you. Those boys didn't deserve it.
> You're going to get what you already got coming to you.

@Themagicofspeech1160

> Fuck all police officers. All those pigs need to be turned
> into bacon. #JUSTICEFORTYSHAWNBRENDAN!

146

@DerrickDaBossman3224

Those cops must've set Tyshawn Brendan up. He was too great, and they sacrificed his life. Pete Gant is a puppet, a patsy. He's part of a bigger agenda. Stay woke out here, people. It's all a conspiracy.

@Artistwiththerock90815

RIP Tyshawn Brendan. The second coming of Michael Jordan. He was the greatest player in the country, and those fucking pigs killed another promising kid. I swear I can't stand these fucking cops, man. They need to put some bullets into Pete Gant's dome and set his ass on fire.

@Rosco1132

Have y'all seen the second video? That was crazy. RIP to Tyshawn. #JusticeforTyshawnBrendan

Pete was shocked to know that there was a second video of the shooting. It did not take long for him to find it on social media. The footage was vivid and in high definition. It looked as if it had been recorded from the second floor of an apartment window. In the video, there was a voice of a woman in the background. "Uh oh," the woman said. "There's some action out here… I hope that cop tells them to turn that rap music down." Pete watched the second video in shame as he already knew the outcome. But to watch it from an unexpected angle was devastating.

"AH!" The woman screamed. "OH MY GOD! OH MY GOD! HE SHOT 'EM! HE SHOT 'EM!" Pete saw the six sparks coming out of his gun. He heard the woman crying in the background as she continued recording. "Oh my God," the woman cried. "There's somebody coming out the car… and he's bleeding—oh, Jesus—oh Jesus." Pete immediately turned the video off as his anxiety went through the roof. He then stuck his head out the window as the vomit bled out.

That second video tore Pete's spirit to shreds. It looked like an execution as you could not hear their commotion in the video. The comments people were leaving were beyond vile, and Pete was on the verge of a nervous breakdown. He exited the car, stepped over the vomit, and walked around the parking lot to clear his head. The tension was rising, and the story of Tyshawn Brendan was spreading faster than the speed of light—growing stronger by the post. Pete, however, had to get his head on straight as he was on his way to meet with the director.

22

DECEMBER 22nd, 2025, MONDAY EVENING:

THANK YOU FOR YOUR SERVICE

Sitting in the Newark Police 5th precinct was a trembling Pete waiting for Director Albert Louis to call him into his office. Albert Louis was the director of the Newark Public Safety Department. He oversaw over 1,100 sworn police officers, 700 firefighters, and several hundred civilian employees. He was in his early sixties, tall and with a short, all-gray Ceaser haircut and a thin salt-and-pepper mustache—a proud man of his Haitian heritage. He had also served as a twenty-seven-year veteran with the Newark Police Department.

Freddy had not shown up yet, and Pete had no intentions of going into Director Louis' office without Freddy's presence. "Gant!" Said Director Louis. Pete took a moment before standing up from the bench—sitting there with a racing heart. Right in the nick of time, Freddy showed up—tightening his tie. "I'm here, Pete," he said. Pete was relieved.

"I don't appreciate the tardiness, Gant," said Louis. "You should know better."

"My apologies, sir," Pete responded.

"I see you've brought a friend."

"*Attorney*, actually," Freddy responded.

"*Attorney?*"

"That's correct, yes. Fredric Gant—*Esquire*."

"*Gant?* Is there a relation here?"

"Yes, sir," Pete said. "He's my uncle."

"Why don't you come in?"

Pete and Freddy entered Director Louis' office. Director Louis was highly decorated as they saw the square ribbon rack pinned to his shirt. His office was decorated with photos, plaques, and credentials. Pete knew that he was in the presence of his superior and had no idea what he was about to tell him. Was his life over? Was he going to prison for the rest of his days? That was all that went through Pete's mind.

"Have a seat, Gant," said Louis.

"You're not going offer *me* a seat, Officer?" Freddy sarcastically asked.

Louis, now with a raised eyebrow. "That's *Director* Louis. Am I going to have trouble with your attorney, Gant?"

"No, sir," Pete responded. "Freddy… please."

Freddy sighed. "So, what's this all about… *Director?*"

"You know what this is about… the prosecutors have reviewed the body cam footage. I myself have watched it dozens of times… from the looks of it… there's not much of a case."

"Exactly!" Freddy said as he pounded his fist on the table. "What did I tell you, Pete? I *told* you this was an open and shut—"

"Wait, hold on, now," Louis said. "This isn't exactly a *celebration*. A *life* was lost here—an *innocent* life at that."

"Well, of course," Freddy said in shame. "I'm not thrilled about *that*."

"Gant… the prosecutors will not charge you with wrongdoing. The teenage driver, RaJohn Brendan—excuse me—RaJohn *Mitchell*, represented a threat as he reached out the window with an electrical device—a phone? That's what you said in the investigation with Detective Bison and Baldwin, yes?"

"Yes, sir… I guess I'm a little relieved about that. But I'm still devastated about what happened to the kid."

"Yes… it was truly unfortunate circumstances."

"So, he can report back to duty, right?" Freddy asked.

"Actually… no."

"No?"

"No, that won't be happening. Not being charged was the *good* news. But there is some bad news."

"*Bad* news? What bad news?" Freddy irritatingly asked.

"Gant… I hate to tell you this… but I'm afraid your years of policing are over."

"What?" Freddy shouted.

"Okay, *Uncle*?" Louis said, now irritated. "What you're *not* going to do is raise your voice in *my* office."

Pete sat there in complete disbelief. He could not begin to process what was happening. He sat there in silence while Freddy went back and forth with Director Louis.

"Gant," Louis said as he looked at Pete. "I know this wasn't the news you wanted to hear, son. It's not easy letting one of our men go. But we're in a *very* complicated situation here."

"*What* fucking situation?" Freddy shouted.

"Excuse me! Can I talk with Mr. Gant, please?"

"You *are* talking to Mr. Gant—*Esquire!*"

"Okay, you know what? *You* can wait outside!"

"No, I'm staying *right* here with *my* client—"

"Freddy, please," Pete said. "Just wait for me outside."

"No, Pete, not on my watch. *I* need him to *explain* this 'complicated' situation."

"Well, maybe if you sit your ass down and shut *up*, I can elaborate."

Freddy chuckled as he sat down. "Wow… *superb* professionalism,

Louis."

Louis shook his head. "Listen, son, the city is under a lot of pressure. Not to mention, the Brendan family has filed a wrongful death lawsuit of $600 *million*—on the city, the police department… and you. And with that weighing over our heads, there are talks about riots. Now, I've been living in Newark my whole life. I was around during the '67 riots. They called it the 'Long, hot summer of 1967.' Many people died—*children* shot down. It was mayhem on those streets. And with this activist, Jaymel Cook-Lynn?"

"Yeah, I know who you're talking about," Pete retorted. "You know that son of a bitch mentioned my daughter's name during his little speech? I was just at her game, and those players were ripping her a new one—fouling her every chance they got."

"And he's an asshole for bringing up your daughter. I'll admit that—entirely out of pocket. However, he's very influential and has a large following, which puts *this* department in a vulnerable position. This is not something I'm proud to do… but we *have* to let you go."

Pete had a moment of silence. "Do you have kids, sir?"

"I *do*. They're *adults*, but yes."

"Well, I have *kids*—two teenagers and a six-year-old. What am I supposed to tell them? What am I supposed to tell my wife?"

"You can tell your family that you won't spend a day in prison. The prosecutors have cleared you of any wrongdoing. As I said, the driver represented a threat, and you acted accordingly under our *policies*. This shooting has been ruled justifiable, Gant…. Unfortunately, we *cannot* keep you on the force."

"Un-*fucking*-believable," Freddy scoffed as he stood up.

"Look… I know this is not going to be easy for you. But we have to do this. It's tough enough that we have to address the public and *tell* them that the shooting of RaJohn Mitchell and Tyshawn Brendan was justifiable. But if there's no delivery of *consequences*… they're going to tear this city down in one night."

"But that's not our fucking *problem*, is it?" Freddy retorted.

"Hey!" Louis shouted as he stood up from his desk. "This my last time telling you—do *not* disrespect my office."

"Oh, for *Christ's* sake," Freddy said as he leaned against the wall.

"Perhaps you don't understand the *magnitude* of problems this incident has *caused*, so, allow me to break it down for you... *Tyshawn Brendan* was *not* your ordinary kid who gets hit by a stray bullet. This story has become *so mainstream* that even the *President* of the *United States* of *America* has shared some words about this basketball star—not to mention that the President is a *huge* Blue Devil fan *and* an alumnus of Duke University. We're talking about the fucking *elites* here. People *raved* about this kid—saying he was the second coming of Michael Jordan. He was known all over the basketball world—in *every* sports magazine out there. He averaged damn near forty points and eight rebounds a *game*—last year alone. That's *unheard* of in high school basketball—it's damn near unheard of in the NBA. He was the greatest basketball player in *America*... probably anywhere in the world. And now he's dead."

"Sir," Pete spoke. "Words cannot express how sorry I am. I am *devastated* about Tyshawn Brendan. I truly am. But... you *can't do this*. You can't do this to me."

"Look, Gant, we're very sorry that it has to end this way.... Listen, I am willing to allow you to step down as an officer and resign."

"Resign? I'm four years away from getting my pension. Can I just transfer to another department?"

"Son, you don't think I've called other departments and asked if you could be transferred to them? With this story attached, no department will *touch* you with a forty-foot pole... take the resignation. At least *that* way, you can still carry some dignity."

"*Dignity?*" Freddy scoffed. "Jesus Christ—can you believe this guy? Did you just say dignity?"

Pete responded. "Sir, you think me resigning as an officer so that you wouldn't have to fire me would give *me dignity*? Where's *your* dignity? Huh? Where's yours?"

"Okay, *Gant*? *Esquire*? This is not tit for tat. I've made my decision—effective immediately, you are no longer an officer of the law… I'm truly sorry."

"Bet your *ass*, you're sorry," Freddy snarled. "You're giving my nephew the fucking boot, and now he can't even get hired by another department—"

"As *I said*… he won't do a day in prison. Not one second. But there is no way he'll be able to waltz out of here and *keep* that badge…

again, not a day in prison. And you have my word, you'll have *full immunity*—"

"*Fuck* your word!" Freddy shouted. "*In writing*—I want that *in writing*

"*Done*! In writing. I need your cooperation on this one, Gant. Do *not* go against the grain. It's not just *your* ass that's on the line here… it's *all* of us. *Take* this one for the team… what do you say?"

Freddy stepped forward. "*I'd* say you're a low-life, sorry sack of *shit* who doesn't stick up for his *officers*!"

Louis looked with a vengeance. "What did you say to me?"

"Oh, you *heard* every fucking word *I* said. You ought to be ashamed of yourself. As much as my nephew did to protect and serve his community, and *this* is the thanks he gets?"

"You get your paralegal ass out of my office—if you *know* what's good for you."

"*Paralegal*? Oh, you didn't like it when I called you *officer*, huh? You know what? This isn't the last you'll hear from *me*. We're going to dispute the termination."

Pete shook his head. "No, we're not."

"Oh, yes, the fuck we are—"

"No, Freddy, we're not, so just *knock it off*!" Pete shouted in frustration. "It's over, Freddy… my days as a cop are over. And I have to accept that."

Freddy brushed his hand over his face as he sighed. "I'm going to be outside waiting for you."

"Okay."

"I want *full fucking* immunity—*in* writing!" Freddy said as he slammed his fist on the desk and stormed out of the office.

Pete sat there with his hand covering his face, feeling drained and defeated. "Please excuse my uncle, sir," Pete sighed. "He's very passionate about his work.... Sir? Is there *anything* I could do to change your mind?" Director Louis looked at Pete in lingering silence. He knew there was nothing more he could do for him. As he sat on the side of his desk, Louis said this to Pete. "Son... I understand what you're feeling right now. I know that shooting someone in the line of duty is never easy—especially when it wasn't intentional. But this is how we have to move forward. I hope that you understand. And as for the full immunity, I'll have that for you, in writing, first thing tomorrow morning. Once again, I'm sorry." Suddenly, Pete stood up and gave Louis a piece of his mind.

"Sir?" Pete said. "May I ask how long you've been on the force?"

"Twenty-seven years as an officer—four years as director."

"You ever shot anyone on the job?"

Louis grew hesitant. "I can't say that I have, son."

"Really? In *twenty-seven years*... you've never shot anyone?"

"Not that I recall, no."

"Then how can you stand there and *tell* me you *understand* what *I'm* going through? You *don't* understand. And you never will, sitting behind a *fucking* desk."

Just as Pete turned around and reached for the doorknob, Director Louis stopped him. "Gant!" He shouted. "*Sit* your ass down, *now.*" Pete knew by Louis' tone of voice that he crossed the line. "Son," he said. "I don't know who the *fuck* you think you're talking to, but you *never* address your superiors in such a condescending manner. How dare you? I had *your* back. And what do you do? You come into *my* office with your arrogant ass, think he's hot-shit *uncle attorney*, and make demands? And you disrespect me by saying that because I never shot anyone in the line of duty, I can't understand *your pain*? Is that right?"

"My apologies, sir. I was way out of line."

"Goddamn *right*, you were."

"I'm just... I'm going through a lot, sir. It's been hell these last couple of days... I feel hopeless."

Louis sighed. "Listen, son... what happened that night was unfortunate. And I take no pleasure in letting go one of our brave men. But remember this... when you walk out that door, you're not going to jail... you're going home... *home*. You'll be with your family. Besides... Christmas is coming up. What better time to spend with family than Christmas? Enjoy it."

"How can I enjoy Christmas when I just killed somebody, sir?"

There was no way Director Louis could respond to that question, and he did not. Instead, he went to his office door and opened it—waiting for Pete to make his exit. Pete turned and looked as if he knew that would be the last time he would step out of that door. He sighed as he said to himself, "*Okay...*" As Pete got up, Director Louis said this one last thing to him. "For what it's worth, I thank you for your service, son... best of luck to you." All Pete could do was nod and walk out of the office. He felt betrayed more than ever—kicked to the curve like a disposable object that no one cared about.

"Pete?" Freddy said, standing up from the bench. "Listen... what happened in there... I'm an asshole. You know this. I'm sorry. You're my nephew and...."

"It's just shitty cards, Freddy," Pete said with a melancholy tone. "I was dealt shitty cards.... Hero."

"*Hero?*" Freddy asked with confusion.

"Ever since I was seven years old, I wanted to be a hero of my community. I wanted to be special… I thought I *was* special. But as I got older, I realized the dark secret about heroes. They only exist in the comic books. So, I settled to be a cop. I thought that was the next best thing. But all I saw in my years was the absolute *worst* in people. Fully grown men raping kids and babies and stabbing them to death. Pedophiles and pimps snatching up every little girl they can get their *sick fucking* hands on. Fentanyl addict boyfriends—fighting their pregnant girlfriends—suicides, thieves, corruption, *greed*… that's all you see out there… *all you see* are *demons—demons* smiling as they roam the streets. And that's when it hit me… heroes are meant to *save* lives and be appreciated for it… cops are only meant to report deaths and be blamed for it. I guess the truth finally caught up to me. I'm *not* a hero. I'm nobody's hero. I was always just a *fucking* pig. But now I'm not even that… I'm not even that."

Minutes later, Pete sat on the bench in the locker room, attempting to clear out his locker. On the door of the locker, Pete had pictures of his family. One by one, he peeled and scrapped off the old tape and removed the pictures—looking at each of them as he reminisced about every moment he had with his family. As he placed his belongings in a black trash bag, one of his fellow officers, Officer Jesse Holm, a stocky, blonde-haired guy, came in and sat on the other end of the bench.

"What's up, brother?" Jesse spoke.

Pete turned his head and saw Jesse. "Hey, Jesse."

"I just heard about the resignation."

"You mean the *bullshit* resignation?"

"Yeah… I heard. I'm sorry, buddy. I'm sorry it has to end this way for you."

"*I'm* sorry it had to end for Tyshawn Brendan. I wish I never took that call."

"Pete… you can't blame yourself for that. If anything, *I* should be the one to blame."

"*You*? Why would you think that?"

"If I had never suggested you transfer here to Newark, none of this would've happened to you."

"Oh, Jesse… the last thing I want is for you to blame yourself. Transferring here was *my* choice. It's just… we never know what's going to come through that radio."

Jesse sighed. "You got that right."

"You know what's so crazy about that night? I was going to take off and get a Christmas tree with my wife, then come home and decorate it with my kids. But I was *so fixated* on just working and getting that overtime. And now they give me no time. No second chances. They just gave me the boot, didn't ask me if I'll be okay, no counseling, *nothing*. I didn't even get a chance to hand over my badge or hold it in my *goddamn* hands for one last time. *All these years*… I thought I was making a difference out there. But now… now I see it was all just a bad dream… with bad memories."

"You know, we have our secret motto around here, 'You delay, you die.' You understand?"

"Yeah… I wish it didn't end the way it did. This is going to be a difficult one to live with."

"You're going to be all right, Pete. Just take it easy. Take it one day at a time."

Pete nodded his head as he wiped away his tears. "I appreciate it, Jesse. You be safe out there."

As Pete stood up, Jesse pulled him in for a brotherly embrace. They had a special bond that only police officers could understand. As Jesse released Pete, he looked at him and said, "They may have taken your badge away. But they can *never* take the truth away. No matter what they say or do, from this point on… they can never take away the truth. You're a great fucking cop, Pete. I know that—the whole goddamn *department* knows that… I'm gonna miss ya, bud."

Pete embraced Jesse once again as tears streamed down the sides of his face.

Pete felt that his destiny had been unfairly confiscated. He wanted to return to that office and demand he be reinstated as a police officer. But he knew the days of wearing that blue uniform he had hanging up in his locker were gone. Pete cleared his locker and headed out the door as his fellow officers watched him walk by. And with all that going on in his mind, he had no idea how he would face Claire and tell her he had lost his dream job.

23

DECEMBER 22nd, 2025, MONDAY LATE EVENING:

I'M JUST PETE NOW

A lingering squeak sound came from the brakes of Pete's Jeep as he pulled into his driveway. Pete sat there in silence… and in pain. He felt as if his identity had been robbed of him—as if his cape was confiscated, and he was no longer a superhero. The job he loved the most was now history. As he sat in the car, he thought about his sixteen years on the force: all the homicides, domestic violence disputes, multiple shootouts, the blood, the bodies… death.

Pete thought about the moment he walked out of the precinct. There was nothing but awkward stares and silence. As he walked, he looked around and saw the faces of his brothers and sisters—thinking that was the last time he would ever see any of them again. There was no happy send-off, no farewells or good riddance. Pete did not even get a chance to radio in and give his final call for end of duty. He remembered how hard the door slammed behind him when he exited the precinct. He turned around and looked up at the building, knowing that was the last time he would see it. Pete wanted to cry, but he was way too numb and drained to show any emotion.

As he sat in the Jeep, Pete scrolled on his phone and looked at some videos on YouTube related to the shooting. There was a nationwide protest for the shooting death of Tyshawn Brendan. Murals were already painted on brick walls in major cities. Tyshawn Brendan's name was becoming more prominent by the hour.

Suddenly, as Pete looked to his left, he saw his next-door neighbor, Stewart Wilkins, waving his hand to him. As Pete waved back, Stewart waved Pete over as he wanted to speak with him. Pete stepped out of the Jeep and walked across his front yard to Stewart. Stewart was a short man with slick back hair and a gut that hung like a kangaroo pouch. But he was a stand-up guy.

"Hey, Pete," Stewart said.

"How are you doing, Stewart?" Pete responded.

"I should be asking *you* that question."

"I've had better ends to the night. I was fired today."

"They fired you?"

"Well, I was told to write a letter of resignation… for my '*dignity.*' But any way you look at it… my policing days are over."

"Wow… I'm terribly sorry to hear that, Pete."

"Yep."

"Well… it could've been worse, you know? They could've thrown the book at you for the shooting."

"It still feels like a slap in the face, though, Stewart. They just took my job away. Just like that."

"It's an unfair world, Pete. I know. But there's nothing we can do about it."

"I guess not… life sucks…. I'm going to head inside, Stewart. I've had a long day. Nice talking with you."

Pete walked away with his head down.

"Wait, Pete. There was something I wanted to share with you."

"What is it, Stewart?"

"My brother-in-law, Brad, he's a former cop. I believe I mentioned him to you before?"

"I'm sure you did."

"Yeah, well, he started this kind of support group meeting for police officers about a year ago. He meets up with other officers who deal with certain traumas from their years on the force."

"Okay… and what does that have to do with me?"

"Well, being that you were involved in a police shooting, I felt that I should share that information with you. I think you should attend the meeting, Pete."

"Listen, Stewart… that's very thoughtful of you to think of me about your brother-in-law's meeting… but I don't think that's for me."

"Oh… okay, well, just wanted to throw that at ya. It's completely discreet, by the way. No one would know that you're attending except the other officers and, of course, Brad. I could give him your information and he'll get in contact with you."

"Stewart, listen—"

"Pete, you've been through a lot, man. You're hurting… I can tell. Just *give* it a go, huh? There will be no judgments there."

Pete thought about it. "No one has to know, right?"

"No one. It's all confidential."

"When?"

"He'll call you. First thing in the morning."

"Okay… thanks, Stewart."

"You're welcome. Get some rest, buddy."

"I'll try."

Stewart then turned around and walked back into his house. Pete stood there in the cold as he thought about the meeting. Stewart's explanation sounded convincing, but Pete still had his doubts. He then grabbed the black trash bag of his belongings from the back seat of the Jeep and walked inside his house.

Moments later, Pete flicked on the light in his study and dropped the trash bag on the floor. He looked around at the awards and pictures of himself when he graduated from the academy. There was an eerie silence in the room that even the *dead* could not deliver—the silence of a fallen hero—a heroic ghost that will not be remembered. Pete stepped toward the wall to look closer at his graduation picture of him and Claire. He unmounted the frame and held the picture, smearing off the years of accumulated dust from the glass with his thumb. He looked at it with a smile that began to warm his cold face. It was one of Pete's proudest moments in life. He had his dream job and his dream woman, all in the same photo—eternally frozen in a good time. But now, that time was just a sacred memory of what he once was.

As Pete placed the photo down, he began to take down his certificates and awards from the wall. He removed his law enforcement glory one by one and piled it on top of the couch. The walls became naked and plain as he unhooked the last thing from the wall; it was a picture of himself and Leo dressed as police officers for Halloween. Suddenly, as he held the photo, the silence was broken as a voice came from behind.

"Pete?" Claire said.

Pete turned and looked at Claire. "Hey."

"Hey... what are you doing?"

"I'm just... redecorating."

"Redecorating? Why are you..." Claire looked at his gloomy face and knew what this meant. "Oh, baby... I'm so sorry."

Claire walked toward Pete and hugged him firmly as he cried in her arms. Claire felt deep sorrow for him losing his position as an officer, But she also felt a sense of immense joy rising in her aching heart. At that moment, Claire knew her worries were over. She knew now that she would never receive that dreadful phone call saying that her husband was killed in the line of duty. She knew that those fears were now laid to rest. As Pete cried tears of gloom, Claire cried tears of salvation.

24

DECEMBER 23^{rd,} 2025, TUESDAY EARLY MORNING:

NIGHT TERROR

A cold sweat blanketed Pete's body as his nightmare became vividly real. In the nightmare, Pete was walking down a long, dark tunnel—the kind of tunnel you would see in an arena. The tunnel was cold as the frost dressed his breath. Suddenly, he began to hear the dribbling of a basketball. The closer he got, the louder the dribbling became. As Pete reached the end of the tunnel, he saw Elle in her basketball uniform, shooting foul shots in a dimly lit gym.

"Hi, Dad," she said with a haunting smile.

"Elle?" Pete spoke as he looked with confusion. "What are you doing here?"

"I'm playing… do you want to play with me?"

"This… this isn't *real*… is it?"

"Of *course*, it's real. Come play with me."

Elle tossed Pete the ball. The ball was defying gravity—slowly rotating in mid-air. As Pete caught the ball, he began to feel a rapid heartbeat coming from inside the ball. It was as if the ball was alive. "Come play with me, Dad," Elle smiled.

Pete was barefooted as he walked on the cold wooden floor of the court. He did not even bother to dribble the ball. He just held

164

it as he walked to the foul line. Elle stepped behind him and said, "Take your best shot, Dad... but don't miss." Pete looked at Elle with startled eyes. He knew something was not right. But he played along. As he turned around and faced the basket, he took a shot and watched the ball float in the air. But the dream was getting stranger. The hoop stretched away as the ball lingered in mid-air, rotating like a planet. Suddenly, the ball exploded—BOOM! Pete jumped as he was in shock.

Suddenly, a familiar voice projected from behind. "Hey, *pig*!" Pete turned around and was shocked at who he saw. It was RaJohnn Mitchell, holding a gun up as he shot the ball down. The ball began to bleed from the bullet hole, resembling the same image from the shooting. It moved as if it was trying to resuscitate, gasping for air. Suddenly, RaJohnn aggressively grabbed Elle and held her at gunpoint like a hostage.

"WOAH! WOAH!" Pete shouted. "Let her go! Let her go *right now*!"

"Or *what*, pig?" RaJohnn yelled. "You gonna shoot me? Huh? You gonna shoot me again, gang? How 'bout I shoot *her*?"

"NO!" Pete screamed.

"Nah... you killed my homeboy... and now, I'm gonna kill this bitch. An eye for an eye, motherfucka!"

Suddenly, Pete felt a heavy weight on his waist. He looked down and realized that he had his duty belt on—with his gun intact. Pete immediately discharged his weapon and aimed it at RaJohnn Mitchell. "Drop the fucking gun! Drop it! *Now*!" Pete screamed. But RaJohnn did not budge. He kept the gun pressed to Elle's temple. "DADDY! HELP ME, *PLEASE*!" Elle cried.

As Pete got ready to take RaJohnn out, his trigger finger would not budge. He squeezed and squeezed—trying to pull the trigger, but it was like a force contained him. Pete then tried to run to Elle, but he could not move. She cried and begged for mercy as

RaJohnn still had the 357-magnum pressed to her temple.

"God, no," Pete said with his startled eyes.

"Kiss this bitch goodbye, pig," RaJohnn said with a sinister smile.

RaJohnn squeezed the trigger without thinking twice—BANG!

"NOOOOOOOOO!" Pete screamed, ripping himself out of his deep sleep. "ELLLEEE!"

Claire was ripped from her sleep.

"PETE! WHAT'S WRONG?" Claire screamed, trying to get a hold on Pete.

Pete jumped out of bed, soaking wet, running across the hall as he burst into Elle's bedroom.

"AH!" Elle screamed.

"ELLE!" Pete cried as he ran towards her.

"Daddy, what's wrong? What's wrong?"

"Pete, stop! You're scaring her! You're scaring her!" Claire cried as she ran into the room.

Claire tried to pull Pete off of Elle. But he held on for dear life and did not let go. Michael and Leo were in Elle's doorway. Leo was hysterical—crying as he did not know what was happening. Even a whimpering Brownie came upstairs, alarmed by Pete's spectacle. Elle lied there in bed as Pete held onto, sobbing his eyes out—rocking her back and forth in his arms. Suddenly, there was calm after the storm. Elle then broke free from Pete's desperate embrace and ran out of her room, crying down the stairs.

"*Jesus*, Dad," Michael said. "You're going crazy again."

"Michael, take your brother back to his room," Claire said. "Pete? Honey, are you okay?"

Pete responded through the traffic of sobs. "Oh, God... I thought she was killed... it was so real. *Everything* felt *so real*... oh, God."

"It was just a dream, Pete... it *wasn't* real."

"It was *real*... I was there."

"Do you want to talk about it?"

Pete shook his head. "No… I just want to talk to Elle."

Pete went back to his bedroom and changed out of his wet clothes. Brownie followed behind him as he went downstairs. Pete looked all over the first floor for Elle, but she was nowhere in sight. He then called for her in the basement, but there was no response. That is when he heard a noise outside. He looked out the kitchen window and saw Elle dribbling a basketball—similar to what he saw in the dream. He grabbed his coat and headed out of the back door. He looked at Elle from a distance. She just stood there, looking up at the hoop in silence. As Pete walked toward her, she turned and looked at him with her tear-stained face. She then turned back to look at the basket, not saying a word to him.

"Elle, I'm sorry," he said. "I didn't mean to scare you… it was a terrible dream. It felt so real."

Elle sighed. "It's fine, Dad."

"What are you staring at?"

"Nothing… I'm just saying goodbye."

"Goodbye? To whom?"

"To the game I love most. I quit the team."

"What?"

"I quit."

"No. No, I won't let you walk away from what you love just because of my actions."

"Dad… it's over. I'm done."

"Elle, you don't have to quit anything. You're too talented—"

"Do you know what those girls on the other team did to me on that court? I got my ass handed to me. I thought I was going to have like a concussion or something. Mom told Coach to take me out of the game, and they booed us out of the gym."

"I know… I saw what was happening."

Elle rolled up her sleeves. "Look at my arms—look at the bruises. Look at my legs. I can never play this game again, Dad. After what you've done to Tyshawn Brendan, they will *never* let me step foot on a court again. They will kill me."

Pete sighed. "I'm so sorry, baby. I didn't mean for any of this."

"This was my dream, Dad… to play college ball and win a national championship. But now that dream is dead. I have no right to play this game any longer… and I saw you walk out."

"Elle, sweetheart… I am so sorry I did that. I had a meeting with the director—"

"Oh God, it's always something, *isn't* it, Dad?" Elle retorted. "Why is everything else more important than *us*?"

"Elle… you, your mother, and your brothers are the most important thing in my life. I'll admit, I haven't shown that to you guys in the last several years. And I'm sorry. I'm sorry for everything that I've put you all through. I know things have been tough for you guys with me always working. I guess my absence has finally caught up to me. But you won't have to worry about that any longer. I'm not a cop anymore."

"You quit?"

"No… I was let go."

Elle shook her head. "Well, what good is *that* going to do? Tyshawn Brendan is gone."

"Elle, listen—"

"He was my *idol*, Dad. The way he played the game… it was magical. He was a *genius*. It's like he was an artist on the court—a poet…. I met him once. They played against Livingston. He was signing autographs for some kids. I walked up to him and introduced myself. He had such a beautiful smile. And he was so sweet and kind-hearted… I told him he was my favorite player. He smiled at me and said, 'Thank you. I appreciate you for telling me that.' I couldn't believe it. *My idol* appreciated *me*… then I woke up that morning, and I saw that he was shot and killed… *by my father*."

"Oh, Elle," Pete sighed.

"You know… I remember when I was eight. Mom had bought some raspberry cheesecake muffins from Mr. Bumpkins' Bakery. They were so good. I had two for dessert. I could've eaten them *all by myself* if I wanted. You had to work late that night, so, you didn't get a chance to have any. I remember I snuck downstairs to get another muffin, and when I got to the kitchen, you were sitting at the table. You were just sitting there in the dark, crying. I never saw you cry before. I hid behind the corner so you wouldn't see me. I felt so sad for you, Dad… and when I walked over to you, and you saw me… you held me tight—just like how you held me in my room, and you didn't let me go… you remember?"

"Of course, I remember."

Pete remembered that night vividly as if it was yesternight—one of the worst moments of his career, and he was hesitant to reminisce about the horrors of that night.

"Tell me… why were you crying that night?" Elle asked.

"I really don't want to talk about that, sweetheart."

"Please, Dad," she begged.

"You really wanna know?"

"Yes, I do."

Pete thought twice. "No. No, I can't—"

"Dad, *please*… I really want you to open up to me. Tell me why you were crying that night… *please*?"

It was Pete's lifelong wish that he would never have to go back to the night. But he knew Elle would not let up until he told her, and he did. He stared at Elle and caressed her cold face.

"Why are you staring at me?" Elle asked.

Pete smiled. "She had the same color eyes as you."

"Who?"

"The little girl… she looked no older than you. It was so cold that night. I was halfway done with my shift and… I was feeling it in my gut all night that something bad was going to happen. I remember it vividly—dispatch radioed me about a disturbance. I got to the residence... all I saw was this little girl... covered in blood. She was screaming and crying. I got out of the car and she ran right into my arms. She was so cold... so lonely... she wouldn't let me go. Once I finally put her down, I asked her what happened. Poor girl couldn't even speak. She just pointed her little finger toward the house. I was scared shitless... but I went in and saw...."

"What? What did you see, Dad?"

Pete became emotional. "Blood... and death. *Oh, Elle*... it was a nightmare. I stepped inside the house and saw her mother on the flood in a puddle of blood... stabbed to death. There was a trail of blood going up the stairs. It was like a horror movie. I didn't know what I was going to see next. And when I got up the stairs... I saw...."

"What... Dad?"

"The bloody crib," Pete cried. "I saw blood seeping through the pillars... that's when I looked over and... and I saw... I saw that *one little foot*.... I ran out of that house as fast as I could."

Elle gasped in disbelief. "Oh my God, Dad... you saw a dead baby?"

Pete nodded his head. "Yes."

"Who would do such a thing?"

"Her father. That's what the little girl said. I thought to myself, 'What kind of a goddamn demon would brutally murder his wife and infant child?' But in that line of work... you never know when or where evil will lurk. For the last sixteen years, I tried to numb the pain and hide it from everyone. But my *God*, Elle... there's just *so much pain* in the world. *Too* much.... *That's* the world we live in. It's full of pain, sweetheart."

It took a moment for Elle to process what Pete had told her. She could not believe the horrors of what her father went through that night. This moment helped Elle better understand Pete's experience as a police officer, but she still wanted to know more.

"Whatever happened to the little girl's father?"

Pete sighed. "He's dead."

"How?"

Pete hesitated. "I rather not say."

"Tell me."

"Elle... why are you doing this to me?"

"I want to know. Tell me how he died—"

"They found his body in the woods!" Pete shouted. "Okay? He put a twelve-gauge shotgun under his chin and blew his *fucking* face off! All right? You satisfied? Is that scary enough for you?"

Elle grew upset as she stood there in silence. She gave Pete a dirty look and stormed her way to the back door. Pete was apologetic and went after her.

"Elle—Elle, wait," he said. "I'm sorry, sweetheart... I wanted to keep that story in the past. But sometimes... I wonder what happened to her... the girl."

Elle turned around and asked, "Do you remember her name?"

"Emilie... her name was Emilie."

"I'm going to go back inside now... I'm cold."

"Okay... good night."

Just as Elle opened the back door, Pete called out to her. "Elle... I didn't share that story with you for your pity. I don't want you or your brothers to feel sorry for me at all. I signed up for this. It was my job... and it came with a price. But now, my job is to take care of my family. But I'm going to need your help. I know I've broken promises. But all that's going to change. There's just one thing that I need from you." Elle took a moment and responded.

"What do you need from me?"

"Love... I need you to love me."

"I've never stopped loving you, Dad... and I never will."

Pete cried. "Okay... thank you."

Pete extended his arms and held her tight, just like he did when she was that seven-year-old girl. Elle appreciated Pete telling her the truth about what happened that night. She knew that was an arduous story for him to revisit. She never knew of the intensity and horrors police officers endure. From that point on, Elle never looked at her father the same again. She sympathized with him and learned things from *his* perspective. But the one thing she assured Pete was that her love for him would never die.

25

DECEMBER 23rd, 2025, TUESDAY EARLY MORNING:

WHY IS EVERYTHING BLACK AND WHITE?

The Gant family was fast asleep. But for Pete, it was another sleepless night. His heavy, baggy eyes were glued to his phone as he sat alone in the basement watching countless minutes of videos on YouTube. Rumors had circulated on social media about a possible riot taking place in Newark, which got the attention of Newark Mayor Tiffani Collins; a forty-five-year-old black woman.

As Pete scrolled through the videos, he came across an interview Mayor Collins did with journalist Jessica Hunter; a white, forty-two-year-old woman sporting a boyish pixie blonde haircut and a mole on her left cheek. Some spectators often referred to her as the Marilyn Monroe of multi-media journalism.

The interview was uploaded five hours earlier and had already accumulated over eight hundred thousand views and thousands of comments. As Pete clicked on the thumbnail, he began to watch the split-screen interview between Mayor Collins and Jessica Hunter.

"Mayor Tiffani Collins, thank you for joining me," said Jessica. "How are you doing this evening?"

A delay before Mayor Collins responded. "I'm fine, Jessica. Thank you for having me."

"Of course. Mayor Collins, I will get right into it. The shooting of seventeen-year-old RaJohnn Mitchell and shooting *death* of *eighteen*-year-old Tyshawn Brendan has made nationwide news. Can you tell me what is the current atmosphere like in Newark, New Jersey right now?"

"Well, first off, I want to offer my deepest condolences, once again, to the family of Tyshawn Brendan. Tyshawn was truly a gifted young man. I had the honor of meeting him at the championship game last year. He was one of the nicest young men I've ever met. Very smart with a bright future ahead of him…. To answer your question, Newark is hurting after such a great loss. But we're managing as best as we can."

"Mayor Collins, there's been rumors circulating on social media that a potential riot may occur. Is there any truth to that?"

"Yes, I was made aware of those rumors and I certainly hope that *doesn't* occur. So far, there has been *peaceful* protesting—which our Newark residents have the right to do. But as far as *riots*, we don't condone that."

"Have you had a chance to speak with the parents of Tyshawn Brendan?"

"Yes, I have. Ms. Jada Brendan is a very strong woman. And I pray for her. She shared a few stories with me about Tyshawn—about his future plans, and it's… it's such a tragic loss for our city."

"Mayor Collins, has there been any contact made with the officer involved in the shooting? Officer Pete Gant?"

"Are you asking if *I* had any contact?"

"Well, what I'm *asking* is, has he been investigated or questioned on the shooting?"

"I was informed that he was investigated, yes. However, I do not have all the details at the moment."

"Will the officer receive termination for the shooting?"

"As I said, Jessica, I don't have any other information other than he was investigated."

"Gotcha... Mayor Collins... the Black Lives Matter movement has been *immensely* vocal about Tyshawn Brendan. Are you at all concerned?"

"Concerned about what?"

"Just the backlash that is coming from the public?"

"Well, *again*, people have the right to a peaceful protest. As for the Black Lives Matter movement, there has only been *virtual* protesting, which I would recommend."

"Mayor Collins... what I'm *getting* at is, being that you *are* a black woman... who is married to a *white* man with bi-racial children, have *you* received any backlash from the black community for marrying outside of your race?"

Dead silence as Mayor Collins had a furious look on her face. "Jessica... my husband has absolutely *nothing* to do with *any* of this. And I am completely mortified and offended that you would even bring him *or* my children up in this interview."

"Oh, Mayor Collins, uh... my *sincerest* apologies—"

"How dare you involve my family in this?"

"I'm *deeply* sorry if I offended you, Mayor Collins."

"Jessica... I love my husband. We have been married for fifteen years and have three *beautiful* children together. I am a *happily* married woman, and for you to bring up my family in this interview is pure, unprofessional atrocity on *your* behalf."

"Um... Mayor Collins, I can't express how sorry I am. Forgive me. Thank you for your time."

Mayor Collins immediately got off the air—leaving Jessica alone in awkward silence. "Uh... Mayor Collins has dropped out, and, um... we will move forward." Jessica Hunter was notorious for being controversial—asking her guests personal and loaded questions. Pete felt that Jessica was in the wrong for bringing up

Mayor Collins's family and understood why she abruptly ended the interview. The well, however, had already been contaminated. In the comments section of the interview, people crucified Mayor Collins. Pete read some of the comments:

@SteveTucker71

Wow! Jessica Hunter is back on her bullshit.

She actually brought up the mayor's bi-racial family.

But I'm not surprised. She ought to be ashamed.

@WillDaGod1969

That coon ass bitch. Collins tries to pretend she loves black people. She laid up in bed with a white man and had three half-breed kids with that cracker who probably hates black people, too. Right on, Jessica Hunter. Put that coon in her place.

@DebbieMichaels1964

People are so cruel in this world. Why would she involve that woman's family? She's trying to make something out of nothing and that mayor put her in her place. Finally, someone had the courage to do that. Jessica Hunter's such a bitch.

@AshleyStevens23

I am a black woman who is married to a white man. We have 4 kids. I really don't understand the backlash of the mayor being married to a non-black man. I mean, isn't that what Dr. Martin Luther King Jr. preached, fought and died for? People calling her an Aunty Tom and a coon? It is so uncomfortable and disgusting that people don't have a conscience, and they will say whatever they have to just to get clicks and views. I'm glad Mayor Tiffani Collins stood up for herself. You can't help but love who you love.

@ThomasSamuel1965

I'm a white man, and my wife is a black woman. Our families didn't really agree with our relationship. But my wife and I didn't care. We were in love. We've been married for 32 years and have 5 beautiful kids together. She's the love of my life, and our passion is growing stronger every day.

@OmarTooReal78

First off, let me say that I don't have any issues with interracial relationships. I think people should love who they love. But we have to be real about this. I think what Jessica Hunter was trying to insinuate was that black people are going to have a hard time trusting the mayor because she is married to a white man. My grandfather always told me you can't speak black and sleep white. And this whole shooting is a black-and-white thing, in my opinion. But whatever, RIP to Tyshawn Brendan.

@SaraPinkwater435

OMG! Why does everything always have to be so black and white with people? Color should never be an issue. The human race is a multifarious species of beauty. History should be our lessons learned so that we evolve and NOT our confinement that keeps us entrapped in ignorance.

It reached a point where Pete had to shut the television off and put his phone in the bathroom to escape technology. He realized that the Tyshawn Brendan shooting took a shift of narrative and created an aggressive public division. It was all black and white now. And according to the minds of the public, this shooting was racially motivated. The entirety of this incident was getting farther and farther away from what truly happened that night; and as for Pete, he had no way to defend himself.

26

DECEMBER 23rd, 2025, TUESDAY AFTERNOON:

THE MOMENT OF FALSE TRUTH

Down in the basement, Pete watched the news as Director Albert Louis took to the podium and addressed the shooting of RaJohnn Mitchell and Tyshawn Brendan. Even though Pete already knew the results, he grew anxious as he sat and waited to see what Director Louis had to say.

Pete scrolled through his phone and looked at the comments of people hoping he would be charged for the death of Tyshawn Brendan. There was a time when Pete would never acknowledge what people had to say about police officers on the internet. But after the shooting, he was desperately vulnerable to public opinion and their harsh criticism of his actions. He wanted to see what others were saying about him and that addiction became his torment.

Moments later, Director Louis went to the podium with his hat tucked under his left arm. Standing behind him were Captain Bernal and Mayor Collins. As Louis placed papers on the podium, he delivered his statement to the press:

Afternoon, everyone.... Before I read this statement, I must warn you that some of what I'm about to say contains graphic content. Please be advised.... On Friday, December 19th, tragedy struck our beloved city. At

8:46 p.m. of that evening, an OIS took place—an 'Officer Involved Shooting.' Two African American teenagers were hit in the line of fire: Seventeen-year-old RaJohnn Mitchell and eighteen-year-old Tyshawn Brendan. From what we were told by Mitchell, he was picking Brendan up from basketball practice that evening, and they went to the 7-Eleven store to get some food. This transpired a little before 8:00 p.m.—forty-six minutes prior to the shooting. At 8:43 p.m., Police Officer Peter Gant radioed in dispatch to report a suspicious vehicle that he was made aware of earlier that evening. Officer Gant pulled over Mitchell and Brendan on Hunterdon Street between 14th and 15th Avenue.

As Officer Gant approached the vehicle, Mitchell, who was the driver, rolled the window down and shared some explicit words with Officer Gant. Mitchell then rolled the window back up, and Officer Gant radioed in for an additional unit. Seconds later, as Officer Gant returned to the vehicle, Mitchell rolled the window down and extended his arm out of the window, holding a black object with a flash. Officer Gant saw it as a threat and immediately drew his weapon and opened fire—firing six rounds. Mitchell was hit twice: once in his left elbow and once in the acetabular rim of his hip—which has temporarily limited his walking abilities. Brendan was *also* hit twice: one in his kidney, and the other bullet ricocheted through his ribcage—piercing his right lung, liver, and intestines—causing internal bleeding. The bullet then exited his navel, entered his left thigh, and was found lodged in the hamstring area. As for the two remaining bullets, one was found in the driver's door of Mitchell's vehicle, and the other traveled through a basketball, then through the passenger door, and landed on the pavement of the sidewalk.

As Officer Gant took cover behind the door of his patrol unit, Mitchell managed to open his door and fell to the ground. Officer Gant then approached Mitchell and detained him. He then applied a tourniquet to Mitchell's left arm to stop the bleeding. At that moment, Officer Gant was unaware of a second occupant in the vehicle. As Officer Gant looked inside, he saw Brendan in the passenger seat and pulled him out of the car. Brendan was going in and out of consciousness while Officer Gant rendered aid until paramedics arrived.

At 9:03 p.m., Tyshawn Brendan succumbed to his injuries. Now,

I say all of that to give you some back story of what transpired that tragic evening, but... after careful consideration, and with the evidence gathered from the body cam footage, this... uh, excuse me....

Pete gazed at the television as he and everyone in that room patiently waited for Director Louis to finish. Director Louis was a nervous wreck—holding on to the edges of the podium. He knew that what he was about to say next would cause an uproar. But he had to deliver the verdict. As Director Louis cleared his throat, he proceeded:

"Excuse me, ladies and gentlemen.... After careful consideration, we deemed this shooting... justifiable. Officer Pete Gant has been cleared of any wrongdoing."

The press created a wave of gags as the shocking news took their breath away. Pete could hear the commotion as he watched. Director Louis then lifted his hand as he tried to calm the roaring crowd. Mayor Collins looked like a deer in headlights, as did Captain Bernal. Director Louis had to pat his forehead with a handkerchief as it was decorated with severe sweat. As he commanded silence, Director Louis continued with his statement:

Ladies and gentlemen, please... if I may finish this up. The prosecutors could not find sufficient evidence in the video that showed foul play or was against our policies. The body cam footage vividly shows RaJohnn Mitchell as a threat. Officer Gant responded as he was *trained* to respond.... Uh... we understand that this may come as a shock and upset some people. But please understand that the prosecutors spent countless hours watching the footage. They felt that Officer Gant handled the situation under accurate policies... and now, um... we—we'll take a few questions.

The press went into a frenzy. Voices projected—one on top of the other, and Director Louis did not know who to pick first. He then, at random, pointed at the reporter with the gold Rolex.

"Yes, sir," said Louis. "You with the gold watch."

"Thank you," said the reporter. "Director Louis, you said the officer has been cleared of any wrongdoing. Does that mean he will be reinstated and back on duty?"

"Uh, no, Pete Gant has been terminated effective immediately and is no longer a Newark police officer."

The commotion grew louder. Another reporter asked, "Wait, he was *terminated*?"

"Co—correct," Louis nervously responded.

"But if he was cleared of *wrongdoing*, why is the officer being terminated?"

"We felt that it was best that Pete Gant be removed from our staff. I don't want to go into any *details*, but... Pete Gant is no longer a law enforcement officer."

Pete turned the television off and sat there in silence. He could not believe what he just heard. Yesterday, Director Louis told him to write a letter of resignation but then told the *public* that he was terminated and is no longer a police officer. Pete felt betrayed—left to hang. He believed Director Louis told the media that he was terminated so that they would get off *his* back about the shooting being justifiable. It was precisely as Pete expected it would be... politics. And because Mayor Collins had been reelected, she did not want this incident to sabotage her reputation.

Pete was livid and also despondent. He felt that it was a complete contradiction of what Director Louis told him. A part of him reconsidered contesting the termination. But after thinking it over, Pete felt that it was a no-win situation. The country knew his name, and they wanted him to pay. At that moment, Pete not only realized but also accepted that this was officially the end of his policing days, and it broke his heart.

Thirty minutes had gone by. Pete was still sitting on the couch in the basement, scrolling away on his iPad. He scrolled through social media and read the horrendous comments people left under the video of Director Louis' statement:

@BookeemWalker917

> How the FUCK could he say that shooting was justifiable? What the hell, man? I've lost all respect for the police, the justice system, and the whole goddamn society. This is an INJUSTICE. Pete "The Pig" Gant, go straight to fucking hell, man. You're a coward, and you'll get yours, you SOB.

@StandfordWebster238

> Justice was served, ladies and gents. It's sad that someone lost their life. But no matter how you look at this situation, the officer did what he had to do. And besides, people die every day.

@LovelyMisty973

> OMG... I'm just so heartbroken for the mother of Tyshawn Brendan. I can tell from his Instagram that they were very close. She didn't even get to see him grow and mature as a man. And now they say that the shooting was justifiable? Shame on America. They aren't going to be satisfied until they kill every black boy and girl... and then what?

@RandellKaufman56

> @LovelyMisty973 And THEN it's a more peaceful world. No more jigaboos, HAHA!

@LovelyMisty973

> @RandellKaufman56 Go fuck yourself! Chances are, you probably already do. I bet you're a fat ass incel still living in your momma's garage and never got laid. FYI, white people are responsible for more violence and bloody wars than any other race on the earth. So no, it WON'T be a more peaceful world. ASSHOLE!

@Witneysworld785

There are some very sick people in this world. Some are just racist to the bone. I hope and pray that the parents of Tyshawn Brendan will find some peace even though the system has failed their son. I can't believe that cop got up on that podium and said the shooting was justifiable. If that cop was black and the two of them were white, they would've charged him. It's so sad that this is the world we live in. I have two sons myself. It scares me because they remind me of the two black teens who were shot. I don't ever want to get that phone call saying that one or both of my boys were shot and killed on the streets. I pray every day and night that my sons will be safe. Even after I'm no longer here.

@KamalJacksontheGod

To that bitch ass cop, Pete Gant. I hope you see this. If I ever see you on the streets, on GOD, it's on sight. Oh, best believe, we going to get some black justice, you bitch ass, ho ass pig. I bet you're at home hiding, sipping on liquor, getting drunk out of your mind because you can't deal with what you've done. I hope the rest of your life is a living hell for you and your fucked up kids. You killed that boy for nothing. Just because he's black. I can't wait until they find your body after you've killed yourself. I know that's what you're going to do. And when they bury you, I'll be the first to piss on your motherfucking grave. I hate you fucking cops, man. Murder to all these pigs.

That last comment disturbed Pete so much that he took a screenshot of it in case he had to report it to authorities. Because that comment mentioned Pete's kids, he felt threatened and triggered. His biggest pet peeve with all of this was people coming after his family—which he never wanted. Pete turned off all his electronics and locked himself in the bathroom. He then turned on the shower and removed his clothes. As he stepped into the hot shower, he closed his eyes and began to relive that night. Even though the shower was loud, Pete could still hear the bullets sounding off in his mind—his body jerked at the sound of each gunshot. The body cam footage was now embedded in his subconscious, playing repeatedly at every waking moment. No matter how much he tried to block the visions out, they would always return… stronger, louder, and bloodier.

27

<u>REBELLIOUS INCOMPETENTS ON THE STREETS</u>

It was a quarter to one in the morning, and Claire's phone received its fourth call in the last two minutes. As Claire woke up, she picked up her phone and looked at the screen; it was Montgomery. She immediately answered.

"Hello?" Claire asked, rubbing the crust from her eyes.

"Jesus *Christ*, Claire," Montgomery shouted.

"What *happened?*"

"Where's Pete? I've been calling his phone for the past hour. He's not answering."

"Uh, he's sleeping in the basement."

"The *basement?* What the fuck is he doing in the basement?"

"He's been sleeping down there because he didn't want to disturb us with his nightmares. But why were you calling him?"

"Oh, God, Claire. Have y'all *not* been watching the *news?*"

"No, it's damn near two o'clock in the morn—"

"Just turn the news on now."

With the phone to her ear, Claire looked around for the remote. She then spotted the remote, hanging off the edge of Pete's nightstand. She crawled over, grabbed it, and hit the power button.

"Do you have it on?" Montgomery impatiently asked.

"Hold on, I'm looking for it!" Claire said. "What exactly am I looking for?"

"The *protestors*! They've gone mad!"

"What?"

Claire finally found the news channel. It was an aerial shot of the city of Newark—coming from the news helicopter. Flames were ablaze outside in front of the police department and three patrol units were set on fire by bomb cocktails. Protestors had vandalized the exterior of the police station. Police officers were all suited up as if they were ready for war. Claire was horrified as she looked at the television screen. She saw hundreds of people standing on the streets—most of their faces were covered with masks and scarves. The whole scene looked like something out of a post-apocalyptic movie—an emerged purge.

"Claire… Claire, you still there?" Montgomery said.

"I'm here," Claire softly responded.

"I *knew* this would happen. It's just like the '67 riots."

"Mr. Gant… I can't talk anymore. I gotta go."

"Wait, Claire—just… look after my son, will ya? Take care of my boy."

"He's a *man*, Mr. Gant… not a boy."

"He's *my* boy, all right? Just take care of him, please. I'll see you all later for the family Christmas."

"Family Christmas? You're not expecting us to *come*, are you?"

"Of *course*, I am. It's a forty-five-year *tradition* in our family."

Claire sighed. "Okay, Mr. Gant… I—I'm gonna go now. Goodnight."

Claire gazed on at the television as the bloodshed had begun. People were getting arrested; teenagers were running around with stolen electronics and liquor bottles as they smashed out the windows of local businesses—vandalizing private property. "Pete," Claire whispered, worried about her husband. She quickly hopped out of bed and ran down the stairs. As she opened the basement door, she called for him. "Pete! *Pete!* Are you down there?" But there was no answer. Claire walked down the stairs as the blue light from the television illuminated the basement floor. As she got down to the basement, she saw Pete sitting there—watching the news with the television on mute. Slowly walking behind him, Claire called his name. "Pete... are you okay?"

Pete turned his head and looked with tears falling from his eyes.

"It's all my fault... this is all my fault."

Claire shook her head. "*No...* don't blame yourself, baby."

"Claire... I don't know if I can go through with this anymore."

"What? What are you saying to me?"

"I... I don't know *what* I'm trying to say. I just... I'm just really fucked up right now."

Suddenly, Claire discovered something odd about Pete. His breath smelt of liquor—*dark* liquor. She looked at the table and saw two bottles of Hennessy: one empty and the other half full.

"You've been drinking?" Claire asked.

"I had to take the pain away," Pete cried. "I just needed a few hours of numbness... why did I have to pull the *trigger*? Huh? Why did that kid have to *die*? Why?"

"Don't cry, baby," Claire said as *she* cried. "Don't cry... it's going to be okay."

Claire hugged Pete as he continued to sob in her arms. With his back facing the television, Claire watched the streets of Newark being garnished with the decoration of malicious chaos. Cops swung their thick, black batons as they landed on bare flesh. Dozens of people were being put in headlocks—dragged across the streets and thrown in patrol units. It was complete and utter mayhem. As Claire released Pete, she looked at him.

"Baby," she said. "Please don't drink anymore… it scares me when you drink."

"The pain is too real. I feel it twenty-four-seven… I can't stop seeing Tyshawn Brendan. He's in every thought, every waking moment… I see him… it's like his ghost is *haunting* me. The nightmares are getting worse…. Oh, *Claire*… I just want the pain to go away… I want to go back and change everything. The world hates me. They hate me for what I've done. That fucking director… he stood at that podium and *lied*—he *lied* about firing me. They took my whole life away from me… those bastards robbed me of my identity."

Claire stepped away from Pete. "But what about *us*? What about our *family*, Pete?"

"I *love* you guys—*you* know that."

"You just don't get it, do you? Your life wasn't just about catching bad guys and writing parking tickets—getting medals and certificates… you have a loving family. What's more important than that? You think your life is over because you can't put on that badge anymore? You are so much more than a fucking badge and blue suit. You're my *husband*. You're the father of our three beautiful kids who *love you*. For you to say that they took your whole fucking *life* away? How *dare* you say something like that?"

"I'm sorry, Claire" Pete softly said. "I… policing is all I know. What am I supposed to do now? I don't even know who the hell I am." Claire looked at him with her startled eyes. "You're unbelievable."

As Claire turned around and walked up the stairs, she said this to Pete before slamming the door. "You might as well make yourself comfortable on that couch because I don't want you nowhere *near* the bedroom until you bring my husband back!" Pete looked up at the stairs and stood there in silence. He thought about what Claire said about having a family who loved him. But after drinking a bottle and a half of Hennessy, Pete felt no love *or* pain… he felt nothing. But the demon within had now awakened.

28

DECEMBER 25th, 2025, THURSDAY MORNING:

I'LL BE STAYING HOME FOR CHRISTMAS

Christmas morning could have had a better start with the Gant family. Every year, the Gant family goes to Montgomery's house to celebrate Christmas. But this year, Pete was not in the Christmas spirit. Pete and Claire argued about his decision to stay home. Montgomery was so furious that he drove to Pete's house to talk with him. As Montgomery arrived at Pete's house, he stormed to the front door and rang the doorbell. But there was no answer. Montgomery knew Pete saw him at the door because there was a Ring doorbell. Montgomery then knocked on the door rapidly.

"Pete, open up! Now!" Montgomery barked.

As Montgomery was banging on the door, Pete was leaned up against it on the other side, looking defeated with baggy eyes and a rugged beard. "Pete!" Montgomery shouted as he continued to bang on the door. "I'll bang on this door all day if I have to. Open up!" Pete, however, was very stubborn. He refused to open the door, but Montgomery kept knocking. "*PETE*!" Finally, Pete swung open the door and shouted, "WHAT?" Montgomery looked Pete up and down as he was in navy blue sweatpants and a dingy white t-shirt.

"*Jesus*," Montgomery said in disgust. "You look like shit."

"And I feel like shit," Pete added. "What'd you expect?"

"What I *expected* was for my son to be at my house—celebrating Christmas with the rest of the family. What the *hell* are you doing here, home alone?"

"I'm *watching* 'Home Alone.'"

"Oh, so you're going to be a wise ass now?"

"Come on, Dad. I don't want to hear this—"

"You're supposed to be over at *my* house—with *your* family— celebrating Christmas with the *rest* of us."

"Dad, *please*—"

"A *forty-five-year* tradition in our family. *Every* year, we celebrate Christmas as a *family*, Pete."

"I'm not exactly in the Christmas spirit right now, Dad. All right? I don't feel very cheerful. I don't want to sing *The Twelve Days of Christmas*, I don't want any eggnog, I *don't* want the turkey, the gravy, the sweet potato and cherry pies, chestnuts roasting on an open fire—*none* of that. Okay? None of that means a damn thing to me right now."

Pete walked into the living room and picked up the half-empty bottle of Hennessey. As he took a drink, Montgomery stared at him in silence. "Don't look at me like that," Pete said. "Don't you dare stand there and judge me." But Montgomery could not help it. He was appalled at the mere sight of Pete's self-destruction.

"*Jesus*..." said Montgomery. "What happened to my son?"

"What happened to your *son*?" Pete responded vilely. "I'll *tell* you what happened to your son—your son *fucked* up, okay? In case you forgot, I *killed* a kid six days ago. He's *dead*... and now everybody expects me to just go on with my life like nothing happened—just go ahead and sip on some hot chocolate and make sure I don't *spill* it on my ugly Christmas sweater. I don't deserve to celebrate *anything*."

"You're *wrong*, Pete! It was *not* your *fault*. But that kid is gone and there's nothing you can *do* about it now. And sitting here all alone, drinking your life away, is *not* going to bring that boy back. You still have a family, Pete—a family who loves you. You *have* to go on with your life, son."

"*How*? How can I go on with my life when I have blood on my hands. Tyshawn Brendan didn't deserve what happened to him... and it's all my fault."

Montgomery sighed. "*Jesus*, Pete... don't make yourself to be this bad guy... huh?"

"But I *am* the bad guy. At least that's what the world is saying about me... and maybe it's true... maybe I am a bigot pig."

"What's going through your *head*?"

Pete stood in brief silence. "You don't understand."

"*What* is it that I need to understand, son? *Tell* me."

"Have you ever killed anybody? Huh? Have you ever taken a life, Dad?"

"Come on. Don't ask me questions like that. Just... just put on your coat and come with me. Spend this time with your family. There's no *harm* in that."

Pete shook his head. "I can't do that, Dad... it's not fair."

Pete made his way to the kitchen. Montgomery, however, was not through talking. He followed behind him and continued the conversation.

"*What's* not *fair*, Pete? Huh? *Huh*? When are you going to get it through your head how lucky you are? What if that little bastard *had* a gun, and he shot you *dead*? *You* would not be here. It would've been me and your *mother* burying you. It would've been Claire and your *kids* crying over *your* casket—holding a folded flag at *your* funeral. You get it?"

"That doesn't change the reality that the kid is gone."

"Oh, *Jesus Christ*!" Montgomery scoffed.

"Look, Dad, I understand what you're saying. I understand how lucky I am to be alive. Hell, there are *plenty* of times in my career where I can say that I'm *so* goddamn fortunate to be *breathing*. But Tyshawn Brendan isn't breathing anymore. And *I* have to live with that. Not you, not Mom, not Claire—"

"Bullshit—"

"Not the kids—"

"Bullshit—"

"Not Greg, not Freddy—"

"Bullshit—BULLSHIT!" Montgomery shouted. "You don't think your mother and I have to live with *this*? You think we don't have *our* nightmares? You think *I* didn't wake up in the middle of the night in cold sweats thinking something happened to you? That you got *shot*? Or in a high-speed chase, and your car flipped over? You don't think *we* were going nuts—stressing about *your* safety out there? You are *not* the only one who's suffering, Pete. *I* take it in, your *mother* takes it in—we *all* have—*just* as much as you do. We've *all* suffered, son—*all* of us."

Pete stood there as he let that one sink in. He then opened the refrigerator door to grab a cold beer. The foam burst out as he cracked it open and took a drink, and Montgomery hated that image of his drunken son.

"Don't do that in front of me," Montgomery said as he looked away. "I *hate* it when you drink."

"So, it's *my* fault, right? It's *my* fault that the family is so dysfunctional? Yet, we ignore the fact that Poppa Dee is an open racist."

"Oh, for the *love* of God, Pete, what are you talking about—"

"Dad, you *can't* deny it. Poppa Dee's—"

"Okay, we're *not* having that conversation. All right? Let's not even go there... unbelievable."

"What's unbelievable?"

192

"Nothing, forget it," Montgomery said as he walked away.

Pete followed behind him. "No, speak your mind, Dad. That's what you came here for, right? To talk down to me. *Right?*"

"I didn't come here to talk down on you. You're my son, and I *love* you. We just want you in our presence, that's all.… You know, ever since this happened, you've been so negative. Your mother and I call you, but you don't answer. We want to make sure you're okay."

"No, Dad. No, I'm *not* okay. I'm *devastated.* For the last six days, I've been in the dark. I can't eat… I can't sleep… some nights, I get up and walk around the block. Every time I close my eyes… I see him… and I see the blood rising up his mouth. All it took was a second, and my whole life changed forever. I'm just not myself."

"And that's why we *call* you—to *check* on you. We *understand* that you've been traumatized by all of this. But this whole isolating yourself—not talking to anyone? That's not going to help you… Pete, you…"

"I what, Dad?"

Montgomery sighed. "*Jesus…* son, you could've been anything you wanted in life— *any*thing you wanted: doctor, engineer—a *lawyer* even. You wanted to be a hero? There's a *million* fucking avenues you could've taken to be a hero. Hell, you could've worked for *me. That* was *my* dream. To build an empire, pass it down to my sons, and you and your family would be set for life… *why* did you have to be a *cop*? *Why?*"

"So, that was your dream? Me working for you? Huh? You think I wanted to be a product of nepotism—follow in your footsteps with my hands out? Looking for *you* to pay for everything and be Daddy's boy—the boy born with a silver spoon in his mouth?"

"Oh, Pete, come on—"

"I'm a *man*, Dad. And a man shouldn't be living his life off of handouts. I wanted to stand on my own two feet. I wanted to make a *difference* in society. *I believed* that I could make a difference and that

that difference would make an impact on people's lives…. I've *always* been a good cop, Dad. *Always*—to the best of my ability. But I've learned something along the way. I've learned that I can't control everything. I learned that every night, when I was done with my shift and lay my head down on that pillow, that the devil was still out there… and he *keeps winning* the *battles*. But every day, I put on that uniform and that badge, and I put my *life* on the line so that he'll *never* win the war. *That* was my purpose. *That* is how I made a difference, and *that* is why I became a cop."

"So, *that's* what it's all about? You didn't want to work for me. You thought working for your old man was a *handout*?"

"It's more than that, Dad—it's the bragging and boasting— whenever we go out for one of your 'Steak dinners,' you always order fifteen-hundred-dollar bottles of wine and wagyu steak— telling the waiters about how you just closed another deal. '*Hey, Ralphie, business is booming as usual. I just made another investment in a hedge fund.*'"

"Don't you *mock me*," Montgomery retorted. "You know, if it *weren't* for those investments, you and *your* family wouldn't be *living* in a house like this—"

"Oh, I *knew* it! I *knew* it! I *knew* it! I *knew* this day would come. You couldn't *wait* to rub it in my face about how you paid for this house."

"So what? You're embarrassed?"

"Something *told* me just take out a mortgage."

"And then what? You spend the next thirty years of your life slaving away, paying it off? I wasn't going to let you do that."

"Why? *Why* couldn't you just let me be a man and take care of my family the way *I* see fit? I wouldn't have had a problem paying a mortgage. Why did you *always* feel the need to pay for *everything*?"

"Because you're my *son*. Is that a fucking *crime*? To take care of my family?"

"Dad—"

"No, no, just listen to me for a second… when I die, the companies are going to *you*. You know I can't trust Gregory to run the businesses. He'll turn the whole shit into a goddamn Ponzi scheme."

"And who said that I wanted that responsibility? Your dreams are not my dreams, Dad. I didn't ask for all of this. I didn't *ask* you to pay for *anything*, but you *fucking insisted*. And I'm tired of it."

"So, what are you saying? Huh? Yo—you're saying I can't take care of my kid—"

"I'm not a *kid* anymore—"

"You're *my* kid, goddamn it! *My* kid—*my* son—*my boy*! I would *die* for you!"

Pete was taken aback as he never heard Montgomery speak like this before. Growing up, Montgomery would pacify Pete and Greg with money, never with love and affection. But that sudden remark gave Pete a warm, tingling feeling inside. He stood there in silence as he processed the moment. He then took a seat on the couch to catch his breath. Montgomery, however, had more to say.

"What makes you so *proud*? What makes you feel that you can't accept a good thing?"

"Oh my God, Dad," Pete scoffed as he walked back into the kitchen.

"Don't you walk *away* from me."

"I just don't want you *paying* for anything anymore."

"Pete… you don't have a job right now, son. And you *don't* have a pension. *What* are you going to do for money?"

"Just let *me* deal with that, Dad. Okay? I'll figure it out—let me be my own man—for *once*. I have just enough money stored away for a rainy day… this is the beginning of that rainy day. I'll pay my taxes and put food on the table for *my* family. But don't you worry about anything. *Your boy* is a man now."

Montgomery shook his head in disappointment. "You're breaking my heart, you know that? I *never* wanted this for my boys."

"What *did* you want for us, Dad? To be some spoiled rich white boys driving around in a brand-new Maserati? Wearing Ralph Lauren Polos, *khakis*, and the leather loafers—*no socks*? Just waiting for Daddy to crack open his piggy bank and soothe us with hundred-dollar bills?"

"You ungrateful bastard… that's what it's all about…. Let me ask you something, son… are you ashamed of being white and privileged?"

"What?"

"Oh, you heard me correctly. *Are you ashamed* of being *white* and *privileged*? Is *that* what it is?"

"What the hell are you talking about—"

"I'll *tell* you what *I'm* talking about, okay? You carry this *race* guilt. You think just because you were born white with a silver spoon in your mouth—and you *were*… you were… you *see* yourself as a *victim* of *my* success."

"That's ridiculous."

"You know… your *great*-grandfather once told me, 'Be careful with how you raise your kids—while having lots of money.' I didn't understand that as a kid. But as I got older, *wiser*… and *richer*… I understood him. He *warned* me that by *having* lots of money, *my* kids would be *victimized* by the lifestyle to the point where *my* success could lead to *their failure*! Is that what happened, son? Did *my* success ruin *your* life? Is being white and privileged a *curse* to you? Huh? I really want to know. Did the money and success *abuse* you and Greg?"

"All right, this is pissing me off now, so I'm going to leave—"

"SIT DOWN!" Montgomery shouted.

It was at that moment Pete was reminded of Montgomery's authority over him. Pete had been an officer for sixteen years, and was not used to anyone outside of the precinct giving him an order, as that was always *his* job. As Pete sat back at the kitchen table, Montgomery sat across from him.

"I'm your father, you're my son, and I *fucking love you*. You're my darling boy… you could've been *anything* you fucking wanted in this life. You wanted to be a cop? I accepted it, but for the *life* of me, I did not understand *why* you would transfer to *Newark*. You were doing just fine in Cedar Grove. Nice house, *nice* neighborhood. Why leave that all behind?"

Pete shook his head as he stood up. "And that's the problem growing up privileged. Right there. Nice neighborhood? Nice house? You think the world is just so beautiful and luxurious. Well, I have news for you, Dad… it's fucking ugly."

"You think I don't know that? I've been on this earth longer than you, my friend."

"No, I don't think you understand how *evil* it is out there—how *wicked* people truly are… that's what happens when you live in the suburbs, Dad. You live in that bubble for too long, you'll go blind and can't see the dangers ahead of you."

"What are you talking about? *What* dangers?"

"Years ago, when I was working in Cedar Grove, we caught some sick bastard trying to link up with an eight-year-old boy at a park. Come to find out, he was my fucking neighbor—just a few houses away. And Leo had just turned four."

Montgomery sighed. "Shit… I remember you told me about that."

"Yeah, and I *refused* to raise *my* kids around a *goddamn pedophile*. Cedar Grove was just as dangerous as the shit you read about in Newark. Maybe even *worse*. Evil has no jurisdiction, Dad… it's *everywhere*."

"Pete," Montgomery sighed. "I really don't know what else to say to you. I just felt that by you putting your life on the line every day, making your family go through all that stress, I just… I expected better for you… and that's all I'm going to say about it."

"Well, you said it—you said it all… so, now what?"

Montgomery reached into his pocket and pulled out an envelope. "Merry Christmas."

"What is it?" Pete frustratingly asked.

"Consider it a Christmas gift… for the family."

Pete, now irritated. "What is it, Dad? *Money*?"

"Just *take* the damn envelope."

"Did you hear a *word* of what I said to you? I'm not accepting any more *handouts* from you."

"All right, fine, you don't want to open it? I'll open it."

Montgomery tore the side of the envelope. Inside was a note along with a check for $100,000. Montgomery read the note to Pete as they stood in the kitchen:

Dear family, I know you're going through some trying times. But I just wanted you to know that Melissa and I are keeping you in our thoughts and prayers and just know that we are family. Family must stick together, and we will get through this. In the meantime, please accept this check for one hundred thousand dollars from us—

Pete snatched the note and check out of Montgomery's hands and immediately tore them to shreds.

"*No… fucking… HANDOUTS*! I'm *not* a charity case!" Pete retorted.

The shreds sprinkled around the floor like paper snowflakes. But the only thing that was melting was Montgomery's heart. "I know you're not," Montgomery said. "I'm sorry if it came off that way… I'll leave you to it."

Montgomery headed straight to the front door. Before he left, he told Pete one last thing. "I really would like for you to think it over and come work for me. You don't have to answer me now… give it a few days. All right?" Pete remained silent as he went down to the basement. Montgomery stood there in the doorway, looking as if he failed as a father. All he could get out before he slammed the door behind him was, "Merry Christmas, son… Merry Christmas."

29

DECEMBER 25^{th,} 2025, THURSDAY EVENING:

THE SLEEPLESS NIGHT

It was a quarter to midnight. Pete was lying in bed, utterly restless as the conversation with his father dwelled in his mind for hours—as well as the shooting. Pete reminisced and brainstormed how he could have made better choices. He questioned his decision to open fire and asked himself, *"Could I have handled that better? Should I have just ran out of the way and dodged it? Or was I just scared?"* All of these questions began to grow like weeds and thorns in a vulnerable garden—scarring his brain—causing a migraine. Pete got out of bed and headed to the bathroom to grab some Advil Migraine. His migraines have occurred off and on for the last several years. The stress and politics that came with being a police officer were a vicious contribution to the development of his migraines.

Pete placed two capsules in his mouth and slurped the tiny puddle of water from the palm of his hand. The whole time in the bathroom, he looked down at the sink as he refused to look at himself in the mirror. He felt so ashamed and disgraceful at the mere sight of his face. Every time he looked at himself, it would make him sick. As he turned the bathroom light off and walked back into the bedroom, Claire began to cough in her sleep. Pete passed on to her the cold he caught a few days ago, which was also passed on to his kids. He then left the bedroom and shut the door as he checked on the kids. As Pete approached Elle's bedroom, he opened the door and looked at her.

Pete had a moment and reminisced about the time he took her to the zoo when she was four. Elle loved the zoo. She had such an obsession with animals. She loved every kind. However, her all-time favorite animal was the lion, which came as no surprise since she was a Leo. That day at the zoo, Pete remembered holding her tiny four-year-old hand as they walked around. He remembered looking at her, and she looked up at him with that gorgeous, innocent smile. Looking back at that moment, Pete realized how much he missed those times. He missed seeing Michael and Elle being those little kids: innocent, pure, happy, and, most importantly, unbothered by the world's troubles. Pete wished he could have kept them frozen at those ages forever. But time flew by like a whisper of mystery that turns your head, and by the time you turn back around, they had grown into teenagers.

Pete slowly shook his head as he stood in the doorway of Elle's bedroom. "My baby girl," he sighed. He then closed the door and headed downstairs. Pete was having difficulty getting adjusted to being at home during the wee hours of the morning. Even when he tried to go to bed, he just could not sleep. He then headed to the living room to start a fire in the fireplace. Brownie was lying on his dog bed when he woke up and saw Pete. Brownie usually was a deep sleeper. But if ever there was an unusual sound, he woke up immediately alert. Pete went over to him and kneeled as he said, "Hey, buddy... sorry I woke you. I couldn't sleep." After Pete petted Brownie, he went ahead and started the fire.

He dusted off his hands as the flames began to flicker and flare over the wood—creating an orange illumination on his grieved face.

He sat on his couch and began to think about the body cam footage. That horrific scene played in his mind hundreds of times. Pete contemplated the multiple decisions that he could have made to prevent the outcome. But Tyshawn Brendan was dead, and there was nothing he could do to change that. As the bark of the crackled, a gentle hand reached across Pete's face. Pete immediately jumped from the couch and looked behind him.

"Leo!" Pete sighed. "You scared me, buddy."

"Sorry, Daddy," Leo said as he stood in his dinosaur pajamas.

"What are you doing up?"

"I had a bad dream and I can't go back to sleep."

"Oh."

"You can't sleep either?"

Pete shook his head. "No... listen, buddy... Daddy's sorry about the other night. I had a bad dream just like you. It's too complicated for you to understand. But I just want you to know I didn't mean to scare you guys. Daddy's just... I'm going through a lot right now."

"Did you kill somebody, Daddy?"

Pete grew hesitant to answer. "I didn't mean to, buddy."

"But Daddy, you always said that it's bad to kill."

"I know, Leo. And—"

"So, does that make *you* bad?"

"No, honey... that doesn't make Daddy a bad man. Your daddy is a *good* man and a good *cop*... I *was* a good cop. I'm a good man who was put in a bad situation. And someday, when you're older, we can revisit this conversation, and I'll explain to you what I mean by that... okay?"

"Okay."

"Okay... why don't you head on up to bed?"

"Can I stay down here with you until I fall asleep?"

Pete smiled. "Sure. Come on, you can sit with me on the couch."

As Leo walked around the couch, he went over to pet

Brownie. As Pete sat on the couch, Leo rest his head on Pete's arm. It was the first time in a long time that Pete had a moment like this with Leo. His busy schedule kept him away from his kids so much. Even under such circumstances, Pete took this moment sincerely and cherished it, and he was sure that Leo appreciated it.

A half-hour later, Leo was comatose. Pete, however, was wide awake, gazing at the dying flames. Suddenly, there was a visitor. Claire came downstairs in her white robe and saw them lying on the couch.

"Pete?" Claire said.

"Hey," Pete responded.

Claire ran her fingers through Leo's hair. "How long he's been asleep?"

"For a little while. He said he had a bad dream, so, I told him he could stay down here with me."

"Oh… well, I'll take him upstairs."

"No, it's okay, I got him—"

"No… I actually want to talk to you. I'll put him in bed."

Pete picked up Leo. "Just wait for me here, I'll take him up."

Claire stayed behind and waited for Pete in the living room. As Pete got up the stairs with Leo, he noticed something on the table in the hallway. It was a gift box and a card with his name on it. Pete had no idea what that was about. He then walked into Leo's bedroom and gently placed Leo in his bed—wrapping his Batman comforter over him as he kissed him on the side of his head. Just as Pete left the room, it hit him like a punch to the gut.

"*Shit*," he pantomimed. Pete realized that the gift box was an anniversary gift. Pete and Claire's wedding anniversary was December 21st, four days ago. Pete stood there in the hallway, cursing himself out as he could not believe he had forgotten his wedding anniversary. Pete and Claire wanted their wedding day to be on Christmas. However, traveling was chaotic during the holidays, so they felt it would be too much for family and friends. So, they scheduled it four days before Christmas—which was still a hassle to orchestrate, but they made it work.

As Pete closed Leo's bedroom door, he walked to the table where the gift was. Pete felt terrible as he looked down through the pillars and of the rail and saw Claire sitting in the living room. Pete shook his head in shame and guilt. He then grabbed the gift box and card and sat on the stairs. The box was beautifully wrapped in black paper with a blue matte ribbon. Pete undid the wrapping and was stunned at what was engraved on the top of the box.

It was a Hublot watch. Pete had been dying for one for years. Yet his guilt overpowered his enthusiasm. He opened the box, revealing an eloquent case with an opening display that showed the watch. As Pete opened the case, he looked at the watch in awe. It was a classic blue fusion chronograph titanium watch. Pete did not know what to be more shocked about, the watch's price or the actual watch itself. He then carefully placed the watch back in its case and picked up the card. He shook his head again as he held the card firmly, still kicking himself for forgetting their anniversary. He opened the envelope and read the front of the card:

To my husband.

The one to whom I said, "I do."

The one whom I vowed to love forever,

Even though forever is not enough.

Think of this card as my heart.

What I honestly have to say and feel lies within.

That part alone warmed Pete's heart. But what Claire wrote on the inside soothed his wounded soul:

Petester,

> *First, I want to get this out of the way and say Happy Anniversary, my love. Can you believe it has been 18 years since we've been married? Eighteen years... time goes at such a hasty pace, doesn't it? But whenever we're together, it feels like time doesn't exist. Or maybe it pauses just for us. Every day that I spend with you is an absolute blessing. I never told you this, but the first day I saw you at the state fair, I knew instantly that you would be my husband someday. I felt it deep within the cartilage of my bones. Maybe that's why I was so weak at the knees that day. But from that day on, I was deeply in love with you.*
>
> *I'll admit, the idea of you being a police officer scared me. I always heard those stories about widowed police wives left behind to take care of the children alone. There were days when I thought that would happen, and it scared me to my soul. But my faith told me that everything would be okay. Besides, whenever I saw you walk out that door with your police uniform on, it just made me want to drool like a hound dog at the mere sight of you. Pete... I love you, baby. So very much. We've had our ups and downs, our struggles, our nightmares, and we've been through our trials and tribulations. But I wouldn't trade a second of it for the universe. You're the lover of my lifetime, my partner, sometimes in crime. You're an incredible father and human being. Please don't ever change. I love you just the way you are, babe. I hope you enjoy the watch. I picked blue because it represents the thin blue line that you proudly serve. I saved up for a whole year to get it. And for you... it was worth every cent. I can't wait to see your face when you open it.*
>
> *Happy 18th Anniversary, Pete.*
> *Your darling wife, Claire Gianna Gant.*

Teardrops hit the card as Pete sobbed. He was devastated that he had forgotten the most important day of their lives. He took a moment to collect himself his return to the living room. As he left the watch and card on the stairs, Pete walked into the living room and saw Claire sitting on the couch, looking straight ahead at the fireplace. Pete stood behind her in silence. He could tell just by her body language that she was distraught. He knew he owed her an apology. "Claire," he said. "I can't express how sorry I am for forgetting our anniversary. I never forget... with everything that has happened... it just slipped my mind. But that's no excuse. I've screwed up, and I'm sorry.... The watch? I love it. Thank you. And the card... that was the most beautiful thing I ever read. I appreciate every word you wrote." Claire, however, did not responded. She sat there and lingered her silence, not moving an inch.

Pete thought what he said would be enough, but it was not. That is when he went deep into his heart and soul and said this to her. "Baby... that very first day we met... there was something that I never told you... when we were dancing at the state fair, I couldn't help but notice the smell of your hair. It smelt of a garden of fresh peaches and cream. I couldn't help it, but I just stood there with my face buried in those long strains of hair—smelling my way into heaven. The way you held me and rubbed my back with your soft hands... it's like *you* were protecting *me*—*you* had my back. And you've had my back ever since. I'm so grateful for that. God knows that I need someone in this *twisted*, *crazy*, *fucked* up world who will give me serenity and peace of mind. Every day and night when I open that door, I see you and the kids; it just made me wanna cry— all those times when I was only an inch away from death. But when I turned the key and saw you and our kids... nothing else in this world mattered. Not that badge, not that uniform... only my family. Claire... I love you more than life itself. Thank you for sharing eighteen years of your life with me. Thank you for giving birth to our beautiful children. *Thank* you for being such a strong, dedicated woman. And thank you for being my best friend through the worst times... Happy Anniversary."

Pete continued to stand there behind Claire as tears rolled down his face. Suddenly, Claire turned and looked at him with tears falling from *her* eyes. She sighed and said, "Happy Anniversary,

Petester." She gave him the smile he fell in love with the first day they met. She then stood up from the couch and walked over to Pete with warm affection. They held each other for what seemed like forever. As they released, they gazed into each other's eyes— pressing their foreheads together as if they were making cognitive love. Then, Pete thought of an idea to celebrate their anniversary. "Stay right here. I'll be right back," he said as he went to the basement. Claire had no idea what Pete had in mind, but he had her attention. He returned with his iPad and opened the music app.

"What are you doing?" Claire asked.

"Taking us back eighteen years ago… back to our wedding."

Pete played a familiar song that instantly put a smile on Claire's face. It was their wedding song, *Wicked Game,* by Chris Isaak. "May I have this dance once again?" Pete asked as he extended his hand to Claire. With her contagious smile, Claire reached for his hand, and they danced in front of the fire. The moment was so perfect. It felt as if they never missed a beat and that they never stopped dancing since their wedding. They just listened to Chris Isaak's seductive voice as he took them back to the best day of their lives. Pete and Claire loved each other more than anything in the world. It was a moment they both needed to rekindle their love. Pete was on a journey—a road to redemption. But a wrathful storm of torment was soon to come in his path.

30

DECEMBER 26^{th,} 2025, FRIDAY MORNING:

THE FUNERAL WILL BE TELEVISED

Cameras were set up across the street as a line of grieving people stretched around the church. Tyshawn's father, Morris Clark, wanted the world to see what happened to his son. He invited every news station to broadcast the service. Jada, however, wanted nothing to do with it as she felt it was exploitation and a publicity stunt. They butted heads about it the whole week. Their dilemma became vile, so much so that they were not on speaking terms, even at their son's funeral. Many people stood in line: coaches, players, classmates, and others who crossed paths with Tyshawn Brendan—waiting patiently with broken hearts as they came to pay their respects to this gifted young man. Even Mayor Tiffani Collins came to pay her respects. And sitting right there in his basement watching this unfold was Pete.

Pete, once again, was home alone as Claire and the kids were spending time with her parents. Pete watched on as Morris Clark appeared on camera. Morris was dressed in all black with his beard neatly groomed. As the cameras rolled, reporter Pat Jolson began to speak with Morris in front of the church.

"I'm outside of the church here with the father of Tyshawn Brendan, Mr. Morris Clark," Pat said as he held his microphone. "Mr. Clark, how are you doing this morning?"

"I'm hanging in there, man. That's the best I can do," Morris responded.

"Mr. Clark, as you can see, many people are in attendance, waiting to pay their respects. You son, obviously, was loved. What does this mean to you and your family?"

"It's breathtaking... to see that my son had such an impact on so many people's lives—even at the young age of eighteen. I just spoke with Mr. Randy Sparks, the head coach of Duke University. Mr. Sparks came to pay his respects and share with me that they will be retiring Tyshawn's Jersey. That means a lot to me and my family. I'm sure Tyshawn would've loved that."

"That will be a beautiful tribute. What will be the next step after this?"

Morris sighed. "I don't know... I'm not thinking about all that. You know? All I'm focused on right now is... saying goodbye to my son. It's... it's still unbelievable to me. I was just talking to him that day. He was telling me something about his free throws and how he wanted to work on them. He was a perfectionist... this is just crazy to me."

"Mr. Clark, I offer my sincerest condolences to you and your family. I thank you for your time."

"Thank you."

Pete saw the sadness in Morris Clark's eyes as he walked off-camera. The dense guilt he felt inside became unbearable. He did not know if he was going to be able to survive watching the funeral, but for some reason, he did not turn off the television. Pete felt this was the only way he could pay his respects, discreetly.

Five minutes went by—no commercial breaks. The news

station began broadcasting inside the church. The flower arrangements were beautiful. It was like a garden in heaven. There was even a flower arrangement shaped like a jersey with the number eleven in white roses. There was music in the background. A song called *We Fall Down* by Donnie McClurkin. The first thing Pete noticed was the fully opened casket. The mere sight of Tyshawn Brendan took his breath away as if a cannonball shot through his body.

They placed Tyshawn Brendan's body in a gold casket with white interior. Tyshawn was dressed in a Duke uniform—number eleven—with a white long-sleeve compression shirt and pants underneath. He was also wearing his favorite Air Jordan sneakers, the *Win like 82* Air Jordan 11s. Morris permitted the news stations to take closer shots of his son. As the camera zoomed in, they showed Tyshawn's face. He looked as if he was resting—unbothered and at peace.

Pete hated funerals, but he has been to many: some were family members, and others were fallen brothers and sisters who were killed in the line of duty. At that moment, a haunting thought came over him. As Pete looked at Tyshawn Brendan, he imagined it being one of *his* kids lying in the casket, and he, as a father, had to bury one of them. But never did he expect to be watching the funeral of the person he shot. That is when it hit him. Pete realized that someday, one way or another, he, too, will be lying in a casket.

The time was ten o'clock, and the viewing had begun. People were making their way down the aisle to pay their respects to Tyshawn Brendan. The casket was blocked off by a red velvet stanchion rope—keeping the viewers at a distance. As people approached Tyshawn Brendan's casket, they collapsed and cried hysterically— teenager girls screamed in pain. Older women waved their hands high as they walked out, enraged. As the line moved, Tyshawn's teammates reached the casket. They held each other as they cried at the sight of their fellow champion. They loved him. They had been playing together since childhood, playing at the same playgrounds. They all were wearing last year's state championship jacket. They had won three in a row and were looking forward to winning their fourth.

The emotions were too intense for Pete. He stood up from the couch and walked away, standing in the corner of his basement. He knew watching the funeral would drain him of emotion, but he had to watch. Pete then walked into the bathroom and splashed hand puddles of water on his face, still unwilling to look at himself in the mirror.

There was a slideshow playing from the projector in the church, showing all these pictures of Tyshawn Brendan. One image was Tyshawn as a baby—smiling and drooling over a rubber duck. Another photo was of him at three years old at a playground, smiling as he held a basketball. The next picture was Tyshawn with his mother at his seventh birthday party. In the picture, Jada had smashed cake in his face, and they shared a good laugh. As Pete looked at the slideshow, he could not help but notice that Tyshawn's father was absent from the pictures in the earlier years of his life. It made Pete wonder if Morris Clark was in the picture at all.

As people took their seats, a woman wearing all white made her way towards the casket… it was Jada. Jada was one of very few who wore white. She stood on the left side of the casket as she greeted and hugged the grieving guests. But as everyone was sobbing in her arms, Jada did not shed a tear… not one.

After two hours of tears, screams, and enragement, it was time for the immediate family to say their final goodbyes. The funeral director went up to the podium to make the announcement. "At this time, we now ask that the immediate family come up to say their last goodbyes." Jada lifted her hand and said to her family, "Please... just let me have a moment with him alone." Jada felt like she was sinking into the floor as she walked toward the casket—the same feeling when she walked toward Tyshawn's body in the operating room. Every step toward the casket was a step to her new reality.

As Jada reached the casket, she looked at Tyshawn and touched him. She felt him, but in the eeriest way, he was not there. She kneeled at his casket and began to speak to him. "Oh, King... baby, don't leave me. We had *plans*. You were going to... *we* were going to travel the world together. You were supposed to take me along the journey. You can't leave Mommy here alone, baby... please come back to me." Jada stayed there, with her forehead up against the rim of the casket.

Pete watched the whole thing with his hands folded—pressed against his mouth. It was a melancholy sight to bear witness. To see a grieving mother at her son's casket. Pete just wanted to die right there in his basement. A woman approached Jada and placed her hand on her back. Jada turned around and looked at her. As she tried to help Jada up, Jada collapsed to the floor. People jumped out of their seats to help her up and took her outside for some air. Morris then made his way up to the casket to take one last look at his son. Right beside him was his ten-year-old daughter, Tianna. Morris leaned on the rim of the casket and sobbed. With Tianna's innocent hand, she rubbed his back and comforted her father. Morris shook his head in disbelief as he rubbed Tyshawn's hand. He then made the sign of the cross with his right hand and kissed his son on his forehead.

Moments later, Jada returned to the casket. She leaned in and kissed Tyshawn over and over like there was no tomorrow. For Jada, she felt that there *was* no tomorrow for her—not without Tyshawn. The morticians proceeded as they removed the banner from the panel, leaving the most difficult part to remain... the closing of the casket.

Morris stood by the foot panel as Jada stood by the cap panel. With tears falling, Morris slowly began closing the foot panel. Jada had her trembling right hand on the panel, but she hesitated to close it as she stared at Tyshawn. She looked at Tyshawn's face, reminiscing about all of her memories of him: all the games she watched him play, the birthdays, the trophies, the excellent report cards, the hugs and kisses... everything. Even the day he was born when the doctors placed his wet infant body on her chest. Jada saw all of that in a matter of seconds.

Her sister, Constance, realized that Jada needed some help and stood beside her. "Sis," said Constance. "I know this is very difficult for you... it's difficult for all of us... but you have to do it. You have to let him go. He's in the Lord's hands now. Let him go, baby." Constance placed her hand on the panel as she helped Jada lower it down. Jada felt like she was falling into an unescapable abyss of lonesome torment. The shade from within the casket grew as the light was eclipsing from Tyshawn's crescent face—moving farther away—disappearing in eternal darkness... click. That was the sound from the casket as it was finally sealed. For Jada, it was a click to her new reality. Her one and only son was now gone. Out of her life forever. "I love you, King... goodbye, baby," she cried stood beside the closed casket.

Pete watched as he was utterly distraught and devastated. His cries could be heard throughout the house. He sat there as he rocked back and forth on the floor, crying, "I'm sorry... I'm sorry... *oh, God*, I'm so sorry." He kept apologizing over and over as the Brendan family continued grieved. It was a somber moment for everyone. And for Pete... he was never going to be the same.

Forty-five minutes later, after the singing and praying, Reverend Stanley Stokes stood at the podium and asked if anyone wanted to speak and share some words about Tyshawn Brendan. Tyshawn's basketball coach, Coach Dutch Stapleton, was the first to come up and talk. Coach Dutch was nicely dressed, wearing a pin button of Tyshawn's face that said, "Justice for Tyshawn."

As Coach Dutch stood up at the podium, he began to talk. "Hello, everyone," he said. "First, I just want to say Justice for Tyshawn." "Justice for Tyshawn!" The entire church of people said in unison. Coach Dutch then continued. "I want to thank Tyshawn's parents, Morris and Jada, for allowing me to be here today under these tragic circumstances. Um… Tyshawn was a gift from God. In the thirty years of coaching the game of basketball, that boy was by far the greatest player I've ever seen on the court.… I've had to attend quite a few of these throughout my years of coaching. But never did I think that I would be standing here at the funeral of this remarkable young man, Tyshawn Brendan. As I stand before you all, I still can't believe it. I still haven't been able to process this. Tyshawn had *everything* going for himself. He was an incredible player—*such* a good kid. Respectful, very smart, professional, and a great human being. Ever since he was seven years old, I followed his game. I knew then that this kid was exceptional. The way he would crossover his defenders, making them look foolish, breaking their ankles from left to right, and taking it to the hole—I mean, you just *had* to have been there. To see him play. He had the whole crowd on their feet. It was magic… *pure magic.*"

Coach Dutch took a moment to collect his thoughts as he wiped away his tears. As he got himself together, he continued to speak. "One time, it was Tyshawn's sophomore year. He was starting in the championship game. It was ten seconds left on the clock, and we were down two. We took our last timeout with the ball in our possession. As I huddled the team up, I was drawing out a play, and the marker had run out of ink. Tyshawn snatched the marker from my hand and said, 'Coach, we got you. In ten seconds, we'll be holding up the championship trophy.' When he said that, he said it with *confidence*, not arrogance. He said it as if he *knew* of his greatness, yet he was humble. They tried to double-team him as we took the ball out, but he was too elusive for them to keep up. Tyshawn got wide open beyond the arc, and Nathaniel, his teammate, passed him the ball. When Tyshawn took that shot... *swish*... all net... state champions."

Sorrow and sobbing in the seats as Coach Dutch continued, saying, "I couldn't have been prouder. He made his teammates great. That's what I loved about that boy. He connected with people. He saw the good in you no matter *who* you were. Ty... you know your coach loves you, man. Always have, and I always will. I'm sorry it had to end like this for you. But I'll never forget you... for as long as I live. Thanks for these last four years. I love you, kid. And I'll miss you."

A round of applause had emerged from the church. Some people stood up and clapped as they appreciated Coach Dutch's words. After the applause faded, a few others shared their stories about Tyshawn. Some were heartwarming, and others were heartbreaking. Then, Morris made his way to the stage. He stood there and held onto the edges of the podium as it took him a minute to gather his words.

"Justice for my son, Tyshawn," Morris said as he looked down, shaking his head in grievance. "First, on behalf of my family, I would like to thank you—from the bottom of my heart for coming out today and paying your respects to my son, Tyshawn Brendan. That was my boy, man. He was a great kid. He wasn't a thug. He wasn't a gangsta or out there gangbanging. He had a good head on his shoulders. A stand-up young brother. He walked with respect, you know? I... uh... I had a lot to say today. But I was never good with public speaking." His daughter, Tianna, stood up and said, "You're doing good, Daddy!"

"Thanks, baby," Morris smiled. "That's my daughter right there—that's my baby…. Tyshawn… our relationship was growing. We were becoming closer every day. I would work with him on his game, but he became so great he no longer needed my assistance. The more I watched his game develop, the happier I was becoming for him. I just saw so many great things to come for him in the future. And, um… to see it all be cut short… it just breaks my heart. Tyshawn, my son, my baby boy… your pops love you, man… Justice for Tyshawn."

After everyone applauded, Jada came up on stage with tissue in her hand. She waited until Morris stepped down before heading to the podium. For a moment, she took a panoramic look at the church, which had a capacity of six hundred people, and all the seats were filled. Jada did not realize how packed the church was until she saw it from the stage. Some people had to stand up on the balcony. At that moment, Jada knew her son was indeed loved and respected, and that brought a smile to her face.

As Jada adjusted the microphone, she gave herself a moment before she spoke. After Jada sighed, she said, "I'm a queen mother. My son, Tyshawn Brendan… he was a true king. I can tell stories about my son for weeks. But there's just not enough time. What I *can* say is that King was more than the game of basketball. *So* much more than that. Believe it or not, he was really into science. He loved chemistry, biology, environmental science, engineering—you name it, he studied it and loved it. I honestly thought he would be a scientist. But then he would always say, 'Ma, basketball *is* a science. It's all chemistry.' He never ceased to amaze me with his intelligence. I loved that about him so much. I knew he would make it out, move on, and do bigger and better things, and just really enjoy his life…. Then one night… I received a call that instantly changed my life. A cop calls and tells me that my son had been shot. I froze for what seemed like forever. I remember saying to the officer, 'He's dead…

isn't he?' He didn't respond right away. But I could tell by his silence that my son was gone. I told the officer that I wanted to see him—I wanted to see my son. I *demanded* they let me see King. I called my sister, Connie, and my friend, Keisha… sorry." Jada took a breather and blotted underneath her eyes as the mascara intertwined with her cries, creating black tears. Pete was still watching, slowly shaking his head as his sobs reoccurred.

"I'm sorry," Jada continued. "Connie and Keisha came with me to the hospital. I don't know how I could've gotten through it without you two. Family is essential to me. But somehow, funerals have become the new family reunions. And that has to change—especially with the black family. But I digress…. When we got to the hospital, I asked the doctor if I could see my son alone. He took me to the operating room, where they left him. When I walked inside… I saw my baby… he looked like he was sleeping. I touched him… he was *so cold*… I just looked at him and asked, 'Why? *Why* did this happen to my baby? Why did God take my son away from me? I know that I shouldn't question God's will. And I hope he forgives me. But sometimes… I don't understand him. I don't understand any of this. And I don't want to. I just want my baby back."

Jada took a deep breath as she finished bidding farewell to her son. "I know that we, black women, have to be strong. We must be strong for our children. But to lose my son on these streets… Lord knows that I'm *so tired* of having to be strong. We keep losing and losing and *losing* our black kings. And for what? *For what*? And for all of this to happen right before *Christmas*? I asked King what he wanted for Christmas… I remember he looked right in my eyes and said, 'All I want for Christmas is to make you proud. That's all I want, Ma. To make you proud.' Well, King… you've made your Momma *very* proud. I couldn't be prouder of you, baby, and all your accomplishments in just eighteen years of life. You've been my companion, the light of my life, and my purpose for living. You were Momma's best friend... I love you so much, King. Please rest well... until we meet again... goodbye."

As Jada left the stage, Rev. Stokes took to the podium as he had this to say. "Praise the Lord.... As we have here today, this young black King is very loved and admired. Can we please stand up and give Tyshawn Brendan a round of applause as we celebrate his life!" People stood on their feet and gave Tyshawn a standing ovation.

"Yes, Lord," Rev. Stokes projected. "Yes, yes... *YES*! We are going to *honor* his legacy!" They stood for several minutes as they continued to applaud. Rev. Stokes then raised his hand to continue. "Praise God," he said. "Before I give the eulogy, sister Jada asked if I could say a few words.... I was aware of this young King, Tyshawn Brendan. My grandson is *also* a basketball player, though *he* plays for East Orange Campus High School. Even though I was rooting for my *grandson*, when I saw Tyshawn step on that court and score twelve points in under two minutes, I said, 'LORD, have mercy, they're about to get destroyed.'"

Everyone began to laugh, which was much needed. Rev. Stokes continued, saying, "I saw Tyshawn do things on that court that took my breath away. The way he played, how he moved up and down the court, and how he could shoot from anywhere *on* the court. I said, '*This* young man is special.' I believe he scored a career-high of sixty-four points that game. After the game, my grandson came to me and said, 'Yo, Pops, I *told* you he's the next Michael Jordan.' I looked at my grandson and told him, 'He's going to be *greater* than Michael Jordan.' Tyshawn Brendan was the truth. This young man was going all the way to the top. But every day, when we least expect it, God shows up and gives us *his* plan. Now, sister Jada, you mentioned that you don't understand why this had to happen—why did God take Tyshawn away from us? Sometimes, my dear, the reasons are not always black and white. They come in layers—layers of understanding, grief, and forgiveness. Basketball consists of strategic game plans and drawing out plays on a clipboard. But in this game of life, *God* draws the plays... and sometimes, we just don't understand them. You may not even *agree* with them. But if you *trust in* him... you *will* find the glory... let us pray."

As Pete watched, he suddenly got off the couch, got on his knees, and prayed along. "Father," said Rev. Stokes. "I pray for sister Jada and brother Morris. I pray that you give them and their family the much-needed guidance. I pray that you give them clarity and understanding of your ways. I pray that they, in time, receive healing. Father, I ask that you watch over them in need. Watch over them as they grieve... in Jesus' name... Amen."

After a two-hour service, Tyshawn Brendan's funeral had concluded. Pete cried so many tears that his eyelids began to swell from the constant rubbing. In his whole life, Pete had never experienced a funeral like that. It gave him some perspective. He realized that Tyshawn Brendan was not some thug or delinquent from the streets who got lucky playing basketball. Tyshawn was loved by many: black people, white people, Latinos, and Asians. He was loved and highly influential.

As they took Tyshawn's casket away, all that was left were the flower arrangements: no more music, no more people, just flowers. As Pete looked at the beautiful flowers, he wondered if that was what heaven looked like. He wondered if heaven was an enchanted place with acres of colorful flowers or just the land of make-believe and that what you saw on earth was what you got. But then, he looked down at the "Man of Faith" tattoo on his arm. At that moment, Pete had mixed feelings about his faith. Even though he got on his knees and prayed, his doubts began to defeat his beliefs.

Jada watched in grief as Coach Dutch and Morris were two of the pallbearers placing Tyshawn's casket in the hearse. Suddenly, Coach

Dutch quickly walked away as he became deeply emotional. Jada looked with concern and followed behind him to the parking lot.

"Coach Dutch? Jada said.

"Jada," Coach Dutch responded as he wiped his eyes.

"That was very nice what you said. I thank you so much for everything that you did for my son. King loved you. He really did." Coach Dutch sighed. "Jada... I have to be honest with you... that night after practice, I had a situation in the gym with Tyshawn."

"What kind of situation?"

"Tyshawn was playing around with one of my former players. RaJohnn Mitchell."

"I know RaJohnn... he was King's best friend. He was the driver."

"Yeah, well, I know the type of kid he is, and I wanted him nowhere near Tyshawn. When I confronted them, I told RaJohnn to leave. Things got heated, and there was an altercation. Tyshawn got in between us. I told him I would take him home. He wanted to ride with RaJohnn. But I wouldn't let him. Not on my watch... I went to my office to grab my keys... by the time I got back, he... he was gone.... *Something told me* to keep my eye on him. The next morning, I turned on the television and saw the news, and that's when I realized he didn't make it home."

"Oh my God," Jada gasped.

"I haven't been able to sleep, Jada. I blame myself. If only I had just told him *not to leave*... he would still be here. You would still have your boy... I'm so sorry. I would lay down my life and *die* to bring him back."

"Coach... please don't blame yourself. King wouldn't want you to burden yourself like that."

"I can't help it," Coach Dutch sniffled. "This will haunt me for the rest of my life."

"I don't blame you... *please* don't carry that burden with you... okay?"

Coach Dutch sighed again. "I'll do my best… It has been an honor to coach your son, Jada."

"The pleasure was all mine, Coach."

As Jada hugged the sobbing coach, they were joined by a woman who was pushing someone in a wheelchair. It was RaJohnn Mitchell and his sister, Neecy. Coach Dutch looked up with a face of disgust as he saw RaJohnn. Jada turned and saw both of them, sharing identical faces of guilt. "Ms. Brendan," said RaJohnn. "I just want to offer my condolences… I swear to you, it wasn't my fault…" Jada walked away as she did not want to hear another word from RaJohnn. Coach Dutch grilled RaJohnn as he could not believe he would even attend the funeral after what he did.

"You got some nerve showin' your face here, boy. Nobody wants you here—*especially* me."

"Well, that's not up to you, is it? Ain't nobody come here to see you anyway. I came here to see my brother one last time. So, why don't you get the fuck out my face, old man?"

"Cussing at the church… you're never going to change, aren't ya, boy?" He looked at Neecy. "You take care of this loser."

"You motherfuck—ow!" RaJohnn screamed as he fell out of his wheelchair.

"Rah!" Neecy said as she helped him back in his wheelchair. "You a'ight?"

RaJohnn dusts off his suit jacket and mumbled, "It's your fault." Neecy looked with a twisted face. "What'd you say?"

"It's *your* fault. Yeah, that's right. *You* were the one who called the cops—you fuckin' *snitch*. If you didn't call the cops, *none* of this would've happened. It's *your* fault my boy's dead."

POW! A smack was heard around the block. Neecy was infuriated that RaJohnn blamed her for Tyshawn's death. Even though she felt some guilt, she refused to be held responsible for RaJohnn's actions. "Don't you *dare* blame this on me," Neecy said. "You take my car without my permission, and you think I'm just going to let you get away with that and do whatever you *want*? Do you have *any idea* what I had to go through to get that car? This is all you, Rah. This is *your* doing, and you *know* it."

"You *knew* I had the car!" RaJohnn growled. "You should've *never* called them pigs. What the fuck you *think* was going to happen? Two black males in the car, and you thought—"

"I didn't *know* Tyshawn was in the *car* with you. *You* did that— *you* put your best friend in harm's way. It was *your* stupid choices that cost him his life."

"Nah… if you'd never called those pigs, my boy would still be alive today. It's *your* fault he's not here."

Neecy scoffed. "Whatever helps you sleep at night, little bro. You made piss poor choices, and you couldn't control your temper. What possessed you to tell that cop to suck your dick? And now look at you… you're lucky the doctors said you'll be able to walk again. Maybe by then, you'll wake up and stop being that stupid kid on the streets… or maybe not."

Neecy left RaJohnn alone in the parking lot. He rolled his way back to his sister's rental car as he thought about Tyshawn. Suddenly, he stopped and pulled out a picture of his friend. It was a folded picture of a cutout of Tyshawn from a newspaper article their Junior year when they won the state championship. Tyshawn held the championship trophy with the net hanging around his neck like a chain of triumph. RaJohnn stood right beside him with his arm over Tyshawn's shoulders. It was a bittersweet moment for him. RaJohnn smiled and cried simultaneously as tears landed on the article. It was the most sacred moment in RaJohnn's life. They rolled together, and they were champions together. That night of the shooting, RaJohnn felt that getting revenge and taking his frustrations out would bring him great triumph. But all it delivered was a Pyrrhic victory.

The front door had opened as Claire came home on her lunch break to check on Pete. Claire worked as a social worker. She had been working in that field for the past fourteen years, helping people who suffer from substance abuse and mental health issues. She studied psychology, earning her doctorate degree from Rutgers University. Claire was a perfect fit for Pete. She knew how to communicate with him and help him get through many of his traumas. But this was a critical trauma—an irreversible tragedy.

Claire took off her hat and coat and looked around for Pete. Coming around the corner was Brownie. Claire kneeled and petted him, saying, "Hey buddy… where's your daddy?" Brownie then walked into the kitchen as Claire followed behind. As she looked out the back window, she saw Pete slouched in the lawn chair with his back turned. She knew something was wrong as she saw a half-empty bottle of Hennessy sitting on the armrest. After putting her coat back on, Claire stepped out the back door onto the wooden deck. She slowly walked towards Pete—stepping on the dead winter leaves.

"Pete?" Claire said. "Honey… what happened?"

Pete, however, did not say a word as he looked straight ahead, blinking and breathing. Claire kneeled before him as she held his cold hand and tried to communicate with him.

"Pete… sweetie," Claire said as she grew emotional. "You're starting to scare me… *talk* to me. *Please.*"

Pete broke his silence. "They had his funeral today… the kid. His mother spoke *so beautifully* about him… why did it have to be him? I'm a killer… I killed that kid, and I hate myself for what I've done."

"Oh, Pete… it wasn't your fault," Claire said as she held Pete. "It wasn't your *fault*, baby."

Pete broke down and cried in Claire's warm embrace. The pain was unbearable—piercing through his core. This situation was not something he could look away from. Even though the funeral had concluded, the pain within would only grow stronger.

31

DECEMBER 27th, 2025, SATURDAY EVENING:

LET THE BLUE BLEED

Pete had just arrived at an undisclosed location—a parking lot of a two-story office building. The lights were on in only one location of the building. Pete looked around the parking lot, only to see five other cars. After the conversation with his neighbor, Stewart, Pete decided to attend one of the meetings ran by Stewart's brother-in-law, Brad Angill.

Pete called Brad ahead of time to ensure he was heading to the correct location. Moments later, Pete saw a man walking out of the building—waving his hand—signaling for him to come over. Pete exited his Jeep and approached him. The man stood tall with a muscular physique, a full beard and salt and pepper combed back hair.

"Pete Gant?" The man asked as he extended his hand. "Brad Angill."

"Oh, hi," Pete said as they shook hands. "Nice to meet you."

"Pleasure… we're all waiting inside."

Pete walked inside the building, unaware of what to expect. As they climb the stairs, Pete asks Brad questions about the meeting.

"So, what's this all about?" Pete asked.

"It's a support group meeting for cops. There's a few who are still on the force."

"Oh."

"So, how are you holding up?"

Pete hesitated to answer. "I'm doing my best. Still haven't been able to sleep much... too afraid of the nightmares."

"Brother, I understand that completely. That's what we're all here for... to get it off our chest."

"Yeah," Pete said with a faux grin.

As Pete and Brad walked down the long hall, they entered the office space. The office had cubicles with old computers and desks. A circle of six chairs seated everyone in the center of the office space. Pete joined the other officers as they welcomed him with open arms. He looked at them and noticed something interesting. They all had the same look in their eyes as he did—that blank thousand-yard stare. These officers felt betrayed by their superiors—who they once believed had their backs... until they did not. As they took their seats, Brad began the meeting.

"Good evening, brothers and sisters," said Brad. "Welcome. And thank you for attending this meeting. Once again, I'm Brad Angill—like *Angel*... but spelled differently. As you all can see, we're in a very discreet location. I know a couple of you are still active police officers. To put your mind at ease, anything you *say* here—*stays* here. No exceptions. That said, you guys are the pioneers of coming together and sharing your stories. I understand this is not what we do. We don't always express ourselves or have a moment to be vulnerable, discussing how this job affects our mental health and our families. We've been trained to *suppress* our emotions, and that's it. However, *we are* human beings."

Pete sat there as he let it all sink in. He looked at the others, wondering who they were and what story they had to tell. Brad continued, saying, "I was inspired to do these meetings by a friend of mine… Stephen Hollis…. Steve was my closest friend. He was an officer for over twenty-five years—highly decorated—served in the Marines. He was a Medal of Valor recipient—a great guy. I loved him, and… one day, he just… he was gone. No warning signs, nothing. His sister found a journal that he kept in his home office. He wrote about everything he was dealing with. Being on the battlefield, crimes, homicides, his ex-wives, everything."

Brad picked up a folded paper from his chair. "This right here is the last page of his journal. I asked his sister if I could have it. If you don't mind, I want to share it with you." Brad then unfolded the page. As he cleared his throat, he read the letter to the group:

To whom it may concern,

I'm sorry you must read this, but I'm afraid I have some bad news… I'm dead. I shot myself in the garage with my 357-magnum. Forgive me for making such a mess. I'm sure you're wondering why this was my final decision. Those of you who knew me know I always had a smile on my face. Well, I'll put it to you like this… a smile is but a curtain that covers the act of misery.

I loved being a cop. It had its perks. But when it came to the dark side of the job, it had its cons (No pun intended). I've been in this business for over twenty-five years. I joined the Marines right after high school. I've been around and seen a lot of things. But the things I've seen on the streets as a cop… It was pure hell. Not many people truly understand what a cop goes through, day in and day out—the bloodshed, the bodies… redrum. You just become numb to it all. You know, I've never told anybody this. This has been a secret of mine for decades. I hate guns. I hate them with a passion. I wish they never existed. But here I am, soon to blow my brains out with my gun. I guess the only thing beneficial about a gun is that it's the quickest way to death. All it takes is a bullet to the brain, and you're out of here. I can't live like this anymore.

I'm holding in all these cases, all these crimes… dark memories turned into nightmares. It's like my brain is a room filled with all these demons attacking me, causing these severe migraines, and I can't take it. I'm hearing all these voices in my head. I can't tell you how many sleepless nights I've had just to avoid any night terrors. I can't tell you how many fights I've had with my ex-wives. I love all four of them, though. I love our children. But for some strange reason... I can't seem to love myself anymore. I'm not sure if I ever did. I don't regret being a cop. I loved my job, as I said. It was more than a job. It was a way of life for me. I loved believing that I could make a difference. My only regret is that I didn't talk to anyone sooner about the pain I kept bottled in for so long.

But it's too late for that now. At least for me, it is. The poison has been in the wound for years now, and the process is irreversible. Anyway... I guess that's all I have to say about my life. I had some good times. But now, I want this nightmare to be over with. To my family, I love you. Please don't hate me for this. It's not your fault. Continue to live on and have an amazing life. Enjoy every single moment. And to my dear, gentle friend, Bradley Angill, who's been like an angel on earth to me. I'm so sorry we lost contact over the years, buddy. I know you always tried to reach out. And I thank you for that. I truly do. But I couldn't get out of my own way. Heaven bless you, brother. I'm sure we'll meet again someday... I love you.

See you all in the next life... I hope. Steven P. Hollis.

P. s. Please make sure that my casket is closed at my funeral. Thank you... it's been real.

The officers sat in silence as they stared at Brad. He stood there, holding the letter as tears fell down his face. "Pardon me," he said as he wiped his eyes. "I've read this letter over a hundred times, and as always, I have a few tears reserved for it.... I shared this with you all because I felt that maybe it would *encourage* you to want to be open here and hold nothing back. As I said, 'there are no judgments here.' So, I guess we can start with you, my friend."

A man stood up, a little taller than Brad, wearing a police officer sweater from the Irvington police department. He had a crooked smile and a bruised eye.

"Should I just start?" The man asked Brad.

"Yeah, go ahead," Brad responded.

"Sho—should I remain standing, or can I sit back down?"

"Whatever makes you more comfortable."

"I think I'll sit then."

As the man took his seat, he began to share his story. "Well... good evening, everyone. My name's Stanley Gannon Jr., uh, you can just call me Stan. I've been a police officer for eleven years now. I'm still an active officer. But right now, I'm on medical leave after suffering a crazy blow to the left side of my face. As you can see, my left eye and mouth are still bruised. Uh... *luckily*, I can see out of it now. About four weeks ago, I was dealing with a domestic violence dispute, and I was going at it with this guy who was beating his wife. As we're going at it, his wife hit me across the face with a metal pipe. The same pipe *he* was using to beat *her*. I didn't even see it coming—just *WHAM*! I couldn't see out of my left eye. My lip was busted, and my tooth's chipped. All I could hear was her screaming, 'Get off my husband!' After she hit me again, her husband ran off. I was going to run after him. But I had to contain his wife until backup got there. Some of my blood was on the metal pipe. I could still taste the blood that was running down my face that night. But you know what the craziest shit—oh, I'm sorry. Are we allowed to curse?"

Brad nodded his head. "Yeah, you're good, Stan." Stan continued. "Cool... so now, whenever I eat something, right? And I'm using silver utensils? I can *taste* my blood. It would happen everywhere: when I go out to restaurants or other people's houses for dinner, if I use silverware, I wouldn't taste the *food*; I'd taste my blood. It scared the shit out of me because I didn't know what was causing this, and I stopped eating for days. I don't know if it had something to do with the metal pipe she hit me with, but I had to stop using silver utensils.... I don't know, did something like that ever occur with any of you guys?"

Pete understood what Stan was talking about. After his

experience with smelling gunpowder and blood on Elle's basketball and the stench of the body of Gabriella del Alto every time he walked past a batch of leaves, Pete knew precisely what Stan was talking about. After Stan finished his story, Brad stood up from his seat and began to speak. "Thank you for sharing your story, Stan. How about a round of applause, everyone?" The group clapped. "All right, who wants to go next?"

The office space went silent for a moment. It was as if no one wanted to stand up and speak. "Well, don't all go at *once*," Brad sarcastically said. "Listen, folks... I know this can't be easy for any of you. Sharing what goes on out there on those streets, in those houses... it's rough out there, I *know*... but I *also* know that if we don't *talk* about it—at least amongst ourselves and let some of this off our chest... one of us could end up like my friend Steve. And I don't want that for *any* of us. So please, one by one, share your story. Tell us what brought you here tonight." Just as Pete was about to stand, another officer sitting across from him stood up and spoke.

"I—I'll go next if that's okay?" Said the woman officer.

"The floor is yours," Brad responded.

The woman officer stood there—her blonde hair neatly combed back in a low bun. She had a beautiful face and the body of a UFC fighter; curvy but fit. On her left elbow, there was a burn mark.

After getting a panoramic look at everyone, she began to share her story. "Good evening, all... my—my name is Andrea Dasani— like the water. I've been a police officer for eight years. Um... I'm here tonight because I wanted to share something that happened to me earlier in my career. I had a partner... Demarco Williamson. He was charming, kind, and... funny. He could always make me laugh. We got along rather swiftly for the first couple of months. But then, things got strange around the third month of working with him. The conversations became very... unprofessional—I'll just say that. He would say things to me that made me terrifyingly uncomfortable. He

228

became aggressive with me. But for some regretful reason, I didn't tell anybody. One night, Demarco and I were on a night shift together. We were stationed on a back road somewhere at a construction site. As we were sitting in the patrol unit, he started to talk to me about... sex. He asked me about all the 'male partners,' I had in my life, and what size penis I preferred. It was *disgusting*. I tried to ignore him because I knew where that was going. But he progressed. Then he said, 'You wanna fuck?' I was shocked that he would even ask me that. But that's just how he said it. I said, 'No, go fuck *yourself*.' Right after I said that, he hit me, and then he proceeded to choke me...." Andrea paused in her speech as she became emotional.

"Do you need a minute, Andrea?" Brad whispered.

Andrea shook her head as she wiped the tears away. "No, let me finish, please."

After handing her some tissues, Brad took a few steps back and gave Andrea some space. She wiped her nose and proceeded. "I couldn't breathe... he was choking me so hard that I started to lose consciousness. I was losing feeling in my hands. I honestly thought he was going to kill me. I felt that the only thing that could've saved me at that moment was for me to tase him. But I didn't grab my taser gun... I accidentally discharged my gun and opened fire. But I didn't shoot him. The bullet went through the driver seat window, and that stopped him from choking me. I just screamed and screamed and screamed.... The next day... after I calmed down, he called me and told me I could get in trouble for this or even be fired. What's worse, he told me that *he* could have me fired, but he would make it all go away *if* we had sex. I told him no and that I would take it up with PR and the agency. I thought my body cam footage would be evidence enough to support my case. But all it did was create a perception that I was having a mental breakdown. It didn't show any foul play on Demarco's behalf. And on top of that... Demarco was the son of the sheriff in my area. I'd rather not say where. But he wouldn't let up. I felt stuck in this situation. I wanted out, but I didn't know how to pull myself out of it and still be able to be a cop. So, I did what I thought was best at that time, and I asked to be transferred to another department."

Pete looked at Andrea with sympathy. He heard of a few stories about female officers being sexually harassed, and Andrea was a beautiful, Puerto Rican woman. After she wiped off her teary face, Andrea finished her story. "I thought transferring would be my answer, but I was wrong. Demarco followed me like a poltergeist. He became this stalker in the night. I had nightmares that he was going to break into my apartment and rape me. I knew that this wouldn't go away until I confronted it. So, I went to my supervisor and told him what had happened to me. Captain Sanchez… he's my hero. My angel. He walked me through everything that I had to do, and Demarco was charged with sexual assault. But of course, with his father being the sheriff, he was given a lesser charge and was suspended—*with* pay—and three years probation—which was a slap on the wrist for *him* but a slap in the face for me. I remember his attorney—a *woman,* by the way, dared to asked me, 'What did you do to lead him on?' She blamed *me* for *his* depredating behavior. But what pissed me off is the fact that *that* motherfucker still gets to wear a badge…. I hate to admit this, but there's a part of me that wished the bullet had hit him when my gun went off—at least in his leg or something. And now, that's another bad memory I fight with mentally. But you know, Karma's a *bad bitch*…. That—that's all I have to say… thank you for listening."

A round of applause emerged—creating an echo throughout the office. "Thank you for sharing your story, Andrea," said Brad. "I know that was not easy for you. And I have to be honest, stories like yours are rarely talked about. They are kept buried and are never brought to the surface. The same thing occurs with women in the military. So, yes, I appreciate you sharing your story. A little ripple

230

for that." The group gave another round of applause.

"Okay," Brad sighed. "Who would like to be next?"

"Um… I guess that'll be me," Pete said as he stood up.

Pete looked across the room at everyone. He did not know where to start or if he should even speak on the shooting of Tyshawn Brendan. He stopped thinking about it and just spoke from his heart.

"Good evening... I'm Pete Gant. I was a police officer for a little over sixteen years. And just like Steve… I loved it. I've wanted to be a cop since I was a little kid. And then I finally got it. But my God… I had no idea of what I was getting myself into. I don't know which nightmares were worse: the ones out there on the streets or the ones I experienced when I slept. They were awful. I don't know how many of you have ever shot anyone… let me tell you, it was *nothing* like what I ever expected it to be. Watching somebody die on the ground after you shot them… I felt like a piece of shit. I thought I would've been able to handle it and say to myself, 'I was only doing my job.' But logic never lasts. I'm sure everybody in this office space recognizes by now who I am. I'm the one who shot and killed Tyshawn Brendan. I was there, trying to save that boy's life… but I failed. It was one of those nights where it was quiet and calm, and then suddenly… a storm came. The last thing he said to me before he closed his eyes was… '*Fuck* you!' Blood shot up in my face when he said that. I'll never forget his face. He looked me in my eyes as if he wanted to ask, 'Why?' I wish I could take it all back. I—I wish I could turn back the clocks and undo *everything*…. I guess that's the thing about life, man. If you work hard enough for what you want, you'll eventually get it… and then some."

32

DECEMBER 27th, 2025, SATURDAY EVENING:

BROTHERHOOD HAS NO COLOR

After the meeting, Pete joined Brad for club soda at a local bar. As they sat at the bar, a college basketball game was on televison, Norte Dame versus Duke. It was difficult for Pete to sit there, being reminded of Tyshawn Brendan and seeing the elite collegiate program he was destined to join. As Brad sat beside Pete, he asked him a question.

"Pete," said Brad. "The last thing you said back at the meeting? What did you mean by that?"

"What was the last thing I said?" Pete asked.

"You know… 'And then some.' What did you mean by that?"

"I just meant that there's always something else waiting for you around the corner. There's always a crude surprise in store for you—especially in this job."

"Oh, I see—like you never know, right?"

"Yeah. I didn't think I was going to shoot somebody that night. I ended up shooting *two* people… kids, and one of them just so happened to be very important to the basketball world."

"It happens, man. Wrong place at the wrong time."

"But you see, it's not that simple for me. *I'm* the one who shot that boy. I have to live with that for the rest of my life. I have to be reminded of it—every single day. When I walk my dog through the park, and I see the basketball court… I think of that kid. Whenever I hear a ball bounce, I think of him and what I did. I think about his family… it's just so fucked up, Brad. Why did it have to be this way?"

"It's real-life shit, Pete. We can't help it. I mean, you can replay that whole scene over and over in your head, and it won't change the outcome. He's gone, man. But *you're* still here, and now *you* have to figure out what's best for you and your family moving forward."

Pete looked up at the television. "Look."

"What?" Brad said as he looked up.

As they watched the television, they saw Duke University paying tribute to Tyshawn Brendan, honoring him with a retired number 11 jersey. Tyshawn's parents, Jada and Morris, were in attendance. Jada held a plaque with Tyshawn's name, while Morris had the framed jersey for a photo. The entire arena stood and applauded as the jersey levitated and aligned with the others. Brad looked to his right as he saw Pete's watery eyes. "It's not your fault, man," Brad said as he grabbed Pete's shoulder. "Don't do this to yourself… you hear me?"

Pete wiped his nose with a napkin. "You don't understand—"

"No, I *do* understand."

"It's just so much pain, Brad… too much."

Brad sighed. "Okay… I wanna share a story with you… my first day on the job, I was a nervous wreck. I didn't know *what* the hell to think. But then, when the day was over, and nothing happened, I said to myself, '*This is policing*?' It was the most miserable day of my life… I went home that night thinking this was going to be a boring ass career. The *very next day*… I got a call about a man who was having a mental health crisis. My partner and I were the first on the scene. When we got there, we saw this young, skinny kid—with thick glasses. He looked like a combination of Urkel and... I don't know, just Urkel. He was sitting on his front steps. He had a gun to his head, threatening to shoot himself. I pleaded with him to put the gun down. But he wouldn't. I kept telling him to drop it, but he wouldn't budge... *seconds* later, he just tossed the gun in the grass and smiled at me."

Pete now confused. "He *smiled* at you?"

"Yeah... he had a very contagious smile. I smiled right back at him and holstered my gun. At that moment, I felt like a hero. I felt so good inside that I wanted to hug this kid just to let him know that everything was going to be all right. *Mind* you, it was my second day on the job. And the back of my ears was *soaking* wet—if you know what I mean. The moment I reached my arms to him, he pulled out a *fucking*... Michael Myers-Halloween knife and slashed me across my forearm."

Brad revealed the scar on his forearm.

"*Shit*," Pete said.

"Yeah, man... it happened so fast. I tried to back away from him, but he just kept coming; he kept swinging that knife. Next thing I know, I'm out in the middle of the street, and he's still charging at me with the knife. That's when my partner had a clear shot and took it. I never forgot those eyes—those *devilish eyes*... I thought that was going to be my last day on this earth."

"Damn, Brad... that's crazy."

Brad took a sip of his club soda. "Mmm... no, I'll tell you what's *crazy* about that moment. I didn't even realize I was bleeding until my partner pointed it out. All that adrenaline, I just couldn't feel nothing. And that shit happened in under a minute—*one fucking minute*, Pete. That's how easy it is to lose your life doing this job, man. When you walk out that door, you never know if you will make it back home. I put my family through that stress for *years*... look at all this gray hair coming out of my head."

"I see. Chances are, I'll look like you within the next year."

"Hey, listen… I told you all of that for a reason. When it comes to policing and seeing a young kid lose his life… you're not alone out here, man. You are *not alone*."

Pete took sip of his club soda. "I'll keep that in mind."

"Please do. I'm gonna hit the head. Be right back."

Brad got up from the stool and went to the restroom. Pete sat there as he dug the straw through the crushed ice in his glass. Suddenly, a man entered the bar and sat beside him. "Hey, what's up, playa?" The man said to the bartender. "Let me just have a beer, please—Heineken Light." The man wore a brown leather jacket and some denim jeans. As Pete continued to dig his straw through the ice, the man began a conversation with Pete.

"What's up, broski?" The man smiled.

"How you doing?" Pete responded as he observed the man's jacket. "Nice jacket."

"Oh, I appreciate it."

"You come here often?"

"Oh nah, not really. I don't like to drink as much. I'm only here because I'm meeting up with a friend. He had a meeting tonight, but I couldn't make it—said he was going to come here afterward. So, I wanted to link up with him."

"Oh… what was the meeting? If you don't mind me asking?"

The man was hesitant to respond. "I can't say."

"Oh, sorry. I was only asking because *I* just came from a meeting. I was wondering if you were talking about the same meeting. It was a meeting for cops, right?"

"*Yeah.* The meeting with Brad?"

"Right, with Brad."

"Oh, that's what's up. So, you're a cop?"

"I *was*… not anymore."

The man extended his hand. "I'm Devin—McCloud."

Pete shook his hand. "Pete Gant."

"*Pete Gant…*" Devin said as he removed his jacket. "Damn, why does your name sound so familiar?"

"I don't know," Pete shrugged, pretending he didn't know.

"Wait a minute… Pete Gant—you're that officer who was involved in… oh wow."

"Yeah," Pete nodded. "I'm *that* guy—unfortunately."

Brad came back from the restroom. "Hey! *There* he is!"

"Oh, what's good, broski," Devin said as he hugged Brad.

"How the fuck are you, man?"

"I'm chillin', man. I'm chillin'. Just trying to live, you know what I'm saying?"

"Hey, I hear you. That's all we *can* do."

"*Facts*, man. How was the meeting?"

"Oh, it went well, yeah. Actually, let me introduce you to—"

"Oh, nah, we just met."

"Oh, you *did*?"

"Yeah, yeah. We met."

"Oh, great. Well, then that's my cue. You can take over. I'm heading out. I have to get up early tomorrow. Sundays are the only days I get visitation rights with my children. Pete… it's been real, buddy."

Pete shook Brad's hand. "Pleasure meeting you, Brad."

"Likewise. And listen, please come back. We're going to have meetings every Saturday from here on out. That door is always open for you whenever you need it."

"I appreciate that, Brad. Thank you."

"All right… yo, D, I'll see ya."

"A'ight, broski. Good seeing you."

Pete noticed something as he looked at Devin and Brad. Brad, a white man, was hugging a black man—something Pete had rarely done in his whole life. It intrigued him to see such affection.

As Devin got settled in, Pete was on his third club soda with a mixture of cranberry juice. Devin was an average-height guy. Young-looking with waves in his faded haircut and a goatee. He also had bushy eyebrows like Tupac Shakur. Pete bought him another round as they furthered their conversation.

"Salute," Devin said as he raised his full beer bottle.

Pete raised and tapped his glass on the bottle. "Salute."

"So, how you been doing with everything going on?"

Pete sighed. "I'm just trying to survive all of this. But it's just… it's rough. It's real rough."

"I hear ya, man. A white cop shoots two black teens in Newark. It fits all the stereotypes, you know?"

"Yeah… I just never thought it would happen to me."

"You mean shooting a black person?"

"Well… *yeah*—kind of. I—I don't know. I—I've just been so confused about this whole incident. I've been fired, the world hates me, and… I don't even know what's going on with my family. I feel like they hate me, too."

"Nah, man. Your family loves you."

"I don't know. Just this morning when I walk into the kitchen, my kids sat there, and… it's like they didn't even want to make eye contact with me. My youngest son, Leo… he doesn't really understand what's going on. I gotta talk to him."

"Yeah, as long as you keep the communication flowing, it's all good. But your family loves you, Pete. *Believe* that."

"Can I ask you something?"

"Of course, fam."

"Do you think I'm a racist for shooting those kids?"

"Woah… just went right into it, huh?" Devin chuckled.

"I'm sorry, maybe I shouldn't ask—"

"Oh, nah, nah, you good, you good… look, I'll keep it a bean with you."

"A *bean*?" Pete asked with confusion.

"Oh, my bad," Devin laughed. "That's my Ebonics talk. It just means that I will be completely *honest* with you.... I was on duty about six years ago, just about to wrap up my shift. I got a call about a situation happening down in Camden. That's where I was originally stationed. I was six months into the job—still a little fresh and naïve, you know what I'm saying? Anyway, when I arrived, it was your typical domestic violence dispute. Dude was beating his girl's *ass* and she got mad and called the cops. So, when I got there, the guy was outside on his phone, just mad fucking loud. So, I tried to get him to calm down. But he wasn't havin' it. He started cussing me out, and you know, I'm like, 'He's going to be a *problem.*' So, I radioed in for backup. I kept asking him where his girl was, right? But every time I asked him, he kept saying, 'Kiss my ass, suck my dick,' you know—typical shit, right? So, as I'm trying to calm *him* down, his girl comes out of the house. Now *mind* you, he *fucked her up*. I'm talking about blood all over her tank top, blood on her face, and even out of her mouth. So, I asked her, 'Did he *do* this to you?'"

"And what did she say?" Pete asked.

"She said, 'Nah... I just got into a car accident. He's just trying to call the ambulance because you cops were taking too long.' So, I looked at homeboy, and I asked *him*. And, once again, he said, 'Suck my dick, pig.' So, I was pissed off because I *knew* he put his hands on his girl. So, I told him to turn around and place his hands behind his back. But of course, he didn't let me just arrest him without putting up a fight. So, as he turned around and I'm placing the cuffs on him, he straight up elbowed to my *face*, and ran off with my cuffs attached to his right hand. So I ended up in a foot chase with dude."

"Black dude?" Pete asked.

"Sorry?" Devin responded.

"Was this a black guy?"

"Oh, yeah, yeah, for sure… he's black… well, *was* black. So, as I'm *chasing* him, I draw my weapon out. Broski… this shit happened *so fucking fast*. He turned around and pointed his phone at me. But what's *crazy* is the flash blinded me. I didn't know if he had a gun or *what* it was, but I didn't… I didn't hesitate. I opened fire and laid him down."

Pete shook his head. "*Shit*, Devin."

"Yeah, man. But here's the kicker, we ran for about four blocks before I took him down. I mean, you can't make this shit up. I didn't even know we were running that far. It was wild, man. But then, by the time I got back to their house, his girl saw me, but she didn't see him. She looked at me with this smirk on her face and said, 'He got away, didn't he?' I just nodded at her and said, 'Yeah… he got away.'"

"So, were y'all able to get him to the hospital?"

"No, he died on the scene."

"*Shit*."

"Yeah, I just couldn't tell her that ole boy was lying *dead* somewhere. But when she found out, I… I *never* heard a woman scream the way she did—damn near made *me* cry, man. But you know how it is. They trained us not to show emotions. She had every curse word known to man for my ass. There was a whole bunch of black people surrounding the scene. His girl was screaming out, telling everybody that I was the one who shot him. People started calling me an Uncle Tom, a coon, just all the things I didn't want to hear…. I look back at that night saying to myself, 'Damn… all I wanted to do was just go home, man, and be with my wife and my daughter.'"

"How did that make you feel?"

"What? Shooting somebody?"

"Yeah. That whole situation."

Devin sighed. "It fucked me up, man. Just like you. And what made it worse was that we had the same birthday."

"You and the guy you *shot*?"

"Yeah—same year, too."

Pete sighed. "*Jesus*—"

"Yeah, *Jesus*…. I'm *telling* you… every time you think you've seen or done it all on those streets… they slap you in the face with *another* twisted scenario. The streets are the most innovative phenomenon—rooted in pure evil."

"Yeah… well said. It's brutal out there."

"Facts. But of course, all my brothers and sisters are talking in my ear, telling me everything will be all right—asking me, 'You good, bro! You *good*!' But I *wasn't* good… I was hurting. I've been through it all: crazy-ass nightmares, waking up soaking wet, scaring my wife and my daughter… it was the worst. And you know what? It got so bad that one day when I took my daughter to the park, she wanted to play a game. I guess the game was *tag* because she wanted me to chase after her. So, as I chased after her, I started to relive that night when I was chasing after that dude. I started to get angry. It was fucking *crazy*, Pete, like… like I was seeing my *daughter* as a *suspect*."

"*Really?*"

"*Yeah*, man… I'm chased after my own fucking daughter as if *she's* a criminal. And then… by the time I caught up to her… I tackled her to the ground, and I got aggressive with her. I put her arms behind her back like I was arresting her."

"Oh, shit, Devin."

"Bro… I just lost my shit that day. I finally snapped out of it because I realized I didn't have my cuffs on me. My baby girl was *screaming* at the top of her lungs—crying for her mother. I *never felt* so low—*ever* in my life. People were looking at me as if I was some predator or something. I just picked my baby girl up and held her so tight. I must've apologized to her a thousand times that day. When

240

we got home, and I told my wife what happened, she slapped me across the face. But my reflexes were so quick, I... I hit her back—in front of our daughter, and she fell to the floor."

"Damn," Pete softly said.

"Yeah, man... my wife looked at me, and I looked at her. It was like I put this huge wedge between us. She packed her bags, took my daughter, and left... they left me. It felt like my whole life was over. I was all alone... alone with a gun and dark thoughts... and *that's* the price we pay for wearing that badge, Pete. It took me a while before I could shake it off."

"I'm sorry, Devin," Pete said with sympathy.

"Hey... it's real-life shit, broski... *real-life shit*."

"Did you ever make things right with your wife?"

Devin sipped his beer. "Nah... she threatened to file domestic violence charges on me if I didn't agree to a divorce. I was only four months in at that time. I didn't want to get a bad reputation so early in my career. So, I signed the divorce papers, she got full custody of our daughter, the house, *and* the car, and I had to start from scratch."

"Did that make you angry?"

"No... I was devastated. Heartbroken. And what's even more hurtful is that when I *do* get to spend time with my daughter, they're *supervised* visits. I can't really be alone with her. And my daughter gives me this look as if she's afraid of me. Like I'm going to attack her or something, you know? To keep it a buck with you, Pete... there was a moment when I contemplated suicide."

Pete shook his head. "Wow, man."

"Yeah. After that incident in the park, I think it traumatized her. And that's understandable. But I tell ya... who would've thought that being a police officer would ruin your family? But you know what? I can't really say that. Because I love my job. I do love being a cop, Pete."

"Why?"

"Excuse me?"

"Why do you love being a cop?"

Devin was taken aback. "*Hmm*… that's a good question. Haven't really thought about that in a while."

"I mean, you don't have to answer it. I was just continuing the conversation—"

"Oh, nah, nah, I'm glad you asked me that… *really*…. It's just something about… *helping* people. I love to help, Pete. Whether it be someone on the side of the road who needs a helping hand or talking someone down from a building who's ready to jump. Every day when I walk out that door, I'm motivated to save someone's life… I just never thought I would *take* a life."

"Neither did I."

At that moment, Pete deeply reflected. After hearing Devin's testimony, Pete realized his situation was one of many, and every man and woman devoted to that blue uniform had a story to tell.

"Devin," Pete said. "I appreciate you sharing your story with me… But I don't think you *specifically* answered my question."

"Oh, my bad, my guy. Damn, I was just venting, ha. It's therapeutic, you feel me? But go ahead, ask again."

"I asked you if you thought I was a racist for shooting those kids?"

"Oh, right, right… you know… just by sitting here with you and having this conversation… nah—*hell* nah. I don't think you're a racist. It was just an unfortunate situation."

Pete felt relieved. "Thank you. That means a lot coming from you."

"Look, Pete… what happened to that kid… it was tragic. I mean, Tyshawn Brendan was legit. Nobody can deny that. And his ball skills? I've never seen *anything* like it before, man. He would've been a *problem* at that next level."

"That's why it bothers me so much. It's like, 'Why did those bullets have to hit him?'"

"Pete, man… you're asking a question that has no answers."

Pete sighed. "Yeah… it's all just fucked up. But you don't think I'm a racist?"

"*Nah*, man. What I just say?"

"Yeah, I know—I *hear* you, I just… I needed to hear it again…. What *do* you think about racism?"

"What do I *think*?"

"Yeah. About racism?"

"*Shit*… well, I hate to say it, but I don't think it's ever going to cease to exist. No matter how much we try to change this crazy, fucked up world. I think racism will always be here. It will always show its ugly face on the most beautiful day. There will always be this black-and-white shit, man. That's like that whole 'Blue Lives Matter' bullshit. *Fuck* that. Because no matter how long I wear that blue uniform, I'll *always* be a black man in America—*just* like those black people on the streets I be chasing after. I still have to deal with racism, Pete. There's been a couple of times I got pulled over by a white cop, and they give me that look."

"What look?"

Devin made a stern expression. "A look like, 'What you doing out at this time of night, boy? Looking for trouble?' But that look disappears once I showed them my badge. Then I get that bullshit ass smile and they say, 'Oh, why didn't you *tell* me you were a cop?' I think *that* hurts me the most, Pete. They're judging their own brother based on the color of my skin. And *that's* why I say when it comes to racism, ain't shit changed but the weather. I mean, I *hope* things change—for the better… but I don't think its gonna be in *this* lifetime."

Pete sighed. "It sucks, Devin."

"Sure does… but enough about me, man. What's your story?"

"*My* story?"

"Yeah. I've been going on and on, but I hardly know anything about you."

"I… I'm just Pete."

"Just Pete, huh?" Devin smiled. "All right, that's cool—I feel ya."

"Yeah… I'm just Pete."

"I respect that. But listen, I'm going to call it a night, man… it's been real, Broski. Thanks for listening."

Pete shook Devin's hand. "It's been a pleasure, Devin, and thank *you*."

Pete and Devin gave each other a much-needed embrace of love and respect. Devin was kind enough to pick up the tab. Right before he left, he exchanged contact information with Pete. Devin also gave Pete the card of his psychologist, Dr. Mary Dune. Devin mentioned to Pete how Dr. Dune helped rekindle his relationship with himself and his grievance. Pete was grateful and told Devin he would make an appointment. For the first time, even after his career ended, Pete had a chance to reflect—to be vacant and vulnerable. He understood that he was not alone in repenting his actions. He mingled with people in the same boat as him who sailed through the same perils of the same storm. After finishing off his fifth club soda, Pete headed to the restroom to take care of some business he had held in for a while.

After leaving the restroom, he checked his phone to see who called. Claire called him six times, and his mother, Melissa, called twice. Pete's attention, however, was focused on the atrocious threats on social media. As he scrolled, he came across an interesting profile name, "@ClaudiaGianna0421." It took a minute for Pete to connect the dots. But when he did, he was shocked at what he discovered:

@ClaudiaGianna0421

> I don't understand you people. How could you all threaten this man as if it was his fault? The driver represented a threat. It's as clear as day in the video. And how could you people suggest he kill himself? You people are disgusting and ought to be ashamed of yourselves.

@RobinMsDiva120469

> @ClaudiaGianna0421 You People? Who the hell are you calling "You People?" You're just as racist as the fucking cop who shot and killed Tyshawn Brendan. Why don't you and Pete "The Pig" go fuck yourselves? How bout that?

@ClaudiaGianna0421

> @RobinMsDiva120469 I'm not a racist. When I said, "You People," I wasn't referring to, "Black People." I'm referring to people on the internet. I understand why black people are upset. But let's not create this narrative every time there's a police shooting, as if every white cop who is involved in an incident with a black person is automatically a racist. It's not fair.

@RobinMsDiva120469

> @ClaudiaGianna0421Exactly! It's NOT fair. It's not fair that Tyshawn Brendan lost his life for no reason. That cop could've handled that situation differently. That's what cops are trained to do, right? But no, he just wanted to kill him a thug and check it off his bucket list. That's why CK took a knee, to protest against these racist ass cops like Pete "The Pig" Gant. He's a piece of shit, and his kids are pieces of shit. He should take that same gun he used to kill Tyshawn Brendan and blow his fucking brains out. It's that simple, sweetie.

@ClaudiaGianna0421

> @RobinMsDiva120469 No! It's not that simple. Because that cop is MY HUSBAND, bitch!

Pete was mortified at the unbelievable discovery. At first, when he looked at the profile name, "*@ClaudiaGianna0421*," he did not think anything of it. But as he read between the lines, it became clear: Claire's *mother's* name was Claudia. Gianna was Claire's *middle* name, and "0421" was her birthday: April 21st. After the constant nagging and lectures of telling Pete to stay off the internet, he was appalled that Claire had been going behind his back and interacting with people on social media. Pete stormed out of the bar and headed to his car as he could not wait to get home.

33

A WORRIED WIFE

It was late in the evening. Claire was in the kitchen drinking green tea with a taste of honey, wondering where Pete was. She sat in the dim kitchen as she waited for Michael's return with Brownie. As Claire looked at the lock screen of her phone to check the time, she smiled at her wedding photo, saved as her screen saver. At that moment, Claire began to reminisce about her wedding day. Claire remembered when she walked down the aisle—escorted by her father. She could not take her eyes off Pete. She was deeply in love with him. No man she had ever met pulled her in like he did.

Claire chuckled as she looked at the wedding photo, picturing that moment vividly in her mind. At their wedding, when Claire and Pete took the picture, Claire suddenly smelt a vile odor. She had an inkling of what it was and whispered in Pete's ear, "Did you just *fart*?" Pete looked at her and responded, "It slipped out." "*Jesus,* Pete," Claire gagged. Pete scoffed and humorously responded, "Get used to it. You're gonna be smelling my 'Silent but *deadly'* bottom burps for life now." Claire burst into laughter, as did Pete, and their Colgate smiles are what their beautiful picture came out to be. She loved and cherished that memory. As she continued to wait in the kitchen, Claire poured herself another cup of green tea. She sipped and sipped as she stared out the window into the midnight hour—existing in silence. Suddenly, the front door opened. Claire stood up in hopes that it was Pete. But it was Michael, along with Brownie.

"Hey," Claire said.

"Hey," Michael responded as he unhooked Brownie's leash.

"No luck, huh?"

"Nope... I didn't see him."

"Oh, God. Where can he *be*?"

"Don't worry about it, Mom."

"No, honey, I *am* worried. I've called your grandpa, and he hasn't heard from him. He told me about this meeting or something. I should call him again."

"Maybe he just went for a walk. Clear his head, you know?"

"For *three hours*?"

"He's probably got a lot on his mind, Mom... you know? I have to be honest... I miss him. Dad used to be so cool and fun to be around... I remember when we were little kids, he always made time for us. No matter what he was doing or how tired he felt after a long workday, he would stop whatever he was doing and come outside and play with us."

"I remember... you guys would always play freeze tag, right?"

"Yeah... only we wouldn't call it '*Freeze*' tag because he hated hearing that word. But I used to love tagging him because he would freeze and not move an inch. He was like a freezing mime or a statue. We had so much fun... we *used* to, at least."

"Michael... your father's been through a lot, sweetheart. His job exposed him to a lot of horrific situations. Things that we wouldn't even imagine. And with this shooting... it's affected him deeply."

"And that's just it, Mom. It affects us too—and *you*."

"Yeah... it has."

248

"And that's what scares me. I'm afraid that I won't get my dad back. I don't know this new guy. I hate to say this, but... he feels like a stranger when he walks past me. It's like nobody's home."

"Oh, honey," Claire said as she caressed Michael's face. "Your father loves you very much. He loves *all* of us. And we love him. We just have to do our best to make him *feel* that... okay?"

"I'll try, Mom... I'll try."

"That's all I can ask from you guys. Everything's going to be all right."

"Okay, Mom," Michael said as he hugged and kissed Claire.

"It's getting late. Why don't you head on up to bed? I'll wait up for your father."

"All right. I love you, Mom."

"I love you, too, sweetie."

Claire watched Michael head upstairs. She returned to the kitchen table, grabbed her "World's Best Mom" mug, and poured the lukewarm tea down the sink. She looked out the window as the hot water ran—steam rising in front of her face as she looked up at the pale crescent moon. She stared and daydreamed—thinking about their honeymoon, a ten-day cruise to Hawaii. It was a surprise honeymoon—a wedding gift from Montgomery.

On the first night at sea, Pete and Claire stood on the balcony—holding each other as they stared at the moon—listening to the natural sounds of the Pacific Ocean. Claire wanted that moment to last forever, as did Pete. More importantly, she wanted their marriage to last a lifetime. But the one thing that scared her to death was the possibility that it would *not* last a lifetime and be tragically cut short by a bullet. From that night on, whenever Claire was scared or could not sleep, she would look out the window for the pale moon. Every time she found it, she would think of that night on the cruise and recite what she called *The Blue Line Poem*:

Baby... you're the only man who could arrest my heart.
If loving you was a crime, I plead my guilt and pray that

our love will serve a life sentence—imprisoned in the cage of our ribs. May our enchanted bond never be paroled.

34

DECEMBER 28th, 2025, EARLY SUNDAY EVENING:

THE ARGUMENT

It was the wee small hours of the morning. Claire was asleep on the couch as well as Brownie—asleep near the fireplace as it illuminated his brown fur. Suddenly, Claire was ripped from her sleep at the sound of Pete stumbling in.

"Where have you been?" Claire said as she walked toward him. "I was losing my fucking *mind*! I didn't know where you… you're *drunk*."

Claire smelled the alcohol on Pete's breath. It was so strong she covered her nose—blocking the stench.

"Is *that* where you've been all this time? At a bar *drinking*?"

Pete looked at Claire with his glassy eyes. "Hypocrite."

"What?"

"You're a *fucking* hypocrite—"

"Don't *curse* at me."

"You told me to stay off the internet, right? Look what I found, Claire."

Pete showed Claire the screenshot of *ClaudiaGianna0421*. She looked at his phone in silence.

"Pete," said Claire. "I'm sorry."

Pete scoffed. "Unbelieve."

"I'm sorry, I just had to see what people were saying. I got caught up and... I couldn't just sit there and let people say all those terrible things about our family. I'll delete the profile."

"You should've never been on it in the *first* place, Claire."

"Look, I'm *sorry*... I'm just trying to keep you in one piece."

"Keep me in one *piece*?"

"Yes."

"When are you going to get it, Claire? Huh? When will you understand that I will *never be* in one *piece*? When I shot that kid, and he died... a piece of me *died with him*. I'm *never* going to be in one piece again."

Claire grew emotional. "Why would you say that? I love you, Pete. I'm sorry that all of this has happened to you. I'm sorry what happened to Tyshawn Brendan... but you can't neglect *us*. You can't neglect your *family*—*we* need you—*I* need you—"

"*I KILLED HIM*!" Pete Shouted and cried. "I *killed* that kid... he's *dead*! He's dead... and it's my fault—it's *my* fault. I can *never* make things right with his family. *Jesus*... people think that being a cop is all about putting on a fucking uniform and having a badge and that *goddamn* gun. But they don't know *shit* when you have to use that gun on somebody and have to *live* with that for the rest of your *life*."

"And you don't think *I* have to live with that? Is *that* what it is? You think I don't have to live with Tyshawn Brendan for the rest of *my* life? That I don't have to take in that pain *every* single *day*? When I look into your eyes and see that pain, *I* take it in—*I* hold you close. *All these years*, *all* the tears—*all* the fear... I took it in with you. You are *not* going through this *alone*. I've been there with you every step of the way, and you *know* it. Every day when you put on that *fucking* uniform, and I see you walk out that door—*knowing* that I may never see your beautiful smile ever *again*! You didn't think that scared the living *shit* out of *me*? Or the *kids*? You didn't think there were days when you didn't answer my calls or texts, that I wasn't *terrified* that something happened to you? Every day—*every fucking day*... I had to go through that. And so did our kids.... It was *hell*, Pete... *hell*."

Pete shrugged his arms. "And here we are. I'm jobless, pension-less, and I have no way to support my family... and everyone hates me."

"We don't hate you... we love you... we *love* you, Pete. Why can't you snap out of this? You're home. You're with your family, and we *love you*."

"But *I* don't love me. I hate myself for what I've done. Tyshawn Brendan was going to the promised land, and I robbed him of *everything*... I'm a terrible man."

"Oh, Pete—"

"I have to leave."

Pete made his way to the door. Claire ran in front of it. "NO! You're not going *anywhere*!"

"Claire, I have to get *outta* here!"

"No, stay here and just *talk* to me—"

"Claire, *move*!"

"No!"

"*STOP*!" Elle screamed from the top of the stairs.

Pete and Claire looked up at Elle, who sobbed as Michael and Leo stood beside her. "Kids," Claire said as she made her way up the stairs. "It's okay. Daddy and I were just a little upset. But we weren't fighting. You can go back to your rooms, okay? Me and Daddy love you guys. We're sorry for yelling." Michael stormed into his room and slammed the door. Claire comforted Elle and Leo as they stood there, holding each other as they cried.

All Pete could do was stand there alone in drunken misery. He walked away from the door and headed down to the basement. As he sat on the couch, he took out his phone and scrolled through YouTube videos. Multiple thumbnails showed his picture, and one by one, he watched them. It was as if the algorithm was in on it—an artificial accomplice that compelled Pete to watch every video that dehumanized him. Pete had become enslaved to public opinions to the point where he believed the discrepancies about him.

Pete started to believe that he *was* a racist pig who hated black people. The more he scrolled up the cracked glass screen of his phone, the more caps he twisted off the glass bottles—letting the foreign alcohol invade his body and abduct the pain. It did not take long for him to fall asleep, nor did it take long for him to wake up in a cold sweat after having another nightmare. Pete was afraid—fearful that this nightmare was never going to end. But the saddest thing was that he believed what the alcohol was telling him. It was as if the alcohol had a sincere voice that manipulated his conscience, and that voice said:

"I'm the only friend you got, buddy. I'll protect you. All you have to do is invite me inside… that's it. I'll take over, and all your worries will go away. Just let me in, Pal. Untwist that cap, and I'll take all the pain away, my friend… just let me in, Pete. I love you."

35

DECEMBER 28[th,] 2025, SUNDAY AFTERNOON:

ONE BAD DAY

It was a quiet ride as Pete and Leo headed to the supermarket to grab some things for dinner. Even though Pete had a hangover from last night, he wanted to spend some quality time with Leo. As Leo sat in the backseat, playing with his Nintendo Switch, Pete began to talk with him.

"What game are you playing?" Pete asked

"Mario," Leo said as his eyes were glued to the screen.

"Is it Mario Kart or... *Super* Mario?"

"Mario Kart."

"Oh okay."

Leo then lifted his head from the game. "Daddy?"

"Yeah, buddy?"

"Can we have that Oreo cookie pie for dessert tonight?"

"We—we'll see, buddy. If they have it at the store."

"Yes!" Leo said with excitement.

"But that's *if* they have it. I don't know if they do."

"Okay... Daddy?"

"Yeah?"

"Were you drinking last night?"

Pete glanced at Leo in the rearview mirror. "Uh... yeah, buddy. Daddy had a few drinks last night. Maybe a few more than I *should* have. But that won't happen again. I'm sorry you guys had to see that."

"You're just upset, right? Because you killed the basketball star?"

"Yes... I'm upset about that. You're right, Leo. And I'm doing my best to cope with it. And do you know what will help me?"

"What?"

"Loving me... just keep loving me, Leo, and I'll be fine... can you keep loving me, bud?"

"Yes, Daddy... I still love you."

An honest smile began to grow on Pete's face. "Thanks, buddy. I needed to hear that... and I love you, too."

To hear Leo say, "I still love you," was the feeling of ice glaciers melting off Pete's lungs, allowing him to breathe again. Pete kept a smile on his face all the way to the supermarket. But that smile was soon to be destroyed.

In the supermarket, Pete was pushing the cart filled with food. Leo was by his side, fully engaged with his Nintendo Switch. As Pete walked down the frozen food aisle, a young black woman began to stare at him. It was a stare as if she knew who he was, but she could not yet put her finger on it. Pete glanced at the woman, who wore a green puffy coat, black leggings, and nineties-styled black leather boots. She had box braids wrapped in a bun and thick, orange-framed glasses.

As Pete opened the freezer door, he saw the reflection of the woman staring at him with her piercing eyes. Pete had a horrific feeling about this woman. Being a police officer for many years, he knew when trouble was near. "Leo... stay close to me, son," Pete said as he gently pulled Leo close. Pete grabbed the Oreo cookie pie from the freezer and swiftly moved to the next aisle. As he turned the corner, he took a breather.

"Leo," he said. "I'm going to need you to stay close to me, okay?"

"Daddy, are you okay—"

"I'm okay, just… just stay close to me. Give me your hand."

Pete held Leo's hand as they walked down the aisle. Suddenly, as he turned and looked, he saw the same woman. "*Fuck me!*" Pete said in his mind. He immediately took the cart and went straight to the checkout line. Every time he looked behind him, the woman was getting closer. The closer she got, the faster his heart raced. But then, Leo let go of Pete's hand as he saw Oreo had their limited-edition strawberry cheesecake cookie.

"Leo, where you going?" Pete said.

"Daddy, they have new Oreos—"

"No, no, no. You have Oreos at home."

"But Daddy—"

"I said '*No.*' Come on."

Leo placed the cookies back on the shelf and moped back over to Pete. But as Pete looked around, the woman was nowhere in sight. He blew out a sigh of relief—thinking she was gone. But then… a voice projected from behind.

"Pete "The Pig" Gant!" The woman shouted as she held up her phone, recording. "You're Pete "The Pig," Gant, right? That cop who shot and killed Tyshawn Brendan?"

Pete stood there in shock. "Ma'am—"

"Don't '*Ma'am*' me, motherfucka! You killed Tyshawn Brendan!"

"No—I—I—don't know what you're talking about—"

"What you *mean* you don't know what I'm talking about? Don't give me that bullshit, you racist ass cracka!"

"Ma'am, I have my son with me. *Please.*"

"I don't give a *fuck*! You didn't care about those parents whose sons you *shot*?"

"Miss, *please*—"

"Everybody! This is the cop who shot and killed Tyshawn Brendan!"

All eyes were on Pete as the formidable woman created a daunting spotlight on him. Pete felt like he was going to shit on himself. He could not move an inch. It was as if he became a statue of guilt and shame, and the whole world stared at him. But as he looked down and saw the fear in Leo's eyes, *Pete's* fear turned into anger. He snapped out of it and took Leo's hand—leaving the shopping cart behind at the register. The woman, however, followed behind them with the camera still rolling.

"Oh, don't you *walk* away from *me*, pig!" The woman shouted. "Everybody, *this* is the cop who killed Tyshawn Brendan! Yeah, this is going *all over* social media!"

"Stop following me," Pete said as they hurried to the car.

"Oh, no, I'm *following* you all the way to your car!"

"Ma'am, *please*—"

"YOU SHOT CORNBREAD! YOU! SHOT! *CORNBREAD*!"

Pete and Leo speed walk out of the supermarket. "Listen, lady, stop *following* me! You're scaring my son!"

"I don't *give* a fuck! I'm sick and tired of you white motherfucking cops killing us and getting away with it. You're a *fucking* disgrace to humanity. You hear me? A *fucking* disgrace—"

"GET THE FUCK AWAY FROM ME!"

"Oh, *oh*! I got that *all on camera*. And it's going right on YouTube—right now! You see that, everybody? You see that? Yeah. Yeah, he *wanted* to kill those boys. Look at that anger in his eyes."

Pete puts Leo in the car. "*Shame* on you."

"Shame on *me*? No, shame on you—shame on *you*! *You* killed that boy. And now the world is going to *see* your true colors. You're a *fucking* racist, just like the rest of those pigs. I hope you burn in hell—*fuck* you!"

258

It happened once again; Pete was triggered. The two-word insult took Pete back to that tragic night when Tyshawn Brendan said those exact words to him. Pete felt like he was going to collapse. The woman kept the camera rolling—taunting him as he leaned against the Jeep. "Aw, look at him, everybody. Now he wants to *cry*... you fucking coward—"

"Hey!" A police officer shouted. "What's going on here?"

"Nothin'—I ain't doin' *nothin'*," The woman said as she kept her phone rolling.

"Don't *look* like nothing. Why are you shouting? What's the problem?"

"I *said*, 'Nothing.'"

The officer looked at Pete. "Sir... is this woman bothering you?"

With his head pressed against his forearms, Pete took a breath and spoke. "Officer... I'm just trying to take my kid home. I don't know this woman."

"This is the cop who shot Tyshawn Brendan," the woman said. "And he's not even sorry. But I'll leave, no problem."

"No, you stay right there," the officer pointed. "Don't you move."

The officer looked at Pete with immediate sympathy. As he walked over to Pete, he touched his shoulder and talked to him.

"Brother... you okay?"

"I just wanna go home... I don't know her. She just started screaming at me and... I want to leave. My kid's in the car... I just want to take him home."

The officer sighed. "Get out of here... I'll take care of it."

As the officer walked away with the woman, Pete took a minute to regain his breath—leaning against the Jeep. He lifted his head and looked at the gloomy clouds and thought, "Jesus... when will this end?" Pete got into the car and saw Leo crying in the backseat.

"Leo, it's okay, buddy, don't cry... it's over. That was just an angry lady."

Leo wiped his eyes. "But *why*? Why was she mad at you, Daddy?"

"Leo… it's complicated for me to explain all of this to you…. When you get older, we'll sit down and have a conversation. But not today… daddy's sorry, bud. We're going straight home, okay?"

Leo sniffled and wiped his nose. "Okay."

Pete sat there for a minute to process what had just happened. He felt like the whole world was against him. With the woman recording everything and his outburst, he knew that the world would believe in the false narrative of who he was, which would lead him to true tribulation.

Twenty minutes later, Pete pulled into his driveway. Sitting there, he thought about how he was going to explain everything to Claire. But he had not a clue.

"Daddy?" Leo spoke. "Who's Cornbread?"

"What?" Pete asked.

"That lady said you shot Cornbread. Who's Cornbread?"

"I don't know, bud. But listen, what happened in the supermarket? Don't tell Mommy, okay? *I'll* tell her."

"Okay."

"All right. Let's go inside."

Just as Pete slid the key in, the door quickly opened. Claire stood there enraged. She picked Leo up and slammed the door on Pete's face. It took Pete a second to realize that not only had the video been uploaded to the internet, but it had also gone viral, making Pete look like the aggressor. As Pete entered the house, he saw Claire sitting on the couch—holding Leo with Elle beside them. Elle looked as if she had been crying for hours.

"Elle?" Pete said. "What's wrong?"

"What do you *think* is wrong?" Claire retorted.

Pete looked at them. "I don't know—*tell* me."

"There's a video of you screaming at some woman all over the internet, Pete."

Pete sighed in disgust. "Oh, God."

"*Why* couldn't you just walk away and keep your mouth *shut*?"

"I *tried*, Claire. All right? I *tried* to walk away. But she *kept nagging* me, and I had Leo, and—"

"Do you know what this is going to do? Huh?"

"Look, it's nothing for you and the kids to worry about. Just let it go."

"Let it *go*?" Claire said as she stood up. "Let it go? There *is* no 'Letting it go,' Pete! She caught it all on camera. It makes *you* look like you didn't have a care in the world about Tyshawn Brendan. And the way you just *snapped* at her? I couldn't *believe* that was my husband."

"Wait a minute… you sound like you're taking *her* side on this."

"Taking *her* side? How dare you? You think I'm taking her side—"

"That's what it sounds like, yes!"

"*Shame* on you, Pete—"

"DON'T SAY THAT TO ME!" Pete shouted as he threw a clear vase across the room.

"Aaahh!" Claire screamed.

"Don't ever say that to me *again*! That's all I hear—people saying to me, 'Oh, you should be ashamed of yourself. *Shame* on you, Pete! *Shame* on you!' I fucked up—*I know* I did! But the last thing I want to come home to is my own *fucking* family telling *me* that I should be *ashamed* of myself. You have *no* fucking idea what it's like to be a *cop*! *NONE*!"

Suddenly, the sounds of footsteps quickly stormed down the stairs. It was Michael, holding a baseball bat with a piercing look in his eyes. Pete looked at Michael, who had every intention of using the bat.

"What you plan on doing with that bat, son?" Pete asked in a heartbreaking tone of voice.

"I'm gonna swing it across your *fucking* face if you don't leave!"

"Don't you *dare* talk to your father with that tone! Show me some respect!"

"You're *not* my father. My father's a good man—who loved his family and never brought work home. My father would *always* make time for his family… I lost my father years ago. I don't know who the *fuck* you are."

Claire grew emotional. "Michael… baby, put the bat down. Please?"

"Yes, son," Pete added. "Put the bat down and calm yourself."

"No," Michael cried. "Don't come any closer."

"Son… I'm your father—"

"You're not my *fucking father*—"

"Do *not* use that *tone* with me!"

"STAY BACK!"

"So, what? You're going to hit me, son? Huh? That's what you're going to do? Well, go ahead! Hit me! Better yet, maybe I should get my gun. That way, you *all* can shoot me! *Everybody* can shoot me! How about that? Is that what you want? To shoot me? To see me *dead*? How bout it, son? Fuck the bat, I'll put the gun right in your hand, you put it *right* to my forehead and *pull* the *fucking trigger*… and it'll all be over. What do you say?"

"You're an asshole, man… I hate you."

"*Wow*…" Pete said as he looked at Claire with a tear rolling down his cheek. "My firstborn hates me. At least I know where you stand now. That's too bad because I *love* you. Since the day you were born… til the day I die… I'm *never* going to stop loving you."

"Just get the fuck out!"

"This is my house, son. Show your father some *goddamn* respect!"

"You want some respect? Here it is!"

SWING… and a miss, but Michael kept swinging. Claire and Elle were hysterically screaming at the top of their lungs, begging

Michael to stop. But Michael took another swing. BOOM! He made contact—hitting Pete in his left arm. Michael took another swing, but Pete grabbed the bat from him and tackled him onto the coffee table. BOOM! The coffee table was destroyed. Pete, however, was having a mental meltdown.

"Get the *fuck* off me!" Michael shouted as Pete had him pinned to the floor.

"Pete, *stop*!" Claire cried. "Get off of him!"

Suddenly, Pete turned Michael over on his stomach and said the most deranged thing. "You have the right to remain silent! Anything you say will be used against you in the court of law. You have the right to an attorn...." Pete froze as he was in complete shock. The room went silent. He looked down and saw that he had Michael's hands behind his back as if he was ready to cuff him. That blue DNA of law enforcement was still coursing rapidly through Pete's veins—so much that Pete forgot he had his blood and flesh pinned to the floor as if he was making an arrest. "Get off me, man!" Michael cried. Pete slowly got off Michael as he looked down at him on the floor.

"I'm so sorry," Pete cried. "Come here, baby... let daddy help you up."

Michael, with blood in his mouth, responded. "*FUCK* YOU!"

"AAAHHHHHHH!" Pete screamed.

Pete suddenly had haunting déjà vu. As he saw Michael lying on the floor, an identical flashback of Tyshawn Brendan lying on the street came to his mind. Pete immediately picked up Michael's bat and began swinging—hitting everything in sight. BOOM! BAM! POW! Smashing holes in the wall, knocking over the plants, and breaking the framed pictures. It was like Pete unleashed all the rage he had built up inside of him for all those years on the force—seeing flashbacks of every case, all the bodies, the pain, the fear, *everything* was coming out, even the devil.

Claire and the kids were terrified as they ran into the kitchen. Brownie was in the backyard, barking as if he knew the family was in shambles. Suddenly, with the bat high in the air—in Pete's firm grip, he stopped swinging and dropped the bat. It was like Pete had come to—awakening from a paranoid psychosis. He looked around, painfully observing the damage he caused. The entire living room was wrecked. The broken glass scattered on the floor like a blanket of forbidden art.

Pete slowly fell to his knees. His mouth was wide open, but no sound was coming through. He began to sob like a boy wanting his Daddy. He looked over and saw his family standing there in fear of him. Pete made gestures with his hands as if he was surrendering—begging for repentance. "I'm sorry," he sobbed. "I'm sorry, I'm sorry, I'm *sorry*… I didn't mean to scare you. I'm *so sorry*… Michael, I'm sorry, baby. Please… I'm so sorry. I'll go. I'll go, okay? I'll leave. I'm so sorry. I—I'll leave."

Pete got up and walked right out of the house. He hopped in the Jeep, drove off, and did not stop until he reached his father's house. He did not realize that his hands were bleeding until he saw the blood on the steering wheel.

Ten minutes later, Pete reached the front of his father's house and slowly approached the front door. He knocked—leaving small blood trails on the white door. The door opened, Pete saw his father and immediately burst into tears. Montgomery was so overwhelmed that *he* began to cry. All Montgomery could get out through the chaos of emotions was, "Oh, *my boy*… what happened? Huh? You're okay, Pete… you're going to be okay. Dad's got you… your father's got you."

36

DECEMBER 29th, 2025, MONDAY MORNING:

A MOTHER'S LOVE

It was 6:47 in the morning and the early birds were beginning to chirp. Pete had just woken up in one of the guest rooms of his parent's house. As he looked over at the nightstand, he grabbed his phone, hoping that Claire or one of the kids had reached out. But all he saw was his wedding photo—no text, no phone calls. That is when he called Claire, hoping that she would answer. But that hope faded as the dial kept ringing. Pete, however, left a voicemail:

Claire… good morning…. Um… about last night… I… that wasn't me. I don't know what got into me. I'm just really *losing* it. But *by God*, I would *never* do anything to hurt you or those kids. I would *never* do anything to hurt Michael. That's my son… my boy, and I love him. I love Elle, and Leo, and you. Please forgive me, okay? I'm at my parents' house. But I'll be home later this afternoon. And when I get home, we'll sit down and get this straight. I love my family, and we have to stay together and survive this. Just… just please… find it in your heart to forgive me. I love you, Claire… I'll see you soon.

Pete ended the voicemail and placed his phone back on the nightstand. As he opened the bedroom door, he saw something unexpected on the floor. It was his childhood teddy bear wearing a police uniform and a Superman cape—the same cape he wore as a kid. Pete picked it up and wiped the dust off. He had not seen the teddy bear in years. A smile slowly grew on his face as he remembered where it came from. His grandmother bought it for him while walking past a toy store. Pete saw it in the window display and begged his grandmother for it. The bear had everything: a badge, a hat, a baton, and the most important thing, a smile. Pete was so happy when he had the bear in his hands. He called it Captain Furry.

Pete then tossed Captain Furry onto the bed and headed to the bathroom. After he finished there, he headed downstairs and into the kitchen. By surprise, he saw his mother, Melissa.

"Mom?" Pete said.

"Good morning, Petey," said Melissa.

"What are you doing up so early?"

"Couldn't sleep. Just came down to get some coffee. You want?"

"No thanks… well, maybe I will."

"Sit down. I'll pour you a cup."

Pete walked over and took a seat at the booth. Melissa poured the black coffee into the cup.

"You want any milk or sugar?" Melissa asked.

Pete shook his head. "No. Black is fine."

"*Black* coffee?" Melissa said with a twisted face. "I don't know how you do it. I could never drink black coffee."

"You get used to it."

"*I* couldn't. Your grandmother would drink black coffee. No milk, no sugar, not even a sweetener. Just straight black. I'd rather die."

Pete grin. "Where's Dad?"

"He went to go pick up your grandfather. He's bringing him over here."

"What for?"

"Just for a visit, he told me."

266

"That's just what I need," Pete unenthusiastically said as he sipped his coffee.

"Your father told me about what happened yesterday."

"Yeah… it was just a very bad day."

"Did you talk to Claire?"

"I called… but she didn't answer. So, I left her a message."

"Petey… Claire loves you. Your children love you. And I know you love them. That's never going to change."

"I don't know, Mom. I don't know what came over me last night. It was like I went completely out of my skull. I broke furniture and tables—the whole living room's a wreck. I don't know how I can even face them."

"Would you like for me to come with you?"

"No. That's okay. I'm going to get myself together and head back home."

"Okay, honey."

"Mom… did you put that in front of the door?"

"Put what, dear?"

"You know, my old teddy bear with the cop uniform? It had my Superman cape tied to it?"

"Oh… no, I didn't do that. Maybe that was your father."

"Are you sure? Because when I came out of the bedroom, it was on the floor."

"No, that wasn't me. Who gave you that bear again?"

"Grandma Beverly. She got it for me when we walked by the toy store."

"Oh, right," Melissa chuckled. "I remember you coming home with it. What did you call him? Captain Fluffy?"

"Pete shook his head. "*Furry*, Mom… Captain Furry"

"Right, ha… you loved him to death. I remember you taking him out in the backyard and playing cops with him. You would salute him. I thought it was so cute."

"Hmm… that's when it all started, Mom. That's when I knew I was going to be a cop. That's when I knew I would make a huge difference…. It's *so strange… life*, I mean. It's strange because when I was a kid, I truly believed that I would *change the world* and save as many lives as I possibly could. But *I've* been changed by the world… and I'm doing everything in my soul to save myself."

"Oh, Pete," Melissa said as she took his hand. "Baby, you *have* made a difference. You put your life on the line for *sixteen years*—protecting your community. You gave it *everything* you had. I'm sorry that it was cut short for you. But you were not a bad cop. And you're *not* a bad man. And don't you go around believing that you are. That is *not* who I raised."

Pete placed his mother's hand on his face. "That means a lot to me, Mom… thank you."

"No, sweetheart… I thank *you* for your service."

Pete stood up from the booth and kissed his mother. He appreciated what she told him, and it put his mind at ease. Unfortunately, that ease would soon be triggered by *dis*-ease.

The clock hit noon and Pete was ready to return home to his family. That was until his father and grandfather came inside the house. As Pete sat outside in the backyard, his grandfather, Poppa Dee, joined him. "*Hey*… there he is," Poppa Dee smiled. Pete, however, was not interested in speaking with him.

"Poppa Dee," he said as he stood from the lounge chair. "I was just leaving."

"Leaving, huh?"

Pete nodded his head. "Yes, I'm going home."

"Eh, what's your hurry? Don't want to talk to the old man?"

"We can talk later, Poppa Dee."

"We can talk *now, too*."

Pete sighed. "Where's my father?"

"He's taking a shit, sit down."

Pete went and sat back down in the lawn chair. Poppa Dee was a standing kind of man. He always liked to stand up while talking, which gave his presence more power. As he lit his cigar, he began to converse with Pete.

"A *lot's* been happening, I see," he said. "I've been reading the papers. The *nerve* of those bastards saying those horrific things about *my* grandson. You did what you had to do, Pete. You know that, right?"

"Poppa Dee... I really don't want to talk about that."

Poppa Dee took a drag. "Okay... we won't talk about it then."

Poppa Dee had this mischievous grin on his wrinkled face. Pete, however, could not bear the sight of it. As Poppa Dee relit his cigar, he took a panoramic look at the beautiful landscape of the backyard.

"They're beautiful, aren't they?" Poppa Dee smiled.

Pete looked around. "What?"

"The *trees*... aren't they beautiful?"

"I guess—whatever."

"I love trees... there's just something about em'. How the wind just *blows the leaves*—from one direction... to another. The *magic* of mother nature.... But you know... *these* trees? They're missing something. You know what they're missing, Pete?"

Pete, now irritated. "I don't know, Poppa Dee... *fruit?*"

"*EXACTLY!*" Poppa Dee optimistically said. "*STRANGE* FRUIT! I always knew you were smart."

"What the hell is strange fruit?"

"You've never heard of strange fruit?"

"No."

Poppa Dee looked around and made sure the coast was clear. "I have a story for you, son... a *true* story. A story I've never shared with anyone in our family. Not even your father."

"What are you talking about?"

"*Years* ago, when I was a green fourteen-year-old living in the great state of Georgia, my old man woke me up one evening and told me to get dressed. He wanted to take me somewhere… *special*. I was so excited. I kept asking, 'Where we going, Pa?' And he would keep on saying, 'Somewhere special.' *I* thought he was going to take me to that secret brothel a few miles down the road. I was a *horny* little bastard—couldn't *wait* to get laid. But we went to no such place... we went somewhere even better. As we drove, I saw a whole crowd of people… *our* people. I didn't know *what* the hell was going on. All I saw were people flocking around these… *trees*… I didn't know *why*… until I looked up and saw something I never would've imagined. I saw… *strange fruit*… *hanging* from the trees."

Pete, now confused. "What the *hell* are you talking about? What is this '*Strange* fruit?'"

Poppa Dee turned and smiled. "The *blacks*… the *blacks* are strange fruit, son. I saw three of them hanging from the trees. At first, I was in shock. I never saw dead bodies just hanging like that. Two of them were men, and the other was a woman—a *pregnant* woman. I remember it *vividly*. I was staring at them, watching them *swing around* with their eyes bulging out—looking like those cartoons—seeing blood dripping from their toes. It was a work of art, really… *all* these people were *smiling* and *pointing* at them. It was as if they were *all*... *happy*. And I wanted to be happy, too."

Pete stared at Poppa Dee with a stern look. "What the fuck?"

"I remember my father placing his hands on my shoulders from behind me… and whispered *this* into my ear… '*You see these apples hanging from that there tree? That'll never be you. That'll never be one of us. We are the elite race of people, my boy. And these tree monkeys are at the bottom of humanity. Don't ever forget that.*'

Pete was enraged—appalled and embarrassed to be in Poppa Dee's presence. He then got up from the lawn chair and headed towards the house.

"You must think I'm a racist," Poppa Dee said from behind. "I'm not a racist… I just always knew my place—from that point on. That's what *my* father taught *me*—to *never forget* my place in this world. And I share that with you, son. So, before you start shedding any more tears for these uppity *blacks*… don't forget who the *fuck you are… don't* forget your place."

Pete turned and looked in disgust. "You're a *sick man*."

"What did you call me—"

"You heard me, you're *fucking sick*. I don't know *why* you would tell me that *despicable* story… I always knew you were a bigot. I'm mortified to call you my grandfather."

"Now, you just hold on a minute there, boy. Remember who the *fuck* you're *talking* to. *I'm* trying to *teach* you something worthwhile, and *this* is how you treat me?"

"Teach me *what*? How to be a racist like *you*? You think you're better than people who don't look like you—"

"*You goddamn right*! Our forefathers paved the way for us. They showed us who *we* are. But *you*? You actually *care* about these… *animals*? Be my guest, son. What do I know, right? I'm just an eighty-three-year-old fart. My opinions don't matter…. But I'll tell you this, boy… before you look down on *me*, you just remember one thing… I didn't decorate that tree with those *black rotting ornaments*. And I didn't kill that black boy… *you* did."

Pete shook his head. "And I have to live with that for the rest of my life. And you know what? Your sick ass story *did* teach me something. I learned that whenever you think you've seen and heard it all… life always has another fucked up lesson to teach you… the poison never ends."

Pete had enough of Poppa Dee and headed towards the back door. Just as he opened the door, Poppa Dee shouted, "*Pete*! You did the world a favor, son. One less jigaboo we need to be *worried* about.

And on top of *that*, you'll never do a day in prison. *GOD FUCKING BLESS AMERICA*! *You* are my *goddamn* hero, Pete Gant. And *I* salute you." Poppa Dee stood there as he raised his wrinkled hand and saluted Pete. Pete, however, could not believe his eyes or ears. "Stay the *fuck* away from me *and* my family," Pete said.

Just as Pete walked into the house, Montgomery came outside.

"What the hell's going on out here?" Montgomery said. "What's all the commotion?"

Pete looked at Poppa Dee. "I'm disowning this racist bastard, *that's* what."

"You can't disown me—*I'm* the head of this family! And I'll be sure to take your name out my will, you ungrateful son of a *bitch*."

"*Hey!*" Montgomery shouted. "You *don't* disrespect Melissa, Pop!"

"No, it's okay, Dad," Pete said. "He said what he had to say… and I have nothing more to say to him… I'm done."

"He's your grandfather, Pete—for *Jesus'* sake."

"*Was*… why don't you tell my father what you just told me?"

"Pete… what are you talking about—"

"I'm done, Dad… I'm done."

As Pete walked into the house, Montgomery looked over at Poppa Dee as he had questions. "What did you say to him, Pop?" Montgomery asked. As he held onto his left arm, Poppa Dee responded, "Pete's under a lot of stress, Monty—and delusion. I tried to talk some sense into him, but it's not his fault… he needs some counseling. Talk to him, Monty. He's *your* son." Montgomery became skeptical of what his father was saying and began to push the envelope further.

"Pop… this has nothing to do with what you saw as a *kid*, does it?"

"A *kid*? Saw what? What you taking bout—"

"You know *exactly* what I'm talking about. The public lynching?"

Poppa Dee was stunned. "You know about that?"

"Yes… what? You thought I *didn't*? Grandpa Thomas told me the whole story. He *told* me that story when I was eleven years old. He told me he took you somewhere 'special,' and you saw those black people hanging from the trees. He *told* me the whole *sick* fucking story. He tried to brainwash me and put that Jim Crow shit into me and Freddy. But *I* refused. I wasn't going to pass that bullshit along to *my* sons. I made *sure* that I broke that cycle... Pop? Pop, what's wrong?"

Suddenly, Poppa Dee grabbed his left shoulder. "I... I can't breathe," Poppa Dee said as he descended to his knees. Montgomery grabbed him and called for Melissa and Pete, but no one was in the house. "Help! Help!" Montgomery screamed. But help was nowhere in sight, and Montgomery was all alone as he watched his father's final breaths.

37

DECEMBER 29^{th,} 2025, MONDAY AFTERNOON:

<u>POLICE WIVES</u>

On the other side of town, Claire was in front of her friend's house, Sarah McCauley. Claire and Sarah have known each other for over ten years. They met through Sarah's husband, Clayton McCauley, who was also a police officer.

Claire stepped to the cherry red door and rang the bell. Hanging on the door was a Christmas wreath with the fresh pine smell. As she waited, she thought about Pete's breakdown. Claire witnessed many of Pete's breakdowns throughout the years. But after what happened last night, Claire needed someone to vent to. Suddenly, the door opened, and Sarah greeted her with open arms. "Oh, Claire," she said as she held onto her. "I've missed you… come in." Claire stepped in and removed her winter boots while Sarah took her coat and placed it in the closet. Sarah looked at Claire and hugged her once more.

"You okay?" Sarah softly asked as she rubbed Claire's back.

Claire shook her head. "No… no, I'm not okay."

"Let's talk in the living room."

As they made their way to the living room, which had all white furniture, Claire looked at the mantel over the fireplace and saw the picture of Sarah's husband, Clayton McCauley, in his police uniform. Next to the photo was a lit candle and a folded American flag in a redwood frame.

They sat down on the couch and got comfortable. Sarah had this long, curly, mouse-brown hair and olive-green eyes. She also had a mole on the left side of her deep cleft chin, which was her beauty mark. Sarah used to be petite. But due to months of stress and depression, she packed on twenty-seven pounds.

"Would you like anything?" Sarah asked. "Some Coffee or tea?"

"Thanks, but I'm fine for now," Claire smiled.

"Okay… thanks for coming over. I really appreciate it."

"Thanks for *having* me over… and for taking my call. I know I probably scared you when you heard me crying. But I needed someone to talk to."

"I'm always here for you," Sarah smiled.

Claire sighed. "I know…. Yesterday was the worst day of my life. If only you could see the look in Pete's eyes. It wasn't him… I didn't see my husband at all. He was saying something about grabbing his gun and for *us* to shoot him. I couldn't *believe* he would say something like that. He just went crazy."

"He's been through a lot, Claire. I'm sure it's just the stress talking."

"Well, no, yesterday he had a mental meltdown. Our living room is a wreck. Him and Michael had an altercation and broke the coffee table. Then he took a baseball bat and smashed all the furniture. I thought he was going to attack us. It was God awful, Sarah."

"I'm sorry to hear that… I know it hasn't been easy for you and the kids either."

"It hasn't. It's been really rough."

"How are the kids?"

Claire sighed. "Confused… upset. I think more in particular with me. I haven't been the best mother these last few days… I don't know what to do, Sarah. My life wasn't like this a couple of weeks ago. I was looking forward to spending Christmas with Pete this year. We hadn't spent Christmas with him in the last three years. I was happy, Pete was happy—we had a happy life—give or take… it's unbelievable how in a split second… your whole life can change. I feel so lost."

Sarah held Claire's hand. "So do I."

"I know," Claire said as she smiled at Sarah. "So… today makes it a year."

"Yeah… a *rough* year. I've been hanging in there as best as I can."

"How are CJ and Katie doing?"

"They're dealing with it. CJ has been having some difficult times since he started high school this school year. And Katie? Katie is just Katie… I don't know what she thinks sometimes."

Claire looked at Clayton's picture. "He was such a good man, wasn't he?"

"Oh *God*, yes… he was," Sarah smiled. "He was the best. I woke up early this morning thinking about him and the night we first met. It was my college roommate's engagement party. I was sitting across from him at the table. We were actually playing footsie with each other."

"*No*…." Claire chuckled.

"*Yes, I swear*… it was like something out of an eighty's movie. And I knew it was him because he kept looking over and smiling at me. Then, he asked me to dance. But silly me said, 'no.'"

"You said, '*no*?'"

"I wasn't much of a dancer. He just raised his hands and said, 'okay.' But I asked him if we could just sit down and talk. He was happy about that. He told me he was a cop. At first, I wasn't as enthusiastic about dating him. But after a while, I said, 'what the hell?' I'll never forget the first time I saw him in that police uniform. *God*, I could've melted. He was *so* hot."

Claire smiled. "I can definitely relate."

"Yeah... I don't know what it is about a man in uniform. Maybe it's just the perception of authority—or leadership. But it was his personality that I fell deeply in love with. He was so positive, Claire—as you already know. He would *always* find a way to bring light into a situation. No matter *what* it was. I mean, I could've had the worst day—the *worst* day. But when that key would hit the door, and I saw his handsome face, I would just run into his arms and give him the kiss of a lifetime—it didn't matter *what* I'd be doing: cooking, cleaning, washing clothes... I would run straight to him, wrap my arms and legs around him and hold him tight. I didn't miss one day... that was our relationship."

"It was a beautiful relationship, Sarah."

"It *was*... it really was. But a year ago today... his key didn't hit the door. Instead, I received a knock on my door at six in the morning. I thought maybe he forgot his keys. When I came downstairs... I looked out the window and saw the two police officers... my heart sunk to the pit of my stomach. I couldn't breathe. The door was only five feet away, but it took me forever to reach it. I didn't have the strength to open it. I was too devastated to hear what I already knew. I just put my head against the door and cried my soul away. I guess the officers heard me through the door and asked if they could come in. I got myself together and finally opened the door. They both took off their hats and looked at me with immense sorrow. The second they looked at my face, they could tell I already knew my husband wasn't coming home... my Claydo wasn't coming home."

Claire rubbed Sarah's back. "I'm so sorry."

Sarah wiped her teary face. "I remember falling to my knees and just *screaming*. I woke up the kids, and they came running down the stairs. They saw the police and knew exactly what happened. They cried right along with me. Even the officers shed a few tears...."

I asked them if I could see the body cam footage. They brought me to the station where I saw it. It happened in a split second. Clay stepped out of his car, walked up to the driver's window, and... the driver just rolled his window down and shot him point blank... nine times... he shot my husband *nine times*.... I just remember hearing Clay screaming, '*Officer down! Officer down! I need a medic right now*!' But the most haunting moment in that video... I'll never forget it... was hearing my baby take his last breath."

Claire sat there and looked at Sarah as she imagined being in her shoes. She looked over at the picture of Clay and imagined it was Pete. She then closed her eyes and sighed.

"You okay?" Sarah asked.

"Yeah," Claire responded as she wiped her eyes. "I'm just...."

"You're just imagining that this could've been you... aren't you?"

Claire sighed. "Yeah... every day, when Pete walked out that door, and there was no guarantee that he would be back... it scared me to death. And when you called me that day and told me about Clay—just hearing you cry... it... it felt like I *was* in your shoes. But at the same time... I was relieved that I *wasn't*.... *Jesus*... Sarah, I'm sorry I said that—"

"No, no, no... I completely understand. I wouldn't wish this for *anyone*."

"Neither do I... this profession does something to your mind.... I remember this one time when Pete worked a sixteen-hour shift. I was asleep. I heard him come into the bedroom. But then the room went silent. Out of *nowhere*... he *screamed*. I jumped out of bed and saw him on the floor, crying hysterically. I asked him what was wrong, but he just kept screaming, '*no white bedsheets*! *No white bedsheets*!' I thought he was losing his mind. I didn't know *what* the hell was going on.... He apologized to me the next day and told me how the white bedsheets reminded him of all the corpses he had seen on the job. And when he saw *me* sleeping under my white bedsheets… it triggered him. He said I looked like I was dead…. You know, Sarah, I never got to apologize to you for walking out during the funeral."

"Oh… I didn't even notice you did. But I understand. It was too much."

"Well, it wasn't that… Pete didn't talk much that morning. And when we got to the funeral, he just sat there and stared at Clay in the casket. I was worried about him. So, I nudged him with my elbow and asked him if he was okay. But he didn't say anything to me… just nodded his head. Maybe like a minute later… he leaned over and whispered, *'that could've been me.'* I looked at him in disbelief. I couldn't believe he would just *say* that to me. That's when I looked at Clay's casket, and I looked back at him… I couldn't take it anymore. I got up from my seat and left… I'm so sorry, Sarah."

"It's *okay*, Claire. I *understand*. I truly do."

"That night of the shooting, when I was on the phone praying with Pete? I had a feeling that something might happen. But I just couldn't put my finger on it. He had to cut things short because he had to take the call. I didn't tell him this but I finished the prayer when I hung up. I prayed to the Lord that Pete would be protected. And you know what? He was… the Lord answered my prayers, Sarah. But now, I can't stay there anymore. I can't have the children around him— being drunk and violent. I really don't know what to do."

"I don't know what to *tell* you to do."

"I think we just need some time apart."

"Do what's best for the family, Claire. That's all I can really say."

"Yeah. You know… I must admit that even though Pete's struggling, I'm overwhelmed with buried joy. I'm so happy I didn't get that call or knock on my door saying he wasn't coming home."

"Yeah… thank God. I kinda envy you."

"Sarah, I'm sorry—"

"No. It's okay. We're going to be all right. And you know why?

Because we're strong. Us police wives, we're strong women. Every day, we face the fear of becoming a widow. And some of us are. But we're strong enough to raise our kids and carry on their legacy. That's why they married us. Because we're *strong*... but *dear God*..." Sarah walked over to the mantel and picked up Clayton's photo. "I wish my husband were here... I wish my baby were here."

38

DECEMBER 29th, 2025, MONDAY EVENING:

EMPTY HOME, EMPTY HEART

Pete opened the front door to his house. Brownie walked right to him, whimpering as if he missed him. "Hey, buddy," he said as he petted Brownie. "Where's everybody?" As Pete hit the lights in the living room, he saw the horrific aftermath of his violent episode. Pete was so out of it yesterday that he did not realize the damage he had done. There was broken glass and furniture and large holes in the wall. But then, in the wreckage, there was a clean, white envelope with his name on it.

"Claire?" Pete projected as he walked over to grab the letter. He held the letter in his hands—hesitant to open it as he feared it was bad news. He looked around and called for Claire again. "Claire? Elle? Michael? Leo?" But no one was home. Pete then ripped open the envelope and pulled out a lengthy letter. As he took a seat on the couch, he began to read:

Pete,

If you're reading this, that means you came home. It breaks my heart what I'm about to tell you... I had to leave you. I've taken the kids, and we're all staying with my parents. Michael just couldn't handle what happened last night. He was so upset. So was Elle and Leo... so was I. I couldn't believe you were reading Miranda rights to Michael. I think you've gone completely insane. These last eighteen years of my life were not easy. And for the sixteen years of you being a police officer... I did the very best I could. I did my best raising our kids without your presence. The last several years of you missing holidays and special occasions... I can't take it anymore. And with everything going on, you're not the same man I fell deeply in love with. You're not the Pete I know. What did you do with him? I love that man so much. But that man is not you.

It frightens me to say this, but I'm starting to believe that my husband must have died that night of the shooting. The only time I can even hold you is when you're having one of your nightmares. I can't tell you anything without you getting angry. And the drinking? You become a monster when you drink. I feel so lost without you... and scared. Please don't be angry with me. I did what I thought was best for everyone. I prayed on it. Maybe we need to leave you be so you can get your head right. I don't know. I'm just so lonely. I just want to cry because I miss you. I miss my husband so much. I know you're dealing with a lot, but I need my husband back. And what scares me the most is that I will never get my Petester back. I don't know. Maybe you're still there inside... I hope. Because we need you. And we love you. I guess this is goodbye for now. I love you so much, Pete.

> *Your wife,*
> *Claire*
> *P.S. Take care of Brownie.*

Tears hit the paper as Pete slid off the couch, sobbing through his broken, empty heart. When Pete lost his position as an officer, he felt that he lost everything. At that moment, he realized policing was just a job and that *family* was everything. But now… he has nothing.

39

DEAR LORD, LET IT END

Another nightmare had imprisoned Pete as he slept on the basement couch. He tossed and turned in a blanket of cold sweat as the nightmare became hauntingly vivid. In the nightmare, Pete was in full uniform as he stumbled down a creepy, dark street during a storm of rain and blood drops—roaring thunder and lightning. Pete pulled out his gun and flashlight as he ran down the street. He looked up and saw the street sign, "Hunterdon Street," the same street where the shooting occurred. Suddenly, a daunting dark figure slowly made its way down the street. Pete saw the dark figure ahead of him, unable to see who it was. "Who's there?" Pete shouted. But then, the chopping sounds of a helicopter made its way over the street—shining a bright light on the dark figure. It was a young woman in her underwear, covered in blood and leaves.

"Hi, Officer Gant," said the woman. "Remember me?"

Pete dropped his gun in shock. "Wh—who are you?"

"You don't remember me? Gabriella Del Alto? You found my body in the woods."

Pete became startled. "*Jesus*... oh, Jesus."

"Don't you remember me? My father raped and impregnated me. Then he raped me again—killed me, and threw my body in the woods…. But I'm okay now. He can never rape me again."

Suddenly, through the thunder and lightning, another dark figure appeared from behind. It was another woman with blood gushing out from her forehead.

"What about me?" the woman said.

"AHH!" Pete screamed as he turned around.

"Don't you remember me? It's me, Patricia. My body was lying by my car in the parking lot."

Pete placed his hands over his face. "No… NO!"

"You don't remember me? Don't you remember my abusive boyfriend? I finally had the courage to leave that bastard. I skipped town… but I knew he would find me. I was walking to my car one night… I didn't even see him coming. He called my name, I turned around, and there he was. The last thing I saw was the gun pointed right at my face—and BANG! *How* could you forget me?"

"Stop," Pete cried. "Please, *stop*!"

The thunder rumbled the ground under Pete's feet, and the blood overflowed the sewer drainage. But then, another dark figure appeared, his friend and fellow officer, Clayton McCauley.

"Hey, brother," Clayton smiled with blood goosing out his mouth. "It's been a while."

"Clayton?" Pete said with startled eyes.

"Yeah, it's me. I miss you, man. Why haven't you talked to me?"

"You're dead, Clay… you're *dead*!"

"That's no excuse, Pete. You could've talked to me through spirit."

"This isn't real… this isn't *real*!"

The nightmare was becoming realer by the millisecond. Suddenly, a glowing figure—a man came from a distance, dribbling a basketball. It got closer and closer until, finally, the glowing figure stood before Pete.

"Yo, Officer Gant," said the glowing figure. "I *know* you remember *me*."

Pete cried, "T—Tyshawn Brendan... oh God."

"Oh *God*? Oh *God*? You didn't say 'Oh, God' when you popped all those fucking bullets through the door, right? You fucking coward... I had big dreams, man—*big* dreams. I was going to be the *greatest*. I was going to be in the league with Lebron James, Kyrie Irving, Jason Tatum, Ja Morant—and Steph Curry. I was going to be the next Michael Jordan. I had a *life*, man! A *life*! I was all my mother had in this world, man. And you took me away from her. Thanks a lot. *I* wasn't *ready* to go. It wasn't my time to check up outta here. I still had a lot of life left to *live*, man. Why? *Why*?"

"I didn't mean it," Pete sobbed. "I'm sorry... I'm *so sorry*. I swear on my life I did *not mean to shoot you*."

"It's too late for that, *Officer Gant*. There's no *coming* back where *I'm* at. And there's no basketball court here, either.... All I ever wanted to do was make my momma proud... I'm sure you made Poppa Dee proud."

The glowing figure of Tyshawn Brendan suddenly disappeared. "Wait, please," Pete said as he reached for Tyshawn Brendan. Then, a sudden presence of children appeared and began to surround Pete. The children were part of a fatal bus crash eleven years ago. They were on their way to a field trip when the front tire of the bus blown out on the freeway and flipped over multiple times down the hill... no survivors. Pete remembered that day, seeing all those kids' bodies. He tried to erase that day from his memories. But the nightmares never failed him. In an eerie, synchronized tone, the children spoke in unison, "Remember me, Officer Gant? Remember me?"

Pete took a panoramic look at his surroundings as the children moved closer to him. "Remember me? Remember me? Remember me?" Pete fell to his knees and cried, "No. I don't want to remember you!" The children formed a closing circle around Pete, saying, "*Save* us, Officer Gant... *save* us. *Save* us!" They all lifted their bloody hands as they reached for Pete. Then a sudden scream, "AHHH!"

Pete screamed right out of his sleep. He got up off the couch, soaking wet. "Claire!" He cried. "Claire! Claire, I need you!" Pete ripped the soaking wet clothes off his body and stood in the basement doorway completely naked. "Claire, Michael... Elle, Leo! Somebody!" But no one was home. Pete was all alone, vulnerable, and terrified. He ran up to his private study, where he kept his guns. He grabbed one, loaded up the clip, and took cover around the house, as if he were part of a drug bust or in a shootout.

Pete had lost it—deluded and paranoid like never before. He then ran his naked body out of the house—into the backyard with his gun pointing at the far end of the yard. That is when everything went quiet. He looked to his left—heavy frost on his breath—no one in sight. He then heard a sound and quickly pointed the gun to his right. Pete caught himself just in the nick of time as he was a millisecond from pulling the trigger. It was Brownie, looking right back at him as he made whimpering sounds.

Pete lowered the gun and dropped it in the grass. "Oh, Brownie," he said as he walked toward Brownie and hugged him. "I'm sorry." Pete then rubbed up and down Brownie's back and cried. "Let it end. Let it end, let it end... oh, *God Almighty*, just let it end... I can't do this anymore. I can't... I just can't."

This was Pete's worst nightmare. But this was the first time Claire was not there by his side, to hold him in comfort, and kiss his worries away. It was at this moment that Pete realized he had hit rock bottom. His family was gone, and he was alone in the dark. Without his family, Pete felt he had no reason to go on.

40

DECEMBER 30^{th,} 2025, TUESDAY MORNING:

<u>E. O. W.</u>

It was 3:16 in the morning. After that nightmare, Pete avoided sleep as much as possible—popping caffeine pills to stay awake. He spent the last several hours lying in a waterless tub—filled with empty beer cans as he scrolled through social media and read the hateful comments from the video of him and Leo in the supermarket. Pete read hundreds of comments. A few comments in particular had put him on the edge, commanding that he jump:

@CraigDaBomb072567

> I hope that son of a bitch kills himself. Look at his eyes. Absolutely no remorse whatsoever. Just die, you fucking pig.

@RoyBookerT020868

> Pete "The pig," you're a sorry excuse for a man. I hope you suffer every day for the rest of your life. And I hope your life is cut short and you die a horrible death, you bastard. Die slow, pig.

@CareyBond051868

I can't believe people are so cruel. He's a human being. Why would you want this man to kill himself? It was an accident.

@JoesphThaTruth051170

@CareyBond051868 Bitch, if you don't get your white ass up out of here. I'm sick of you motherfuckers taking this pig's side as if he's the victim. Look at the video. He knew exactly what he was doing, and he should get the needle for what he did to Tyshawn Brendan. Idc what any of you white crackers have to say. Pete "the pig" deserves to die and rot in hell.

@CareyBond051868

@JoesphThaTruth051170 I did see the video, and that woman 100% harassed him in that supermarket. Simple. My heart goes out to the family of Tyshawn Brendan. However, that situation gives no one the right to harass the officer. You have no idea what he's going through. And for people to tell him that he should just kill himself is atrocious and should be arrested for cyberbullying.

@BlackMoorsNeverDie100374

Hey Pete "The Pig," idc what anybody says, you must pay for your sins. It's evident that you have no remorse for shooting those two black kids. Salute to Bianca Jennings, who recorded the video. She showed the world what a heartless, racist ass cop looks like. And what's sad is that there are so many more Pete Gants out there who still wear a badge. But God will make you pay for your sins. Everybody has a day of judgment. And when that pig stands before his maker, I know he will send him straight to the fire and brimstone of hell.

@MonicaDaSistahSoldier022778

Tyshawn Brendan was going to shake up this world. He was ours. He was our king. And for this cop to do what he did and show all that anger in the video, I'm just so disappointed in the American judicial system. The fact that they let that cop just get away with murder. It's insane. When is this going to stop? When are they going to stop? Sometimes, I just want to walk into a crowd and scream, "STOP KILLING US!" To the police officer, you deserve everything bad that comes to you. You better pray that God Almighty has mercy on your soul.

@WillGamble121779

Idk why people are stressing out about this cop. He's probably going to off himself in his basement any day now. He'll never be able to live with what he's done. Karma is a bitch, bruh. And she never disappoints. Yo, Pete "The Pig," how bout you take the gun you used to kill Tyshawn Brendan to kill yourself? Just saying.

There was a time when Pete did not believe that words could hurt him. Not only did the words of others hurt like daggers piercing through his body, but they also influenced him to harm himself. A tear slowly streamed down his right cheek as he read more. But then, he picked up a brand-new bottle of dark liquor. He looked at the bottle as if it was talking to him once again. And in his mind, it was. The liquor began to speak:

Don't listen to those people, Pete. Listen to me. I'm the only friend you need. I'm your family now. And I have what you need to get well. I know what it's like to be alone. To have nobody. To be a nobody. But now, I have you, my friend... and you have me. We have each other. All you have to do is twist the cap, and I'll give you the magic. I'll give your body the medicine it needs.... Come on, buddy... taste my bottled tears.

Pete broke the seal and consumed the poison. But the *poison* was coming back up. He hopped out of the tub—barely making the toilet as he puked. After the vomiting, Pete laid down on the cold tile of his bathroom floor. Looking up at the ceiling—with a hazy vision, he began to think about Claire and sang their wedding song, *Wicked Games*. Suddenly, through the lyrics, he broke down and sobbed. Through his tears, he softly said, "Oh, dear *God*... I can't do this anymore. I'm so tired. I just want it to end. No more pain... no more Pete."

Hours later, the tears had faded from Pete's red puffy eyes. In his bedroom, Pete sat quietly on his bed as he held an envelope with Claire's name on it. After he spent the last few minutes staring at the envelope, Pete gave it a gentle kiss, placed it against Claire's pillow, and left the room. He then went downstairs and put on his jacket and grabbed the keys to the Jeep. Just as Pete opened the door, Brownie came toward him, whimpering with his puppy dog eyes. Pete kneeled and rubbed the back of Brownie's ears. "Hey, buddy," he said. "I'm sorry I have to leave you like this. I'm just tired... I'm so tired... take care of everybody for me, okay?" Pete hugged Brownie as his free-falling tears landed in his brown fur. "I love you."

As Pete let go, Brownie began to lick his face. And yet, Pete did not chuckle or even smile. He was too far gone. He stood up, walked backward towards the front door, and waved goodbye as Brownie whimpered.

Moments later, Pete was out on the road, listening to a song that one of his fellow officers put him onto, *Free Bird* by Lynyrd Skynyrd. Pete played the song on a loop—driving to a lake his father used to take him to when he was a kid. It was the lake where Pete saved Gregory from drowning. Gregory swam too far out into the lake. He was not the best swimmer, but Pete was. Pete kept stroking his arms and kicking his legs until he reached his brother. He caught him just in time before he went under. Gregory held onto Pete as he swam back to the beach. Montgomery was so grateful and proud of Pete. He called him a hero, and that stuck with Pete ever since.

Forty-five minutes later, Pete pulled up to the lake. He sat there as he reminisced about his childhood there—remembering the good times vividly, as well as the bad. He then looked over on the passenger seat at his black case. Pete stared at it for a moment in silence. He then looked at himself in the rearview mirror, looking as if he was ready. He prepared himself for what was to come after opening the case. He carefully opened the case and looked at what was inside. He then looked at the lake once more and made that his destination. He then closed the case and brought it with him to the dock.

It was the longest walk Pete had ever taken in his life. It was like he was walking on a dock to heaven or in his mind, hell. As he reached the end of the dock, he sat with his legs dangling off the edge. Right beside him was the case. Pete opened it once again and took out his toy; a Glock 45 9mm Pistol. Pete had reached the very end of the spirit he had left. He felt utterly empty, useless... cast out by everyone. And now that the world knew him as the cop who killed who *could* have been one of the greatest basketball players ever to live, Pete felt that there was no reason for *him* to live.

Pete took one last look at the lake—the last sight his eyes would ever cast upon. He wanted his last sight to be beautiful, enchanted, and peaceful. But nothing was more beautiful than the photo of him with his family. Pete took one last look of the picture, kissed it, and placed it in the pocket that was over his broken heart. He then took a deep breath, closed his eyes, and put the gun in his mouth. Tears began to descend his face while his finger was on the trigger and his saliva streaming down the barrel. But then, Pete changed his mind as he pressed the pistol to his temple. He opened his eyes for a moment as the beautiful sight became a hazy vision.

"God?" Pete cried. "Please have mercy on my soul." As his finger was back on the trigger, slowly squeezing it to the end of life, something astonishing had occurred. A striped bass fish jumped out of the water—jump after jump—immediately catching Pete's attention. It was as if the fish was putting on a show at SeaWorld. Pete slowly removed the barrel from his temple and focused on the fish. He then looked at the gun and came to his senses. He then discharged the magazine and removed the bullet from the chamber, and seconds later, the fish was gone. Pete could not believe it. He could not believe that the presence of a fish prevented him from pulling the trigger. In his mind, he suddenly thought, "Did this fish just save my life?"

Pete put his gun back in the case, got up from the deck, and walked away—puzzled at what just happened. He got into his Jeep and sat there momentarily as he looked at the lake. As he sat there, another thought dawned upon him. For the first time in his life, Pete realized that *all* life on this earth was connected, and sometimes, it could be the most unexpected thing that could save your life.

41

DECEMBER 30th, 2025, TUESDAY EVENING:

THE LOST DAUGHTER

Later that evening, Pete took a relaxing drive on the I95 highway to Camden County. As he drove, Pete could not get the jumping fish out of his mind, unsure if it was a coincidence or a sign. Pete was grateful of the fish, but in deep sorrow for contemplating suicide.

As Pete stopped at the light, he saw a church to the far right, still neatly decorated with enchanted Christmas lights. It was an exquisite site to see. As the traffic light turned green, Pete drove up in front of the church and pulled over. He looked at the church and thought about how close he was to ending his life. With him being a man of faith, he felt that he needed God's forgiveness. As he sat there, he closed his eyes and took a breather. The church doors were open, and he decided to go in.

Pete walked up to the church and stepped inside. The church was stunningly beautiful. It had twenty-foot stain-glass windows telling the most vivid biblical stories. Pete looked around as he was immersed in the sight of it all. As he walked down the long aisle, there was a young woman on the far end of the bench who noticed him. Pete, however, was unaware of her presence. He then stood before the altar and kneeled on the prayer bench. As he kneeled, he folded his hands and began to pray:

Father... forgive me.... For these last several days, I've been living in misery.... As you know, I have sinned. I have taken a life that was not meant to be taken. Tyshawn Brendan didn't deserve to die. He was a good kid. I didn't mean to shoot him... why did this happen? *Why? Why* did you take away one of your gifts to the world? *Why* did it have to be *me*? Why is the world so ugly? Why, why, why, *why*? Does this all serve some unprecedented purpose? Never in a million years would I ever *think* to put a gun to my head. If that fish hadn't jumped out of the water, I... I probably would be at your feet, Father—begging for your forgiveness, begging you to let me through the pearly gates. Life is filled with pain, Father—suffering, melancholy... there's just too much of it—the pain. It runs *so deep*... and I'm drowning in it.

As Pete bowed his head, a gentle presence came behind him. "Son?" said The Priest. Pete turned around, wiping his tears away as he stood up from the prayer bench.

"Um... I'm sorry, Father," Pete said. "I thought I was alone."

"Oh? Well, then, who were you talking to?"

"That's a good point. I was talking to God. So, I guess I'm *not* alone."

The Priest pointed to the bench. "Please, take a seat."

The Priest was a tall, slender gentleman, standing in his white garment with a gold stole and cross. His hair was short and silver, and he had a clean-shaven face. His eyes were gray like gloomy clouds, but he was honest. As he sat beside Pete, the Priest inquired about him being there.

"What seems to be your troubles, my son?" The Priest asked.

Pete hesitated. "Everything."

"*Everything*? And just what is that... 'everything?'"

"My whole life is in shambles, Father. My wife left me a few days ago. She took my kids with her, and... and now I'm all alone."

"Why did she leave?"

"Because I screwed up... I did an evil thing, Father."

"What evil did you do, my son?"

"I took a life—accidently. I was a cop. I was involved in a shooting over a week ago."

"Oh, yes... I remember reading about that in the paper."

"Yeah... the driver had become hostile. I thought he had a gun, and I... I opened fire. Unbeknownst to me, there was another person in the car, and he was hit... he didn't make it.... The whole world knows now. People hate me, Father. They call me the worst things you could ever imagine. So many people want to see me dead. And today... today, I almost granted their wish."

"What do you mean, my son?"

"I had a gun to my head, Father... I was going to end it all. I was so defeated. I couldn't take it anymore.... For *sixteen years*, I put my life on the line to protect and serve my communities. Day in and day out, I was treated like an animal—like I wasn't even a human being. People treated me like I didn't have a conscience.... You work hard *every day*—*thinking* you're making a difference... *thinking* it may be your last... but now I realize that all *I* was ever doing was hurting my family."

"My son... are you a man of faith?"

Pete took off his coat and rolled up his sleeve. "I *am*... I have it inked on my body."

"Oh... well, I can't say I agree with permanently marking your *body*. But that's neither here nor there. I asked because, with your line of work, it could be very conflicting for you to *keep* your faith. I can't imagine the things you've seen as an officer. Death must present itself in many ways."

"It *does*... gunshots, car accidents, fires, suicide, stabbings, drownings... and the bodies keep piling up. You never know what you'll come across.... What do you think happens when people die, Father?"

"Well… according to my beliefs… those who do bad, if they repent and pray for forgiveness, their souls go to heaven. But those who do bad with no remorse go to hell."

"Oh," Pete unenthusiastically said.

"Were you expecting a different answer?"

"I *was*, actually… I used to think that when people die that… there was nothing but eternal darkness, and their bodies rot in a grave forever."

"Is *that* what you believe?"

"A part of me does, yes."

"Yet you say you're a man of faith and that you contemplated suicide. And what if you had gone through with it? You wouldn't be talking to me right now."

"Yeah… I know… but I just… I felt that everyone would be better off if I just wasn't here anymore."

"And you believe that?"

"I don't know, Father… I don't know what to believe anymore. I *do* have faith in God… but after all of what happened… I've lost faith in people."

"Could I share with you some words of wisdom?"

"Yes, Father."

"You said that you're a man of faith, yes?"

"Yes."

"Good. But there's something you must understand about faith, son. You can't just believe… you have to protect it. There are things in life that will happen that will compel your subconscious with doubt—*things* that will try to *destroy* your faith. Protecting our faith is the hardest thing for us to do."

"But Father… how will I *ever* survive this?"

"Hope, my son. Hope is a muscle that we must train and build. But our *faith*… our faith is the veins that we *must* keep pure… pure and clean. God knows that in the world we live in, keeping our faith pure and clean in a war of temptation and chaos... that's hard to ask of anyone.... That's the thing about chaos. It's a very patient phenomenon. It always knows when to deliver. It's like a chess move. It sets you up for an attack you would least expect—one you wouldn't see coming... and boom. It's all over.... The world is filled with pain, my son. And so many people consume products like alcohol and drugs to *ease* that pain. Have you consumed?"

"To alcohol, yes."

"And I pass no judgments onto you. Your situation was a heavy catastrophe. But I'm afraid there's no alcohol here for you to consume. The only service that *I* have for you is prayer. And it costs you nothing."

"Prayer... right. But how do I make things right with Tyshawn Brendan's family? Is that even possible?"

"How about you pray on it, my son? Prayer is the answer. It may not be the answer you're *looking* for. It may not come at the time you want it... but *God will answer you.* He listens... he answers. Just keep your faith."

"Okay... Father? Can I share one last thing with you?"

"Of course, my son."

"Earlier today, I was sitting on a dock with... with my gun to my head. Just as I was squeezing the trigger, a bass fish came jumping out of the lake. It just kept jumping and jumping and jumping. I don't know what that meant, but... it felt like the fish was telling me to stop. It was the strangest feeling. It's like... like the fish was my guardian angel protecting me or something... it saved my life."

"You know that wasn't by coincidence, right? Are you *familiar* with the history of bass fish?"

Pete shook his head. "No."

"It has been said in history that bass fish are messengers. They provide guidance and protection. They're spiritual creatures representing vitality, strength, and leadership—similar to what you were as an officer of law. They are also known to be a bringer of peace. So, in a way, that fish *was* your guardian angel."

"I like to believe that.... Father, I can't thank you enough for listening."

"You're welcome, my son. And may God bless you."

Pete stood up with a paused look. "Wait... will God forgive me, Father? And what about Tyshawn Brendan's family?"

The Priest slowly extended his arm toward the kneeling bench. "Pray, my son... he will listen."

Once again, Pete kneeled on the kneeling bench and prayed. After he finished praying, he turned around and noticed the Priest was gone. He looked around the church but he was nowhere in sight. But then, as Pete looked down the aisle, a dark figure walked towards him—similar to the dark figures of the nightmare.

"Who's that?" Pete fearfully asked.

The dark figure spoke. "Are—are you Officer Pete Gant?"

"Who are you? Step into the light."

The dark figure slowly stepped into the light. It was the young woman who was sitting on the bench. She wore a black peacoat, some black leggings, and Ugg boots. Her dirty-blonde hair was braided in two pigtails and she looked no older than nineteen.

"You're Officer Gant... right?"

Pete hesitated to answer. "I'm not an officer anymore... but I'm Pete Gant, yes... who are you?"

"You don't remember me—"

"Please," Pete said as he covered is ears. "Please don't say that 'R' word... please."

"I'm sorry."

After Pete's recent nightmare, he was triggered by the word "remember," and kept his distance from the young woman. "Just stay there... please," he anxiously said. The young woman stood there silently as she stared at Pete.

"So... it *is* you," the young woman smiled. "But you don't remem... sorry. You don't recognize me, do you?"

"I'm sorry... my mind's not in a good place today... maybe if you gave me a *hint*?"

"I'm Emilie... Emilie Graham?"

Pete, stood there in shock. "*Oh my God... Emilie*? The little girl—you're the little girl who... the *bloody pajamas*."

"Yeah... that was me."

"I... I'm sorry... I thought I'd never see you again."

"I thought that, too."

Pete sighed. "Emilie... how are you?"

"I've been okay... and you?"

"I haven't been in good spirits, to be honest with you. My life's been in shambles."

"I can understand that. I've been trying to give my life meaning again ever since... that night. It hasn't been easy for me at all. But how could it, you know? What I've been through... that's not something you can get over. I'm still in therapy to this day for it. I go twice a week. I used to go every day when I was a kid. But that doesn't stop me from coming to church and praying. It's been a rough road."

"I know it has."

"Officer Gant—"

"No, please... call me Pete... let's take a seat."

"Okay."

Pete and Emilie sat on the bench and had a moment of silence. They both observed each other, getting a feel of their energy.

"You know," she spoked. "I never got a chance to thank you."

"Thank me for what?" Pete asked.

"Maybe you don't remem... I'm so sorry. Perhaps you don't *recall* this moment, but you came by to check on me when I was in the ambulance. I asked if you could sing me a song. My momma sang to me every night when she tucked me in. It relaxed me... you had the most beautiful, soothing voice. Do you recall the song?"

Pete nodded his head. "Yeah... yeah, I do."

"I know this might be awkward, but can you sing it with me?"

"Oh, Emilie... I'm not in the right state of mind for that."

"Please? It would mean a lot to me."

Pete sighed. "Okay... let's see if I still know the lyrics... *all the leaves are brown, and the sky is gray... I've been for a walk on the winter's—*"

"*Day...*" Emilie joined in. "*I'd be safe and warm if I was in L.A. California Dreamin', on such a winter's day....* You put me at ease when you sang to me that night. Who made that song again?"

"The Mamas and the Papas... California Dreamin'."

"I'll be sure to put that in my playlist. So much of that night is now a blur for me, and I'm grateful for that. But then again... there are just some things you can never forget."

"That's very true... Emilie... I know you may not want to talk about it, and I understand if you don't. Tell me... what *happened* that night?"

For a moment, Emilie went silent. She stood up from the bench and walked over to the altar—looking up at Jesus on the cross. She then closed her eyes and sighed as she shared with Pete her story. "I had a mother once... a brother, a father... I had a family. I adored my father more than *anything* in this world. He was such a good daddy to me. I loved him... but that one night... it all came to an end.... My mother and father were having a fight. They were so loud that Sebastian—my baby brother, woke up crying. I shared my room with him, so, I got out of bed and picked him up from his crib. I remember holding him—looking him in his eyes. He had the most beautiful, icy blue eyes... they looked like glaciers. As I held him, he fell asleep, and things began to calm down with my parents downstairs. The last thing I said to Sebastian before I kissed him goodnight was, 'I love you.' I stood over his crib and watched him dreaming his baby dreams... and then it happened."

Pete looked and listened as Emilie cried. "I heard my mother *scream* for her life. That's when I ran downstairs and... my mother was holding a knife in her hand. My father had this sinister look in his eye... the eyes of a demon. I just remember him laughing as he said, 'til death do us part.' That's when he grabbed the knife from my mother and stabbed her several times in her stomach.... I couldn't move. I couldn't speak. I couldn't do anything... except watch my father stab her to death. When he turned around and looked at me... there was no humanity left in his eyes. No soul, no conscience... no Daddy. That's when he made his way toward the stairs. I was so scared that he was going to come after me next. So, I ran back to my room and hid under my bed. I can still hear the sound of my bedroom door creaking open and his dark shadow slowly moving on the floor... and my mother's blood dripping from the knife. And then... I saw him standing next to Sebastian's crib. Sebastian was crying again. I liked to believe he was crying for me and wanted me to hold him one more time. But I just couldn't. And that's when..." Emilie, began to sob uncontrollably with her hands covering her face.

"Emilie," Pete said as he stepped to her. "It's okay, we don't have to talk about—"

"No," Emilie said as she sniffled and wiped her eyes. "Please... just let me finish."

"Go ahead... I'm sorry."

Emilie sighed. "I *never*, in *all my life*, heard the sounds of a baby screaming like that... to hear my baby brother squirming out his *last breath*... I could've died right there under my bed. How could a human being just stab an infant child to death? And that's when I realized that my father wasn't a human being... he was a monster... and that was the first time I saw the devil."

"*Jesus*," Pete sighed in disbelief.

"After my father left my room, I stayed under my bed for what seemed like *forever*. I was too afraid to crawl out. I was too afraid to see Sebastian lying dead in his crib. But I did… I crawled from under my bed, and I saw him—lying there in a bloody crib. I never screamed so loud before. I screamed all the way down the stairs and ran to my mommy. I turned her around and *begged* her to wake up. I held onto her and just cried and cried. My mommy always told me that if I was ever in danger, I should call the police… and that's when you came into my life."

The more Emilie told Pete, the more questions came up in his mind, as that was just the cop in him. Pete wanted to know what her father's motive was to kill his wife and infant child.

"Emilie," he said. "Did you ever find out why your father did what he did?"

Emilie nodded her head as she sniffled. "Yes… I know why. My dad was always busy with work and wasn't around much… I guess my mom just became lonely, and things started to change with her behavior. That's when my father's best friend would come over— which I thought was weird because he'd always come when my father wasn't home. I didn't understand that until I finally did. He and my mom were having an affair."

"But why your baby broth… *oh*…"

Emilie slowly nodded her head. "Yeah… my dad's best friend was Sebastian's father. When my dad found out about the affair and that Sebastian wasn't his son… he *snapped*…. But you know what? I forgave him. I forgave my dad. It took a long time. But I forgave him. I even wrote him a letter."

"A letter?"

"Yes. I went out to the woods, where they found his body. I felt that maybe his soul was still out there somewhere. I just read the letter to him aloud, hoping he would hear me."

"Did that help? Writing the letter?"

302

"It *did*. It felt like a great weight was lifted off my shoulders. Not just writing the letter but… my forgiveness. I wouldn't have survived if I had stayed angry with him forever. I still miss him, Mr. Pete. I hate what he *did*. But I miss him terribly. Does that sound insane?"

"No, Emilie. It doesn't sound insane at all. It's understandable."

"I was Daddy's little girl. But I don't *have* a daddy anymore… I have no one… I am *so lonely*, Mr. Pete… so lonely."

Pete felt for Emilie as he watched her walk away. He felt the need to give her some encouragement and guidance. But with everything *he* was going through, he did not have the words for her. Suddenly, Pete thought of an idea. He stood from the bench and began to sing. "*Stopped into a church… I passed along the way. Well, I got down on my knees, and I pretend to pray. You know the preacher liked the cold. He knows I'm gonna stay… California Dreamin' on such a winter's day….*" Emilie turned around with descending tears and a smile on her face. She walked back to Pete with a warm feeling in her heart. Emilie looked up at Pete with her beautiful smile.

"You remind me so much of my daughter," Pete said.

"Really?"

"Yeah… you both have the same eyes."

"She's lucky to have a father like you. I don't have a father."

Pete then opened his arms and gave Emilie a heartwarming embrace—an embrace that only a father would know how to give.

"Thank you," Emilie smiled, wiping away her tears. "I really needed that."

"That makes two of us."

"I can't believe we crossed paths again. And of all places."

"Emilie… I had the worst day. I didn't think I was going to make it through. But by the grace of God… I'm still here. I'm *still breathing*… but I'm still hurting. I took a life… a young man named Tyshawn Brendan. He was a gifted basketball player… it was just a bad situation. He was in the passenger seat of a car I pulled over. The driver pulled out what I thought was a gun but it was his phone and... I opened fire. I hit them both... Tyshawn Brendan didn't make it. I lost my position as a police officer, and I think I lost my family... I'm just like you now, sweetheart... I'm all alone."

Pete kneeled on the prayer bench with his hands folded. Emilie then kneeled beside him and made a suggestion.

"Mr. Pete? What if *you* wrote a letter?"

"What?"

"Write a letter to *his* family—Tyshawn Brendan's."

"Oh, Emilie... that's not possible."

"Why not?"

"Because they hate me. I know they do. And I don't blame them."

"I don't believe they hate you, Mr. Pete. I believe if you reach out to his parents, you could really make a difference. It wouldn't hurt to try, you know?"

Pete shook his head in doubt. "I don't know, Emilie... I don't think it's a good idea. I mean, what would I even say?"

"Just listen to your heart. It will give you the words. What do you have to lose?"

"I don't know," Pete said as he stood up. "My life wasn't like this a couple of weeks ago. I was happy. My *wife* was happy—my children. I had my career... I had a happy life, Emilie. And within *seconds*... that all changed. I was only four years away from getting my pension.... You know... when I was a kid, I wanted to c*hange the world* and save as many lives as I possibly could. But *I've* been changed by the world, and I have to do everything in my power to save myself.... I guess I was just trying too hard to be a hero. And now... I'm nobody's hero. I'm nothing... I'm just Pete."

"Mr. Pete... you have *always* been *my* hero. I never forgot you or what you did for me. And the fact that we're here, reunited... this was all God's plan. He brought us back together for a reason. You know? And seeing you, it... it gives me hope."

"Hope for what?"

"A better day."

Pete gently smiled. "I'm so glad I saw you again, Emilie."

"Likewise, Mr. Pete… please write that letter."

"I will… thank you."

"No, Mr. Pete… *thank you*," Emilie said as she kissed Pete on his cheek. "Oh… Happy New Year."

"Right… Happy New Year."

Pete watched as Emilie walked down the aisle and left the church. He thought he would never see her again. But after tonight, he felt that spark of faith once again, and this time, he was going to protect it.

42

DECEMBER 31^{st,} 2025, WEDNESDAY MORNING:

<u>BROTHERS</u>

It was one in the morning. Pete had just pulled up his driveway. To his surprise, Greg was waiting on the front steps. Greg stood up with a furious look on his face as he had been waiting for hours. Pete, however, was in no mood for Greg's antics. As he stepped out of the Jeep with his black case, Greg confronted him with a vengeance.

"Where the *hell* have you been?" Greg retorted.

"What are you doing here, Greg?" Pete asked. "Looking for trouble as usual?"

"No… I was looking for *you*. Have you checked your phone? Everyone has been calling you since yesterday."

"Calling me for what?"

"*Shit…* you don't *know?*"

"*What*, Greg?"

"Poppa *Dee…* he's *dead*."

Pete was stunned. "What?"

"He's *dead*, Pete. Heart attack. Dad said it happened right after you left—he collapsed in the backyard… Dad called the paramedics, but… he was D.O.A."

Pete sighed. "As if I need any more shit news for the day."

"Shit *news*? What, you still worried about that Brendan kid?"

"I'm going inside, Greg," Pete said as he walked inside the house.

"Oh, no, we're not *done* with this conversation—"

"I think we *are*, Greg."

"Look, people die every day, Pete. Tyshawn Brendan's water under the bridge now."

"Greg, please. I've had a *terrible* day. You don't even know the *half* of it."

"Well, why don't you sit down with your brother, have a *beer* with me… and let's have a conversation, huh?"

Pete sighed. "Fine."

As Greg stepped inside, he was stunned to see the wreckage in the living room.

"*Jesus Christ*," he said. "What the hell happened in *here*?"

Pete ignored Greg's question. "The kitchen's this way."

"Yeah, I *know* that… I didn't know you were *redecorating*."

"Do you want a beer or not?"

"Lead the way, little brother," Greg smiled.

Pete and Greg made their way into the kitchen. Greg stood by the island as he looked at Pete who was grabbing some beers from the refrigerator. Pete pulled out two Heinekens and slid one across the island down to Greg.

"Thanks," Greg said as he twisted the cap off and took a sip. "You know… you don't seem too upset about Poppa Dee. Not one tear?"

"I've cried enough tears for one day," Pete said.

"Hmm…. So, where's the family?"

Pete looked at Greg as he took a sip. "At Claire's parents' house."

"Well, are they coming back?"

"*Yes*, Greg."

"Okay… are they coming back *tomorrow*? Next week? Next

year—"

"I don't know, Greg. All right? They'll be back when they're back."

Greg put his beer on the table. "Okay, *okay*... don't have to bite my head off about it."

"Look... I'm very tired. How about you just finish your beer... and call it a night? You can let yourself out." Pete walked out of the kitchen.

"So, that's it?"

"Make sure you lock my door on your way out."

Greg chuckled. "*Wow*."

Pete returned to the kitchen. "What's so funny?"

"Oh, nothing. Nothing at all—"

"No, go ahead and tell me—*enlighten* me with your sense of humor."

"Oh *no*, buddy, the sense of humor is *all you*. I just think it's funny how you said to me, 'Lock *my* door,' as if this is *your* house—when in *actuality*, this is and has always been *Dad's* house."

"Jesus," Pete scoffed. "Can you go *one goddamn day* without being an asshole?"

"Oh, for *Christ's sake*, Pete. You know, since when did you become a *poo*-butt ass? I'm just fooling around here. We used to bust each other's balls *all* the time. What the *hell* happened to your sense of humor?"

"I don't *know*, Greg. Shit—maybe I just saw too much shit out there. Maybe my sense of humor is a little numb right now. It hasn't been the best couple of weeks lately."

"Whatever," Greg said as he took another drink.

"You wanna talk, Greg? You got something you want to get off your chest? Then go ahead."

"Well, since it's *your* house, maybe *you* should say whatever it is that *you* have to say. Let's discuss what *your* problems are with me."

"I don't have no problems with you, Greg."

"Oh, I *know* that's bullshit.... Look, Pete... I'm an asshole. I know *that* much about myself. I say whatever I want, and I have no filter. I like to party, and I *love* to roll the dice. That's just who the hell I am. I have my flaws, and so what? Who doesn't? But for the *most* part? I'm a pretty okay fucking guy."

Pete remained silent as he had no words for Greg. He then went into the refrigerator and grabbed another beer. Greg became very agitated at Pete's silence.

"So what? You're just going to stand there and not say shit?"

"You know what, Greg? I think it's *you* who really has something to get off your chest."

"What are you talking about?"

"You say you have no filter, right? So why don't you get whatever it is you've had built up inside *you*—for *years* and just let that shit out... go ahead."

Greg chuckled as he finished his beer. "That's a bet.... Little brother... we were always close as kids. Thick as thieves. Wherever I went, you were right behind me. You were my right-hand guy— loved you to death. I still do. But then the adolescence kicked in. Yours kicked in a little earlier than mine and you started growing facial hair. When we were teenagers, I peeked in the crack of the bathroom door and saw Dad showing you how to shave. I could barely grow a peach fuzz at fifteen. But *you*? You were the *fucking man*. You had the beard growing, the chicks chased after you, and *I* was flunking out of school. Dad paid for the *best* tutors that money could buy... but I *just couldn't get* my shit *together*. You did everything right, Pete. Graduated high school, went off to college, got a degree, went into the academy, started a family, and fucking *made* something of yourself. Mom was so proud of you. You should've seen her face when you got on stage to accept your certificate. We were all so *fucking* proud of you.... Mom would always say to me, '*Gregory, why can't you be like your brother? Why can't you be more like Pete?'"*

Pete was taken aback. "She said that?"

"Sure did. What a slap in the face, right? Why the hell couldn't they just accept me for *me*? What the hell was wrong with *me*? But, *you*? *You* were their guy—*you* were the family hero. And *I* was the goddamn heel. Then, one night… oh, how the *tables turned*… my little brother became a *killer*!" Greg clapped his hands in joy. "*Look at God! Finally*, Mr. Perfect *fucked* up! When Mom called and told me the news, oh, *believe me* when I *tell* you—I slept like a *goddamn king* that night. I couldn't *wait* to come over here and see the look on your face—the same look you got on your face right now. It felt *so fucking good*… to finally see *you* hit bottom, become the fucking heel, and *I* take the crown as the *family hero*… and you can't have it back…. Is *that* what you meant about getting shit off my chest? Spare no punches? There's plenty more where that came from."

Pete was appalled at what he just heard—appalled and heartbroken. He shook his head and said, "I think it's best that you get out of my fucking house now." Greg laughed in his face. "Are you still under the impression that this is *your house*? I thought we addressed that, Pete. This is *not* your fucking house. You didn't put up the money, so this is not your shit—"

"*Go* to hell, Greg!" Pete shouted in anger.

Greg stepped toward Pete. "Oh, go to *hell*, huh? And where the hell do you think *you're* going after this? *Heaven*? 'Thou shall not kill,' right? *Right*?"

"Get outta my face, Greg—"

"No, I'm *in* your face! Huh? *Huh*? Because I didn't *kill* anybody, Pete—*you* did—*you* fucked up! *You're* not the fucking man anymore! *You're* not the hero—*I'm* the fucking hero! And I bet *money* on *this*… it's only a matter of *fucking time* before *Claire* finds *herself*… a *new* hero."

"You *motherfucker*!" Pete shouted as he pushed Greg up against the wall.

A sibling rivalry became a sibling war as they brawled. POW! Pete got hit with a right hook to the face. BOOM! Greg received a blow to the gut. Now there was a tussle—knocking over glasses and putting dents in the wall. BAM! Pete hit Greg with a right uppercut he did not see coming. Greg fell to the floor with Pete now on top of him. Pete, with his fist balled up, looked as if he is ready to put Greg in the hospital. "What, Pete?" Greg shouted. "You're going to kill me next? Killing that black kid wasn't enough for you, huh? You going to kill me too? You fucking loser. Go ahead, kill me! *Kill me*! Or better yet, why don't you off your *fucking* self? You *pig*!"

Suddenly, there was silence in the war. Pete's fist slowly unraveled to a trembling hand. He finally got off of Greg and walked away without saying a word. Greg then stood up and wipe the blood from his busted eyebrow. As Greg fixed his suit jacket, he walked toward the living room. Suddenly, he stopped in fear as he saw Pete holding a gun—looking at the picture of his family on the wall. "You're absolutely right," Pete cried. "I *am* a loser. I lost my job... my family... I even lost my fucking mind... all because some stupid kid pulled out a goddamn phone." A startled Greg pleaded with Pete to drop the gun.

"Pete... what are you doing, man?"

"I was at the lake this morning. Lake Hopatcong. Where Dad used to take us when we were kids?"

"Yeah, yeah, I remember, but just, please... put the gun down."

Pete looked down at the gun. "When I was there... I sat at the dock. I had a picture of Claire, me, and the kids. I kissed them goodbye, took one last drink... that's when I took this baby out of its case... and I put it to my temple... *just... like... this*."

Pete turned around with the gun to his head and faced a startled Greg. "*Jesus Christ*, Pete. Put the gun down," Greg said in fear. But Pete did not budge. He kept the gun to his head, looking like a statue of suicide.

"I was going to take my own life, Greg... I still could—right here... right now."

"All right, *stop* this, Pete! *Stop*! I'm sorry, all right? I'm sorry. I should've never said what I said—I didn't mean it."

"No... *you* meant it. You meant every word that you said. No filter, right?"

"Pete, put the gun down—"

"Maybe I should... maybe I should end it all. That way, you'll forever be the family hero."

A crying Greg moved toward Pete. "Brother, *please*... don't do this. *Don't do this*... I'm sorry. You're my brother, Pete. You're my brother, and I love you. I don't want to see anything bad happen to you. I'm sorry. I'm just... I'm just a jealous guy. Don't go out like this. Give me the gun. Come on, Pete... give me the gun."

Pete slowly lowered the gun from his temple and stood there looking defeated. "That's it, buddy," said Greg. "Give me the gun." Pete had a firm grip on the gun. One by one, Greg removed Pete's fingers and took the gun. Greg sighed in relief while Pete stood there in grief.

"I'm a killer, Greg," Pete cried. "I killed that kid."

"Come here, buddy," Greg said as he hugged Pete. "I got you... I got you. I'm sorry. You're my brother, and I love you... I love you, Pete."

43

DECEMBER 31st, 2025, WEDNESDAY MORNING:

EVERYTHING BURNS

After an hour long conversation, Pete and Greg reconciled and settled their differences. Pete shared with Greg some cop stories that he never shared with anyone before. It took hearing those stories for Greg to understand what Pete went through for the last sixteen years of his life, and he respected Pete more than ever.

Pete sat on the living room couch as he needed a rest. He spent the last two hours cleaning up the damage from the other night. Some furniture could not be salvaged and had to be put out for garbage. Piled on top of the coffee table were Pete's certificates of recognition he accumulated over the years. He tossed them into the fireplace one by one and watched as the white sheets turned to black soot. He also threw in a few pictures he took with people he held in high regard but were not there for him in a time of need. All that was left was the letter he had written to Claire he left on the bed.

Pete looked at the envelope that the letter was in—thinking that was the last thing on this earth he would leave behind. As he opened the envelope, he read the letter. It was short and melancholy:

Dearest Claire,

My lover of a lifetime. I'm free now. Free as a bird. Michael, I'm sorry, son. Elle, you'll always be Daddy's little girl. And Leo, I'll always watch over you.

   I love you all.
   Take care.
      Peter Arthur Gant

Pete tossed the letter into the fire and burned his regrets. As he sat and stared at the fire, he began to think about writing another letter—a letter to Tyshawn Brendan's parents. Pete had no idea of what he would write. That is when he remembered what Emilie said to him—to ensure it came from his heart. But it was hard for Pete to write something while his heart was broken. But he was willing to try. He got up from the couch and grabbed a few sheets of paper from his office. As he looked for a pen, his phone began to ring… Elle was calling. Pete grabbed his phone and answered.

"Elle, baby?" Pete said.

"Daddy?" Elle said in her broken voice. *"Hi…"*

"Hi, sweetie… oh, I'm so glad to hear your voice."

"Me too… how are you?"

"I'm… I'm better now. I had a rough day today. But I'm okay. And you?"

"I'm fine… I miss you so much."

"I miss you more, baby. I'm so sorry about the other night. I swear to you, I didn't mean to scare you guys. I… I lost control. I would never hurt you or your brothers—*or* your mother."

"I know, Daddy. I know you've been having a tough time. Mom's having a hard time, too. She's taken a leave of absence from work. Michael's been very quiet around us, and I try to be there for Leo. He misses you too."

"Jesus… baby, I know I've messed up our family."

"No, Daddy. You didn't mess things up—"

"No, no, I did. Over these last several years… I wasn't there for you guys. Your mother was damn near a single parent, you know? I haven't been around. I've missed so much with you guys. I didn't even know Leo's favorite cereal. You all have paid such a horrific price along with me. And I will do everything in my power to make that up to you. I love you guys so much and *I will* be the good father you once knew and loved. I *promise* you, Elle… I'll get our family back together… you'll see, we—we'll be just fine… okay?"

Elle cried. "Okay, Daddy… I trust you."

"Thank you for trusting me…. Does your mother talk about me?"

"Only when she's upset. She told me not to call you. But I just wanted to speak to you. I wanted to hear your voice."

"I'm so grateful that you called, baby. You don't know how much that means to your Daddy. But listen, it's almost four in the morning. You should get your rest. We'll talk again at another time, okay?"

"Okay… I love you, Daddy."

"And I love *you*, Elle."

A silent five seconds went by before Elle ended the call. The phone slowly slid down Pete's teary cheek as he closed his eyes and thought of a happier time when he and his family were at a playground. Pete remembered that day vividly. He remembered Michael going down the slide and a pregnant Claire pushing Elle on the swing. There was nothing but smiles and graceful laughter. It was Pete's day off, and he did not have a worry in the world. Pete wished he could return to that innocent time—back when he was their hero. But that hero within had been lost for quite some time, and he must do everything in his power to find Pete again.

After burning his past, Pete went into the kitchen, grabbed several bottles of dark liquor, and decided it was time to pour out the poison. As he took the bottles to the sink, that inner voice came back into his conscience:

Hey, buddy. I know what you're thinking. Don't do it. I'm your friend, remember? Don't pour me out... pour me in. Pour me inside. Let me get into your bloodstream so you can have better dreams. I'll make you feel better. Come on, Pete. Don't do this to me, buddy. We need each other. We're two of a kind. Let me take over, and I'll keep you warm through the night.

Pete, however, ignored the voice as he twisted off the caps of the bottles. One by one, he tilted the bottles forward and poured. The inner voice grew more aggressive, screaming as the liquor streamed down the dark drain. It was then that Pete felt he was gaining his power back. Suddenly, it was down to the last bottle, his favorite drink: Vodka—that clear liquid that would burn his throat like a watery flame. But the Vodka had an inner voice of its own. And it was not going down without a fight:

Coward! You fucking piece of shit! How dare you do this to me? After all I helped you through, and this is how you repay me? Your only friend in the world? Oh, how the betrayal hurts. Judas! I should've killed you when I had the chance. Fine, go ahead, pour me out. You'll see me again. I'm everywhere, Pete. In every liquor store, in every bar, at every party. You can't escape me forever. You know where to find me. All it takes is another taste... I'm the disease that never dies.

Pete poured out the Vodka and said this in *his* voice. "You were *never* a friend. You caused me nothing but hell. You were just an enemy who pretended to care. And now... you're out of my life... for good."

44

JANUARY 12^{th,} 2026, MONDAY AFTERNOON:

<u>A LETTER OF HOPE</u>

It had been a long ten days. The remains of dozens of balled-up papers were decorated on the floor of Pete's study. Pete had been struggling with the letter he was writing for Tyshawn Brendan's mother, Jada Brennan. After seeing a heated press interview with Tyshawn's father, Morris Clark, Pete felt he would not get through to him with a letter and decided that the letter should only be addressed to Jada. Even though Pete was no longer a police officer, he still had connections on the force. He made some phone calls and asked for a home address to mail the letter. But that was the easy part. The hard part was *writing* the letter. And after twenty-seven tries, Pete finally had a letter from the heart. As he sat there in his leather chair as he read the letter aloud:

Dear Mrs. Jada Brendan,

I am sure that this letter comes unexpected and unwanted, and you probably have no intentions of reading any further and might want to burn this letter. But I beg of you, please don't. I've spent days working up the strength and the nerve to write to you. I wanted to reach out to you to offer my deepest and sincerest apologies for all the pain and heartache I have caused you and your family. Before that horrific night, I was just an officer protecting and serving the community. It was my only wish that I would not be involved in a situation where I would have to use my weapon and open fire, as I'm sure you would never think that your son, Tyshawn, would be involved in such a tragic situation.

That night was the worst night of not just my career but of my entire life. I haven't been able to sleep at night. I see Tyshawn's face every time I close my eyes, and I carry such guilt and misery. I've lost everything. My wife left me and took the kids. I've been dismissed as a law enforcement officer, and now... I'm all alone, and it's been a living hell. But by no means am I trying to paint myself as a victim. I am the one who's responsible for what happened to your son, and I am so, very sorry for what happened. Every day since it happened, I've played that night in my head and asked myself, "What could I have done differently?" "Why did it have to be your son?"

I know this never happens. Here I am, the officer who is responsible for your son's death, and I'm writing you a letter. I wish I could take it all back, Mrs. Brendan. I wish I could have that moment back and let those boys go on. I wish I never took that call. I don't understand why this happened. But now, like you, I have to live with this for the rest of my life. And I must be honest with you... I'm in a lot of pain. There is no way I can just go on with my life knowing that I took someone away who was so gifted and so special to many people. How can I possibly live on with that on my conscience? I can't.

Mrs. Brendan... I don't know if you'll respond or not. And I completely understand if you don't. And you have my word that I will never write or contact you again. But I just want you to know that not a day will go by that I don't think of your son. I don't know how I will survive through all of this moving forward, if I can move forward. I don't know if I'll ever get my family back. But I just wanted you to know how truly sorry I am for the loss of your son, Tyshawn Brendan.

Thank you very much for your time.
Sincerely, Peter Gant

Thirty minutes later, Pete was at the local post office. He watched as the window clerk put the stamps on the letter and transported it off with the other mail. Pete stood in a daze as he had doubts about if the letter was a good idea. But all he could do was hope for the best.

"Sir… you okay?" said the window clerk.

"Huh? Oh, yes. I'm fine," Pete responded as he pinched the bridge of his nose.

"Is there anything else I can help you with today?"

"No… that'll be all. Thank you. Have a great day."

Pete walked out of the post office and headed to his Jeep. As he got in, he sat there and did what the Priest suggested he do… pray. He prayed that Jada Brendan would receive and read the letter. After he finished praying, he drove off in search of healing and finding his life again. Pete knew this journey of recovery would not be easy, but this time, he was not going to give up.

45

HEALING FROM THE BADGE

Eight months had come and gone. The seasons had changed and the summer was almost through. But as much time as had gone by, Pete was stuck—struggling with his demons.

It was the afternoon and Pete had an appointment with his psychologist, Dr. Mary Dune, the same psychologist Officer Devin McCloud referred. Pete had been seeing Dr. Dune for the last several months—gradually opening up to her. Since the shooting, some things have changed with Pete and his appearance. The months of stress, depression, and being apart from his family had taken its toll. He was twenty pounds lighter, and gray hair was scattered all over his head. He and Claire were legally separated, with Claire having full custody of the children. Pete was granted visitation rights and would spend quality time with Elle and Leo. Michael, however, avoided Pete as they still had a perpetuating dilemma. It hurt Pete that his oldest child did not want to see him. But he was grateful for Elle and Leo's presence and love.

As for Montgomery, he and Pete had not spoken since their argument back in May. Montgomery was angry with Pete for not attending Poppa Dee's funeral. He told Pete he would regret it for the rest of his life. Pete, however, thought otherwise. Because they both had stubborn personalities, they had not spoken to each other in months.

In the office of Dr. Dune, Pete sat and waited patiently as he was reading a newspaper. One of the articles was about Tyshawn Brendan and how his parents, Morris and Jada, settled the wrongful death lawsuit for $65 million. To the left of the article was a photo of Tyshawn Brendan with his mother Jada at his basketball game. Up to that day, Jada had not responded to Pete's letter.

Suddenly, the door to Dr. Dune's office had opened. "Hey, Pete, come on in," said Dr. Dune. Pete entered the office and took his regular seat on the couch. Dr. Dune was a woman of great logic. She had been a psychologist for over thirty years. Over the years, Dr. Dune had received great notoriety for her work with over eight thousand patients throughout her career. She was tall and very well-dressed every day she came to the office. She had a gray lob haircut and thick, red-framed Gucci eyeglasses. One thing Pete liked about Dr. Dune was that she had these honest brown eyes with crow's feet wrinkles. Looking at her eyes, he could tell that she lived life and had much experience. As they both sat there, Dr. Dune opened the conversation.

"How are you feeling today, Pete?" Dr. Dune asked.

"I'm having a good day so far," Pete responded. "Got a good night's sleep."

"That's good… any nightmares?"

"No… not for a while now. They've been clearing up."

"*Good*… and how is everything going with the kids?"

"I had them for the weekend. We went to the movies for Leo's birthday. He wanted to see the new Lego movie. Then afterward, we stopped to have a pizza and ice cream cake at Carvel."

"Wonderful. It sounds like you guys enjoyed yourselves."

"We did, yeah. It was the best time *I* had in a while."

"And Michael?"

Pete combed his hair back and sighed. "Michael and I haven't really connected since that night we had that… altercation. I really miss him. But he just refuses to talk to me."

"Have you made attempts to talk with *him*?"

"No. I haven't. Well… I texted him a few months back, wishing him a happy birthday. I remember looking at the three dots—you know—when someone is responding? But then they disappeared. I was hoping he'd respond… what are you going to do, right?"

"I think it's time that we try harder, Pete. How about we invite him to a session? Let's have the both of you sit down and have that conversation."

"Oh, I don't know, Doc. Michael's not the kind of kid who just opens up like that to people."

"It wouldn't hurt to try. We have to get you two reacquainted. I think it would help. It's been six months, yes?"

"*Seven* months—off and on. I really would like to see him."

"Then we'll make that happen…. What else is on your mind?"

Pete thought about it. "I need a job—something to keep me busy. My mom's been sending money. Even though I know it's coming from my father… I feel like a little boy again."

"Have you been *looking* for a job?"

"It's complicated. I'm still dealing with social anxiety. I also feel like I have a lot of unfinished business."

"What kind of unfinished business?"

"Just… not being able to have closure with what happened. And my father and I are not in communication."

"Let's focus on your father. What is your current relationship with him?"

"There *is* no relationship right now. We haven't been speaking. And as much as I hate handouts… it's been a struggle keeping up with my bills… my taxes were crazy this year…. My life has gone downhill, Doc. And my family's destroyed."

"No, Pete. It's not. And we've *talked* about this. It's *broken*... but it's not destroyed. It can and *will* be healed."

"I just... I don't feel like a man right now. A man is supposed to protect and provide for his family."

"A *man* is a *human being*, Pete. *You* are a human being. And life for us human beings can be unpredictable and challenging. You never know *what* could happen to you in life."

"You got that right. I'm living proof of that."

"You know, for the two months you've been coming here, you've shared with me the stories of Gabriella del Alto, Emilie Graham, and Brady Willis... you have many more of these stories bottled up inside, don't you?"

Pete sighed. "You have no idea. It was a brutal sixteen years out there. I've seen things that a regular person wouldn't even see in their worst nightmares. I've crossed paths with the worst people—*evil* people... people who, somewhere down the line, just... fell off the path. Predators, victims who had their throats slit. There was one case when a nine-year-old kid poured lighter fluid on his mom while she was sleeping and set her on fire—just because she took his Xbox away as a punishment for bad behavior. She survived though—by the skin of her teeth."

"And this happened in Cedar Grove?"

"Oh, *yeah*. See, that's the thing, Doc. People think they're safe once they move into the suburbs. Nothing could be farther from the truth. People don't seem to realize that *violence*... it's everywhere."

"That's very true."

"You mentioned Brady Willis. I was hoping you wouldn't, though."

"You still don't want to talk about him?"

"There's nothing really to talk *about*. A drunk driver drove up on the sidewalk—struck Brady from behind—he died instantly... never saw it coming. He was only twelve years old."

"Were you the first responder?"

"I was… his father asked him to take out the trash. I just remember seeing Brady's father holding his body. I never heard a man cry the way he did. It was like you could hear his cries throughout the universe."

"What happened to the drunk driver?"

"He took off, but not too far. He crashed his car a couple blocks away. *He* survived. But the Judge gave him forty years for hit and run and manslaughter. That image of Brady, though… it's still in me. I went home that morning and hugged Michael so tight. It was awful, Doc."

"What else is in you, Pete? Share it with me."

Since day one, Dr. Dune had been chipping away at the wall Pete had placed before him. He shared things with her that he never mentioned to anyone before. That is when he thought of Virginia Garfield-Smith.

"Doc… have I ever mentioned the name Virginia Garfield-Smith?"

"Not that I recall."

"Her family called her 'Ginny.' She was a cheerleader in high school—straight-A student—*beautiful* girl. One night, she went to a house party with some of her friends. They played this game called 'What would you do in the closet?' When it was her turn, she went into a closet with a guy. From what I read in the report, the guy tried to rape her. She ran out of the closet screaming. She screamed all the way out of the house. I was one of the officers sent to shut down the party. As I got out of my car, Ginny ran straight to me with her shirt ripped and her body exposed, and she just held onto me for dear life—crying hysterically."

"That's terrible."

"Yeah… after I got her to calm down, she told me what happened. I remember becoming very angry when she told me because I imagined her being Elle. I pictured *Elle* running to me and telling me that some kid or even some *man* tried to rape her. I stormed into that house—looking for that kid. I was ready to slam that kid on his *face* and cuff him."

"Did you arrest the kid?"

"Well... here's the kicker, Ginny didn't want him to get in trouble. She wasn't willing to cooperate or press charges. She didn't even give me the guy's name."

"Why?"

Pete chuckled. "Doc, that's a question I will *never* get an answer to. There have been so many cases where women are attacked by their husband or boyfriend, and whenever the police arrive on the scene, it's the *woman* who ends up protecting their abuser and attacking the officer. *Why* do they protect their abuser? I have no idea."

"What about the boy?"

"Well, after hours of convincing her, Ginny gave the boy's name. Philip Sterling."

"Was he brought in?"

"Of *course* he was. Officers brought him in for questioning. He denied everything, of course. But you know what's so crazy about that Sterling kid? Both of his parents were hot-shot attorneys."

"Oh... so, I take it he didn't serve any time?"

"Not one day. Technically speaking, it wasn't "*Rape*-rape," as his father said in the courtroom... whatever the hell *that* means. Being that the kid didn't *penetrate* Ginny, it couldn't be ruled a rape, so they settled for sexual assault. But there was a plea deal. Two-year probation—which was a slap on the wrist for *him*, but a slap in the face for Ginny."

"And what happened to her? Ginny?"

Pete went silent. "I ran into her mother at a store about three years ago. I asked her how Ginny was doing...."

Dr. Dune waited. "And what did she say?"

"'She's dead...' that's what she told me. She overdosed on

prescription pills. She said that Ginny never recovered from that night.... And that boy? Philip Sterling? It was *his* house where the incident occurred. I drove past his house a few nights during my shift—sometimes even when I was off-duty. I would see that bastard in the front yard. It took me everything in my *power* not to get out of my car and beat the living shit out of him. There was a part of me that thought, 'instead of Brady Willis getting struck by the drunk driver, it should be *this* rapist piece of shit. But that's not how life works, does it? It's always the *good* ones who check out first, right?"

Dr. Dune nodded in agreement. "Unfortunately."

"Yeah... it's a shame, too. That kid was captain of his Lacrosse team—All-American athlete. And he pissed that all away. That's what's so frustrating about this job. You want to save as many people as you possibly can... but you can't. All you ever really save are the bad memories... and I hate them."

Dr. Dune took a moment to observe Pete in silence. She saw the pain in his eyes as he shared stories of his days and nights of policing. She sympathized with Pete deeply.

Dr. Dune coughed. "Excuse me... well... we're almost out of time. Was there anything else you wanted to discuss?"

"Well... I don't want to discuss any more cases I was involved in. Some of them I'd just like to forget about completely."

"Pete... in these sessions you've had with me, you mentioned all the bad things that came with the job. Were there any *good* things?"

"Yeah. There was *one* good thing that came out of it."

"What?"

"Survival... I always made it home. And that's what so strange about it because when I got home to my family, I would forget the bad stuff and leave it all outside my house. But sometimes, the bad stuff would leak through the cracks of my conscience and terrorize me with wicked thoughts. But on the good days, I would play with my kids, help them with their homework, and spend quality time with my family. Claire and my kids… they have been my sanity. They are my purpose for why I did the job. To protect them and try my best to make the world a better place for them. Boy, did I fail."

"You didn't fail, Pete. You just have a lot of healing to catch up on."

"Could I ask you for a favor, Doc?"

"Absolutely."

"If I could invite Claire in for a session as well, would you be willing to talk with the both of us?"

"Well, that depends. If it's about trying to save your *marriage*, I'm not a marriage counselor—per se. But if the two of you would like to discuss co-parenting, the kids, or how you're dealing with the separation *mentally*, I think I could be of some assistance."

"Thank you, Doc."

"You're welcome. Is there anything else you want to discuss before we wrap things up?"

"No, Doc. I think I've tortured you enough with my crazy cop stories."

"Wait a minute, Pete. I almost forgot. Have you heard back from Jada Brendan?"

"Um… no. I haven't heard back from her," Pete said with sorrow.

"I'm sorry to hear that."

"Yeah. I don't think I'll ever hear from that family, Doc. But I understand… I just wish her and her family the best."

"That's nice of you, Pete. It's good that you feel these things. And I'm sure she would want the best for you."

Pete scoffed. "I doubt that."

"Pete… I've had the privilege of knowing who you are for the last several months. Your character, your demeanor, it doesn't fit the narrative of you being a racist cop looking to hunt down black people. I think what happened that night was a tragic incident that cannot be undone. And now, *you* have to find within yourself how to move

JORDAN WELLS

forward in your life and look at what's right in front of you... family. Like you said, '*family* is what kept you sane.' Now's the time to heal, Pete. Not just for your family but for yourself... okay?"

"Okay, Doc... thank you."

"You're very welcome.... Now, that's it for the day. And hopefully, the next time we see each other, we'll have some guests with us?"

"I hope so... thanks again."

Pete got a lot off his chest in that session. That was the first time he shared the stories of Brady Willis and Virginia Garfield-Smith. Pete learned that therapy indeed worked. His mind was clearer and he felt the demons within were finally heading to the exit. But his number one priority was to bring his family back together.

46

SEPTEMBER 13^{th,} 2026, SUNDAY EVENING:

KARMA AND REDEMPTION

It had been a long road to recovery, but RaJohnn Mitchell was back on his feet, walking on his own again. Alone on a basketball court in Branch Brook Park, RaJohnn dribbled around and took a few shots. Being that he was a lefty, his sharp release was derailed from the bullet fragments lodged in his left elbow. As RaJohnn held the ball, he began to think about Tyshawn—reminiscing about their playing days on that same court as little kids. RaJohnn knew way back then that Tyshawn was going to be great. He knew that he was going to make it.

As RaJohnn took another shot, a voice shouted from behind. "Ayo, *Rah!*" RaJohnn turned around and saw three of his homeboys from around the way: Wally, Quah, and Budda. Wally had a babyface, not even a chin hair. His dreadlocks were down, and he sported denim jean shorts, a black hoodie, and Timberland boots. Quah was heavy-set and wore a silver durag, a white t-shirt, and jeans. As for Budda, he also wore a black hoodie with the hood over his black Yankees fitted hat with the brim tilted left.

"*Oh, shit!*" RaJohnn said with enthusiasm as he dapped them up. "What up, what up, what *up!* What it do, gang?"

"Ain't nothin', my guy," said Wally. "What's good with you?"

"*Shit*... I'm *chillin'*. Just getting some exercise. Doctors say I gotta keep moving to get my hip right. So, I just be walking on the track and shit, keeping my legs in shape, you feel me?"

"A'ight, a'ight... heard you got that three mil from the lawsuit."

"Who told you that?" RaJohnn asked with a twisted face.

"That's what the streets been *saying*," Quah said.

RaJohnn was in denial. "Nah, I don't know *nothing* about *that*."

Quah chuckled. "*Word*, gang?"

"*Word*—I don't know what the fuck you *talkin'* bout'."

"*A'ight, homie*," Wally said. "You ain't gotta be all *salty* about it...."

RaJohnn sighed. "Yo, I'm just trying to get my shit together and get the hell outta Newark, a'ight? Fuck the hood."

"Fuck the *hood*?" Said Budda.

"Yeah, *fuck* this place, gang. All these bums around here ain't about nothin'. I'm tryin' be about somethin', ya feel me?"

"A'ight, *a'ight*," Wally chuckled. "Ain't nothin' wrong with leaving the hood. I ain't mad at ya... but before you go... how's bout' we get a two-on-two going?"

RaJohnn scoffed. "Yo, you really fin to play in *Timbs*?"

"Hell yeah, and we *still* gonna whip your ass. Yo, Budda... you rock with Rah."

"A'ight, bet," Budda said as he rubbed his hands together like an evil scientist.

"Yo, Rah... let me get the rock, homie," Wally said with a sinister smile.

RaJohnn looked at the three of them: their demeanor said it all. He began to feel a sense of danger. He went from feeling like he was surrounded by friends to being surrounded by sharks—ready to tear the flesh off his bones. At that moment, RaJohnn looked at his gym bag on the ground. Inside was his Glock 9mm. He thought about running to his bag to pull it out and start dumping on them. But as soon as that thought entered his mind, Wally got his attention.

"Yo, Rah! You ready?" Said Wally.

"Yeah," RaJohnn said unconfidently. "To—toss me the rock, gang."

Wally looked at the ball with his sinister smile. "You know what? I don't think we *need* the rock. Right, fellas?"

"Nah," Budda smiled. "We don't need it all, ain't that right, Budda?"

"*Goddamn* right, Budda!" Budda added.

RaJohnn took a panoramic look at the three of them as he knew exactly what was about to happen. But he *also* knew that if he were going out, he would take the first hit, and that was exactly what he did. BOOM! RaJohnn punched Budda to the ground and made a run for his bag. Quah swiftly swept RaJohnn's leg and watched him fall face first on the court. They then formed a circle around RaJohnn and began to stomp him out. All RaJohnn could see was the soles of Wally's size twelve Timberland boots smashing his face. "*Yeah, motherfucka!*" Quah said as he punched RaJohnn in the face. Suddenly, Wally reached behind him and pulled out a gun. As he pointed the gun down at RaJohnn, he looked into his eyes as if he had every intention of letting the lemon squeeze.

"You already knew you had this one coming to you, homeboy," Wally said, with the gun aimed at RaJohnn's head. "It was *you… you* fucked up."

"*Hell yeah!*" Quah added. "If you had kept your fucking cool and not crash out, Ty would still be alive."

Budda then walked over to Wally. "Do it, Wah… *blast* his bitch ass."

RaJohnn looked at them in a bloody haze. He could feel this was it. But deep down, he was ready to die. The trigger was pulled, but no bullet was dispensed. "Mother*fucka!*" Wally said as the gun jammed. He tried to cock the gun, but it wouldn't budge. Suddenly the sounds of police sirens grew louder and closer. "Yo, Wah! *Fuck* him. Let's roll," Quah said as he and Budda began to run off. Wally, however, did not budge. "Yo, Wah! Bring your ass on!" Budda shouted. With the gun jammed and still pointed at RaJohnn, Wally said, "You live to run again, fool…. On *God…* I'm gonna finish this shit. *You* killed Tyshawn… *you* don't deserve to live." RaJohnn gave Wally a stern look and responded. "*Fuck* you!" Wally immediately kicked RaJohnn in the face and ran off—leaving RaJohnn lying on the court, bloodied and battered. Wally knew about RaJohnn's short temper, and after seeing the body cam footage, he knew—more than anyone, that RaJohnn was at fault, and he wanted to avenge Tyshawn. But RaJohnn's life was spared, and he lived to see another day.

Hours later, RaJohnn was home, lying on his bed with Ziploc bags of ice on his bruised legs and one covering the right side of his face. He had minor cuts on his face that he blotted down with peroxide. Mounted on the wall of his room was a custom poster of him and Tyshawn. It was the same picture from the newspaper cutout of them at the state championship. RaJohnn had spent timeless nights staring at that picture, reminiscing with fresh tears. Suddenly, his sister, Neecy, barged into his room—shocked at his condition.

"What the *fuck* happened to you?" Neecy said.

"Ain't *nothin'* happened to me," RaJohnn aggressively responded.

"*Nothing?*"

"Yeah, that's right, *nothin'*."

"Don't *look* like nothing. Looks like you got your *ass* whipped. You just can't stay out of trouble, can you?"

"Why don't you mind your own business, Neecy? *Damn!*"

"Okay, we not doing that—not when I'm paying all the bills. You're *going* to tell me what happened."

RaJohnn hesitated. "I slipped, and I fell—"

"Don't bullshit me, Rah. I *told* you about that."

"It ain't *nothin'*, a'ight? Just some low-life, thug ass bitches hating on me. But it's all good—I *got* something for their ass."

Neecy sighed. "When are you going to learn, Rah? Huh? When are you going to grow up and take responsibility for *your actions*? Don't you realize this way of living is what got you *in* that situation last year?"

"Go ahead and say it, Neecy. Go ahead. Go ahead and say it was all *my* fault."

"Rah, I am *so sick* and tired of this. Here you are, living in *my* house, not doing *shit* with your life except smoking weed all day long—*talking* to yourself about Tyshawn. *Enough* is *enough*!"

RaJohnn sucked his teeth. "Man, go ahead with that."

"Listen… I talked with Ma today… she thinks it's best if you move down to North Carolina and live with her."

RaJohnn grew furious. "What?"

"Look, she can enroll you in a good school down there. She lives in a very nice neighborhood—gated community and everything… this could be a great opportunity, Rah."

"Opportunity? *What* opportunity?"

"An opportunity to get your life back on track."

"Neecy, I'm a black man from *Newark*. *What* opportunities are *out* there for black men that don't involve rapping, trapping, running or shooting a goddamn *ball*? Nobody gives a *shit* about us—*especially* the ones like *me*."

"Oh, so *that's* what we're doing now? Playing the victim?"

"What do you expect, Neecy?"

"I expect you to have a little more faith in yourself."

"Well, I *don't*, a'ight?"

Neecy stood up. "Okay… Rah? What I'm about to tell you is something you *obviously* need to hear… if you keep going on living your life like this, you'll be dead by the end of this year… or in prison… and I do *not* want you to end up like your friend."

RaJohnn went silent. "I almost was."

"That's right. You lucky that cop—"

"No, no… I'm talking about tonight. They almost popped my ass."

Neecy was startled. "*What*?"

"I was at the basketball court. Some dudes from the block came running up on me and jumped me. Then one of them pulled out the blickie… I thought it was a wrap… but it jammed… that's when I heard the cops coming. But I wasn't trying to get caught up with *them*, so I bounced."

"Oh my Lord," Neecy said. "Do you… why didn't you *call* me?"

"I wasn't even in my right mind. I was just trying to get the hell outta there. That's when I came home."

"*Shit*, Rah, we need to get you to the hospital—"

"No, I ain't with that hospital shit right now. I've seen *enough* of that place."

"Rah… do you know how lucky you are? Not everybody can face death twice and win."

"Yeah… I know…. I'm not even going to hold you, Sis… I *am* tired of living this way. I'm not trying to go out like that on these streets."

"And that's why you need to take this opportunity, move down south, and live with Ma. These second and third chances of changing your life don't happen like that."

"I miss him, Neecy," RaJohnn cried. "I miss my brother so much. Ty told me to keep my cool, and I didn't… *I* fucked up… and now he's gone."

"Rah… Tyshawn would've want you to get your life together. You *owe* that to him—you owe that to *yourself*."

RaJohnn nodded his head as he wiped away the tears. "Yeah, you right… he was such a good dude. He was *real* smart. The shorties loved him… he had his whole life set. He was *our* king. He was going to be the GOAT… he was going to be the greatest."

"I think you know what you need to do now."

"Yeah... I'll go down there... and start over. But I'm leaving tonight."

"*Tonight?*"

"Yup, I'm going to book me a plane ticket right now... um... you think you could spot me the money for the ticket?"

Neecy smiled. "I got you, boo... I got you. I love you, Rah."

"I know you do, Neecy," RaJohnn smirked. "Got love for you, too."

"Uh, no, I need you to *say*, 'I love you, Neecy.'"

RaJohnn chuckled. "A'ight, a'ight... I *love* you, Neecy."

Neecy gave RaJohnn a gentle hug and a kiss. She was grateful RaJohnn had told her the truth. After an hour of helping him pack, Neecy finally convinced RaJohnn to go to the emergency room to get checked out. Luckily, there were no broken bones or head injuries. As soon as he was discharged from the hospital, Neecy took him straight to Newark International Airport, and he hopped on the next flight out to North Carolina. Even though RaJohnn was conflicted, he felt he owed it to Tyshawn to leave a troubled life of nonsense behind and live a more meaningful and promising life.

47

Pete had returned to Dr. Dune's office, but this time, he had company. Claire and Michael were sitting in the waiting room while Pete spoke with Dr. Dune. Pete sat there in silence as he attempted to solve a Rubik's cube.

"You've gotten better since last time," said Dr. Dune. "You almost got it."

"Yeah," Pete said as he twist the Rubik's cube.

"Don't have much to say today?"

Pete shook his head. "Not really. Usually, I would have a *lot* to say… but not today."

"Are you still reading people's comments?"

Pete placed the Rubik's cube on the table. "Not as much as before. I've deleted my social media accounts. But sometimes, I read the comments people leave on YouTube."

"What do they say?"

"The usual. They call me a pig, a racist—saying that I was determined to shoot and kill those kids because they were black."

"How does that make you feel?"

"It makes me feel terrible—like I'm not even a human being. But they *just don't understand*. They don't understand that we're trained to handle a threat a certain way as an officer. I remember in the academy, my supervisor once told us, 'You delay, you die.' I didn't delay. I didn't hesitate. And now... I'm the most hated man in America."

"Pete... you mentioned that people have called you a racist... do you feel that?"

"Feel what?"

"That you're a racist?"

Pete paused as he thought about it. "Before all of this happened... No. I didn't feel that way. But now... I don't know. Something inside me has been indoctrinated ever since I was a kid. But I never had to address it. I asked myself if RaJohnn Mitchell and Tyshawn Brendan were *white*, would I have opened fire the same way without hesitation?"

"And what's your answer to that?"

"I *can't* answer that. Because it shouldn't be a black or white thing... but it is."

"Was there something rooted in your family that may have caused some kind of trauma?"

"Well... back in January, Poppa Dee told me this story about how *his* father took him to a public lynching."

Dr. Dune was stunned. "A public *lynching*?"

"Yes... it was the most disgusting story I ever heard. He told me about never forgetting your place as a white man—not just in America... but the world.... I'm just stuck. For the first time in my life, after the shooting, I questioned myself and asked, 'Am I a racist?'"

"Is that what *you're* asking or people on the internet?"

Pete hesitated. "Both."

"Okay, so let me ask you again. Do you feel that you're a racist?"

Pete shook his head. "No... no, I'm not a racist."

"Then that's it. You've answered your question. There's nothing more to say about that."

"But that's what people *don't* know. They don't *care* to know."

"Pete, you have to stop concerning yourself with what other people *think* of you. Those people are on the outside looking in, and they only go off speculation. But as long as you can look in the mirror and see and know the *real* you... that's all that matters."

"Yeah... I guess you're right."

"Pete... what is it that you want?"

"What do I want?"

"Yes."

"I just want people to leave me alone. I want them to stop harassing me and my family... and I want my family back."

"You have Claire and Michael waiting out there, yes?"

"Yeah, they're sitting down on the couch."

"Okay, I want you to sit down with Michael first. Is that okay?"

"Okay."

"All right. Just a moment."

Dr. Dune opened her door and invited Michael into her office. Michael came in with a look that said, "What am I doing here?" As he sat beside Pete, Dr. Dune brought Michael into the conversation.

"How are you, Michael?" Dr. Dune asked.

Michael hesitated. "I'm good."

"Thank you for joining us."

"Yeah, sure."

Michael did not have much to say, not to Dr. Dune or to Pete. Pete looked and looked at him—reminiscing about the day Michael was born. He remembered holding him in the hospital, thinking it was the happiest day of his life.

"Pete," Dr. Dune said as he was in a daze. "Pete!"

"What? Yes?" Pete said as he snapped out of it.

"Is there something you would like to say to Michael?"

"Uh... yes. There is.... Michael? Son... I know these last several years haven't been easy for you. I know I haven't been the best father. And what happened months ago? I... I'm still struggling with it mentally. We *all* are.... What happened to Tyshawn Brendan... I didn't mean to shoot him. Before that night, I'd never taken a life. It screwed me up, and I haven't been the same since. This tragedy is going to follow me for the rest of my life. I can never escape it. I can never let it go. But somehow, I've let *you* go. And I miss you. I miss you so much, Michael."

Michael wiped his eyes. "I miss you, too, Dad."

"Do you remember when you were eight years old, and you had a hard time sleeping because you thought monsters were hiding in your closet?"

Michael chuckled. "Yeah... yeah I remember that."

"You asked me if I could stay with you for the night. Not only did I stay with you, I wore my uniform—as if I was on patrol. You woke up with the biggest smile on your face when you saw me guarding the room. I told you that I'll always protect you from those monsters. You hugged me and called me your hero.... Well, son... I have to be honest with you... *I* need a hero now... and I was hoping *you* would be up for that role."

"*Me*?" Michael emotionally said.

"Yes."

"Be your *hero*?"

"Yes," Pete said as tears streamed down his face. "Be *my* hero, son."

"*How*? How am I going to be *your* hero, Dad? You're *my* father! How can I be a hero to *you*?"

"Forgiveness... and love. I believe you still love me, Michael. Love is a given... and respect is earned. But forgiveness is a choice. I know it may take some *time*, but... if you can forgive me... it would save *my* life."

Michael did not know how to respond. He was confused and

at a loss for words. Dr. Dune then interjected.

"Michael?" Dr. Dune said. "You love your father, yes?"

Michael shook his head. "Yes... I love him."

"Can you forgive him?"

"Yeah... I can forgive. I love you, Dad. I'm sorry that you're still in a lot of pain. But I forgive you."

Pete sobbed. "Thank you... thank you."

Michael slid over on the couch and hugged Pete. Pete kissed him on the side of his head. Their tears were genuine and in sync. As they released, Pete said, "I'm going to talk with your mother now, okay? I have to make things right with her, too. Just hang tight in the waiting room." Michael stepped out of the office as Claire walked in. Claire sat on the far end of the couch, leaving a significant gap between her and Pete. As they sat there, Dr. Dune began to speak with Claire.

"Hi, Claire," said Dr. Dune. "Thank you for coming today."

"Thank you for having me," Claire softly responded.

"So, Pete and Michael were able to reconcile."

"That's good."

"Pete, would you care to tell Claire what's on your mind?"

Pete turned his body toward Claire. "Claire... I've *never* loved someone... more than love can *ever* exist... than the way I love you. Since the first moment of sight that my eyes cast on you, I said to myself, 'God, if she's my future wife, give me the courage to approach her. But if she's not, I don't care because I gotta have her.' I've dedicated over sixteen years of my life to my badge. Every day, before I walked out of that house, I'd kissed you and told you I would be back unharmed. And every day... you would be right there, waiting for me with open arms. For sixteen years... I've kept my word—physically. But mentally... I've never felt so much pain. There were so many incidents that I've kept secret from you and the kids—so many tragic scenes playing over and over in my head—too many deaths… too many nightmares. I wouldn't have survived without you by my side. You are my rock and… and I appreciate everything you did to keep our family together."

Claire grabbed a few tissues as she blotted her eyes. She then cleared her throat as she had something to say to Pete. "I appreciate your appreciation. But now, I want you to hear *my* point of view… *my* nightmares. You have *no idea* the pain that *I* went through, the secrets that *I've* kept away from the kids… and taking care of them alone? So many sleepless nights of me lying in bed thinking at any given second, you could be shot down—*dead*. I must've cried *pools* over my pillows, worrying if you were safe out there. You would always tell me that I was strong. But if something would've happened to you? That would've broken me, Pete. I understand how hard that job was for you. How disposable you are—how they don't care about you after they've used you and sucked you dry of life. Just like those soldiers at war. I was there for all of it, Pete. I signed up for it just as much as you did—knowing the price I'd paid. But I'm so tired. I'm tired of the drinking, I'm tired of having nightmares, I'm tired of arguing, and I'm tired of…" Pete looked at Claire as if he knew what she would say next.

"*Me?*" Pete asked. "You're tired of *me*… aren't you?"

"I'm just tired, period. I thought I would be strong enough to go the whole way with you. But I don't think I can anymore."

"Claire?" Dr. Dune spoke. "You don't have to finalize anything right now. Keep in mind that I'm *not* a marriage counselor. But what I *can* say is this… whatever decision is made, it *has* to be in the children's best interest. Not just the two of you."

"Doctor. If I may ask, what would *you* do if you were in my situation?"

"I'm afraid I can't answer that, Claire. That is something that you have to discuss with Pete. And as I said, a decision does not have to be made overnight. Pete has mentioned that you both are legally separated?"

"Yes, we are."

"Okay. Sometimes, a separation is beneficial. It allows both parties to have time apart and process what you want for yourselves.... Do you know what you want, Claire?"

"I don't know *what* I want, Dr. Dune... I really don't know."

"Pete? What about you?"

As tears fell, Pete said, "At this point in my life, all I want is for Claire and the kids to be happy.... Maybe my father was right. I could've been anything I wanted in life—*anything*... I chose to be a cop. That badge damaged my life and the lives of others and cost me time away from my family. And that's the price I've paid for wearing that blue uniform. The thing is... being a cop is not just a job... it's a way of life—*for* life. And I can't just undo everything that I've been through. I wish I could, Claire... but I can't. And for what it's worth, in the sixteen years... I *never* meant to hurt you or those kids.... If you can find it in your soul to give *us* another chance, I promise I will not fail this time... I will not fail my family."

Claire held Pete's hand. "I still need my time, Pete. Please understand that."

"Take your time then," Pete said as he stood and walked toward the door.

"Wait, Pete," Dr. Dune said as Pete exited the office.

As Pete left the office, Claire buried her face in her hands and sobbed. Dr. Dune then sat beside Claire to comfort her.

"Are you okay?" Dr. Dune asked as she rubbed Claire's back.

"No," Claire sniffled. "Dr. Dune... I have no regrets about marrying Pete—*none*. I love him. I don't think I'll ever stop loving him. I never would've imagined leaving him. But I'm just so *tired*, doctor."

"What are you tired of, Claire? Specifically."

"I'm tired of being afraid. For so many years, I was afraid of losing him. I was afraid that one day, he was going to reach his breaking point and just kill himself—or one of us. I'm afraid a day would come when I would no longer love him. And that scares me to death."

"What is it about Pete that you love?"

Through the sobbing storm, a smile emerged like an honest rainbow. *"Everything… everything."*

Dr. Dune empathized with Claire. She understood what Claire was going through because her *first* husband was also a police officer. Dr. Dune shared some stories with Claire about her years as a police wife. Some stories were heartwarming, others you could not imagine. Claire walked out that office with a better understanding of what she wanted—not just with Pete, but for herself.

48

OCTOBER 21st, 2026, WEDNESDAY MORNING:

THE RESPONSE

Another month had gone by. Dead autumn leaves had blanketed the grounds, keeping their everlasting promise of the changing seasons. As Pete took Brownie for a walk, he observed the Halloween decorations in the neighborhood. The decorations were hysterically spooky, as houses had giant skeletons and inflatable pumpkins on the front yards.

As Pete walked under a bridge, he spotted this colossal mural of Tyshawn Brendan on the wall of an abandon building. The mural was a multi-color portrait of Tyshawn Brendan with a background of the sun-setting clouds of heaven. It was exquisitely detailed—beautifully capturing the essence of the promising, gifted young man that Tyshawn Brendan was. Pete stared at the mural as he played back the night of the shooting in his mind. "I'm sorry, kid... I'm so sorry," Pete said as he looked at the mural. At first, Pete did not think anything of it, but as he continued to look at the mural, he could not help but stare at the eyes as they had a haunting resemblance to Tyshawn Brendan's eyes that night. Even though the nightmares were not recurring as often, the heartache was still effective.

Back at home, Pete ran into the mailman, who was holding a stack of envelopes. "Good morning," said the mailman. "You have a lot today." After Pete collected the mail, he went inside his house and unhooked Brownie from his leash. One by one, Pete shuffled through the envelopes with disappointment—similar to having a bad hand in poker as he saw only bills and ads. But then, he dropped the envelopes as he came upon the last one. Pete was shocked as he saw who it was from. A sudden rush of adrenaline rapidly flowed through his body. Pete grew hesitant as he did not know how this would play out. He had no idea whether it was a good letter or a letter he would soon regret opening.

For ten minutes, Pete walked back and forth in the living room as he looked down at the envelope on the coffee table. After another five minutes went by, Pete sat down and picked up the envelope. He then turned it around, opened the envelope, and pulled out a letter. It was longer than Pete expected, but he was prepared to read every word. As he held the letter, he began to read:

Dear Officer Pete Gant,

First, please pardon my delay in responding. I know this comes to you at an unexpected time. It's been ten long months since you sent me your letter. I must be honest with you, Officer Gant. I wasn't sure if I would ever respond to you. Initially, I intended to just tear it to shreds and burn the remains. I was too angry with you to even think about reading anything you had to say. For months, I've carried around this hatred for you. Carrying it around like a weapon, waiting for the right moment to attack you with it. I hated you so much for what you did. You took my son away from me... forever. Do you have any idea what pain you've caused me? When I got that phone call that night... I was devastated. I couldn't believe that my son was gone. He was my only child. And when I saw your mugshot on the television, I literally spit on the screen. I was enraged. I wanted you to suffer. I wanted you to feel every ounce of misery that I felt. Please don't blame me for saying this... but I wanted you dead. But then I asked myself a question. I asked myself, "What good would that do?" You have a family, too. Another reason for my delay was that I simply didn't know what to say. Of all people, for you to reach out to me... I was utterly dumbfounded. I never heard of anything like this before. For an officer to send a letter. It hasn't been an easy ten months for me, as you may already know. But then again, after reading your letter, I understand that it hasn't been easy for you, either. I know you may not think what I ask of you will be appropriate. But I was hoping that you would be willing to meet me in person. I do appreciate the letter. But for myself, I just want to see you. I want to look into your eyes and see who you are. And please don't worry. In no way am I looking for any trouble or to cause you harm. It would be just me and you. Face to face, one-on-one. We can meet up at a local park during the day. Let's meet at Paulette D'Aldouri Park, at the basketball court. That's where I used to bring King for his basketball camps. Hope that's not too far away from you. I don't want to waste time, so let's meet this Saturday at noon. It will mean a lot to me, Officer. Gant.

Thank you for your time. I hope to see you soon.
Jada Brendan

Pete was against meeting up with Jada. He felt that it would be a trap and that someone else could be behind all of this—plotting a hit on him. But for some reason, Pete was willing to go through with it. Even though he was nervous, he prayed for this opportunity that night in the church, and his prayer was finally answered. But now, *he* is the one who must deliver. All Pete could say as he sat on the couch with his eyes closed was… "Thank you, Emilie."

49

OCTOBER 24^{th,} 2026, SATURDAY AFTERNOON:

A MOTHER'S PAIN: A COP'S GUILT

It was ten minutes past noon. The sun was piercing through the October sky, and a cool breeze was blowing through Pete's salt and pepper hair as he waited on the park bench next to the basketball court. Oddly enough, there were not many people around in the park. Pete grew more nervous by the minute. He stood up and began to walk back and forth with his hand over his mouth—thinking about what the initial reaction was going to be.

As he looked ahead, he saw someone walking toward him from a distance. Pete could not tell who it was as there was a distance of what seemed like a football field between them. But the person was getting closer. Pete saw these long braids blowing in the wind as he stood there. At that moment, he knew it was Jada Brendan.

The closer Jada approached, the more nervous Pete became. And then, there she was, standing in front of him. They stood there in silence—not uttering a word to each other. Pete was surprised at how young Jada looked. She looked like a teenager—standing in her black leggings, Yeezy Boost 700 Wave Runner sneakers, and a long sleeve t-shirt with a picture of Tyshawn. In her hands she held a cardboard box, which made Pete nervous as he thought there was a weapon inside. Suddenly… words were exchanged.

"Are you Officer Pete Gant?" Jada asked.

"I—I'm not an officer anymore," Pete said nervously. "But I'm Pete Gant, yes. Yo—you can call me Pete... and you're Jada Brendan?"

Jada nodded her head. "I'm Jada, yes."

They looked at each other as if they were from two different worlds—two different species. In a way, they were. Suddenly, paranoia began to creep into Pete's conscience as he looked at his surroundings. "Oh, no. Please," Jada said. "I didn't bring anyone here with me. I didn't come here to harm you. I'm just here to talk... one-on-one." Pete sighed. "Okay... shou—should we sit down?" Jada nodded as they walked over to the park bench. As they sat there, an awkward occurrence of looks began. Pete glanced over at Jada, and *Jada* glanced over at him.

"This... this isn't what I expected it to be," said Jada.

"Neither did I," Pete responded. "To be honest with you... I wasn't even sure I would come. I was so nervous."

"I understand."

"Mrs. Brendan—"

"No, no, no... please, call me Jada."

"Jada... there are no words that I could say to you to express how sorry I am for what happened to your son. Every single day since that night... I think about him. I think about what I could've done differently to prevent that incident. But I wake up every day, realizing I can't change what happened. And every day... that eats me alive."

"Mr. Gant... the video of the shooting is all over the internet. To this day, I've never watched it. I can't watch my son take his last breath.... I want to hear from you... *what happened* that night?"

Pete looked at Jada as if he wanted to cry in tremendous guilt. But he kept himself together and told her as much of the truth as he could remember. "I received a call about a suspicious vehicle. I told dispatch that I would be on the lookout. I drove around for a little while before I spotted the car. When I pulled the car over, I walked up to the door and knocked on the window. The driver, um... RayJohn?

Jada corrected him. "*Ra*Johnn. His name is RaJohnn."

"*Ra*Johnn... okay.... RaJohnn rolled the window down and said something like, 'What you want?' The music was so loud. I could barely hear him. I asked if he could turn the car off. He said, 'Suck my dick,' and rolled the window back up. That's when I turned my back and radioed in for a second unit... it all happened so fast. I turned around, and... RaJohnn rolled the window down and extended his arm out the window. He had something in his hand— something with a flash... I thought it was a gun. I thought I was going to die. So many of my friends on the force lost their lives in a routine traffic stop. One of my best friends, Clayton... was shot and killed that way. When you're in those situations, there's just no time to think about anything except to protect yourself, and I didn't want to end up like Clayton... I didn't want to leave my wife and kids behind. So, I took my gun out and opened fire."

Jada stood up as she needed a moment. "Oh, God."

Pete looked at Jada with growing emotion as he continued to speak, "I'm sorry... he kept calling for his friend. RaJohnn kept screaming out for Tyshawn. But he wasn't *answering.* I had no idea there was somebody else in the car. I *swear* to you I didn't.... I picked up my flashlight to look inside and... I saw him. I saw Tyshawn curled up inside. I pulled him out and laid him on the ground. He gave me this look—a look as if he was... transitioning. And that's when he said his last two words to me... '*Fuck* you!' To this day, those words trigger me. It takes me right back to that night.... Mrs. Brendan... I wish I never took that call. I wish I never saw that car. Your son would still be alive today if I didn't see it. I'm *so sorry*. But I know that's not enough. I know that apologies can't bring him back. And I have to live with my actions for the rest of my life... but the reality is I *still* get to live. From the bottom of my heart, I am truly sorry."

Jada looked at Pete with tears running down her face. She then turned and looked forward at the basketball court. She wiped her eyes and sighed.

"Is that the whole story?" She asked.

Pete sniffled. "Yes."

As Jada looked at the basket, she shared a story about Tyshawn with Pete. "King truly loved this game. When he was six, I took him to his first basketball camp in this very same park. He was the only black boy in the camp, so he stood out very easily. But when that basketball was in his hands, he stood out even more. King was a… *magician*—an artist—poet, telling a story through dribbling. It was like seeing an adult with decades of basketball experience in a little six-year-old body. All the coaches were in awe of him. They've never seen anyone like him before. The president of the camp said to me, 'Ms. Brendan, I just want you to know that your son *will be* number one in the world. *He* is going to be the next Michael Jordan.' And I believed him. I can't tell you how many games I've been to. But when I tell you that I never saw *anyone* play the game the way my son played… he was… *amazing*…. I wish I could see him again. I wish I could touch him. I wish he could just come down the stairs, hug and kiss me, and ask, 'What ya cookin', Ma?' He was my companion. We were going to travel the world together. We were going to go to Africa and visit Egypt, Ethiopia, and then Paris… all the places he and I dreamed about traveling to and living comfortably for the rest of our lives. That was *our* American dream. But now… I'm just living in this nightmare… and I can't wake up from it."

Pete had no words for Jada. There was nothing he could say that would cease her pain. He then got up from the bench and stood beside Jada as he looked at her tear-stained face.

"I would give my life if that could bring him back," Pete said.

"Would you? You don't have to say those things... I don't hate you."

"You don't?"

"No. Not anymore, at least. I hate what you *did*. But I don't hate you. I don't even know if that makes sense. It took me a long time to let that hatred go. I realized that in order for me to move on and live my life, there is something essential that I must do first... I have to forgive you."

Pete was stunned. "Forgive?"

"Yes."

Pete shook his head. "No... you don't have to forgive me at all, Mrs. Brendan."

"No, I *do*. Otherwise, I'll end up hating you forever."

"No, Mrs. Brendan—"

"Please... just call me Jada."

"Jada, I... I took your son away from you. I can't let you—"

"I *forgive* you, Pete Gant... I cannot go on with my life carrying all that hatred and pain with me. And I know now that *you* can't go on holding that same pain inside of *you*. I'm tired of suffering. We've all suffered enough, you know?"

"You... you really do forgive me?"

Jada walked toward Pete. "Yes... I do."

"I don't deserve your forgiveness," Pete cried. "I know I don't. But I thank you... I thank you very much."

"I didn't forgive you for a 'thank you,' Pete. But I appreciate it."

Pete suddenly extended his arms out to hug Jada. But Jada immediately stepped back in shock. "Oh," a startled Pete said. "I—I'm terribly sorry." Jada shook her head as she looked at Pete. Suddenly, she balled up her hands and slowly pounded her fist onto Pete's chest—*pounding* like she was banging on a door with anguish. Jada gave Pete a look as if she forgave him, but was releasing all the pain, hatred, and anger through her pounding fist. She then broke down and sobbed into his chest. Pete sobbed as he understood her pain and embraced her with linger hug. "I'm sorry," He cried. "I'm terribly, terribly sorry." They both cried in each other's arms as they released all the hurt that was built up inside of them.

"I know forgiving me wasn't easy," Pete said. "But I thank you a million times."

"No... it wasn't," Jada said as she looked at her tear-stained hands. "If only our tears could reverse reality... we'd all be better off."

Pete looked at her hands. "Amen."

"Officer Gant—"

"No, please, just Pete."

"Pete... I hope you understand why I was hitting you."

"I understand. I guess I even deserve it... what happens now?"

"I don't know. Go our separate ways? Try to find some balance in life again?"

"Are you going to be okay?"

"You don't have to worry about me. I'll be just fine... and so will you."

"What about your husband? Tyshawn's father—"

"He's not my husband. In fact, we were never married."

"Oh... sorry, um, I just assumed."

"It's fine. He was never really in King's life. It's a long story."

"Can I ask you something? Why do you call your son, 'King?'"

Jada smiled. "I've called him King ever since he was a little boy. It's an acronym for '**K**eep **I**nspiring **N**ever **G**ive up.'"

Pete smiled. "I like that."

"You would've loved him, Pete. I wish you two could've crossed paths a better way."

Pete sighed. "So do I... would it be okay with you if I went to his grave and apologized to him?"

Jada smiled. "That would be nice of you... but I didn't bury him."

"You didn't?"

"No. I have him right here… close to my heart."

Pete looked at Jada as she held onto the basketball charm hanging from her neck. "I'm not one who visits gravesites. So, I had King cremated and put some of his ashes in this basketball charm. That way, he's always near my heart. And right there is a small box of some more of his ashes. I wanted to scatter them on this court so that a piece of him would be here forever." Pete looked over at the box and sighed deeply in guilt.

"I was a good cop, Jada," he said. "I played by the rules, was never corrupt, and I loved what I did, even though most of the people out there didn't love me. I just never thought my career would end so tragically. I wish I could go back and change things, you know?"

Suddenly, Jada had a thought. "Perhaps we should go *forward…* and change things *that* way."

"What do you mean?"

"I'll explain later. But right now, I want to lay my son to rest—where he belongs."

"Jada? Before you set him free, can I apologize to him?"

Jada looked down at the box. "I'm okay with that."

Jada placed the box on the foul line. As Pete looked down at the box that held Tyshawn's ashes, he began to say a few words. "Tyshawn… this is Pete Gant. I was the police officer who was there that night. I was the one who pulled the trigger. When I got the call that night… I thought I was just pulling someone over to diffuse a situation and go on with my shift. But that didn't happen. You were in the car, you were probably scared, and you wanted out. But what sat between us was trouble. Trouble that neither of us wanted. I swear to you, I did not know you were in the car. I did not want to shoot you. I didn't want *any* of this to happen…. For *months*, I've questioned why this happened. But I'm sure for the rest of my life, I'll never find the answer. You didn't deserve this, Tyshawn. I wish I could take this all back. But I can't… I'm sorry, kid… I'm *so sorry*.

Wherever you are… I hope and pray that you can forgive me as well."

Jada wiped her eyes and stood beside Pete as he stared at the box. "That was very thoughtful of you," she said as she placed her hand on Pete's shoulder. "Okay, King… Momma's going to set you free now—at your eternal kingdom." Jada opened the box and took out a wooden, box-shaped urn. As she removed the top, she gave her son's ashes one final look and tossed them to the sky. Tyshawn's ashes flew through the autumn wind. Jada stood still with her eyes closed as she had a moment. Pete looked on as he grieved with her.

"I'm terribly sorry, Jada," he said.

"I know you are," Jada responded. "But we're going to get through this… okay?"

"Okay… thank you for everything. I know it wasn't easy to forgive me. But I'm forever grateful that you have."

Jada gently placed her hand on Pete's shoulder. "I'll be in touch."

Jada then took her leave, leaving Pete behind with his thoughts and her forgiveness. He looked down at the court and saw what remained of Tyshawn's ashes—slowly fading as the wind picked up. Pete wondered what Jada had in mind about making a change. But whatever she was willing to do, he was going to support her, come what may.

50

NOVEMBER 17^{th,} 2025, TUESDAY MORNING:

THANK YOU, MAYOR COLLINS

Weeks have passed since Jada's epic rendezvous with Pete. Meeting with Pete took the burdening weight off her shoulders. Her mind was at ease, and her broken heart was on the road to a very long recovery. She had made an appointment to meet with Newark Mayor Tiffani Collins as she hoped for a favor. Moments later, the door opened, and Mayor Collins's assistant looked to Jada and said, "Hi, Ms. Brendan. Mayor Collins is ready for you now." Jada grabbed her bag and headed inside the office. Mayor Collins stood up from her desk and walked over to greet Jada with a warm embrace.

"Oh, Jada," said Mayor Collins. "How are you, my sister?"

"I'm hanging in there," Jada smiled. "Thank you so much for taking the time to meet with me."

"*Absolutely*. Please, have a seat."

Jada sat down across from Mayor Collins. "How have you been?"

"I've been a very busy woman. A lot of things had occurred since… since it happened. Some cops have resigned, and others put in transfers. *Surprisingly*, the crime rate has been stable. And I'm grateful for that. Um… my husband, Tobey, asked of you. I told him that I was having a meeting with you. He sends his love—and belated condolences."

"That's very nice of him. Please tell him I said thank you."

"Will do…. *So*, what brings you here today?"

"Mayor Collins… last month, I met with former Officer Pete Gant."

Mayor Collins looked at Jada with startled eyes. "Wha… *what*?"

"I just had to meet him. I had to look him in the eyes and see him— see who he *really* is. And he's a really nice man."

"Oh… I… I—I'm sorry. I'm a little caught off guard. I wouldn't have expected you to want to meet with the person who… you know."

"Yeah. I wasn't sure that I was going to go through with it. But I'm glad I did. He told me what happened that night—the truth, I mean. And it wasn't his fault. It was painful to hear, but I needed to know… and I forgave him."

"*Wow*… I'm… I'm sorry, I'm just really taken aback by this. So, you met Pete Gant, *talked* with him, and you've *forgiven* him?"

"Yes. I need to heal from this. But there was no way that I would be able to do that if I didn't *first* forgive the person responsible for my son's death. Now, the reason that I came here today is because I need a favor from you."

"I will do whatever is in my *power* to help you, Jada. Just say it, and it's done."

"I want to hold a press conference. I want every news station to come and broadcast me and Pete Gant so that we can show the world that even though this man is responsible for King's death, I can still stand beside him—with no hatred or malice in my heart and forgive him. I want the world to see that law enforcement officers are *not* to be feared but embraced as human beings with families who love them. Every day, people are crucifying these cops—calling them pigs or racists… and I was one of them. But after meeting Pete Gant, nothing can be farther from the truth. He showed me that there are good ones out there. I was just too devastated to embrace any of them."

Mayor Tiffani Collins was stunned at what she just heard.

Never in her life would she have believed that a mother who tragically lost her son in a police shooting would want to stand beside the officer who was responsible. Mayor Collins stood up from her chair and sat beside Jada.

"My sister… you are, by *far*, the strongest woman I have ever met. By you forgiving the person who shot your son—who had a promising life ahead of him and want to share your story with the world… I commend you. I know this cannot be easy for you—to lose your son so tragically… I don't know *what* I would do if it were one of my kids."

"Mayor Collins… we as black women have the toughest job in America… raising black children. I worked *so hard* to keep my son flying straight. To keep him on the right track and *away* from those streets. I did the absolute best I could. But I guess God had other plans for him. And for me. I just wish I knew what that plan was. I feel this is terrible to admit… but I feel like I failed as a mother."

"Oh, *God*, no," Mayor Collins said as she held Jada's hands. "Jada, look at me… don't *ever* think that about yourself. You did *not* fail as a mother. You did a *wonderful* job with Tyshawn. You kept him on the right path and gave him purpose and direction in his life. You *gave* him life. By no means should you blame yourself for what happened."

"You know… that morning before it all happened, I had the worst stomachache. I woke up feeling like I was punched in my gut about twenty times, back-to-back. But when I went to use the bathroom, I realized it was just that time of the month, you know? I went downstairs and saw King sitting in the kitchen watching his film on his iPad. I came behind him and gave him a kiss. As we were eating breakfast and talking, he looked at me and said, 'Ma… if basketball doesn't work out… I'm still going to make you proud of me. I have so many dreams that I want to fulfill. And no matter what I do, just know I will make you proud.' I kissed his hand and said, 'You've already made me proud, baby… the sky is the limit… the sky is the limit.' *That* was my son… a caring, loving, young black king."

Mayor Collins shed tears. "Jada, my sister… *you* are my *idol*. We're going to make this happen. You name the time and place, and we *will* make this a reality."

Jada stood up and hugged Mayor Collins. She was so happy to have her support on this. They began to discuss more in detail what Jada had in mind. Mayor Collins loved the idea and worked with her team to make all the arrangements for what was to be a historical moment that would demand change. At least, that was what Jada hoped for.

51

DECEMBER 19^{th,} 2026, SATURDAY AFTERNOON:

A CHANGE IS GOING TO COME

The cameras were lined up facing the podium. News channels from all over the country and internationally were in attendance as the press were ready to hear from Jada Brendan. Mayor Collins and her team spent countless hours and weeks planning to make this happen. Jada and Pete were nervous wrecks as they stood off stage, waiting to be called up by Mayor Collins.

"Jeez," Pete nervously said. "I didn't think I would be this nervous."

"Me neither," Jada added. "But I think this will be worthwhile. We just have to be ourselves out there."

"Right.... You know, Jada? For what it's worth, I want to say thanks again."

"For what?"

"For everything. For believing in me, for your forgiveness, and for... well... I don't know if you would approve of this. Forgive me again if I'm overstepping boundaries with you. But I would like to thank you for your friendship as well."

Jada looked at Pete with a face of stillness. "Well... I don't want us to be enemies, Pete. A friendship would be better than us hating each other... so, I welcome it."

Pete smiled. "You're a great woman."

As Jada and Pete waited, Mayor Collins addressed the press:

Good afternoon, ladies and gentlemen. I thank you all for coming in today. A year ago today, the city of Newark was struck with tragedy. Two African American teenage boys were involved in a police shooting. One of those teenagers was an *exceptional* scholar-athlete… Tyshawn Brendan. Tyshawn Brendan was a straight-A student, a basketball phenom, and a son. He was the son of Jada Brendan. A year ago today, Jada's life was changed forever when her son succumbed to his injuries. For a parent to lose their child—in *any* circumstance, is tragic. But today, Jada Brendan is here to share her vision to remedy how we perceive the men and women in blue.… At this moment, I would like to invite Jada Brendan to the podium as she would like to share some words with you. Jada?

Jada stepped onto the stage and stood behind the podium. The cameras flashed and clicked as if she was a movie star walking down the red carpet. After Mayor Collins hugged her and stepped off stage, Jada took a deep breath and began her speech:

Good afternoon, everyone. I thank you all for coming today. I am sure many of you are wondering why I decided to make a public announcement after a year. To be honest with you, I was too hurt to want to talk with anyone. I was distraught—not willing to face the reality that my son was no longer here. I had to face it every day for a year. But I still get up every day and do my best to make every moment count. My son, Tyshawn Brendan… was one of a kind. He wasn't the one who would always express himself emotionally. But being his mother, I found ways to open him up and share things with me. And when he did, he was the most charismatic, charming, *handsome* human being. He was my companion for many years. Then one night—*this* night soon to be, I got a phone call with the worst news a mother could *ever* receive. I was told that my son was not coming home that night. I was completely numb. I couldn't believe it. It's still surreal to me. But that night, I made sure that I saw King… I call him *King* because he was one.

After all this time, I felt I wasn't getting any closure. I thought I would have closure and *justice* when the lawsuit was settled. But I knew that all the money in the world would not heal the burning hole in my heart.

The only thing I felt would heal that hole was forgiveness. I had to do some serious soul-searching and healing to forgive.... Ladies and gentlemen, I am here today to show you what forgiveness looks like. I want to show you that forgiving someone who took the life of a loved one is worthy and necessary. Today, I have Peter Gant with me. Pete, can you come on out, please?

Pete froze backstage as he was unwilling to step out in the spotlight. He could not move his legs. Across the room was the exit. He wanted to run to the exit as fast as he could and leave it all behind. But he knew that would be a cowardly act, and Pete was no coward. He took a deep breath and stepped up to the podium. But then, something had occurred. Pete was getting triggered as the flashing cameras were going off. He leaned over and whispered something in Jada's ear. After Pete said what he said, she looked up at him and nodded. "Um, ladies and gentlemen," said Jada. "If you don't mind, can you please take off the flashes on your cameras?" As Pete stood there next to Jada, she continued with her speech:

Without question, I miss my son terribly. Not a day goes by that I don't think of him or what else he would've accomplished in his life. Earlier this year, I received a letter from this man... Pete Gant. I could not believe it. I did not open it for weeks. I was too heartbroken to read a word. But something in my soul insisted that I read it. When I finally read the letter... I knew this man was a *real* human being. Pete Gant opened my eyes, my mind, and my heart again. He showed me that there was a good heart beneath that badge.

After reading the letter, Pete Gant helped me believe in humanity again. I began to care about people and how they felt. But I was still far from responding to him. Then one day... I prayed on it and built up the strength to respond. Ladies and gentlemen, I must say that was the best decision I could've made. I've been carrying around so much anger and hatred— simply because people around me told me that I *should*. Social media had become a living hell. People said that this man should take his own life. I started to believe in what those people were saying and hated this man. I hated Officer Pete Gant for taking my son away from me.

But I was wrong. Because *hate* is wrong.... This man is a *human being*. He is a husband, a father, and a good man.... I learned some things over this past year. I realized that nobody's perfect. We all have our flaws, our mistakes, *and* our regrets. But if we can learn to forgive, *we* can change our world. I know that I'm not the first mother to lose her child to unfortunate circumstances. But I knew that if I did not forgive this man and carried that hatred with me, I would not survive. And neither would he.... Before I hand it over to Mr. Gant, I'd like to address this. Leave this man and his family alone. Our families have suffered enough, and all we want to do is move forward with our lives. And this is coming from *me*—Tyshawn Brendan's mother. *Leave Pete Gant alone.* I have forgiven him. Do not write any derogative comments online. If you happen to see him in public, do *not* harass him. I ask that you listen to this man—listen with an open mind and an open heart.

As Jada stepped aside, Pete stood behind the podium. He had no clue of what to say as he did not have anything prepared on paper. But then, he remembered Emilie Graham saying, "*Just let it come from the heart.*" As Pete took a breath and cleared his throat, he said this to the public:

Good afternoon, everyone. Uh, first off, Jada? Thank you for everything. I haven't said this to you before, but... you have taken this broken man who hit rock bottom, and you gave him the one thing I thought didn't exist anymore... forgiveness. You forgave me when the rest of the world wouldn't. And I am forever grateful to you for that. You're my hero.... In this life, we *all* need a hero at times. Someone who we look up to. Someone who will protect us from harm's way. Someone who makes it their duty to protect and serve their community. For years, I thought I *was* a hero. I felt I was placed on this earth to save lives and help others in need. But, for the first time in my life, I understood what it truly means to be a hero. Being a hero is not about putting on a costume and a cape. It's not about putting on a blue uniform and a shiny badge. It's about knowing that you're not always in control of what life throws at you. It's about holding yourself accountable when you've done wrong and knowing you've hurt people. Being a hero is forgiving someone who couldn't help or save you in a time of need.

In my sixteen years as a police officer, there were many times when I could not save a person whose life was in danger, and for *years*, I blamed myself. Heroes are not perfect. *Cops* are not perfect—none of us are. But day in and day out, we do our best. But even at our best, it's nowhere near good enough. But if people can learn to forgive, open their minds, and *see* the fuller picture, they will understand that even *cops* need a hero. And I'm grateful to say that Jada Brendan is *my* hero… because she forgave me. Now, I know that this world will always have its problems, and life will permanently preserve its violent ways.

But as long as you have forgiveness, *we* can change anything. We could change our world for the better. It is time. It's time for the American public and law enforcement officers to come together and learn how to peacefully coexist and respect one another so that there is not another tragedy like Tyshawn Brendan. And also, we should not wait for *another* tragedy to occur before we sit down and have that conversation. Let us change our world with the power of forgiveness and the magic of hope. Let us change the social dilemmas of culture, race, politics, and religion, and, most importantly, let's change *ourselves* for the better. We can change… we can change…. Lastly, to my family, know that I love you, and I'm healing every day. And Emilie? You know who you are. If you're watching this, thank you for your advice… Heaven bless you.

52

DECEMBER 19th, 2026, SATURDAY EVENING:

JADA'S CLOSURE

Jada and Pete filled up the rest of their day with several meetings—setting dates for appearances on talk shows and news stations to get their message across. And after a long train of questions from the press, it was time for Pete and Jada to call it a day and go home.

Their cars were parked on the third level of the building's lot. As they walked, they began to recap their public statement.

"How did we do?" Pete asked.

"Couldn't have been better," Jada responded. "I wish I could've done something different with my *hair*, though... black women problems, don't worry about it."

Pete laughed but immediately regretted it.

"Hey," Jada said with concern. "What's the matter?"

"I laughed," Pete said with shame. "I haven't really been able to laugh much since it happened. I thought my sense of humor died after that night."

"You can laugh now. Laugh, sing, dance, smile... *live*. Please live your life now. And don't worry about what the world has to say. As long as you know that *I* have forgiven you... that's all that matters, Pete."

Pete smiled. "Okay... thank you."

Suddenly, a loud voice ripped through the moment and shouted, "JADA!" It was Tyshawn's father, Morris—standing there in his black fur coat with a burgundy turtleneck underneath and black Versace shades.

"Morris?" Jada said. "What are you doing here?"

"Looking for you."

Jada looked at Pete. "Um… Morris, this is Pete—"

"*I* know who the fuck this is!" Morris retorted. "And *no*, I *don't* wanna shake your hand, don't *talk* to me, don't even *look* at me, and kiss my *black* ass with your apologies…. You killed my son. You're lucky I'm not *fucking* your ass up right now, pig—"

"Morris!" Jada said as she stood between Morris and Pete.

Pete grew nervous. "I should go."

"You goddamn *right*, you should go—get your cracker ass up outta here, pig."

"Morris, *stop* it!" Jada shouted.

Morris removed his shades. "You still here, pig?"

"*Enough*!"

Pete looked into Morris' hazel eyes and saw nothing but pure hatred. He knew there would be no forgiveness from him. "Pete?" Jada said. "I think it's best we go our separate ways now. It's okay." Pete nodded his head in understanding. "Goodbye, Jada." She smiled and said, "Goodbye, Pete." Morris kept his eyes on Pete every step of the way until he made it to his Jeep. As Pete took off, Morris turned and looked at Jada as if he had a bone to pick with her.

"You fucking *kidding* me?" Morris shouted.

"Morris, don't use that tone with me," Jada retorted.

"You doing this soap-opera bullshit with this *white* boy? Do I need to remind you who the *fuck* he is or what he *did*?"

"No, I *know* what he did. Just like I know what *you* did—or *didn't* do—being an absentee *father*."

"*Absentee*?"

Jada observed Morris' wardrobe. "And I see you're spending that settlement money very well. *You'll* be broke within a year."

Morris scoffed. "Look, I know what to do with *my* money."

"*Your* money? That's *blood* money, you sorry-ass bastard! You're *lucky* I gave you *anything*. Because you don't even deserve the copper off a *penny* of that money."

"Look, Jada, I'm not here for all that bullshit. I saw what you did today, and I ain't fucking like it."

"What are you talking about?"

"What I'm *talking*—you go on national television with that racist ass cop—making a *fool* of yourself—*that's* what I'm talking about."

"Excuse me?"

"What the *fuck* were you thinking? I couldn't believe my *eyes*—watching you stand there next to that murderer. I mean, what was going through your *mind*? *That's* what we're doing now? *That's* the type of time you're on?"

"Morris, listen—"

"No, Jada. How about *you* listen? A'ight? You listen to *me* right now. That little stunt you pulled today? Giving that racist ass cop a *pass*? He killed my son. He ain't *getting* no fucking passes from *me*."

"Well, *I* forgave him, Morris. I can't control how *you* feel… are you done now?"

"*No*, I'm not done, goddamn it."

"Oh, *God*, Morris, don't you think it's a little too late to try to be a father to *my* son?"

"What'd you just say?"

"Yeah, that's right—*my* son—he was *my* son. For the first fourteen years of his life, you didn't even *exist*—nothing more than a *fucking* sperm donor."

"A *sperm* donor? Woman, have you lost your nerve—"

"*Where were you*, Morris?" Jada shouted. "Where were you when he *needed* you? Do you know how many nights he woke up with tears running down his face—asking me, 'Where's my father? *When am I going to meet my father?'* I had to *lie* to my own son. I *lied* to King—*telling* him that you were in *prison*.... Every time I told him that, it *crushed* my heart, Morris. And what's even sad about that whole situation? You were only a *five fucking minute drive* away. Yet you didn't even *care* to see him. You didn't care to see your own kid."

Morris went silent. "I didn't know what to do, Jada. I was a kid my *damn* self. I didn't know what it meant to *be* a father. I never had one. I never had *any* fucking father figure in my *life*. When you told me you were pregnant... I bugged out.... Besides, you told me you were getting an abortion, so—"

"That's *bullshit*, Morris, and you *fucking* know it. I *never* said I was getting an abortion."

"Listen, you didn't deserve to be left alone with a child. But I was still *learning*. I was *learning* how to be a man. I didn't feel like my presence would be of any benefit *to* him. So, I just stayed away."

"Then why *did* you come into his life, Morris? Huh? Why did you?"

"I wanted to see my son. I—I wanted to see him *shine*. I wanted to be there to support him—"

"*Don't bullshit* me, Morris! You wanted a slice of the pie—*just* like everybody else. When word spread about King, you *saw* the potential—*everybody* did. You never gave that boy a goddamn *dime*. And *then*, after fourteen years, you just come barging into his life—telling him that you're his father. Do you know what that does to a teenage black boy? To come into his life out of nowhere and *demand* his love and respect?"

"I fucked up, all right? I *know* I did. I should've been there for him—*and* for *you*. But I just..."

"Just what, Morris?"

"I just didn't think I would be a good father."

"Well, like I said, it's too late to try to be his father now, Morris. King is gone. You missed a lot of good years. And yet, you *still* reaped the benefits of him…. Look at you—fur coat, Versace shades—diamond chains and rings—a *Rolex*—*and* a Lambo truck. You're living off of *my* son's blood."

Morris removed his shades. "A'ight, first of all, that was *my* blood that went through that boy's veins—"

"Oh, *Jesus Christ*—"

"A'ight—a'ight, so, what do you want, Jada? Huh? What do you *want*? Would you like to be reimbursed? You want the money back?"

"No, Morris. How about you use some of that money and buy a *fucking clue*? The *money* doesn't make me feel better. You know, I wasn't able to sleep for *months* after King's death. But now… I finally can. And I'm sleeping well at night. And it's *not* because of *money*… it's forgiveness. *Forgiveness* is what helps me sleep at night. I don't carry that hatred in my heart anymore. *That's* what forgiveness did for me. That's something that money can *never* give *you*. But you go ahead, *burn* through *every last dollar*. You enjoy living off the son you never truly cared for."

As Jada walked away, Morris carried on as he was not happy with her making him out to be a neglectful monster. "I *cared* for him!" Morris shouted. "He was *my* son, *too*! You want me to say it again? I *fucked* up, Jada, a'ight? *I* bailed out, and I regret every *fucking* day I missed with him. Not a *day* went by that I didn't think about that boy… not one day." Jada shook her head as long-awaited tears fell from her face.

"And now he's gone. He's *gone*, Morris. It's over. Good night."

"Jada, wait."

Jada stopped and turned around. "What, Morris?"

"You said you forgave that pig, right? But what about me? Can you forgive *me*?"

In the eighteen years of Tyshawn's life, Jada never stopped to think about forgiving Morris for his absence—not just in

Tyshawn's life but her life. She stood there as the frost on her breath created a vanishing cloud of mist. After she gave it some thought, Jada responded and said, "You know… I remember one time when I was at one of King's games. He was having a bad night. His shots just weren't going in—turnover after turnover. It seemed like nothing was working for him. But they still won. Later that night, I talked to him about the game. As we talked, he started to cry. I never saw King cry like that. I thought it was because of the game. But when I asked him what was wrong and he *told* me… it took my breath away. He told me about what you discussed with him earlier that day. He told me that you were trying to make him sign a *contract* to be his manager and that you would take *thirty percent* of *all* his career earnings… *thirty percent.*"

Morris had a face of guilt. "He told you about that?"

"Yes… I kept my mouth shut about a *lot* of your bullshit. But when he told me about *that*… I was *never* able to look at you the same again. And neither did he. I guess bloodline doesn't guarantee trust."

Morris sighed. "I was only trying to protect him."

"You mean protect *your* investment. Your own fucking son."

"Look, we *both* agreed to file that lawsuit. Don't put that all on me. Besides, I wasn't going to let those corrupt motherfuckas get away with murdering *my* son, a'ight? We should've sued them for a *billion.*"

"And you thought you were *entitled* to his future earnings?"

"See? There you go again… trying to paint me as the villain. And *that's* one of the reasons I stayed away."

Jada shook her head. "Morris—for *once* in your *pathetic life, keep* it real… if King didn't play basketball, would you have been in his life?"

The silence grew solid as Morris stood there with a blank face. He turned away as he did not have an answer for Jada. "Wow," said Jada. "Dead silence… typical Morris to go ghost." As Jada walked away, Morris tried to pull her back in with his guilt.

"I should've been there, a'ight? I should've been there since the very beginning... but I wasn't. It was my fault."

Jada turned and looked at Morris. "You asked me if I could ever forgive you... right?"

"Yeah, can you?"

"I don't hate you, Morris. I really don't. I can't even say that I ever *loved* you.... Hell, was there ever a time that you loved *me*?"

Morris delayed his answer. "We were just kids, Jada... *kids*. Two kids that made a baby."

Jada became emotional. "And now that baby's gone... *he's* gone. There's nothing more for us to talk about. You got the money, so let's just leave it at that."

"Look, Jada... I'm not *perfect*, a'ight? I've made some bad choices, and I've *paid* for them."

"No, Morris, you *didn't*. Some people pay for their bad choices. But *you*? You *got* paid for *yours*. You got paid for *not* being in his life... and at the end of the day... you still got your thirty percent."

Morris responded with a piercing look. "At the end of the day... we *all* gotta *eat*, baby girl."

Jada looked as if her eyes would pop out of her head as she could not believe what Morris had just said. "*Wow*," she sighed. "'*We all gotta eat*,' huh? And off *my* baby's blood.... That's what's so fucked up about this sick world... the goddamn leeches. And what's so pathetically *sick* about *you* is you're feeding off your *own* flesh and blood... just another vampire... I'm so done with you." Just as Jada walked to her car and opened the door, Morris asked one final question. "Do you forgive me, Jada? That's *all* I'm asking." Jada slammed her car door and walked back towards Morris. As she stood in front of him, she calmly responded.

"*Fuck* no... and *fuck* you."

Morris looked with a twisted face. "Fuck *me*? So, you can forgive that racist ass pig who *killed* my son? But you can't forgive *me*? You *see*? That's black folks' *problem*, man. We can't forgive ourselves— *yet,* we're willing to go on fucking television and show the *world* how *black* people can *forgive white* people for killing *us*! What about *me,* Jada? You can't forgive *me*?"

"Morris—"

"No, don't *Morris* me! I fucking *loved* that boy—with *all* my heart! I may not have *showed* that to him, but I always told him that I loved him—*every fucking* time I was with him…. Maybe I don't deserve your forgiveness. That's *cool*, a'ight? I won't ever ask again."

"Morris! I can forgive someone who made a mistake. But you didn't *make* a mistake. *You* made a *choice not* to be in your son's life. *You* made that choice… but even in King's death… you're *still* an asshole."

Morris felt defeated. "Only God can Judge me."

"So, what? You're fucking *Tupac* now?" Jada said in disgust.

Morris raised his arms. "Only God can judge me."

"Fine, Morris… only God can judge you. And how do you think you'll be judged?"

"I don't give a shit… I'm out."

Morris turned around and got into his brand-new, black Lamborghini Urus. Jada stood there and watched as he skirred off down the ramp. She closed her eyes as tears slid down her cold, smooth cheeks—firmly holding onto her basketball charm that held Tyshawn's ashes. "I'm sorry, baby," she said. "But I just couldn't do it. You deserved better. I'm sorry I couldn't give you a better father. But it's okay now. He's out of my life… for good."

53

DECEMBER 21st, 2026, MONDAY EVENING:

A DATE OF REKINDLE

It was a perfect night for a date. It was the first date Pete and Claire had together since their separation. Pete took her to a local restaurant called *Piazza's*. *Piazza's* was a five-star restaurant. Inside was a dim-light dining area and a pianist playing eloquent tunes to set the mood.

Claire wore a beautiful red dress and a necklace with a diamond charm. Her hair was down in gorgeous curls. Pete had on his navy blue suit jacket with his shirt collar unbuttoned. As they took their seats and skimmed through the menu, Pete sparked a long-awaited conversation with Claire.

"You look great tonight," Pete said as he complimented Claire.

"Thank you," Claire smiled. "So do you."

"Thanks… what do you think of this gray hair?"

"I think it looks good on you… why? You don't like it?"

"Well, I was *hoping* I wouldn't get any until *after* I turned forty. But it is what it is."

Claire chuckled. "Yeah."

As Claire picked up her glass of water, Pete noticed she was not wearing her wedding ring. Even though they were separated, its absence broke his heart—seeing the woman he loved not wearing the symbol of their eternal bond. Pete looked down at the table and grew quiet, deep in his thoughts.

"Hey," Claire said with concern. "Where'd you go?"

"Oh, I'm sorry," Pete said as he pinched the bridge of his nose. "I was just thinking."

"About?"

"The future. And what it beholds."

"Oh... well, we don't *know* what it beholds. Maybe that's what makes life so interesting."

"Maybe."

"So... how have you been?"

"I've been all right. Still having sessions with Dr. Dune. She recommended that I attend an Alcoholics Anonymous class. It's ninety sessions for ninety days. They've been helping. Besides, I've just been taking things one day at a time.... Things have been better after I made that public appearance with Jada Brendan. I think we really touched people by coming together the way we did. We did a few podcasts and possibly some talk shows in the future."

"That's great to hear, Pete."

"Yeah. There's been a lot of feedback from family members who were speaking out, saying how they forgave the person who was responsible for the death of *their* loved ones. I think we made an impact, Claire."

"I'm very proud of you," Claire smiled. "You've come a long way. I can't imagine how difficult it has been for you... but you survived."

"Thanks," Pete smiled as he sipped his water. "So... what about *you*? How are things?"

"I'm good. I've done a lot of reflecting. On *my* life, and what I want out of it—as of now."

"Okay... and what is it that you want?"

"Well, that's just it... I don't *know* what I want right now. These last several months have been an eye-opener for me. I've been contemplating a career change for *weeks* now. I don't want to be a social worker anymore."

"But Claire... that was your *dream*."

"I know. And I fulfilled that dream. But now I think it's time for me to move on and find another dream... and there's other things."

"What other things? You mean the kids?"

"No.... I... I—I've been dating someone."

Pete looked at her with a troubled face. His knees shook underneath the table and could barely breathe as that news took him by surprise. The waiter returned to the table with a bottle of wine.

"Okay, have we decided—"

"Could—could you give us a minute, please?" Pete interjected. "We're having a personal conversation."

"Not a problem, sir," The waiter said as he placed the bottle on the table and walked off.

"Pete, are you okay?" Claire asked.

"I'm just a little... *unsettled* about what you just told me. Who... *who* are you dating?"

"A guy at my job—well, no, I'm sorry—a guy at my job's best *friend*. There was a Halloween party back in October at my job. He brought his friend and introduced us. We began to talk, and... the talking led to dating."

Pete's face had a look of devastation. "I see.... Listen, Claire... I know we're separated, and whatever you do on your own time is your business. But... I just gotta know... did you sleep with this guy?"

Claire went silent—not a single word as her face gave Pete an answer. She then poured herself a glass of wine and guzzled it down. Pete looked as if the world had ended—*his* world, at least. As he looked up at Claire, she turned away—wiping the tears from her eyes.

"You don't have to cry," said Pete. "I understand. I wasn't around."

"No," Claire said as she blotted her eyes with her handkerchief. "I didn't sleep with him. After we went on our date, he took me to his place. But as I got there… I felt that I was making the biggest mistake of my life. I wanted out, but at the same time, I couldn't leave. I was just tired of being alone. All those years of lying in bed by myself and you not by my side… made me feel like I wasn't even a wife. Like you never existed."

Pete sighed. "I know."

"Oh, Pete… I just wanted to feel *alive* again. I wanted to feel like I mattered—I *needed* to feel *loved*. But as he was getting on top of me… I didn't feel the love that I desperately desired. All I felt was forbidden lust—deliberate infidelity. I just couldn't go through with it."

Pete placed his hand over his forehead. "*Oh, Claire—*"

"I'm so sorry… I've been so lonely without you being there. I miss all the good times we had. I miss your smile. You used to be so happy in the beginning. I don't know… I just thought maybe you saw too much out there and felt that you had no reason to smile anymore."

Pete lifted his head. "I have to use the restroom. Excuse me."

Pete stood up and headed to the restroom. He slammed his hand on the frosted glass door as he walked in the restroom, infuriated. He then punched the tiled wall, creating an echo of his heartbreak. Pete felt betrayed—stabbed deeply in his back. He had never stepped out on Claire—never had an interest in another woman since he met her. But hearing the news of her affair, he felt that their bond was broken—*broken* but not gone. As he exited the restroom, Pete noticed that Claire was gone. He looked around, but she was nowhere in sight. That is when he saw the waiter.

"Excuse me," Pete called to the waiter. "Did you see my wife? She was wearing a red dress?"

"Yes, sir. She took her belongings and left."

"Oh, *shit*," Pete said as he grabbed his coat and headed for the door. "Oh. I'm sorry… a little something for the wine and your trouble."

Pete placed some money on the table and rushed out of *Piazza's*. As he was outside, with frost coming out his mouth, he looked to his left, but there was no Claire. He turned to his right... there she was—getting into an Uber. "Claire! CLAIRE!" Pete projected as he ran after her. But the car had taken off, leaving Pete in the same place he feared the most... alone.

Back at the house, Pete had just pulled up in his driveway. But there was something odd going on. He noticed that the lights were on in the living room. He remembered turning the lights off. The inner cop in him would expect a home invasion. But the inner Pete expected that Claire had come home. As he opened the door, Brownie approached him. But then, he looked in the living room and saw Claire sitting on the couch with tears dripping on the glass frame of their wedding photo.

"Claire?" Pete said.

"Pete," Claire responded as she wiped her eyes.

"You came home?"

"I didn't want to go anywhere else."

"Oh, Claire... my wife. My beautiful... *beautiful* wife. *How* did I screw up so badly?"

Claire sniffled. "Don't blame yourself."

"You know... the very first day we met, there was something that I never told you. Remember when we were dancing at the state fair? We danced to Chris Isaak's *Wicked Love*. You remember?"

Claire smiled. "Of course, I remember... that's our wedding song."

"Yeah... as we danced, I couldn't help but notice the smell of your hair. It smelt of a garden of fresh peaches and cream. I just stood there with my face buried in those *long strains* of hair—smelling my way into heaven. The way you held me, rubbing my back with your soft hands... it's like you were protecting *me*. Like it was *you* who had my back. You've had my back ever since, and I'm so grateful for that. God knows that I needed someone in this *twisted, crazy, fucked* up world who would give me serenity and peace of mind."

"I did my very best."

"You did great, *Claire*... there's no woman in this life—on this earth, I want to share the rest of my life with other than you. You are *all* of my heart... but that badge covered my heart. That badge rested on my heart for *sixteen years*, and it weighed heavy on it—blocking all the love that came my way. I began to believe that my whole identity was immersed within that badge. But I was wrong... I screwed up, and they took that badge away from me forever. It felt like they took my life away. I felt naked to the world... naked and unwelcomed. But you... you loved and supported me since day one. You gave birth to our beautiful kids. But I never took the time to stop and say thank you—for everything."

Claire sighed. "Oh, Pete."

"I'm not blaming my job. I loved being an officer of the law. But I should've loved you guys more than *any*thing in this world. I didn't show that side of me enough and took you for granted. You have my word that *nothing* will *ever* come between us again. The badge is long gone now. But I'm still here... I'm *still Pete*. I'm *your* Pete."

As Claire stood up from the couch, she walked over to Pete and placed her hands on his tear-stained face. They stared into each other's eyes—looking like two statues in love.

"Claire," he said. "I'm in a better place now. My conscience is clear... and as certain as the sun will rise... I love you more at the birth of every day."

"Pete," Claire cried. "I betrayed you. I stepped outside—"

"No... *I'm* the one who owes you an apology. I betrayed *you* long ago when I put that job before you and those kids. *I'm* sorry. Can you forgive me?"

"I forgive you... Petester," Claire smiled.

With his gentle smile, Pete leaned in and kissed Claire like never before—running his fingers through the sacred strains of her hair. "Alexa," Pete said. "Play Wicked Games by Chris Isaak." Suddenly, the song began to play.

"May I have this dance, baby?" Pete asked.

Claire extended her hand. "Yes, you may."

Pete took her hand, and they danced angelically as they marked the end of a chapter of that beautiful evening.

"I love you, Pete... I love you, baby," Claire said through the traffic of his warm kisses.

"I love you more—to the moon and back. And I'm sorry about—"

"Shh... no more apologies... just kiss me."

The bedroom floor was romantically decorated with clothes as Pete and Claire rekindled their love with the act of fornication. The past was now behind them, and all that was ahead was the mystery of tomorrow... and Christmas.

54

DECEMBER 24th, 2026, THURSDAY EVENING:

FATHER AND SON

Christmas Eve had returned, and so did Claire and the kids. After Pete and Claire's evening of romantic forgiveness, she and the kids settled back home, which made Pete a happy family man again.

Outside in his front yard, Pete had just finished setting up the Christmas lights on the front lawn. Suddenly, laughter came from behind.

"Ah, just like you to put up your Christmas decorations at the last minute," Montgomery laughed.

"Dad," Pete said, surprised to see Montgomery. "Hey."

"How are you doing, son?" Montgomery hugged Pete.

"I'm doing fine. How about you?"

"Oh, I'm *doing*… business has been booming with the holidays. We had a twenty-seven percent increase in the profit margin."

"Oh. Well, congratulations, Dad. That sounds… rewarding."

"Yeah. I guess you don't understand all that business talk."

"How's Mom?"

"Oh, your mother's your mother—the same. She's looking forward to tomorrow. She found this new casserole recipe that she was *dying* to try. She made it for dinner the other night—not bad. But I *warn* you, *chew with caution*."

Pete laughed. "I'll keep that in mind."

"Oh, God," Montgomery sighed as he stared at Pete.

"What?"

"I almost forgot how handsome you are when you smile. I always told your mother that your smile could brighten the darkest day. I'm just happy to see you smiling again, son."

"I'm grateful that I *can* smile again, you know?"

"Yeah. I know... you've come full circle, Pete. And now you're home—reunited with the family."

"Yeah.... Dad, um... about Poppa Dee—the funeral? My absence was not to hurt you. I... I had my reasons for not attending. I'm sorry."

Montgomery sighed. "Well... he's gone. You know? It is what it is."

"Yep," Pete said as he untangled the Christmas lights.

"Son? Son, look at me. Put the lights down."

Pete dropped the lights in the snow. "What?"

"I just want you to know that regardless of your life decisions— you being a police officer, I must confess, I... I was jealous of you."

"*Jealous*?" Pete asked with confusion.

"Yes—*very* jealous. I never understood why a man would want to be a cop. Day in—day out, you deal with the *shittiest* sons of bitches the world's ever created. You deal with people calling you every name in the *book*. But you got up—day after day, put on that uniform, and went out into the Devil's playground. And here you are. My boy's still standing... standing strong... I wish I had a *tenth* of your courage.... You know, I just... I want you to know that I have *never* been prouder of someone than I am of you. And I couldn't be prouder to be your father."

Pete had been wanting to hear those words his whole life. To hear Montgomery say that he was proud of him. It brought immense satisfaction to Pete's core.

"Thanks, Dad," Pete said as he hugged Montgomery. "I love you so much."

"I love *you*, son," Montgomery responded as he kissed Pete.

"Dad?"

"Yes, son?"

"Earlier this year, when I was at the house, I opened the bedroom door and saw my old teddy bear on the floor. Captain Furry? Did you put him there?"

Montgomery paused for a moment. "I was looking for something in your old room—where we keep the boxes. I saw him in the box. I thought of your Grandma Beverly when I looked at him. She bought the bear for you, right?"

"Yeah, she did."

"I remember you used to play with him all the time. He was your partner in crime. Coincidently, that was the anniversary of the day she passed away. I thought by putting the cape on Captain... *Stuffy?*"

Pete chuckled. "Furry, Dad—Furry."

"Right. I felt that maybe seeing him with the cape on would cheer you up, you know? Remind you that you *are* a hero. And to also remind you of your Grandma Beverly.... She was delightful to you."

"She was. I loved her very much."

"And she loved *you*."

"I know she did.... But to be honest with you, Dad, I'm not a hero. Jada Brendan is a hero... she saved *my* life... through forgiveness."

It took Montgomery a moment to comprehend Pete's heroic concept. But after some thought, he smiled and touched Pete gently on his shoulder.

"I respect that, son... I really do. You're all heart, Pete."

Pete smiled. "Thanks, Dad. Um... I thought about taking you up on that offer you made me some time ago."

"Oh? What offer was that?"

"The job offer... if it's still available."

Montgomery smiled. "It *is*, and it's yours. And don't you worry. You're going to *love* the position I have for you. I'm going to make you head of my security team."

Pete was shocked. "Really?"

"Uh-huh, it's the perfect timing, too. The guy who's in charge of it now? Bob Cummings? He's retiring in two weeks. I've been looking for a replacement. And with your background in law enforcement, who could be more qualified than you? A six-figure salary and more fringe benefits than policing would've *ever* provided for you. It's yours, buddy."

"Thanks, Dad... and for what it's worth... you've always been my hero. Thank you for always being a great father."

Montgomery grew emotional. "That's a man's job. You know? To look out for his family."

They hugged once more and spent the next hour setting up the Christmas decorations. It had been a long time coming for Pete, but he was beginning to regain his strength and a healthy relationship with his father. Most importantly, he was aligned again with his true purpose in life: a family man.

An hour and a half later, Pete headed upstairs to change out of his sweaty clothes. As he got to the top, he heard the melodic sounds of a guitar coming from Michael's room. He walked toward Michael's bedroom and looked through the door's crack. Michael's back was turned as he played. Pete knocked on the door—making Michael aware of his presence.

"Hey," Pete smiled.

"Hey, Dad," Michael responded, still holding the guitar.

"I thought you were going ice skating with Elle and Leo."

"Changed my mind last minute. Mom went instead."

"Oh... I hear you were playing some music."

"Oh, yeah, I was... just going over some of the chords and lyrics."

"Oh, okay… well… I guess I'll leave you to it."

"Uh, Dad? Would you care to hear the song?"

"Yeah," Pete said with enthusiasm. "Yeah, of course. I wish *I* knew how to play."

Pete went and sat across from Michael on the bed. He looked as Michael adjusted the strings on his guitar. "You got a name for the song?" Pete asked. Michael handed Pete the crinkled notebook paper and said, "It's called *Hero*." Pete looked at Michael, waiting to hear what his creative son had to say—not just with his mind, but with his heart. Michael began to play some chords: (*Capo 3, G to E minor 7, A minor 7, C over D (D Major)*. As Michael played the chords, he began to sing:

A hero,
Have you ever needed a hero?
One who's seen the darkest times,
Who's seen the darkest crimes,
Have you ever needed a hero?

A hero,
Have you ever needed a hero?
One who's felt less than a zero,
One who's seen the darkest nights,
Who's fought the toughest fights,
Have you ever needed a hero?

You're my hero,
You picked me up and said, "I love you, kiddo,"
You hugged me tight when I used to cry,
A love you cannot buy,
Daddy, you're my hero.

Michael continued to play more chords. It was as if the

strings were plucking at Pete's emotions—making him cry on cue. After a minute of playing chords, Michael finished with the final verse:

My hero,
Ugly monsters shaking my windows,
I'm scared to death, hiding under my pillows.
But you protected me through the night,
Said, "Everything will be all right."
Oh, Daddy, you're my hero…
I love you.

There was a moment of silence as Pete wiped his eyes—sitting there with his head down. "What do you think?" Michael asked. Pete looked up at him and said, "Encore." Michael smiled at Pete's approval. Pete then took the guitar from Michael's hands and placed it on the bed.

"Michael… you wrote that?"

"Yeah… you like it?"

"I *love* it, kid… that one came from your heart."

"It did… and I meant every word."

"I know you did."

"I remember we talked about it with Dr. Dune. I was too afraid to go to sleep because I thought ugly monsters were hiding under my bed and in my closet. Instead of you telling me to toughen up and be a man, you stayed with me and said that you would protect me throughout the night. But I never expected you to wear your uniform and stand guard in my room all night. I never felt so protected in my life… and I always loved you for that, Dad."

Pete smiled. "I remember that, too. You were just a little boy hiding under your Dark Knight blanket…. *God*… one second, you guys were *babies*… and in the blink of an eye… you're all little grown-ups. You'll be heading off to college next year—Elle's a junior now, and Leo's in second grade. You kids grew up too fast. Time was *not* on my side. I missed a lot. I really did… I just couldn't keep up. I'm sorry, buddy."

"I'm sorry too, Dad. I should've never swung the bat at you."

"It's okay, Michael. I understand. You weren't swinging it at me… you were swinging it at the monster I had become. You were just protecting your mother and your brother and sister. For the last several years, you had to be the man of the house. I regret that on your behalf. You were supposed to be a kid, doing kid things. I put a lot on you guys—so that *I* can be a hero to strangers… but I've lost that."

"You'll always be my hero, Dad."

Pete smiled and hugged Michael. "Thanks, buddy. You have no idea how much that means to your Dad."

"You're welcome."

Pete sighed. "Everything's going to be just fine now. You hear me? My family is my top priority, and that's a promise I *will* keep…. So, are we cool now? We're good? There's no bad blood between us?"

Michael chuckled. "No, Dad. We're cool."

"That's what I love to hear. Listen, I'm going to go to the ice skating rink. You wanna come with?"

"No thanks. I'm just gonna stay here and work on the song. It's the only time I get peace around here without Leo or Elle bugging me."

Pete laughed. "I understand… well, I'll see you in a bit."

"Uh, Dad?"

"Yeah, buddy?"

"I've had something on my mind for a while now that I wanted to ask you… if I wanted to be a cop, would you support my decision?"

Pete was stunned as he was not prepared for such a question. After sixteen years on the force and all that he experienced, Pete said this to Michael. "Michael… I will support you in *whatever* it is you so choose to do with your life. And if you choose to be a cop, I will be behind you one hundred percent. We need good cops in this country. Period. Being a cop is one of the bravest things a man or woman can do. It is a privilege. But know this... Tyshawn Brendan is now a part of my life. He will be with me until the day I *die*.... I was fortunate not to be prosecuted, and I'm *truly* blessed that his mother forgave me. That is something that doesn't happen every day. You want to be a cop, son? Go ahead. I would never stand in your way... but Satan's out there, son, and he's only getting bigger and stronger and *uglier* by the second. But he doesn't have horns or a long red tail. He looks like you, like me, like anybody. He disguises himself through humans. But don't let him fool you, Michael. His heart is dark and wicked, and he'll always be out there on those streets—building his army... laughing as he wins. You have to protect yourself. And *no matter what*... protect your faith and keep your family close and first. Because at the end of the day, when you open that door to your house and see your family... that is *all* that matters in this world, son... family... understand?"

Michael nodded his head as he plucked the liquid strings of tears from his face and hugged his father. Pete kissed Michael as he said, "I just want the best for you, son. You can be anything you want in this life. But just know, you're already a hero. Thanks for saving my life."

55

DECEMBER 24^{th,} 2026, THURSDAY EVENING:

<u>10-42</u>

After Pete and Michael reconciled their bond, Pete made it to the ice skating rink. It was a perfect night to be out and about on the ice. As Pete watched from a distance, he looked at Elle and Leo on the ice, skating and having endless fun. Then, he looked over to Claire. "Leo, be careful," Claire said. "Hold Elle's hand." It was a sacred moment for Pete. He felt like the luckiest man on earth to have a second chance at having a good life. As he walked up behind Claire, he called to her.

"Hey, babe," he smiled.

Claire turned around and returned a smile. "Pete, you came."

"Yeah. I just wanted to see the kids in action. How's Leo doing out there?"

"Well, surprisingly, he hasn't fallen once—*oh*!" Claire watched as Leo fell. "I jinx him…. Come on, let's go sit over there."

Pete and Claire sat on the bench as they watched Elle and Leo have the time of their lives.

"Don't you just love their bond?" Claire smiled. "Elle has always been so protective of him…. I remember when we first came home with Leo. She jumped all around the house, screaming, 'Yay, I have a little brother! I have a little brother!' She said it was the happiest day of her life. That time just *flew* by. Now look at them."

Pete, however, remained silent as he looked out at the ice skating rink and watched Elle and Leo skate around in circles.

"Pete? What's wrong?" Claire asked with concern.

"Nothing," he smiled. "I'm just looking at them—not missing a second. I've missed too much as is…. Maybe we should go ice fishing someday. That would be a good family trip."

"Yeah… *speaking* of fish, why did you get a tattoo of a bass fish on your arm? You said you would tell me when the time was right."

Pete looked at Claire with a silent smile. A few weeks ago, he got a tattoo of a striped bass fish, the same fish he saw at the lake. He put a halo above it with a writing titled "*My Guardian Angel.*" Pete, however, did not want to disclose why. He felt that it was best to leave the past in the past. But then again, he did not wish to keep any more secrets from Claire and decided to tell her the truth.

"Back when everything was happening, and I hit rock bottom, I felt so alone without you guys. The only thing that kept me company was the booze and the nightmares. And one day… I took a trip out to Lake Hopatcong and… I was just ready."

"Ready for what, babe?"

"To say goodbye. And be free of it all. But then a bass fish came jumping out of the water. It was like the fish was cheering me up or something. I like to think it saved my life… that's why I got the tattoo."

Claire stared at Pete. "Pete… baby, you didn't… you didn't try to *kill* yourself… did you?"

Pete looked at Claire without saying a word. He then looked straight ahead and continued to watch Elle and Leo on the ice. Claire knew his answer but did not press it. She laid her head on his shoulder—comforting him as they watched their kids have fun.

"Promise me this stays between us, all right?" Pete softly said. "Don't ever mention this to the kids."

"No… I—I wouldn't ever do that."

"And *please* don't worry... I'm not suicidal... I still have my appointments with Dr. Dune, and I'm taking care of myself one day at a time."

Claire sighed. "Oh, baby... I'm so glad that's all over with. You did your service, and you survived it."

Pete sighed. "Yep."

"Do you miss it?"

"The job? I can't say that I do. I just only wish I could've had a proper farewell. I didn't get to say goodbye or even retire. They just pushed me away. I was as disposable as the garbage you see on the streets."

"You *do* miss it. Don't you?"

Pete looked into Claire's eyes. "I missed you more, Claire. I missed the kids. And now, you'll never have to worry about getting that phone call."

"I know," she smiled. "And that's going to help me sleep better at night."

"I love you, Claire."

"I love you, too... *Petester*."

"Oh my *God*..." Pete rolled his eyes and laughed. "I wish we *never* walked inside that pet store—that *damn* parrot."

Claire laughed. "He was *so funny*. And he said it so clearly, '*Petester*! *Petester*!' We should've brought him home."

"Why, so he could '*Petester*' me to death?"

"Ha, *yes*, that would've been *hilarious*."

"I don't know. Brownie would've been too jealous to have another pet member in the family. He probably would've eaten him."

"No, they would've been best friends."

"I guess that was pretty funny. That was a good memory."

"It was... some really good times. And this? Right here? This is one of many more good times to come. Let's cherish these moments now. As a family... okay?"

"You got it," Pete smiled.

Suddenly, Claire received a phone call. It was Elle. "Wait, why is Elle calling me—why are you calling me?" Claire said with the phone to her ear. "What? Where are you—oh, I see you. Yes, I see you and your brother waving." Claire waved back. "*Hi*, yes, we *see* you... oh, you're waving at us to *skate*? Oh, okay. Okay, I'll ask your father. Okay, bye.... They wanted to know if you'll skate with us?" Pete refused as he was not a skater.

"Ah... I think I'll pass," he said.

"Babe, what did I just say? *Cherish* these good times. That clock is ticking, and it never goes backward—only forward. We have to enjoy every minute of this life now."

Pete smiled. "You're right, babe. But you go on ahead. I just want to enjoy watching you guys have fun."

Claire sighed. "All right, *square*... enjoy watching us skate... I love you, Pete."

"And I love *you*."

Pete and Claire shared one of the most passionate kisses ever shared by two humans. It was a kiss that was more like a toast to life... the good life. But then, a flickering of red and blue lights cast on the side of Pete's face and caught his attention. As he turned and looked, he saw two patrol units on the side of the road while the officers were handing out gifts to the local kids. That visual put a smile on Pete's face.

"Pete?" Claire said from behind. "Baby, you okay?"

Pete turned and smiled. "Yeah... I was just saying goodbye."

"Oh..." Claire said with confusion. "Are you sure you don't want to skate with us?"

Pete thought about it. "You know what? I'd love to... I'll be right there, okay?"

Claire smiled. "Okay, sweetheart."

As Claire walked away, Pete turned to see those flickering lights fade beyond the distance. Pete never had the opportunity to get a proper farewell from his dream job, until this moment. Pete learned a lot this past year. A lot about himself, about people, about life *and* death. He realized that heroes don't always wear capes or blue uniforms, but sometimes, they are dressed in regular clothes, just regular people. And Jada Brendan was one of those heroes. He also learned that forgiveness is the most essential thing to ever exist on this earth. *Forgiveness* is what changes the world. And people *can* change… if they so choose.

Just before the flickering lights faded down the road, Pete put his diagonal hand to his head in a salute and gave his final sign-off call to himself:

"Officer Pete Gant… badge number: eight-two-one… it has been an honor and a privilege… Ten-Forty-Two."

About the Author

Jordan Wells was born in Orange, New Jersey, but was raised in East Orange, New Jersey. He graduated from Centenary University, earning a bachelor's degree in business, with concentrations in finance and marketing. Jordan Wells is a professional actor and a member of Screen Actors Guild-American Federation of Television and Radio Artists. He is the author of twenty-one books. He lives in New Jersey.